THE FOUR-
NIGHT
RUN

Other Titles by William Lashner

Guaranteed Heroes

The Barkeep

The Accounting

Blood and Bone

The Victor Carl Novels

Bagmen

A Killer's Kiss

Marked Man

Falls the Shadow

Past Due

Fatal Flaw

Bitter Truth

Hostile Witness

Writing as Tyler Knox

Kockroach

WILLIAM LASHNER

THE FOUR-NIGHT RUN

THOMAS & MERCER

Published by Thomas & Mercer, Seattle

www.apub.com

Amazon, the Amazon logo, and Thomas & Mercer are trademarks of Amazon.com, Inc., or its affiliates.

ISBN-13: 9781503933248
ISBN-10: 1503933245

Cover design by Mark Ecob

Printed in the United States of America

For my sister Suzanne

FIRST NIGHT

1

CALEB BREEST

They say Caleb Breest killed his father when Breest was just fourteen, buried him in the basement, and dug him up each Father's Day to piss on his bones. They say Caleb Breest cracked the skull of a motorcycle freak who looked at him wrong, and then pried the skull open like a coconut. They say Caleb Breest once fought Satan in a barroom brawl, wrestled the demon to the floor, bit off his nose, and spit the stub into his ugly maw.

Caleb Breest ruled like a dark feudal lord over the forgotten western sector of an old shore town on the eastern coast, a sordid landscape of tenements and saloons and old hotels with shattered balustrades lining their dank, rotting porches, a forgotten place its denizens called Crapstown.

You know the city we're talking about. It had once been a famous family resort, but having grown decrepit over long decades of neglect, it turned to gambling to reverse its flagging fortunes. Now the length of its seaside was stacked with giant cash registers attached to high-rise garages, and for three blocks in from the once-renowned boardwalk there were busy streets and neon-lit buildings and the splash of life. This narrow strip was dubbed Casinoland, and it was favored by the politicians and protected by the police and ruled by the corporate owners of the high-toned towers that fronted the sea. But the revitalization promised by the politicians never progressed beyond Casinoland. The baccarat games and roulette wheels, the slot machines and dice pits and blackjack tables did more than drain money from hundreds of miles up and down the coast and west to the mountains. They drained the very light from that part of the old resort town outside the neon's embrace, casting it into perpetual shadow.

The city had now become a world of contrasts. The brittle brightness of Casinoland, promising so much even as it picked your pocket clean, and the darkness of Crapstown—the failed factories, the listing houses, the heaving sea of cracked cement and rusting steel—promising nothing and meting out worse. And for the unlucky residents of Crapstown, their view of the ocean blocked by the casino towers, there was nothing left but to kick away the rats and pick their uncertain way through the rubble between the Charybdis of Casinoland and the Scylla that was Caleb Breest.

They say Caleb Breest, cut from his high school football team because of his grossly enlarged heart, was so bitter at the slight he beat the first-string fullback until the boy's face fell apart. They say Caleb Breest once lost a poker pot to a man with an aces-over-boat and proceeded to flatten the man's Mercedes with a steamroller while the man was still inside the car. They say Caleb Breest grabbed by the neck a labor leader named Malloy, beat him to within an inch of his life, and then went the extra mile. Malloy was reportedly trying to expunge Breest's influence from the local hotel-workers' union before he was found naked and dead in an alley, his face smashed so brutally that his wife could identify him only from a scar on the left side of his chest.

After a three-month investigation, a grand jury indicted Caleb Breest for the murder of Peter Malloy, and Breest was brought before the bar of justice at the county courthouse that sat in the uneasy penumbra between the light of Casinoland and the darkness of Crapstown. Standing for the state were two special agents of the State Bureau of Investigation, three police detectives, and a team of four prosecutors, led by the first assistant county prosecutor himself, Thomas Surwin. Representing Caleb Breest, with only an intern from the local university by his side, was a thirty-year-old attorney with a smashing wardrobe and a beguiling smirk he practiced daily in front of the mirror.

It is fair to say the prosecution found itself shorthanded.

If you had asked J.D. Scrbacek why he had agreed to represent a monster like Caleb Breest, he would have given you a long lecture on the Sixth Amendment to the Constitution of the United States, but suffice it to say that he was a criminal defense attorney and Breest was a criminal, and so they were made one for the other.

Representing a man like Caleb Breest severely limited Scrbacek's options for his defense. He couldn't, for example, stand behind the hulking figure of the defendant, put his hands on his client's massive shoulders, and say, "Is this the face of a murderer?" because the inevitable answer would be, "Absolutely." And he couldn't bring in a parade of character witnesses, because the character of Caleb Breest was appallingly evident. Even Breest's mother showed the terror of a whipped dog whenever the defendant's eyes, hidden behind the prescription-free spectacles Scrbacek had provided, were trained upon her. And Scrbacek couldn't demonstrate for the jury all the good Breest had done for the community, because he had done no good for the community, had for the whole of his life only taken what he wanted and given nothing but his fists and his spit and the blood of countless victims he had spilled upon the dirt.

No, in the face of the prosecution's considerable evidence against Caleb Breest, Scrbacek had no choice but to attack the prosecution itself, which meant attacking Thomas Surwin, whose name Scrbacek dutifully mispronounced as "Sour-Wine" during the whole of the trial, to the first assistant county prosecutor's obvious distress.

In his examination of the cop who first found Malloy's body:

Q: And how long did it take for Mr. Sour-Wine to show up at the crime scene?

A: No more than half an hour.

Q: And he examined everything very carefully, didn't he?

A: Yes, sir.

Q: Kneeled here, kneeled there, bent over the naked body to get a close look at every cut and slash, every inch of mortified flesh.

A: He was quite interested in everything, sir.

Q: And was it usual for the first assistant county prosecutor, with so many important things to do in the office, to show up at a crime scene and fuss so much over a naked corpse?

A: I'd never seen it before, sir.

In his examination of the crime scene search officer:

Q: And as you found the drop of blood you labeled Stain 37, Mr. Sour-Wine was there the whole time, looking over your shoulder?

A: Yes, he was.

Q: Asking questions was he? Making comments? Offering suggestions?

A: The choice is 'D,' sir. All of the above.

In his examination of the lab technician who worked with the blood:

Q: And who was there, with you, as you performed your tests on Stain 37 and prepared it for DNA analysis?

A: Mr. Surwin.

Q: Surprise, surprise. Mr. Sour-Wine just happened to drop by the lab, and have access to all your equipment, at the very moment you were performing your tests?

A: Yes, sir.

In his examination of the coroner:

Q: And the autopsy on Mr. Malloy was done in a closed procedure, isn't that right, Doctor?

A: Only authorized personnel were allowed.

Q: And call it just a lucky guess, Doctor, but did authorized personnel include the ubiquitous Mr. Sour-Wine? Was Mr. Sour-Wine there as you cut up the corpse of Mr. Malloy and made your crucial determinations as to the circumstances surrounding his tragic and violent death?

A: That is correct.

And in his examination of the deal-making scum-sucking sell-his-momma-for-a-buck prison stoolie:

Q: And when you thought you had information relevant to Mr. Malloy's murder, with whom did you first speak?

A: I think it was with that Mr. Surwin over there.

Q: Mr. Sour-Wine? Are you sure?

A: Yep.

Q: And as you had this first meeting with Mr. Sour-Wine and worked out what you should say in this testimony, was there anyone else there?

A: Not that I remember.

Q: Just you and Mr. Sour-Wine, hatching up the stories you would tell to this jury.

A: I don't know if we was hatching nothing. We was just talking.

Q: Just talking. Just you and Mr. Sour-Wine, chatting, chatting, chatting, like a couple of old society ladies out to lunch.

A: I guess so.

It was not a subtle strategy, but this was not a subtle crime, Caleb Breest was not a subtle man, and the DNA analysis that matched Stain 37 with Caleb Breest's own blood was not itself a subtle piece of evidence. The motive proposed by the prosecution was weak and unconvincing, Scrbacek knew, but if that DNA evidence stood, his client fell, and so he went tooth and claw after Thomas Sour-Wine. The jury could deduce Surwin's penchant for dirty tricks from the way his face reddened and fists clenched every time Scrbacek mispronounced his name. And it wasn't as if Surwin didn't fit the part. With a long, pinched face, flattop crew cut, boxy blue suit, and narrow tie, he looked like something that had wandered zombielike straight out of the Nixon White House.

So went the trial of Caleb Breest. It was featured on the front pages of the papers each day, it was updated on the news broadcasts each evening, it was argued over in the seedy bars of Crapstown and discussed in the gambling pits of Casinoland. For its two-month length, it held the entire city in its thrall.

Caleb Breest didn't testify, of course. The biggest problem in the defense of Caleb Breest was always Caleb Breest himself, so he sat silent and immobile the whole of the trial, staring at the witnesses through those fake glasses, his face as expressive as a granite cliff. And he kept the same still posture as J.D. Scrbacek stood before the jury and delivered, with clarity and passion, his closing argument.

"They say Caleb Breest once shot a man because he didn't like the color of his eyes. They say Caleb Breest burned down a bar just to hear the screams. They say Caleb Breest is a monster from the deep, wearing a suit to hide his scales, and glasses to disguise his demon eyes. They say all these things about Caleb Breest in the hope that you will put him in jail for something he did not do. For what does it matter if Caleb Breest didn't kill Peter Malloy, when he just as well might have?

"Thomas Sour-Wine surely knows what Caleb Breest is. He has heard all the stories and has grown certain as to Caleb Breest's malignancy. So what does it matter if Thomas Sour-Wine creates out of thin air a labor dispute to provide motive for Caleb Breest to murder Peter Malloy? What does it matter if Thomas Sour-Wine leans over the corpse of Peter Malloy and drops on Peter Malloy's chest the tiniest spatter of Caleb Breest's blood, conveniently stored in the police lab from his prior arrest? What does it matter if Thomas Sour-Wine instructs the crime scene search officer to take a sample of just that drop, or instructs the lab technician to find a match, or instructs the coroner to state that the killer had beastly strength, or hatches plots with criminal riffraff to spread malicious untruths about the defendant on this very witness stand? What does all that matter when we know what Caleb Breest is, when to find him guilty would be a public service?

"Well, I'll tell you what Caleb Breest is, first and foremost. He is an American, the same as you, born under the protections of our Constitution, endowed with the same rights given to all of us at birth. The presumption of innocence. The right to face his accusers. The right not to be framed by an overzealous prosecutor whose high-minded self-righteousness compels him to manufacture evidence and place before you lies, in an effort to purge from his city a man he believes has no right to walk freely along the same streets as he.

"And who is next, I wonder, to fall under Thomas Sour-Wine's evil eye? Me, for defending a man like Caleb Breest? The pharmacist who sells him the heart medicine that keeps him alive? The tavern owner who sells him his whiskey? The passerby who tips his hat in greeting? Who is safe if Caleb Breest is not? And let me ask you, ladies and gentlemen: What are they saying about you, and what is Thomas Sour-Wine going to do about it?"

J.D. Scrbacek would never have admitted it, but he felt fear as he sat beside Caleb Breest, awaiting the jury's decision.

Breest was a big man, with the shoulders of a steer, and Scrbacek wasn't sure how that bull would react to a guilty verdict. Loaded in the back of Scrbacek's Ford Explorer was a change of clothes for

Breest: black pants, black turtleneck, long camel coat. The plan was for Scrbacek to drive Breest directly from the courthouse to Dirty Dirk's, Breest's regular hangout, for a gala celebration of the acquittal. There would be fireworks in Crapstown that night, Scrbacek had been assured, when the big man got off—so long as the big man got off. But what would happen if Breest was found guilty? Would Breest, in a paroxysm of rage, lash out at the closest person to him, the man upon whom he had rested all his hopes for freedom and who, in the crucible of the trial, had failed him? They say Caleb Breest once crushed the throat of a Frenchman with one blow, just because he was French. Scrbacek showered regularly, sure, but still he couldn't be certain Breest wouldn't do the same to him. So it was with genuine concern for his own neck that Scrbacek watched the jury file back into the courtroom.

"All rise," said the bailiff.

Caleb Breest put his massive hands on the table and pushed himself to his feet. Scrbacek stood beside him like a thin willow shaking in the breeze.

"Ladies and gentlemen of the jury," said the judge, "have you reached a verdict?"

"We have," said the jury foreman, before handing the verdict form to the bailiff to take to the judge.

The judge reviewed the paper, her face impassive, and then said to the foreman, "In the matter of the *People versus Caleb Breest*, on the charge of murder in the first degree, how do you find?"

Not a breath stirred as the jury foreman prepared to speak.

2
Mortis Ex Machina

On his rush out of the courtroom in search of the nearest camera, Scrbacek ran smack into Thomas Surwin. The prosecutor's expression was understandably darker and more pinched than usual.

"I hope you're proud of your fine work in there," said Surwin.

"Very."

"Take my advice, Scrbacek, and watch your ass."

"Oh, I will," said Scrbacek, with a wink. "On the evening news."

The lovely glow of Casinoland was just infiltrating the darkening sky to the east when J.D. Scrbacek stood on the courthouse steps with the cameras on and the heavy white lights picking up his rugged features. His tie was tight; the collar of his raincoat was turned rakishly up. His intern had already been dispatched to drive the Explorer from the parking lot behind the courthouse to the front steps, so as to provide the cameras a view of Scrbacek's dramatic exit with his client. All was as it should have been, except that his client wasn't by his side. Surwin had unexpectedly kept Caleb Breest locked up one more night, pending a probation revocation hearing scheduled for the next morning. But still the scene was as near perfect as Scrbacek could have wished when he began to crow to the crowd of reporters.

"The jury's verdict wasn't just a victory for Mr. Breest, it was a victory for us all. This was a case without motive or evidence, a case that should never have been brought, a case hatched in the mind of First Assistant County Prosecutor Thomas Sour-Wine simply because he doesn't like my client. Well, I'm not sure I like my client either, but if that's enough to put a man in jail and kill him dead, then we all have much to fear."

He gave good press, Scrbacek, especially on the courthouse steps after a high-profile win.

"Now that Mr. Breest has been found innocent of Mr. Malloy's murder, I hope the police redouble their efforts to find exactly who committed this horrible crime. My sympathies and the sympathies of Mr. Breest remain, as they have all through this ordeal, with the Malloy family. Nothing that happened in this courtroom can disguise the fact that a man is dead and his murderer still at large. There might be celebrating tonight by Mr. Breest's friends and associates, there might be fireworks in the night sky over this fine city, but our thoughts will also be with the brave—"

A loud pop, followed by a deafening explosion from behind the courthouse.

The crowd ducked. Some reporters dived to the ground, others threw their arms over their heads as if mortars were incoming. Scrbacek alone remained standing tall, his anger rising at the goons who had started the celebration before he had finished his speechifying. He raised his voice and began again.

"As I was saying, there may be fireworks in the night sky over this fine city, but our . . ."

It was no good. The cameras were off him now. The reporters were running in a pack down the steps, circling the building. TV crews lugged their equipment, straining to keep up. There were calls, yelps, the poundings of hard-soled shoes on cement.

"What I'm trying to say," Scrbacek shouted to the retreating backs of the media, "what is important to remember . . ." But no one anymore was listening.

Standing alone on the steps of the courthouse, Scrbacek cocked his head at the commotion before following the mob down the steps. People were now running away from the explosion, running madly, with terror etched on their faces, as they passed the reporters. The two groups were shouting back and forth, the reporters heading to the rear of the courthouse and the sane civilians running away.

"What was it?"

"A car, I think."

"A car?"

"I think. Oh God, it's a mess."

"Whose car?"

"Who knows?"

"How?"

"I don't know."

Scrbacek stopped and looked up and down the street. He was searching for his Explorer, high and shiny black, with chrome enough to blind on a sunny day, wondering what was keeping his intern.

There was another explosion, soft, muffled, along with a crescendo of shouts. Scrbacek turned. Behind the courthouse the glow of a great spitting bonfire broke through the twilight and, from out of that glow, thick black smoke rose in tortuous billows, even as a horrible thought began to rise within him.

Scrbacek spun around and again searched up and down the street, up and down the street, looking for his SUV, his head twisting ever more desperately. He pulled his phone out of his raincoat pocket and pressed his finger on the reader to unlock the screen when he heard:

"Scrbacek."

His name, being called by a woman, her voice sharp enough to cut through the shouts, the crackles of fire, the sirens racing their way to the courthouse. Scrbacek turned with a lurch.

Coming at him was one of the State Bureau of Investigation special agents who had worked the Malloy murder with Surwin. The agent was running at Scrbacek full bore, her jacket flapping, her knees driving beneath her gray skirt, her heavy black shoes slapping the pavement. She was a thickly built blonde woman with a pocked face and the muscled hands of a longshoreman. Her name was Dyer, Stephanie Dyer, and she was rushing at Scrbacek like a linebacker on the blitz.

Scrbacek grabbed his phone tight and braced for the blow. But instead of slamming him to the ground, Dyer took hold of his biceps and started yanking him up the stairs.

Scrbacek pulled his arm away.

"Scrbacek," Dyer said, "we have to get inside." She gasped for air. "Right away."

"I'm waiting for my Explorer."

"It's gone. We have to get inside." Dyer tugged at Scrbacek's arm. "Hurry. You'll be safer inside."

"What about my Explorer? What happened to my Explorer?"

"We have to get inside. Now."

She yanked again at his arm, and this time Scrbacek let Dyer drag him up the stairs and into the courthouse.

In the brutal nights to come, J.D. Scrbacek would wonder if it was a mark of how very far he had traveled in his legal career and in his life that after the explosion he had asked first about his sport-utility vehicle and only later, much later, about his intern, who had been sitting inside.

3
STEPHANIE DYER

Agent Dyer sat with Scrbacek in a windowless witness room on the third floor of the courthouse. A low-hanging fixture cast a funnel of light upon the Formica tabletop, strewn with ashes, but left the edges of the room in shadow. Two uniformed police officers stood guard outside. It was hot in that room, stuffy, but even in his raincoat and suit jacket Scrbacek was shivering. He had tried to convince Dyer to tell him exactly what had happened behind the courthouse, but instead of information, Dyer offered Scrbacek a cigarette and a light.

Scrbacek put the cigarette in his mouth with a shaking hand and leaned toward the flame. Dyer gently removed the cigarette from Scrbacek's lips and flipped it around so that the filter was facing away from the fire.

When the cigarette was lit, Scrbacek took too deep a drag before coughing out a fit of smoke.

"Easy there, Tenderfoot," said Dyer. "Can I get you something else? Coffee?"

"I think I'm jittery enough, don't you?"

"Don't know if it's any consolation, but if what happened to your car just happened to my car, I'd be shaking, too."

"It wasn't a car. It was an SUV."

"My mistake," said Dyer. "You get off-road much?"

"No, not really."

"But it gets pretty rugged, doesn't it, in the parking lot of the Super Fresh."

They sat quietly for a long moment as the cigarette burned to a nub and the thickening smoke twisted slowly within the funnel of light. When the cigarette died of its own accord, Scrbacek tossed it into the pinched foil ashtray and pulled out his phone, still in silent mode from court. He had scores of texts, mostly from reporters he now had no desire to deal with, and a slew of voice messages, which he ignored. He called Dirty Dirk's, but the line was busy. A quick check of the local newspaper's website informed him the police were giving no information beyond that a vehicle had exploded into flames behind the courthouse. He checked the Phillies score and then tried Dirty Dirk's again, and again the line was busy. Finally, Scrbacek wondered who might be worried about his welfare and, coming up with no one locally, called his mother, ensconced behind the gates of The Villages, billed as Florida's friendliest retirement hometown. His mother was pleased to hear from her son, and happy that he had won his big important case, but somewhat baffled at his repeated assurances that he was okay when, from behind the gates of Florida's friendliest retirement hometown, she had no concerns whatsoever about his safety. His mother off the line, he turned off the phone, slipped it back into his raincoat, and accepted another cigarette.

"Thanks," he said. "Mine are in the Explorer."

He had just lit the cigarette when the door opened and a big-bellied agent from the State Bureau of Investigation stuck his head in the opening.

"What was the name of the kid in the vehicle?" he asked Dyer.

Dyer looked at Scrbacek.

"Brummel," Scrbacek said. "Ethan Brummel."

Addressing Dyer only, as if he couldn't see Scrbacek through the smoke, the man said, "Any idea where he lived?"

Dyer again turned to Scrbacek and arched an eyebrow.

"His family lives on an inlet about twenty miles south." Scrbacek told him the name of the beach town. "How is he?"

For the first time, the man looked at Scrbacek, his face filled with a bitter incredulity. "Your car blew up with him inside. The blast destroyed the cars parked on either side and shattered half the windows on the rear wall of the courthouse. How the hell do you think he is?"

"I was just . . ."

The agent turned back to Dyer. "Don't let him leave until we talk to him."

"Are you holding me here?" Scrbacek said in a lawyerly reflex. "Am I under arrest?"

The man looked at Scrbacek again, the incredulity replaced now with disgust. "Shut up," he said, and then he closed the door behind him.

Scrbacek stared at the now closed door. "I didn't realize about Ethan," he said. "I can't believe this. I didn't think . . ."

Dyer didn't say anything, just looked at the back wall of the room as if there were a window there.

In the smoky quiet, Scrbacek thought of Ethan Brummel, tall and gawky and blond, anxious to learn and eager to please. He had come to Scrbacek's office looking to satisfy his senior internship requirement, excited at the opportunity to slave for no pay so as to learn about the criminal law. Ethan Brummel told Scrbacek he had been a hero to him ever since Scrbacek had proven Amber Grace, seven years on death row, innocent of murder. It had been Scrbacek's big break, the Amber Grace case, had made his name, such as it was, but Scrbacek didn't smile and warmly offer Brummel the job after Ethan mentioned his great victory. "Go to med school," he said instead. "Go to journalism school, save the whales, become a game show host. Do anything other than this." But Ethan knew what he wanted with the certainty of innocence, and Scrbacek, with a sad shake of his head, had given way. And Ethan Brummel had in fact proved to be a likable young man, sharp, hard-working, sincere. So Scrbacek was surprised that he couldn't summon a tear for his now-dead intern. He wiped at his eyes for Dyer's benefit.

"He was a good kid," Scrbacek said. "He was just a . . . a good kid. He didn't deserve that."

"Who does?" said Dyer, still facing the wall.

"What do you mean?"

Dyer turned to Scrbacek, her pocked cheeks rising in a smile. "Someone was trying kill somebody, and the best guess here is that the somebody this someone was trying to kill was you."

"Huh?"

Dyer just stared at him as the meaning of the sentence came clear in Scrbacek's head.

"Who would want to kill me?" said Scrbacek.

"That's the question, isn't it?"

"No one hates me that much."

"Maybe not," said Dyer, "but in my experience, vehicles aren't rock-and-roll drummers, they don't spontaneously combust."

Shaken by the thought, Scrbacek began to sort through his enemies like trading cards, moving forward from his childhood, searching for anyone who might have a motive to kill. There were scores of possibilities: kids from the schoolyard, women from the dating wars, opponents in the courtroom. A parade of names from his past flitted across his mind like words on the news ticker in Times Square. It was as sobering as a funeral, raising up the list of his potential enemies, a crude and nasty self-portrait. Still, he had only come up with one name that caused him to shudder, when the door of the stuffy little room suddenly opened.

Dyer stood quickly.

Into the room strode a uniformed police officer, and then the big-bellied special agent, and then two prosecutors, and then a plainclothes detective with a badge hanging from his jacket pocket. All of these, including Dyer, stood stiffly up against the wall, facing Scrbacek from the shadows as, through the door, sweeping in like Elliot Ness at a beer bash, came First Assistant County Prosecutor Thomas Surwin.

4
THOMAS SURWIN

Surwin sat across the table from Scrbacek, laid his hands flat on the Formica, tilted his flattop forward so that his narrow, pinched features were cut deep by shadow from the overhead light.

"From what we can tell," said Surwin, getting right to it without even the semblance of pleasantry, "there were two explosive charges set on the bottom of your chassis, one underneath the front seat, one attached to your gas tank. We have to wait for confirmation from the lab, but it appears to have been a plastic explosive. Semtex or the like."

"What about Ethan?" said Scrbacek.

"I notified his parents already. I advised them not to look at the body, as it was burned beyond recognition. If dental records don't help, we'll need to do a DNA analysis to prove it was Mr. Brummel in the Explorer. Some might find that definitive."

Surwin pursed his lips, and Scrbacek knew enough to say not a word.

"Did you have any accelerants in your vehicle?" asked Surwin.

"Gasoline."

"In containers?"

"In the tank. I filled it up this morning."

"How much did the car hold?"

"It wasn't a car," said Dyer, dryly, from the back wall. "It was an SUV."

Scrbacek glanced with annoyance at Special Agent Dyer and then said, "I think maybe twenty gallons."

Surwin nodded. "A clerk entering the courthouse noted someone working on the underside of an Explorer in the parking lot at about four in the afternoon. A guy in jeans and work boots. She didn't see his face. She figured it was simply car trouble and didn't think to mention it until after an Explorer in the lot blew to smithereens. Were you having car trouble?"

"No."

"Any idea who it might have been beneath the car?"

"None."

"Had Mr. Brummel received any threats in the past weeks?"

"Not that I know of. He was a good kid. He wasn't the type to have gotten in any trouble."

"Well, it found him, didn't it," said Surwin. "How about you? Have you received any threats?"

"Just one."

Surwin leaned forward. "From whom?"

"You. Today. After the verdict came down."

Surwin let a smile slip across his lips and then stifled it. "That wasn't a threat. That was a warning, for your own benefit."

"It warms my heart to know the prosecutor's office is so concerned with my benefit."

Surwin pursed his lips again, bowed his head, and scratched his chin with his folded hands. "You beat me today, Scrbacek," he said.

"For the second time," said Scrbacek.

Surwin's eyes tightened in annoyance and then eased as he regained control. "You beat me today for the second time. And I won't pretend it didn't hurt. Caleb Breest is an animal, and he needs to be put away. But as far as I know, you beat me fair and square under the law. As much as I despise Caleb Breest, I love the law, so you can go about your day knowing I bear you no ill will. All you are to me is a misguided punk with a flair in court. Now if someone succeeds in killing you, I won't mourn, true, but you can rest assured I will still prosecute the son of a bitch to the fullest extent of the law."

"Comforting," said Scrbacek.

"Now I have a murder case to investigate and I need your help. Who wants you dead?"

"I've been considering it."

"And?" said Surwin, one eyebrow arching.

"I keep coming back to the last time we matched up," said Scrbacek.

"You're thinking of Bozant," said Surwin, nodding. "Any word from him?"

"Not since you put him in prison. But in the middle of the Amber Grace case, when they pulled his badge, he promised to twist me into some very unpleasant positions."

"Well, you'll be gratified to know I already checked with Remi Bozant's parole officer. He's in Las Vegas, doing private security at one of the hotels. Apparently, he's made a new life for himself."

"Isn't that sweet?"

"We have someone there right now checking up on him. But if not Bozant, then who?"

"No one else I can think of. It must have been some kind of mistake."

"The Semtex slipped under your car by accident, is that the theory?" Surwin leaned back, smiled. "You know, I've been wondering for years. What kind of name is Scrbacek?"

"Dutch."

"Dutch? I never would have guessed. Dutch. How about that? Anything else that might be of some use?"

"My mother was Ukrainian, if that helps."

"Do you ever worry that the families of the victims of the guys you get off might be out for payback?"

"I'm just a lawyer. All I do is my job. I'm sure they understand that. I would guess they'd have more of a beef with the prosecutors that didn't do their jobs as well as I did mine."

"What were your plans for the evening?"

"There was going to be a party if Breest was acquitted."

"Where?"

"Dirty Dirk's."

"Who was going with you in the Explorer other than Mr. Brummel?"

"My client."

Surwin's eyes suddenly snapped into focus. "Breest was supposed to leave the courthouse in your Explorer?"

"That was the plan, until you kept him in the lockup for tomorrow's hearing."

Surwin closed his eyes for a moment. "Who else knew of Breest's travel plans?"

"Joey Torresdale."

"The turkey man?"

"Mr. Torresdale gives out his Thanksgiving turkeys to the poor as a goodwill gesture to the entire community."

"Bleed the city all year as Breest's number two, sure, but dump a pile of frozen turkeys onto the street in November for the television cameras and suddenly you're a saint. Anyone else?"

"Other people Breest or Torresdale might have told, and, of course, Dirty Dirk himself."

"That means everybody in the damn city."

"So you think it was Breest they were after?"

"Don't you?"

"That actually makes sense," said Scrbacek, the edge of his fear sanded smooth by the switch in targets. "Ironic, if it's true, isn't it? By keeping him in lockup, you saved his life."

"Had your client received any threats? Anyone let it be known he was ready to step to the top over Breest's corpse?"

"Besides you?"

"Besides me."

"Not that I know of."

"The turkey man, Torresdale. Do you think he was stepping up?"

"He's Breest's oldest friend."

"Since when does that matter?" Surwin paused. "Ever hear of a gang called the Furies?"

"The Furies?" said Scrbacek, shaking his head. "Sounds like a Roller Derby team."

"The C-Town Furies. Did Breest or Torresdale ever mention them to you?"

"Torresdale never did. Anything Breest said or didn't say to me is privileged. You'll have to ask him. I'm sure he'll be cooperative."

"He'll be as cooperative as always," said Surwin. "I'll ask him a question, he'll spit on the floor. I'll ask him another question, he'll spit on my shoe."

"His heart medicine acts as an expectorant."

"I just thought he didn't approve of my footwear," said Surwin before slapping the table as he stood. "I'll have Dyer drive you to your building, make sure you get in safe and sound. Wouldn't want anything to happen to you on your way home from our courthouse."

"I appreciate it," said Scrbacek, "but I'm not worried."

Surwin headed off toward the door but then stopped, turned around. "It must be wonderful, Scrbacek, to be so universally well loved."

"I told you, other than Remi Bozant, who you say is fat and happy in Vegas, I have no enemies."

"Maybe not. But the secretary saw the killer set the bomb at four in the afternoon. The jury had informed the judge it had reached a verdict by then, true, but the actual verdict wasn't announced until six."

"So?"

"So Caleb Breest could only have been in that car with an acquittal, but the plan, I'm sure, was for you to have turned the ignition key, win or lose."

Scrbacek's eye twitched.

"Sweet dreams, baby," said Surwin before striding out of the room.

5
THE CLIENT

Scrbacek insisted that Dyer take him one place first before dropping him at his home. Dyer shrugged and said, "No problem."

The courthouse elevator sank slowly down.

The subbasement lockup was a dank warren of concrete tunnels and maintenance offices, with one large section divided into six holding cells. Each morning the stillness of the subbasement was trampled by a herd of prisoners brought in from the buses, thick leather belts around their waists, hands cuffed to the belts. Group by group, they were guided into the various cells by sheriff's deputies, where, shackles removed, they were left to await their perfunctory moments in court, after which they would be returned to their temporary cells. As the day wore on, the decibel level rose, the stench of prisoner sweat filled the stifling air, the catcalls and hoots and bodies bashing against bars grew more frequent, more dangerous. To call it bedlam would be an insult to Bedlam. Then, in the evening, one by one, the cells were emptied. Group by group, the prisoners, belts and shackles in place, were led back to the buses. Cell by cell, the floors were mopped with a heavy concentration of ammonia to hide the stink of sweat and fear and blood. And a stillness fell once again upon the lockup.

Because of the late announcement of the verdict, and the probation revocation hearing scheduled for the next day, the sheriff had left Caleb Breest to stay overnight in one of the lockup cells. But Breest was not a talkative man and did nothing to disturb the subbasement's quiet. Instead he sat on his cot, massive torso leaning forward, heavy black shoes flat on the floor, elbows resting on knees, huge hands clasped together, silent and still.

Normally, Scrbacek would have been required to talk to a client in the courthouse lockup through the thick cell bars, but since Breest had been just that day acquitted of capital murder, and there were no other prisoners, the sheriff allowed Scrbacek to bring a chair into the cell. Scrbacek would have preferred, actually, the protection of sturdy steel between himself and his client.

His client.

It was how Scrbacek referred to Caleb Breest, as his client, but his relationship to Caleb Breest was like no lawyer-client relationship he had ever experienced. Through the whole of Scrbacek's representation of Caleb Breest, the client had spit no more than a few monosyllabic words at his lawyer. Instead, Scrbacek dealt almost exclusively with Breest's number two.

It was Joey Torresdale who had appeared at Scrbacek's storefront office one afternoon and dropped a briefcase filled with cash onto his desk. Scrbacek had a busy practice and wasn't actively searching for new clients, but a briefcase filled with cash always got his attention, as did a high-profile client and the mash of publicity that would inevitably come with him. Short and dapper, with razor-cut gray hair and a nose like a blob of putty, Joey Torresdale told Scrbacek he came highly recommended, though Torresdale wouldn't say by whom. It was Joey Torresdale who laid the ground rules for the attorney-client relationship: (1) Scrbacek would refrain from asking Caleb Breest any questions about his past or specific matters relating to the crime, (2) all legal strategies were to be approved in advance by Torresdale, (3) any investigative work had to be conducted by a PI named Trent Fallow, whose work was to be reviewed by Torresdale, and the most important rule of all, (4) Scrbacek must never ever anger Caleb Breest, lest the surfeit of emotion injure Breest's fragile, oversize heart.

In the weeks leading to the trial, during numerous late-night strategy meetings at Dirty Dirk's with Joey Torresdale, Scrbacek had discovered Torresdale's mind to be sharp as a shiv. Torresdale would have been a crackerjack attorney, Scrbacek was certain, had he chosen law school over the rule of the streets. Some of the ideas Torresdale casually floated in their meetings had been beyond brilliant and greatly aided in the crafting of Breest's defense. Torresdale's innate street smarts, and the way he had insinuated himself into every aspect of Breest's defense, had caused Scrbacek to wonder if Caleb Breest was merely a puppet, being manipulated by the small but insanely clever Joey Torresdale. It was because of that suspicion that Scrbacek had taken more than due care in keeping his client informed of all trial preparations, though Caleb Breest, in the county jail, had rarely acknowledged Scrbacek's words, except with a nod or a cruelly curled lip.

Now, as Scrbacek brought his little metal chair into the cell, unfolded it, and placed it in front of Breest, his client's huge body stayed immobile while his eyes followed Scrbacek's halting steps. They were strange, Caleb Breest's eyes, the palest blue with a character of derangement. One of his eyes wandered up and to the left, so that you could never be sure whether Caleb Breest was staring at you or over your left shoulder, whether he was contemplating ripping out your lungs or the lungs of the man behind you. It was this very character that had prompted Scrbacek to purchase the fake glasses for Breest, so as to hide those eyes as much as possible from the jury. Scrbacek wished the glasses were still in place. The two eyes stared crazily at Scrbacek and behind Scrbacek and, as there was no one standing now behind Scrbacek, he had a pretty good idea of whose lungs Breest was contemplating at this very moment.

Scrbacek sat and leaned forward so his voice couldn't be heard by Special Agent Dyer. "Did anyone tell you what happened behind the courthouse?" said Scrbacek softly and slowly.

Breest didn't move.

"Someone placed a bomb under my Ford Explorer after word went out that the jury had reached a verdict. It blew up when my intern started the engine. You may have heard the explosion. My intern was incinerated immediately. This was the same car you and I were supposed to take from the courthouse to Dirty Dirk's after the acquittal."

Breest still didn't move, but his eyes narrowed.

"Surwin kept me for questioning. He thinks someone was trying to kill you, and possibly me, too. He is setting up a task force to determine who set the bomb. He asked me if I knew of anyone who might be making a move to take over your territory. I told him I had no idea."

Breest remained motionless.

"He also mentioned something about a gang. A gang called the Furies."

Breest's eyes widened and then narrowed again. It took only an instant, this widening and narrowing, but still it was the greatest show of emotion Scrbacek had ever seen from Caleb Breest.

"I haven't spoken to Joey or anyone else since the explosion. I don't know any other details. I thought you ought to know."

Breest stared at Scrbacek for a long moment, a stare that unnerved Scrbacek with its intensity, like Breest was accusing Scrbacek of blowing up his own car. Then Breest, still with that awful stare, nodded, the movement so slight Scrbacek wondered if it had happened at all.

"Is there anything you want me to do?" said Scrbacek.

"No," said Caleb Breest in the slow graveled whisper that was his normal speaking tone, the snarl of a great predator cat.

Scrbacek sat there for a moment more before slapping his own thigh and standing. "Fine, then. I'll see you tomorrow at the hearing.

Surwin's yanking at straws on this probation thing. The state's burden of proof is lower for a revocation, but the jury's verdict should convince the judge to rule in our favor."

Breest's body didn't stir as his deviated gaze followed Scrbacek's movements.

"Have a nice night, Mr. Breest."

Scrbacek lifted the chair, folded it, carried it out. The sheriff slammed shut the cell door, locking it with a resounding clang.

On his way out of the basement, Scrbacek took one last glance into the cell. Caleb Breest sat on his cot, massive torso leaning forward, heavy black shoes flat on the floor, elbows resting on knees, huge hands clasped together, silent and still.

In the elevator, rising from the depths, Dyer said to Scrbacek, "He seemed cheery for a guy who was acquitted of capital murder."

"He's still in jail."

"Thank God for minor miracles. Is there anyplace else you need to go?"

"Home is fine. I'm exhausted."

"Are you sure?" said Dyer.

Scrbacek squinted at her. "You like playing chauffeur?"

"Only if you've got someplace you need to go."

Scrbacek thought for a moment. "I can't think of any."

"You sure?" said Dyer. "You sure you've got no place you still need to go tonight? Because if you've got someplace you really need to go tonight, I will take you there. Yes, I will. No problem. All you have to do is ask."

"No," said Scrbacek. "Home is fine."

"You sure?"

Scrbacek squinted at her again. "My guess, Special Agent Dyer, is that you have someplace in mind."

"Well," said Dyer, nodding as the elevator doors opened at street level, "now that you mention it, maybe I do."

6

THE CONSTITUTION

After a forty-minute drive along parkways, across bridges, through the centers of beach towns strung along the shore like bright beads on a string, Dyer stopped her unmarked brown sedan on a wide residential street. The street was lined with newly constructed, multistory houses that hovered like well-lit dollar signs over the last remnant of a more modest era. The one-story soon-to-be teardown in front of which they now parked was dim and gray, the flat windowless front of the garage as welcoming as a bolted door.

Scrbacek sat in the car and stared for a long moment at Ethan Brummel's boyhood home until Dyer gently said, "Go on."

"You're not coming?"

"Oh, no," said Dyer. "No, no, no. I'll stay right out here in case you need me."

"I appreciate the support."

"Right out here," said Dyer, settling back into the seat of her car, "in case you need me."

Scrbacek waited a moment more, then climbed out of the car and made his way around the garage to the door on the house's side.

There was no answer to his first knock, no answer to his second. The lights were dim inside, and he secretly hoped no one was home, but he tried once more and this time, in response, the door opened slowly.

She was tall but bent, sturdily built but shaking as if from some deep cold that had invaded her bones. She looked at him out of glassy eyes set deep within their sockets and said not a word.

"Mrs. Brummel, I'm J.D. Scrbacek."

"I know who you are," she said, her brogue Dublin-sharp.

"I came to offer my condolences, Mrs. Brummel. Your son was a good man and would have made a fine lawyer."

"I know who you are," she said.

"May I come in?"

She looked at him out of those glassy eyes and then backed away, opening the door in the process. Scrbacek stepped warily inside.

The lights were low in the Brummel house. Scrbacek had entered a kitchen area. To the left was a hallway, to the right a living room and then a dark glass-enclosed porch, through which he could see a sandy path, illuminated by security lights, which led to a broad inlet. Even in the dimness, Scrbacek could spot the pictures of Ethan Brummel on the walls. A school photo, a large portrait, a blown-up snapshot of Ethan on his sailboat like a young Kennedy.

"I'm sure you've naught to say to me," said Mrs. Brummel. "I'll take you to my husband."

She walked out of the kitchen, through the living room area, into the glassed-in porch. Scrbacek followed. Mrs. Brummel switched on a floor lamp, and suddenly Scrbacek could see a man sitting stiffly in an extended lounge chair, sitting in stockinged feet, eyes open but unfocused, the clear plastic tube from an oxygen tank wrapping around his neck and under his nose.

"This is Mr. Scrbacek," said Mrs. Brummel loudly. "He was the lawyer Ethan was working for. He has come to offer his condolences."

The man turned his head and focused on Scrbacek. "You're the lawyer?" His voice was a mere rasp.

"That's right, Mr. Brummel."

"Ethan works for you?"

"As an intern, yes."

"Is he a good worker? A hard worker?"

"Yes, Mr. Brummel. He was exemplary. A fine young man."

"That's how I raised him. I raised him to work."

"You raised him well."

"He made dean's list. Twice. He says he wants to be a lawyer. He wants to help people."

"He was a fine young man."

"It sounds to me like a stupid plan, becoming a lawyer to help people."

"We try our best."

"Does Ethan help people when he works for you?"

"I think so."

"I hope you more than think so, young man."

"Yes, he helped people when he worked for me."

"I'm glad he works for you, then. Take care of my boy. He's a good boy. I'll trust you to take care of him."

"My husband is tired, Mr. Scrbacek," said Mrs. Brummel. "I think we ought leave him be for now."

"Good-bye, Mr. Brummel, and again, I'm so sorry for your loss."

Mrs. Brummel turned off the lamp and led Scrbacek back to the kitchen. She opened the door and held it as she bowed her head. "You'll be on your way," she said.

"I'm so sorry, Mrs. Brummel. So very, very sorry."

"So you've said. Do they know any more about how it happened?"

"They're not sure. Did Ethan tell you anything, give you any reason to make you think he was scared?"

"No, nothing."

"No threats? No concerns he might have had about anything?"

"None."

"They think the bomb was meant not for Ethan but for our client, Mr. Breest."

"Oh my God," she said, her chin rising as her hand jumped to her mouth. "Oh my dear God. They killed Ethan instead of that Caleb Breest?"

"That's what the authorities now believe."

"That monster murdered that man, Malloy, with the four daughters he had, and now my son is dead."

"Mr. Breest was acquitted by the jury, and your son was a great help in gaining that verdict."

"Oh Jaysis, no," she said, bending now at the waist, as if suddenly overcome with cramps. "Don't be making it any worse than it is."

"I'm sorry, Mrs. Brummel. So sorry."

"You've said that already." With much difficulty, she struggled to straighten enough to look into Scrbacek's eyes. "But my son, he came to you searching for a future, and you brought him to that monster."

"Mr. Breest is my client."

"Your client? Has your client ever done anything other than destroy whatever it was he touched? Wouldn't the world now be a better place if your Caleb Breest was on death row waiting the hangman and my son was still alive? Couldn't we all then rejoice? Isn't that the end you should have been working for, Mr. Scrbacek?"

"Mrs. Brummel, the Constitution provides—"

She threw up a hand and slapped his face. It wasn't hard, the blow, but it shocked him with its naked intimacy.

"Don't. Don't you dare," she said. "He came to you searching for a future, and you dragged him down to the level of that monster, to the

35

level of filth, to your level. Wasn't it inevitable that at the end of it, your Caleb Breest would be as free as a gull, and my boy, my sweet innocent boy, would be the one burned so badly they won't even let me see his face a final time, won't let me wash his flesh with my tears? And, you, you shifty bastard, you try to quote to me the Constitution?"

"Mrs. Brummel—"

"Get out of my house."

"Mrs. Brummel, I—"

"Get the hell out of my house. Out. Out. Get out."

***

It was a quiet ride back through the center of the beach towns, across the bridges, along the parkways into the city. Scrbacek wasn't talking, and Dyer, after her few conversational gambits fell flat as a drunkard over a stoop, was tactful enough to maintain her quiet. Dyer offered a cigarette, and Scrbacek accepted, and they smoked in silence as they headed north.

Without asking for directions, Dyer found her way to the side street just a block off the boardwalk where sat J.D. Scrbacek's building. The bottom floor was a storefront office with his name painted on the plate-glass window in gold. The second and third floors were a duplex apartment with exposed brick, thick beams of old-growth wood, and a wide sleeping loft with a bed, a huge flat-screen, and a skylight that leaked during heavy rains but through which at night, after sex, you could see the glister of stars.

"Thanks for the ride," said Scrbacek.

"I'm sure it wasn't so bad as you may think," said Dyer. "It's a hard thing when a child dies. It can't but seem that everything you say is wrong."

"It was worse than you could imagine."

"I'm sure it wasn't."

"I tried to quote the Constitution to Mrs. Brummel."

"Oh." Dyer turned to stare out the windshield without saying anything more.

Scrbacek got out of the car and then leaned back through the open doorway. "But even so," he said, "I appreciate you taking me. Sometimes I forget the things I should be doing, forget what's important."

"I saw the way you were with the kid in court," said Dyer. "You never bossed him. You listened to what he said. Some people are better at the eulogies than at being with the living."

"I suppose."

"In the Bureau they say you aren't worth the shit we wipe off our shoes, but from here on I'll stand up for you."

"Thanks, Stephanie, I think. You going to be at the hearing tomorrow?"

"I'm testifying against your scum client."

"So I get to cross-examine you. Won't that be fun." Scrbacek glanced up at the bright neon glow of the casinos and then turned to face the darkness in the west. "This thing Surwin was talking about, the Furies, what the hell is that all about?"

"Some Crapstown gang," said Dyer. "One of a half dozen or so, though this one seems to rule the rest. We can't get a handle on them, but they're bad eggs for sure, pure killers. So scary we hear even your client is worried."

"Nasty enough to blow up cars?"

"Nasty enough to blow up towns. Be careful, Tenderfoot. There's still danger out there. Stay home tonight."

"I will."

"I'm serious now. To keep your street safe, we cleared away the reporters who were camped out here looking for a quote, but we can't do anything if you don't stay put."

"Don't worry, Stephanie. I'm too exhausted to do anything other than sleep, even if I wanted to."

As Scrbacek was opening the front door of his building, Dyer called out through the car window. "Is Scrbacek really a Dutch name?"

Scrbacek shook his head. "Flemish."

"Flemish?" said Dyer. "I never would have guessed."

Inside his office the answering machine was blinking like an idiot, soundless but full of fury. He dropped his briefcase and played the first few messages, all from reporters asking about the Breest trial and the bomb. Scrbacek loved talking to the press, was an unabashed publicity hound, glad to howl to even the lowliest members of the fourth estate, but tonight he simply wasn't in the mood. Tomorrow. He'd give them all the choicest of quotes tomorrow.

But tonight the office was dark as a hole and felt like work, and so instead of hanging around, he climbed the spiral stairwell to his apartment. He turned on the light and took off his raincoat, threw his shirt into the hamper, carefully hung his suit pants and jacket on a hanger, placed his tie upon the tie carousel in his closet. He took a drink of water, brushed his teeth, flossed, gargled, climbed into his loft, and turned off the light.

Then he sneaked down the loft stairs, peered out the window, and watched as Dyer sat in her car for five minutes, ten minutes, fifteen minutes, before driving off.

In the darkness of his apartment, lit only by the city light drifting through his windows, he put on a pair of jeans, his boots, a white shirt, his raincoat. He grabbed his wallet and keys, his last pack of cigs, his lighter, and his phone, which he placed into his raincoat pocket. Then he slipped down the spiral stairs and out the back door leading to the alley where they picked up the trash. On the horizon, rising above the tops of the low buildings, he could see already the bright glow, the herald of a night where there was more than the agony of a lost child, where there was glitter and laughter and risk and the possibility, no matter how dim, of real possibility.

He took a quick look around to be sure there was no one from the State Bureau of Investigation watching over him for his own damn good, and then, with a spring in his step, headed off toward the dazzling neon lights of Casinoland.

7

CASINOLAND

The casinos on the boardwalk stood bright as silver dollars and high as pipe dreams on a line fronting the utter blackness of the sea. The Castle. The Seaside. Diamond's Alhambra. Diamond's Pyramid. Parade Parade. LondonTown. How Fat's House of Luck. And in the middle, higher than the others, grander, lit brighter, topped by twin domes of shimmering gold surrounded by full-color statues of Greek gods, rose Diamond's Mount Olympus.

Mount Olympus had the largest casino floor space, the greatest number of rooms, the most slot machines, the biggest jackpots, and the highest table drop and table win of any casino east of the Rockies. It was a palace of profit and pleasure, with gold trim on every fixture and gold rims on every glass, with air cooled by Freon and doped with oxygen, with cocktail waitresses in black high heels and little gold tops that covered just the bottoms, with second-rate singers in the lounges and first-rate acts on the main stage, and a soundtrack like the voice of Daisy Buchanan on speed, overdubbed a hundred thousand times. Diamond's Mount Olympus.

"Good to see you, Mr. Scrbacek," said a greeter at the first of two sets of doors.

"Way to go, Mr. Scrbacek," said one of the men brushing cigarette butts into a dustbin in the foyer.

And then he was past the second set of doors, into the impossible flash of the casino. Every time he stepped inside Mount Olympus, he couldn't help the quickening of his pace, the jiggling of his fingers, the sense of expectation that stole upon him like a burgeoning erection. He was always after something in the casino—sometimes luck, sometimes money, sometimes the thrill of losing more than he could afford, sometimes a quiet drink, sometimes a noisy drunk, but most times, like tonight, Dolores.

Even late on a Tuesday night, the floor was mobbed with gamblers, and the minimums were jacked high. Scrbacek stood amidst the sea of gaming tables, examining the waitresses as they paraded by with their full trays and skimpy tops. As he searched, he sidled up to one of the blackjack tables.

"Hey, Chris," he said.

The dealer, short and thin with hands quick enough to hide his boredom, glanced up from the table for just an instant. "J.D." The table was full, all except one place with a clear chip over its betting spot. Chris continued dealing while he talked. "Heard there was some excitement down at the courthouse."

"Some," said Scrbacek.

"Congrats, dude."

"Thanks."

"I thought the bastard was finally cooked. You're some kind of a magician, you are."

"My client was innocent."

"Not since the day he was born. But I've been telling everyone for a long time now—I ever get in trouble, I'm going straight to J.D. Scrbacek."

"Have you seen Dolores?"

"She's on tonight, somewheres. And how about that car blowing up like that?"

"How about it?"

"Kaboom. I heard someone was inside."

"That's right."

"Son of a bitch. Tough way to go. Whose car was it, anyways?"

"It wasn't a car, it was a Ford Explorer. And it was mine."

"You're kidding me."

"Unfortunately not."

"And the guy inside was turning the key instead of you?"

"That's the way it looks."

Chris paid the winners, scooped up the cards still on the table, and looked straight at Scrbacek. "You want to sit, there's a seat open. I've been saving it for some joker who's been gone past his time."

"No, thanks. I'm just looking for Dolores."

"Hey, J.D., I don't know about you, but if I won a case with the DNA against me and then my car blew up with someone else inside, I'd figure it was my lucky day."

Scrbacek looked at Chris for a moment and then down at the sign on the table. Twenty-five-dollar minimum. He thought a moment more before taking his wallet from his pants, pulling out what he had—six twenties, a five, two ones—and dropping it on the table.

Chris spread the bills out before him and said loudly, "Change one hundred twenty-seven."

Scrbacek stood behind the open seat as Chris jammed the bills down the cash slot and gave him five green chips and two white.

"Good luck," said Chris.

Scrbacek bet a green chip and pulled a three and an eight. Chris showed six. Without a word Scrbacek placed a second green chip beside the first and Chris slipped Scrbacek's third card beneath his others, face-down. When the deal came back to him, Chris pulled out his bottom card, a jack, dealt a nine on top, and just like that Scrbacek was up fifty bucks.

"Maybe you're right," said Scrbacek. He took off his raincoat, hung it over the chair, and sat. He pulled two greens back into his stack, leaving two for the next hand.

What followed was uncanny. Whenever he stayed pat with a twelve or thirteen, Chris would bust. Whenever he squinted and took a hit, the right card, like magic, flipped atop his others. With a hand of fifteen, he pulled an ace and a five; with a hand of fourteen he pulled a seven; twice when Chris had a twenty, Scrbacek pounded his hand into a twenty-one. And the pile of greens he placed before him grew until they turned to blacks, and then they grew some more.

He toked Chris a few chips every couple of hands, first the greens then the blacks, and when Chris was replaced by a woman named Thuy, he tipped her, too, because toking kept the luck moving through him, and it was moving through him like a current. The cocktail waitress brought him a stream of scotches on the rocks and another pack of cigarettes after he ran through his first, supplying as he was not only his own vile habit but the vile habit of the guy sitting next to him, who was cheerily bumming Marlboros even as his losses mounted. Scrbacek drank and smoked and tried to keep his hands steady as he placed his chips before him and signaled his plays. He won with a fourteen when Thuy pulled an eight to her six-jack. She placed three black chips in front of him as he turned his head to the left just in time to spot another cocktail waitress coming toward him, her round tray full of gold-rimmed glasses.

She had long thin legs, breasts bursting out of her top, black hair falling in waves around her pretty face. She smiled at Scrbacek, and he smiled back and took a long, satisfied drag of his cigarette.

"When did you get in?" said Dolores.

"A few thousand dollars ago."

"Up or down?"

"Up."

"Good for you."

"Farther up since you showed."

"How sweet."

She searched the glasses in her tray and pulled out a scotch on the rocks. "I'm working craps, but the guy this is for only tips when he's winning, and the tables have been ice all night."

"Not this one," he said before sucking down a long draw of the scotch.

"I heard you were having quite a day. You want to celebrate tonight?"

"That's why I came. Do you have the kid?"

"She's with her father."

"That's good. That's great. When do you get off?"

"It's your play."

Scrbacek turned back to the table. He was showing an ace-five. The dealer had a jack. He took a card, another five, and nodded, like it was the easiest thing in the world.

"I can get there by two," said Dolores.

"I'll be waiting."

"Good," she said, and then she leaned in close to whisper. "But J.D., don't climb up to your loft before I get there. Pretend I'm worth waiting up for."

Before he could answer, she sashayed off.

He watched as she carried her tray away, the twitch of her rear in that skimpy gold skirt bringing him hard. He had a burning for Dolores that he found inexplicable. Her perfect breasts were false, her red nails were glued on, the lavish frizz of black that framed her face was a fall pinned to her lank brown hair, her pouting lips were injected, her cute pinched nose was carved, her straight white teeth were corrected. Even her orgasms, as she squirmed atop of him and squeezed her own breasts and let out that hungry moan, were false, or at least he hoped so.

Somehow he found all this artificiality so erotic he could barely think straight around Dolores until after he twisted inside her and let loose his desire, before lapsing into a sweet and lonely sleep.

When he turned back to the table, something had changed. Where before there had been a current, now there was a dead calm. He bet three hundred and pulled a jack to his twelve and knew that whatever had been with him at the table had disappeared. Normally, he'd try to force it to come back to papa, keep betting against the deadness, waiting for the current to turn live again. Something inside him didn't like to win, but tonight his luck held. The scotch and the long day with its traumatic coda finally hit him all at once with a sickening weariness. It was time to go. He tossed another black chip at Thuy, gave the man beside him the rest of his cigarettes, slipped on his raincoat, and gathered his chips into a pile to take to the cashier.

Twenty-one hundred and seventy-five dollars.

He was too tired to let out a cheer or pump his fist as the cashier counted out the bills. He had thought a win like that would somehow make him happier and was disappointed that it didn't. He put a hundred seventy-five dollars into his wallet and folded the twenty remaining Ben Franklins in half and stuffed them into the top of his boot. On his way out he stopped at a bar in one of the lounges.

"I need a bottle of champagne," he told the bartender.

"What table you at?"

"I need it to go."

"Sorry, pal. No bottles to go. House rule."

"Well, you see, I got this girl coming over."

"I know the story."

"And she's been feeling unappreciated lately."

"What else is new."

"And she's had the best surgeons money can buy."

The barkeep glanced around. "All right, this once. You want the good stuff or the very good stuff?"

"I want the hundred-and-fifty-dollar stuff."

On his way out of the bar, holding the brown paper bag like a football, he heard the man sweeping the foyer say, "Good evening, Mr. Scrbacek."

He heard the doorman say, "Hope you had a good run, Mr. Scrbacek."

And then he was back outside, surrounded by the cool of the brightly lit night. He walked to the edge of the boardwalk, heard the uneven but steady roar of the waves in the darkness that crouched beyond the reach of the casino lights, breathed in the sweet salty-rot scent of the sea. He turned around and faced the gaudy grandeur that was Diamond's Mount Olympus.

Between the two golden domes was a post with a flag flapping in the wind, the word **SINGAPORE** printed upon the rippling fabric. The owner of Mount Olympus and three other casinos on the boardwalk, James E. Diamond—billionaire, high-flying jet-setter, author of three ghostwritten books detailing his brilliant business strategies—was such a famous personage that the patrons always wanted to know where he was. Management had taken to putting up a flag each morning to announce his location. Sometimes it was Hong Kong, sometimes London, sometimes Vegas or New York or Hollywood. And then, on those special days when he came to inspect his flagship casino or to work on his grand plan to put a mammoth casino resort on the swath of land on the northern bay of the city, known as the Marina District, they put up a great red flag that simply said IN THE HOUSE.

So, thought Scrbacek, the great James E. Diamond is in Singapore this evening. Singapore. Sweet. But I'll bet he didn't have a day like mine. I'll bet he didn't single-handedly whip the government in a court of law with nothing but his wiles and his wit. I'll bet he didn't feel death brush past his cheek and land on someone else's shoulder. I'll bet he didn't take all his ready cash and increase it twentyfold in a game of chance with the odds set dead against him. I'll bet he's not looking to a long night of champagne and sex with a surgically enhanced cocktail waitress with magic hands and a mouth like velvet.

He raised his brown paper bag and said out loud, "You might be a billionaire, Mr. Diamond, but tonight I kicked your ass."

And then, alone, he headed home.

8
FINAL CIGARETTE

As Scrbacek climbed the stairway from his office to his apartment, he thought about how nice it would be to keep climbing, to shuck off his raincoat, his shirt, his shoes, his pants, to keep climbing and keep shucking until he was in his sleeping loft, naked, feeling the pressure of the blankets on his body as slumber caressed his brow. One of his favorite things in the world was being awoken for sex by Dolores when she came in after her shift, the smoky taste of scotch in her mouth, the urgency of her hands as they kneaded him to wakefulness. It all took place in a hazy netherworld of pleasure. And afterward he would drift back into sleep as if he had just passed through the most perfect of dreams.

But he stopped short of the loft. He put the champagne in the freezer and dropped onto his couch. He was too tired even to take off his raincoat, but he would wait for Dolores as she had asked.

He just needed to keep his eyes open.

If he could keep his eyes open, then he would be ready for her when she opened the door with the key he left behind a loose brick, and made her way up the stairs. His smile and a glass of very good champagne would act as salve upon all the slights that had marred the strange thing that had grown between them—an acquaintanceship charged with random bouts of goatish sex but always, at heart, an acquaintanceship. Their relationship was as convenient a thing as he could ever have hoped for, but it left her, he could sense, more than vaguely disappointed. Maybe tonight would be different. Maybe tonight he would kiss her gently without trying to rip off her shirt. Maybe tonight he would ask about her day and listen to what she said and feign real interest in how wonderfully her daughter was doing in school. Maybe tonight he would try to make her a little happy.

He just needed to keep his eyes open.

A cigarette. He could use a cigarette. He patted the pockets of his raincoat—nothing. He had foolishly given what he'd had left to the cheerful man sitting next to him at the blackjack table, and now Scrbacek had zilch. He rose and quickly searched the apartment, coming up empty before he dropped down again in his chair. He didn't need to smoke, he just wanted to. He knew the difference.

He had quit smoking once, for a girl. Jenny Ling. Everybody has one great failed love, and Jenny Ling was his. She was an earnest, liberal help-thy-fellow-human type who found the stink, the stray litter of ash, the yellowed teeth, the cancerous tumors, found all the by-products of Scrbacek's habit decidedly uncool. Despite the startling banality of her insights into smoking, he had given it up for her, and had felt decidedly virtuous. It was his virtuous epoch, his time with Jenny Ling, but that love had failed, decidedly so, and he had taken up the practice once again.

Now, trying to stay awake for a different lover, he could use a cigarette. But Dolores would bring him one, sweet Dolores—she was always good for a spare. He closed his eyes and thought about the way Dolores would purse her pretty lips as she tossed him her pack of Benson & Hedges. He would tap the pack against the arm of his chair, shake out a single slim cigarette, place its smooth surface within his lips, flick to life his lighter, bring the flame close to his face, breathe in the fire, fill his nose and throat with the rich dark pleasure of the smoke, redolent of the burning leaves of autumn, the crackling hearths of winter, the sparks of a campfire spiraling into the summer night. He inhaled deeply, the warm tug of the nicotine suffusing into his blood, the heat of the red glow upon his fingers, filling his lungs and turning his dream into a gorgeous chiaroscuro of smolder and smoke.

He woke with a cough.

The smoke of his dream was surrounding him, thick, warm.

He sat up and coughed again.

"What the . . ."

There was only smoke. The lit digital displays on his stove, his cable box, his stereo, all were lost in the haze.

He stood and coughed, dashed to his window, pushed up the bottom sash. Fresh air washed upon him. He punched out the screen and looked down. The glow of flame within his office on the bottom floor danced upon the darkened street. He yelled for help, but nothing outside moved except the dance of the firelight.

He took a deep breath and rushed halfway down the spiral stairs. The heat hit his face like a fist. A carpet of flame covered the floor of his office. Fire danced wildly up the stairway. He stepped down farther into the roar as a tongue of flame shot high enough to lick his boot. He wrapped the coat around himself in preparation for a race through the fire to the safety of the street and took a deep breath. It felt like raw flame had leaped into his throat and seared his lungs. The pain buckled his legs. As he gripped the handrail, a cinder burned into his palm. He threw up his hand and collapsed down the circular stairwell, twisting until he lay in a curve, facing the steps. Fire danced about him as if he were the guest of honor on a funeral pyre. He took another breath. The pain was beyond pain. He fell into a fit of coughing as the heat overwhelmed him.

Slowly, desperately, hand over enfeebled hand, he dragged himself back up the stairway and into his apartment.

On his knees he crawled to the window, grabbed the sill, pulled himself up, stuck out his head. He gulped at the air. He knew the air he breathed to be cool, delicious, sweet, but still each inhalation burned as if he were again breathing in the hot smoke of the fire. He had to get out, somehow. He thought of jumping; it was only the second floor, but still. There was a drainpipe leading from the roof just a few feet from the window. That could be his ticket. He turned to take a look back into the apartment. What did he need? What must he save? What in his life was absolutely essential? A suit? His flat-screen? The diploma he was awarded by his law school? No, nothing. Nothing worth saving. He leaned back through the window and lunged for the pipe.

It groaned audibly when he grabbed hold of it. His burned right hand slammed into a brace, and the metal sliced his skin, but even so he whipped his other arm around to grab the drainpipe with both hands. It wasn't as steady as he had hoped, nothing more than folded sheet metal, but he saw no choice except to hold on tight and swing his body out of the window, away from the fire.

He steadied his grip, took a painful breath, swung.

His legs hung loose. He scrabbled at the brick wall with his boots, trying to find purchase, as if to climb up instead of down. Suddenly he stopped moving altogether, as if suspended in time as well as midair. With a groan and the sound of snapping braces, the pipe broke from the building, falling away even as it collapsed in on itself.

And Scrbacek fell with it, shouting, shouting.

The bending and collapsing of the metal slowed his fall just enough so that when he hit the asphalt unevenly, his left leg jammed but did not shatter. He lay on the ground, stunned. Slowly he raised his torso so he could stare head-on at the wall of fire inside the plate-glass window of his office. With much effort he stood, took a step forward and then another, and stopped before the flames, watching his entire career incinerate before his eyes. He wondered what he had done to cause the fire, what appliance he had forgotten to turn off, what combustible he had left too close to a source of heat. He wondered why the fire alarm hadn't gone off, tried to remember when he last changed the batteries. He thought for a moment of the twenty-six years remaining on his mortgage.

There came a rustling sound from behind him, and then something else.

"Scrbacek."

It was less than a whisper, as soft as a thought. He turned his head, and in that instant the fire before him was linked in his mind with the explosion behind the courthouse and he knew, with all certainty, that the car bomb had been meant for him and the fire had been purposely set and there was someone behind him intent on finishing the job.

He dived to the left at the same time he heard an insect buzz by his ear. He rolled along the ground and rose, running as fast as his jammed leg and seared lungs would allow, running, gasping for air, running, running for his life.

He pumped hard with both fists until he felt something like a baseball bat slam into his left arm, knocking him to the ground, and when he rose and started running again, the left arm refused to move, just hung there, lifeless. But he kept running, gasping and running, pumping now with one fist only, the singed tail of his raincoat sweeping behind him as he kept running, kept running.

He came to a cross street and turned quickly right. He grabbed his left biceps, and his hand came away slick—his arm was bleeding and the blood was coming fast—but he kept running.

Until he came to another intersection. Where he slowed. And then stopped. Bent over, grabbing again his bloodied biceps, gasping for breath. Gasping. For breath. Gasping. He coughed out a gob of black phlegm and searched desperately around him.

To the right, the neon glow of Casinoland beckoned. Within the reach of that light were the police, the hospitals, the Department of Human Services, whole industries designed to track and help a man in trouble. Within the reach of that light were friends, colleagues, Dolores. To the left were the hostile shadows of Crapstown.

Our brains have evolved over the eons by growing up and out. It is the forebrain, a rather recent addition, that controls all the higher functions: reason, mercy, love. In contrast, the hindbrain is a vestige of the lower-order mammals out of which we rose in the far recesses of the misty past. It sits at the base of our skulls like a rat, with a tail that runs down our spines, and controls our involuntary functions: heartbeat, breathing, vomiting, the release of adrenaline at the scent of danger. Our forebrains wrestle with the grand unanswerable questions of existence—our places in the world, the interconnectedness of all things, the intricacies of the infield fly rule—but when the worst dangers rear their ugly heads, it is that little rat at the base of the skull that takes control.

Put a rat between light and darkness, give it a shock, it will always, always run to the dark. Always. J.D. Scrbacek was marked for death for no reason he could fathom, his vehicle was gone, his home and office were destroyed, he was leaking blood with every step, and there was no one he could trust. J.D. Scrbacek was in mortal danger, and the rat at the base of his skull knew exactly what to do.

Scrbacek took off to the left, running as fast as lungs and legs would allow, running away from a killer, away from the light, running dead straight into the heart of darkness that was Crapstown.

9
CRAPSTOWN

He cut into an alley, veered up a wide street, darted into another alley. He ran like an asthmatic kick returner with the legions of hell out to tackle him and the whole of Crapstown as his field.

The cityscape he ran through was barely lit, the odd streetlight here, the odd porch light there, a wall vaguely illumined by the blue-gray flicker of a television. But even in the shadows, Scrbacek could feel the changes as he made his way farther from the boardwalk. The windows became first barred, then shattered, then boarded up with planks of splintering plywood. The lines of houses were first pitted with the occasional empty lot here and there, then held as much empty rubble as a standing building, then were reduced to swaths where the few standing buildings looked like the tottering teeth of a decrepit old man too poor to afford his daily orange. The stench of decay grew ever stronger, the sounds grew more desperate: the wails of a siren, the clash of a metal can overturning, a moan, a cry, something like the shattering of bones.

He ran past whores with silvered tops and fishnet stockings, who hooted at him and laughed as if it were they he was running from. He ran past packs of men standing in the shadows on dark corners, men who danced uneasily from foot to foot and called out to him as he ran past. A long-toothed boy spied him and gave maniacal chase before surrendering the pursuit with a shouted expletive. An old woman without any teeth rocked on a porch and stared down as he ran by. Dogs, eyes glowing red, heads bowed menacingly, tracked him as he made his way. And rats, big as small cats, sometimes held their ground as he approached, rearing upon their hind legs, snarling.

Lungs bursting, muscles screaming, heart failing, Scrbacek ran blindly on, pushed by fear, careering here and there but always heading west, until his jammed leg wobbled and he swerved off course, hitting the wall, literally, smashing his face into brick. He spun until his back was against the rutted surface, and looked behind him. Nothing. No one. He took a long breath, coughed it out, took another. He grabbed his arm, and slid to sitting on the ground.

He was bleeding too much, he knew. He tried to take his arm out of the raincoat, but it was swollen grotesquely and limp with pain. With his other hand he unbuttoned the front of his shirt, reached for the collar of his tee, and pulled. A sharp pressure at the back of his neck. He pulled again, resisting with his neck, gave it a sharp yank, and suddenly the whole front of his T-shirt ripped free. He tied it into a loop and slipped it over his hand and up his arm on the outside of the coat until it sat above the wound. He looked around the ground and found a thick splinter of wood. He scraped the points off the ends, slipped the stick into the loop of cotton, twisted it, and twisted it again until the loop was brutally tight upon his arm. He packed the stick and knot into his armpit so it wouldn't spin loose.

Tourniquet in place, he looked up and down the street. He wondered if maybe he had lost his pursuer, if maybe he wasn't really being chased at all, wondered if the whole thing was indeed a mistake, despite the explosion and the fire and the bullet wound. But the screech of a cat jolted his bones, and he scrabbled up and staggered forward again. He was reduced by terror to his raw essentials: joints and bones and lungs, the pain in his arm, the stitch in his side, the demented cough, the need to move, to get away, to be someplace else, anyplace else, to run.

As he made his way past a stack of metal trash cans, a hand reached out and tripped him. When he hit the ground, he saw the hand retract and a large shadow emerge from between the cans. Before the shadow could approach any closer, he pushed himself back to his feet and kept on moving. Along one sidewalk a silhouette lifted up an arm to try to stop him and he put a shoulder into the figure, knocking it aside, so he could continue his run.

Finally, on a dark narrow street with trash strewn and its buildings reduced to rubble, exhaustion caught him by the scruff of the neck and threw him facedown onto the cracked cement. A stone stoop stood out from the rubbled brick of a ruined house, and he crawled into the dark corner between the stoop and the brick. As he twisted into a sitting position, something scurried away, its claws scraping the cement.

He grabbed at the air with his lungs, coughed, grabbed for more, and fought to beat back the fear. Calm yourself, he thought. You must have lost the bastard by now. Probably even lost him when you made that first cut off your street. And if the shooter is right behind the ruined wall ready to take you out here and now, what the hell are you going to do about it anyway? So calm yourself. Make a plan.

The first plan that came to his mind was to get up and run, but as he tried to stand, a violent vertigo pounced, throwing him back down to the cement. No more running. Calm down. Make a plan.

He touched his wounded arm. The raincoat was now sticky and stiff with drying blood. He gently felt for the damage, and a pole of pain shot into his shoulder. He probed further and woke another pole of pain, and he shouted out despite himself. There were two wounds, one on either side. The bullet must have gone right through his arm; it wasn't stuck in there to torture the muscle. Chris at Mount Olympus had been right—it was his lucky night. It was unbelievable how lucky he felt. So damn lucky he wanted to wring a neck. He pressed the wounds again, two poles of pain ripped into his shoulder, and he shouted out:

"I'm so fucking lucky!"

Stop, he told himself. Calm down. Make a plan. His arm was still oozing blood despite the tourniquet. He opened his shirt and ripped himself another swath from his T-shirt. He wrapped the white cloth as tightly as he could bear around his bicep, twisting the loose end into itself so it would stay in place.

Now what? He would need a hospital. But to walk into an emergency room in the city—the bright fluorescents, the nurses rushing back and forth, the other patients watching him, the doctor calling the police to report a bullet wound—to place himself in that much light now seemed impossible. Someone was out to kill him, someone who could blow up his car and burn down his building, someone with the gall to shoot at him in the middle of his own street. Checking himself into a hospital in this city seemed a certain way to give himself over to that someone. No, he needed to get away, far away. But how?

His hand jerked to his raincoat. He felt for it. Here, no here. He pushed himself up to his knees and patted the pockets. There it was. He pulled out his phone and turned it on. The screen lit, and he let out a great breath of relief as he pressed his finger to the reader.

Who to call? His first thought was of his mother, but that was the reflex of a scared little boy; there was nothing she could do for him from The Villages. And 911 was an impossibility, what with the corruption that riddled the police force like a ruinous case of clap. Some cop had probably already been paid off to issue an APB with his description, all in the hope of leading the killer to his quarry. He thought of Dolores, but how reliable was she, really? He thought of his friends, his colleagues, friendly beat reporters, but could come up with no one in whom he had absolute confidence and who had the wherewithal to help. His secretary talked too much. Ethan Brummel was dead. Jenny Ling had dropped a restraining order on his ass, not that he didn't have it coming. And then there was Cirilio Vega, friend and fellow member of both the defense bar and Sweeney's Sunrise Club, where a pack of criminal defense attorneys shared strategies and swapped stories each morning before court. They were as close as rival attorneys could be, but there was something slippery about Cirilio, and his clients all were criminals. Could he trust his fate to a man who spent his entire life working for criminals?

Thirty years of life, and Scrbacek could come up with no name he absolutely trusted. His frustration rose within him and welled into a sob.

Calm down. Make a plan. He wiped his nose with the sleeve of his raincoat, went through his options one more time, and suddenly he knew. He found the number on the Internet.

"State Bureau of Investigation," said the voice.

"I'm looking for Special Agent Stephanie Dyer," he said, as softly as he could.

"I'm sorry," said the voice, "but I'm showing her not on duty now. Is there a message?"

"This is an absolute stone-cold emergency. Can you give me her home number?"

"That's not allowed, sir, but if it is an emergency, I can page her for you. Would you like me to do that for you, sir?"

"Yes. Of course, yes."

"What is the nature of the emergency?"

"Someone is trying to kill me."

"I see. Yes. That would be an emergency. And can you give me your name?"

"Scrbacek. J.D. Scrbacek. And please hurry."

"Oh, Mr. Scrbacek. Of course," said the woman, her voice quickening in recognition. "Stay on the line, please, and I'll find her right away."

He was put on hold. Music was pumped through his phone, nice cheery music with violins. He closed his eyes and listened to the music as if it were a lifeline, the sweep of the strings like the sweep of a rope as it flew in the air to save him. When he opened his eyes to catch sight of the rope, he saw the shadowy figures, three of them, walking in a line down the street toward him, three of them, walking in a line.

And the music in Scrbacek's ear was suddenly as loud as a Sousa march played by a great brass band.

10

ANSONIA ROAD

They had to hear it, the three walking toward him, the music was so damn loud.

Scrbacek pressed the phone tighter to his ear, and the crazy music grew even louder as the figures stepped closer. With a rush of panic, he ripped the phone from his ear, disconnected the call, and pressed the device against his chest to hide the light as he scrunched backward to fit as tightly as possible in the darkened corner of the stoop.

The three figures approached, their footsteps growing louder, their voices more distinct. Scrbacek couldn't yet make out the words but could read the tone: young, arrogant, slow. He scrunched up even tighter and kept his breath as silent as his fear would let him, fighting the compulsion to cough.

Closer they came, closer.

The tall shadow was doing most of the talking, the short shadow was letting out the occasional "Yes" and "Oh man," the middle shadow was saying nothing, but walking with a speed and purpose that forced the other two shadows to keep up their pace.

"They're like great bowls of Jell-O, and it don't take much of a joke to get her laughing and them two bowls going."

"No, man, it does not."

"Just a little joke, a three-priests-on-a-boat joke, and the Jell-O, it be jiggling and joggling."

"That's right."

"Makes you want to go in with a can a whipped cream and a spoon and get you some, all that jiggling and joggling."

"Oh man, yes, it does."

As the three shadowy figures approached his spot, Scrbacek jammed himself as far into the corner as his bones would allow and held his breath. Except for his heart, which was thumping madly in his ears, he was totally silent.

"She'd be good-looking, too, Rita, yes, if it wasn't for them teeth. I'd be afraid to stick anything near them teeth, she'd a bite it right off."

"Yes, she would."

"Like a beaver going after a big old oak tree."

"Now you're getting proud."

"What?"

"You heard me."

Scrbacek was sure they could see him, certain of it, wincing involuntarily at the recognition of his presence he was sure would come. But they kept walking and talking, coming ever closer, right up to the stoop where he hid. And then, quick as that, they were past.

He didn't dare breathe yet, waited as step by step they moved past him, step by step, their footsteps dropping in tone, their voices growing lower, quieter. He couldn't hold it any longer and slowly let out a breath, and as soon as he did, he heard the loud blaring of some techno-jazz.

He jerked when he heard it, sending pain crashing through his shoulder. It was his damn ringtone. Crap. He answered the call as quickly as his shaking fingers would allow, jamming the phone to his ear.

"Mr. Scrbacek? Are you there, Mr. Scrbacek? I've paged Special Agent Dyer, and she should be calling in shortly. We were disconnected somehow."

He was shaking so hard he couldn't answer, just listened to the phone, shaking, staring down at the cracked cement beneath him as if to do so made him smaller, less obvious.

"Mr. Scrbacek, are you there? Are you there?"

"Yes," he said softly, "I'm here."

"Can you tell me where you are, Mr. Scrbacek?"

When he looked up, there was a man bending over him.

The man was young and squat and said nothing. Behind him were the tall figure and the short figure. The man bending over him and saying nothing reached out, took the phone away from Scrbacek, canceled the call, and passed it to the tall figure.

"Oh man," said the tall one, gazing down at the phone. "This sucker was just released. The Freak's gonna love this."

"Nice," said the short one.

"The Freak, he's gonna pay top dollar for this one, not like that old flip unit we took out from that van last week."

The man bending over Scrbacek started searching through Scrbacek's front pants pockets. When Scrbacek said something, the man ignored him, and when Scrbacek tried to grab the man's arm to stop the search, the man just slapped his hand away before reaching in a pocket and pulling out his keys. He looked at them and handed them to the man behind him.

"Now what are we going to do with these? What the hell use are keys?"

The man bending over Scrbacek grabbed Scrbacek's hip and rolled him over onto his side. Scrbacek landed on his wounded arm and screamed in pain. The silent figure checked Scrbacek's back pockets and pulled out his wallet. He handed the wallet to the tall figure behind him.

"Now look at this, look at this," said the tall man. "I told you stuff was happening on the street tonight. I told you we ought to get off our fat asses and find us some trouble, and now look at this. Cash, cards, the whole shooting match. We're going to have us a time with this."

"Is there an address?" said the short man.

"Of course there's an address. What does that matter?"

"The keys."

"The keys? Oh yeah, the keys. We got the house, we got the car, we got the cash. Oh, we're going to have us a time. Let's get what we can get and then go to Stinger's, man, scarf some shrimp, have us a time. What else that dude got there, Jorge?"

The techno-jazz played, and the tall man answered the call, saying, "Hello, no one home," before hanging up.

The silent man grabbed Scrbacek's right arm and yanked up the sleeve of his raincoat, then dropped it and grabbed the left arm. Scrbacek screamed again in pain as the silent figure shoved up the sleeve on the left arm, grabbed hold of Scrbacek's metal wristwatch band, flicked it loose, and pulled it off the wrist. He handed it to the tall man.

"What's this? Tag who? You think we could luck at least once into a Rolex."

"You'd think."

"A Rolex would look sharp on my arm, yes, it would."

The silent man stepped back and lifted up Scrbacek's leg. He eyed the sole of Scrbacek's boot, did a rough measurement with his hand, let the leg fall back to the cement. Then, still without saying anything, the man stood up straight, turned away, and started walking again down the street.

"Is that all?" said the tall one, hurrying now after the silent man. "No shoes, no belt, nothing else? What about the raincoat? Even filthy as it is, it's got to be worth something."

"At least something," said the small one, following behind.

"Jorge, man, what's the rush? I mean, we can't just throw away these opportunities. Jorge, come on, man."

They continued down the street, their voices growing less distinct until Scrbacek could no longer make out the words, just the tone: young, arrogant, slow. In the distance he could hear the techno-jazz ringtone play and then die, play and then die.

Scrbacek leaned back against the edge of the stoop and held his arm and gasped. He had never felt so lost, so scared, so hurt, so weak, so hopeless. It was as if even the air, as it burned his lungs with every breath, had betrayed him. He closed his eyes and tried to make it all go away, tried to force himself to wake up back in his apartment, whole and uninjured, ready to start another day as the brilliant legal hotshot with the whole city at his feet. But then his eyes snapped open. He thought he heard something. He thought he heard them, Jorge and his two lemmings, coming back for the raincoat, the belt, the boots. He pulled himself up to standing, fought the wooziness, looked down the street the way they had gone. Even though he saw nothing, he headed in the opposite direction.

He wasn't running now. He was too tired, too weak and dizzy, in too much pain. He was walking, slowly, limping from his jammed leg, holding his injured arm tight to his chest, coughing and shivering with every painful step. When he reached a cross street he turned, and when he reached another cross street he turned again. He wasn't going anywhere in particular, just going. At the next intersection he looked at the street signs to see if he could get his bearings.

Taft and Ansonia.

Ansonia?

It was somehow familiar.

Ansonia Road.

He had represented someone who lived on Ansonia Road, a man picked up on a weapons violation. Donatino Guillen. Donnie. The case had been a loser except for a minor search-and-seizure issue, which Scrbacek had built into a major problem for the County Prosecutor's Office, allowing Donnie to plead to a gift—three years, suspended, with two years' probation. He remembered Donnie Guillen because Donnie had been very grateful after everything and because Donnie hadn't seemed the type to play with guns. He had been small, quiet, sweet, actually, without the aura of violence that usually attached to his gun defendants, which was peculiar because they had found on Donnie Guillen enough weaponry to arm a battalion: seventeen handguns, two automatic rifles, a hand grenade, a silencer. And he remembered Donnie Guillen's address because it combined the number of home runs Babe Ruth had hit with the Babe's New York home, the Ansonia hotel. When Scrbacek had mentioned the coincidence, Donnie had said, "Who's Babe Ruth?"

714 Ansonia Road.

Scrbacek was on the five-hundred block of Ansonia Road. He started to make his way north, through the five hundreds and the six hundreds, staying in the shadows, hiding when a police cruiser slid by. The street, he could see, dead-ended at the bay, there was only so much farther he could go, and still it seemed like he would never get there. He grew weaker with each step. The dizziness increased, the coughing, the shaking. Twice he felt like he was about to faint before he caught himself. He wrapped the raincoat as tight around him as he could, but still he couldn't stop his shivering.

He staggered on and on, and finally he was there: 714 Ansonia Road. And his hopes sank until they pooled at his feet.

An old tenement building near the very end of the street, dark and ruined, with all but one of the windows planked with plywood and this last showing not the faintest ray of light. Looming behind was an abandoned warehouse with bricked-up doors and windows. The warehouse's lot was ringed with a fence topped by barbed wire. Trash was piled high outside the warehouse, sat in drifts along the fence, spilled out from beneath the house's porch. The whole place was as forlorn as anything Scrbacek had ever seen. If Donnie Guillen had lived there once, he lived there no more, unless he had fallen lower than a rat. Still, without a choice, Scrbacek struggled to climb the steps. He crossed the rotted beams of the porch and banged on the door.

Nothing.

He banged again, harder and longer, feeling the reverberations in his injured arm, banged until his right hand was numb from banging. He leaned against the door and felt a wave of weakness fall through him. He closed his eyes and thought of sleeping, and his knees buckled and he barely caught himself. And then he heard a sound. From inside the building. A shuffling, growing louder, coming closer.

He banged again and shouted, "I'm looking for Donnie. Donnie Guillen."

Slowly the door opened.

A face appeared out of the darkness.

"Mr. Scrbacek?"

"Donnie, thank God. I need . . . I need . . ."

"What are you doing here?"

"I need . . ."

"You're bleeding. Let me call an ambulance."

"No ambulance. No hospitals. No one can know where I . . . where I . . . They're after me. They're . . ."

"Mr. Scrbacek?"

And then he fainted, J.D. Scrbacek, fainted right into the ruin that was 714 Ansonia Road.

If you were looking from across the street, you would next have seen an unsettling sight. A man in a bloodied raincoat, lying on the doorstep of an all-but-abandoned house, his body half inside the black doorway, his legs on the porch. And then you would have seen those legs slowly disappearing, dragged into the building inch by inch, until their entirety was inside, and the door was closed, and everything was again as it should have been on Ansonia Road in the heart of Crapstown. Dark, deserted, despairing.

Desolation.

SECOND NIGHT

11
SQUIRREL

Scrbacek dreamed his clothes were being stripped off his body until suddenly he awoke to find his clothes being stripped off his body. He opened his eyes to see a score of hands clutching at him, shouted out from the pain in his arm, and fell hard back into unconsciousness.

***

He woke again from the pain twisting inside his arm and called out into the darkness. A woman with a broad face and a great halo of blonde hair appeared over him and smiled as she stroked his brow with her hand. He knew then, with all certainty, that she was an angel and he was dead. She disappeared for a moment, and he felt a stinger slip into his arm, and the angel came back and stroked his brow, and he grew light, and the pain eased, and he rose sweetly back into unconsciousness.

***

For a period of time, the length of which he couldn't fathom, he slipped in and out of a dream state. His constant companions, whether asleep or awake, were the sound of intense muffled conversation from somewhere distant and the dank smell of deterioration.

A sharp pressure on his chest jolted him to consciousness, and he found himself lying naked on a mattress, covered from the waist down by a blanket, doused with light from a bare bulb inside a cone hanging overhead. A hunched little man with spectacles, big ears, and too many teeth, was twisting a piece of Scrbacek's chest between his fingers.

"Three," said the man, a stethoscope draped around his scrawny neck. He sucked air through pursed lips and leaned close to the piece of flesh between his fingers. "Interesting." The little man raised his other hand. Light gleamed off the short curved blade of a scalpel.

Scrbacek tried to sit up, but a weight of dizziness pushed him down onto the mattress.

The hunched man pulled his hand away with a loud intake of air. "He's awake." He took a step back and squealed, "Someone come and hold him down. He's awake."

Scrbacek could feel the pain in his left arm but only at a far remove, as if he were somehow floating above the wreck that was his body. His left arm was bloodied, a long strip of gauze was wrapped tightly around his right hand, his chest was mottled with bruises. He tried again to sit up against the dizziness, pushing with his right arm despite the pain in his palm, and this time he succeeded in lifting his upper body. Slowly he looked around.

He was on a bed in the middle of a small, seedy room with stained yellow wallpaper. Holes had been punched through the walls. A single wooden chair, with an open black medicine bag on its seat, sat directly beneath a window through which no light flowed. At first he assumed that meant it was night, but when he raised his hand to cover his eyes from the bulb he saw that the window was boarded up from the inside, and so he had no idea of the time of day. There was the same muffled conversation that had been his constant companion, but now he could identify it as a television, somewhere down a hallway, with the volume on loud. In a dark corner of the room stood a ragged bureau with some sort of large dark object perched atop it.

Scrbacek turned to the little man. "Where's Donnie?"

"Donnie is currently indisposed," said the little man. "He asked me if it wouldn't be too much of an imposition to treat your deteriorating condition. I told him it was, but he implored me to come anyway, so here I am."

"Are you a doctor?"

"Not exactly."

"Then stay the hell away from me."

"Suit yourself," said the little man. "You're the patient, and the patient is always right. But be aware the infection in your arm is spreading every minute." The little man smiled. "Every second." He dropped the scalpel into the black bag, clasped it shut, and carried it out of the room, leaving Scrbacek alone.

Scrbacek tried to swing his legs off the bed and stand, but the blood drained too quickly from his head and nausea forced him to lie down again. He closed his eyes and felt the nausea subside, and he disappeared into some dark, dreamless sleep.

***

When he awoke, the television was still blaring, the same endless conversation going on and on about absolutely nothing. The angel was now sitting on his mattress, wiping his face with a wet towel.

"Finally," she said in flat, bored voice. "I thought maybe I had given you too much. It's a sin to waste."

Scrbacek shook his head and sat up in the bed. He was still dazed, though the pain had returned to roost in his left arm, flaring sharply whenever he moved. The woman with the towel was pale and pretty and as all-American as football and pom-poms and butter statues at the Iowa State Fair. She wore jeans and a T-shirt pressed to its limits by her sharply nippled breasts, and as he stared at her, he thought she looked vaguely familiar, though he couldn't place her. A client? A blackjack dealer? A woman he had hit on once in a bar? Probably that, because he surely would have hit on her in a bar. Standing behind her was the hunched little man with the stethoscope and the scalpel, and when Scrbacek saw him, he started scooting away before a sharp bolt of pain stopped him.

"Calm down, sweetie," said the woman. "You'll hurt yourself. My name's Elisha."

"Where's Donnie?" said Scrbacek.

"He went with Reggie and Blixen," she said, "getting you your drugs."

"No. No more drugs."

"Take it easy now," said Elisha, pushing the wet towel into his chest and forcing him back down on the bed. "You're cut off from the good stuff. I gave you a taste to stop the pain, but I've never been good at sharing. They went to fill a scrip. What was it, Squirrel?"

"Keflex," said the hunched little man, stepping forward nervously. "We could use Cipro, or Bactrim if forced, fine antibiotics both, but with gunshot wounds Keflex is generally indicated."

"I thought you weren't a doctor," said Scrbacek.

"Squirrel went to medical school," said Elisha.

"And I told them I needed peroxide," said Squirrel. "It can be a very effective cleanser."

"And that's great," said the blonde, "because I can always use whatever you have left over."

"Can I have a cigarette?"

"Sure," said Elisha, pulling a crumpled pack out of her jeans.

"I would recommend against it," said Squirrel.

"And if you were maybe a doctor," said Scrbacek, "I would maybe listen."

"It's your funeral," said the little man with a toothy smile.

Elisha extracted a cigarette from the pack, lit it, took a drag herself, and then handed it to Scrbacek, who stared at it longingly for a moment before placing it in his lips, dragging deep.

He twisted on the bed and coughed the smoke out in brutal spasms. His lungs burned as if he had spent the night swallowing flaming shots of tequila. As he coughed, his throat closed in on him, tightening, until he could barely breathe. He threw away the cigarette. Squirrel hopped around, stamping on the still-lit butt as Scrbacek grabbed at his neck, coughed, fought for breath, and coughed some more. Slowly the spasms stopped, and his airway eased open.

"I guess he's not used to menthols," said Elisha.

"He burned the crap out of his lungs," said Squirrel. "From the smell of him and the burns on his coat and the way he was hacking all night, it was obvious. Frankly, I wouldn't mind a peek inside that chest. His lungs would be quite interesting specimens."

"Keep your stinking hands off me," Scrbacek coughed out.

"It's only a matter of time, I suppose."

"No more cigs for you," said Elisha. "At least for a while."

"Forever, I would suggest," said Squirrel. "But what do I know?"

"Other than my lungs," said Scrbacek, "how am I?"

"You should be dead. But the tourniquet, however crude, saved much blood, and there's no pulsatile bleeding. The bullet missed the bone and a major artery. You might just survive."

"Squirrel is disappointed," said Elisha.

"You were lucky," spit out the little man with much bitterness.

"That's just how I feel," said Scrbacek. "Lucky, lucky, lucky. Call me Mr. Lucky."

"Still," said Squirrel, "we may need to amputate."

"What?" Scrbacek bolted upright, suddenly hyperalert. The pain shot through his shoulder and into his back, but he hardly noticed. Something moved atop the bureau, and he pulled back. It was the dark object he had seen before, but now it had a shape. It looked like a gargoyle holding a pike. He put his hands over his eyes to get a better look. It was a girl, in fatigue pants and a green tank top, holding in her muscled arms some sort of assault rifle.

"Who's that?" said Scrbacek.

"The Nightingale," said Elisha. "Consider her your guardian angel. And don't worry about the amputation. Squirrel's only kidding."

"No, I'm not," said the man. "Not kidding at all."

"You're not going to lose your arm," said Elisha.

"It won't be lost," said Squirrel.

"Don't mind him," said Elisha. "He's just a silly little man with a dream and a hacksaw. I brought you some broth."

"No, my stomach—"

"Shut up and drink," she said as she brought a mug to his lips. It was warm and rich and it made him gag, but she forced him to finish it, and when he did he felt nauseated again.

"Better?" she said.

"No," said Scrbacek. "Where's Donnie?"

"I told you, Donnie's out getting help," she said. "You need some, don't you think? I cleaned your clothes, got as much of the blood off them as I could. The raincoat said dry-clean only, but I washed it anyway, got most of the blacking out, though there are still burn spots. The shirt was too stained to save, so Donnie's getting you a new one, same size, and some T-shirts from the mission thrift shop. And a toothbrush, which you could use."

Scrbacek rubbed his tongue along his upper teeth.

"Definitely," she said.

Scrbacek stared at her. "Do I know you? I have this feeling I've seen you before."

She smiled dimly for a moment, the smile of a movie star when someone comes up to her in a bathroom and says, *I recognize you. You're somebody.* She waited a moment and then shrugged. "Some say I'm unforgettable. But I know you. You're the lawyer who was representing Caleb Breest and now has gone seriously missing."

The whole thing flooded back into Scrbacek's consciousness, and he remembered the courthouse and Ethan Brummel and the fire in his building and the shot that tore through his arm and the someone out there who was trying to kill him. His breathing suddenly constricted again as if his lungs were filling with fear.

"I have to get out of here," he gasped. "I have to get out, now. I have to get help."

"You need to get your arm fixed first," said Squirrel.

"No time," said Scrbacek. "I have to go."

"Where to?" said Elisha calmly. "Where are you going to go?"

He thought for a moment as the panic flowed through him. There was no home anymore, no office, no Ford Explorer to take him away from all of this. He needed Stephanie Dyer. He needed Caleb Breest. He needed his mother. His mother. In Florida. He could go to Florida. Yeah, Florida. But how would he get there? And what would he do? Hide out in The Villages, play mah-jongg, save coupons, eat dinner at four, sit by the pool in his Speedo, chatting with seventy-five-year-old women on the make, waiting for someone to kill him?

"Right now you're safer here than anyplace else," said Elisha. "So stop being a baby and let him look at your arm."

Squirrel stepped hesitantly to the mattress as Scrbacek, buoyed by Elisha's high-wattage smile, offered the little man his left arm. Squirrel unraveled the cloth around the wounds, took a magnifying glass out of his bag, and began his examination.

"Interesting," said Squirrel as he studied the still-seeping holes in Scrbacek's arm and the grotesquely swollen biceps, streaked yellow and purple from the blood that had drained through the muscle. Almost gleefully, he added, "The infection is spreading."

"You're not taking it off," said Scrbacek.

"We shall see what we shall see," said Squirrel as he leaned in to get a closer look at the wounds. "I only do what I must."

"Don't grow too attached to it, you little rodent," came a raucous voice, crisply twanged.

Scrbacek turned to see, blocking the whole of the doorway, a concrete slab of a woman, with reddish dreads thick as snakes and large yellow teeth. She stood wide as a barn and haughty as a queen and brandished as her mace of state an automatic the size of a salami. Squirrel sucked in a wet breath when he saw her.

"I'm only looking, Reggie," he said. "No harm is there in looking?"

"He's not taking off my arm," said Scrbacek.

"Don't worry about your arm there, Stifferdeck," said the woman, sliding back the barrel of the huge gun before pointing it at Scrbacek's chest. "You got bigger things to be sweating over now."

12
REGINA

The woman known as Reggie, with the dreads and the automatic, squinted at Scrbacek as she kept her gun pointed at his chest. She wore black buckled boots and faded jeans and a leather motorcycle vest over a stained T-shirt, and her arms were like tattooed girders of iron. Behind her an old woman wearing the ragged, layered clothing of the chronically homeless clutched a paper bag as she hobbled to Reggie's side. The old woman, stooped and aged, barely came up to Reggie's hip.

"Is Donnie back?" said the woman with the gun.

"I thought he was with you," said Elisha.

"He skipped off before we could fill the scrip, said he had an important errand. Has Stifferdeck explained what he's doing here?"

"We haven't gotten there yet."

"He ask you any suspicious questions?"

"Not even my sign. He's mostly been sleeping."

"Then it's about time he woke up." Reggie swaggered toward Scrbacek and pressed the gun into his cheek. It was cold and hard and had the slick dark scent of oil. "We got some questions that need answering, Stifferdeck. Like, what the hell you doing in this part of town?"

"Hiding," said Scrbacek, keeping his head as still as possible.

"But why here?"

"Where else?" said Scrbacek. "Someone tried to kill me. I ran into Crapstown and remembered Donnie's address."

"How damn convenient for you," said Reggie, raising the gun into the air and turning around as if giving a speech to the multitudes. "Just happened to remember Donnie's address. Just happened. No one just stumbles into Crapstown. No one just happens to show up on Ansonia Road. Especially not no high-flying briefcase who defended the monster that killed Malloy and who's now supposedly on the run."

"Supposedly?"

She slapped the gun into his jaw; it cracked painfully against the bone. "Oh, they looking for you all right, Stifferdeck, but I still got questions. What's your game?"

"Staying alive."

"When Malloy appointed me Sentinel, he said a fool would come dancing our way, and that this fool would wreak havoc and change everything. And then, lo and behold, here you come, prancing on in. Something's going on, and I'm going to smoke it out, all right." She leaned forward, pressed the gun into Scrbacek's neck, opened her eyes wide.

The old woman in rags took a step forward as Reggie backed off to lean against the wall. "You're the beagle," the old woman said in a rapid, cragged voice. Gray tufts of hair curled out of her chin. Her breath smelled of rotgut whiskey and rot. "The one that was mouthing for Caleb Breest. The one that's gone missing. The one they think is dead."

"I suppose that's me," said Scrbacek.

"Blixen has one question for you, beagle. Do you play chess? Do you?"

"I used to," said Scrbacek.

"Then I'll get the board."

"Not until I take care of his arm," said Squirrel.

Scrbacek quickly said to him, "Forget it."

"Don't worry," said the old woman. "Squirrel's not taking it off. Blixen won't let him. He'd probably kill you doing it, and then we'd never have our game. But Squirrel's about the best healer you can find in this part of the city. He was top of his class at medical school until—"

"Quiet, you old fool," squealed Squirrel.

"Until he was expelled—"

"Must we go into this every time?"

"For collecting."

Scrbacek looked at Squirrel for a moment and then yanked his arm away from the little man.

"It's just a hobby," said Squirrel. "A man needs a hobby."

"I told you to take up golf," said Elisha.

"You listen to Baltimore," said the old woman, "before someone starts collecting parts off of you. Those ears of yours must be worth something."

"Elisha Baltimore?" said Scrbacek, taking in anew the woman's all-American face and well-filled T-shirt. "The Lady Baltimore?" Of course he knew her. He simply hadn't recognized her with her clothes on. The Lady Baltimore was one of the headlining strippers at Dirty Dirk's. He had seen her during his strategy meetings with Joey Torresdale, had seen her strut to the stage in a short mink jacket and wrap her long legs around the pole as the satin-lined fur slid languorously down her pale, firm skin. He remembered the way she faced away from the crowd and bent at the waist to reach through her legs for the ten-dollar bills thrust at her by trembling, eager hands. He remembered the way her breasts had kept their remarkable shape even as she hiked herself upside down on the pole.

"You are unforgettable," said Scrbacek.

"So they say," she said, standing. "You thirsty?"

"Yes, actually, I am."

"You know, Stifferdeck," said Reggie, still leaning against the wall, "even if we don't ax you, you're not going to last long anyhow, the way things are. Everyone and his whore is out looking for you. We just don't want to end up laid out on the street alongside your worthless body. Like the Freak. I don't think it's no coincidence that a day after they burn down your building, they burn down the Freak's place with him still inside. And word has been passed that the scavenger who finds you is in line to collect for himself a fat fee."

Squirrel turned his head and his eyes opened with curiosity. "How fat?"

"You remember my Sheila?" said Reggie.

"That's fat," said Squirrel, toothy smile growing. "That's positively obese."

"Don't even think it, you perverse piece of gristle," said the old woman. "Not a word to anyone, or Blixen will twist your head off like a chicken and toss it into the bay for crab bait. Blixen and the beagle, we're going to play. He promised. As soon as he is able. And we won't let the likes of you spoil it." She hobbled over to the bed and tossed the paper bag to Squirrel. "Now heal."

As Squirrel rummaged through the bag, Reggie turned and spoke to the girl sitting on the bureau with the gun. "You keep your eye on him. One false move, and ffft." She pushed herself off the wall and slid a finger across her own throat. "What the hell kind of name is Stifferdeck, anyway?"

"My father's from Scandinavia," said Scrbacek.

"Figures. Damn Scandinoovians . . .-navinians . . . Just don't be getting too comfortable. I want you gone. One way or the other." And then she swaggered out of the room.

"I don't think she likes me," said Scrbacek.

"Don't mind Regina," said the old woman, pulling out a flask from the rags wrapped around her body. "Underneath she's just a lonely country girl."

"And underneath that," said Elisha, coming back in the room with a glass of murky water, "she's a murderous bitch."

"Just what the doctor ordered," said Squirrel as he searched through the contents out of the bag. "Keflex, Tylenol No. 3, saline, gauze, peroxide." He took an empty coffee can and mixed the peroxide with the saline. "We'll see now if the limb can be saved, though I have my doubts. Take this."

Squirrel took two of the spiked Tylenols out of the bottle, and Scrbacek chased the pills with the foul glass of water.

"Better give him two more," said Elisha. "He doesn't take well to pain." Squirrel did as she said, and Scrbacek gratefully downed those also.

"Now if one of you will gently restrain my patient's arm, I can begin."

"Just a cleaning, right?" said Scrbacek.

"Don't you worry, beagle," said the old woman before taking a snatch from her flask and then hobbling over to the bed. She took hold of Scrbacek's left wrist and clamped her filthy, gnarled hands around it with shocking strength. "I'll be here the whole time, keeping my eyes on the little thief. And right after he's through, we'll play our little game. That's the deal. Our little game. Now hold on to your socks."

"I'm not wearing any socks."

"That's a shame," she said.

Squirrel dabbed a piece of gauze in the peroxide solution. It boiled and sizzled as Squirrel slowly brought it to the wounds in Scrbacek's biceps.

The scream fell upon Ansonia Road like the mating call of a mammal long extinct.

13
BLIXEN

After the ordeal of the treatment, Scrbacek lay back, closed his eyes, listened to the drone of the immortal television, and waited for the codeine in the Tylenol to ease both his pain and his urge to cough. Squirrel had flushed Scrbacek's wounds with the peroxide and saline solution, applied a pressure dressing, and given him strict orders to take the Tylenol as needed and the Keflex four times daily for ten full days. Before the ersatz doctor left, he took one more look at Scrbacek's arm and shook his head sadly. Scrbacek couldn't tell if the sadness came because Squirrel thought the wounds wouldn't heal or because he thought they would.

Now, his eyes still closed and the drugs just starting to take effect, Scrbacek plotted out his next move. He needed to find out who was trying to kill him, that much was certain. And he needed to find someplace safer to hide than this ruined house with its deranged ex-medical student, its peroxided stripper, its homeless old woman, its gargoyle with a gun, and its dreadlocked sentinel who wanted him gone, one way or the other. But most of all he needed help, was desperate for help, for it was not within the realm of his imaginings that he, J.D. Scrbacek, on his own, might save himself.

As far as he could determine, there were only two people to whom he might turn. Special Agent Dyer could put Scrbacek in a safe house, send her fellow agents out to discover who was after him, solve the whole problem through the finely tuned mechanisms of the law. But who knew better than Scrbacek the flaws in that machinery? And the state bureaucracy was incapable of keeping a secret; as soon as Dyer knew where he was hiding, everyone would know where he was hiding, including his would-be killer. Caleb Breest had the strength to protect Scrbacek, the sources to discover who was behind the attempts on his life, the brute power to annihilate the assassin and those behind him. But Breest could just as easily turn that brutality against Scrbacek if it served his purposes. There had been something in the way Breest had stared at him during their meeting in the courthouse lockup that had left him deeply unsettled.

So that was it: turn to the law, whose enforcers he had opposed for the entirety of his career; or turn to the lawless, whom he had defended but whom now he feared. How in the world, Scrbacek wondered, had his life come to hinge on such an unpalatable choice?

He smelled something unpleasant, acrid, like a mélange of freshly piled garbage, lightly scented with warm piss. He opened one eye. Staring at him from a chair beside his bed, a chessboard with the pieces arrayed in her shaking hands, was the old woman with the wisp of beard, the one called Blixen.

"Our game," she croaked.

"I'm not sure I feel quite up to it," said Scrbacek, groggy with codeine.

The old woman put the board on the side of his bed, white pieces facing him. It was a small leather-tooled chess set with pewter pieces. Two of the black pawns had been replaced by pennies; the role of a white bishop was being played by a pebble.

"Oh, you're up for it, all right," said the old woman. "Make your move. Pawn to king four is the old standby. Pawn to king four. Or to queen four, if you're the adventurous sort."

"I really don't—"

"Make your move," said the old woman. "Make it. Hurry." And then her eyes locked into Scrbacek's, and her voice softened so he could barely hear it above the television. "It could be worth your life. Make your move."

Scrbacek sat up in the bed, the blanket falling from his bare chest, and stared at the woman for a moment before looking around. There was no one else in the room except the girl with the gun atop the bureau. Her face was in shadow, and she sat with a stillness that gave not the slightest indication she was alive.

"The Nightingale can be trusted," said the old woman. "Make your move."

"All right," said Scrbacek, and he pushed his pawn to queen four.

"Excellent," cackled the old woman. "We're off on the hunt now. Hear the hounds? And already you're in more danger than you know."

"I made one move," complained Scrbacek.

"One's enough," said the old woman before pushing her queen's pawn to meet Scrbacek's. "Too much." And then, in a lower voice, she said, "Who sent you?"

"No one sent me," said Scrbacek. "I'm just trying to stay alive."

"Thar she blows," said the old woman, pointing at Scrbacek's naked chest. "Squirrel said that you had it. It's a sign, a message from the moon."

"It's nothing."

"It's an extra nipple," barked the old woman. "A third tit."

"I've had it all my life." Scrbacek covered his chest with the blanket as he pushed his king's pawn up two spaces.

"Oh, the King's Gambit," howled Blixen. "Should Blixen wipe the pawn off the face of the board or let it be? What says the moon? Can the pawn be trusted? You tell me."

"Let it be," said Scrbacek.

The old woman stared at him as her hand hovered above the pawn, whose only move was to capture his pawn, and then her hand shifted her king's knight, moving it to threaten the pawn, but keeping it alive for the moment.

"Regina is afraid of you," said the old woman softly. "She thinks you've come to destroy us all. Is it true?"

"Of course not."

"You'd be dead already if it wasn't for Donatino's say-so. Regina listens to Donatino. But not to Blixen. To Regina, Blixen's a cantankerous loon. She thinks insanity runs in the family." She extracted her flask, flicked it open, poured a slug down her throat, wiped her mouth with the back of her hand. "And she may be right. Still, Blixen knows things. The beagle can help, Blixen tells her. He can be our knight, jumping from place to place, but Regina won't listen. She sees a threat and wants to eliminate it."

"Why? I don't understand."

"You're Caleb Breest's lawyer. You come into Crapstown looking for our Donatino. Our Ares. You're here just one day, and already the place is on fire. A friend was killed this morning, as honest a criminal as you could ever hope to find. Killed, and his entire storehouse of filched merchandise destroyed. Your name was shouted by the attackers." The old woman raised her voice and said, "Make your move."

Scrbacek moved the pebble, his king's bishop, to protect his pawn. "How could I be connected to a fence? Was he a client?"

"Freddie Margolis."

"I don't know him."

"Freddie 'the Freak' Margolis, friend of the forgotten. Give us your hubcaps, your car batteries, give us your stolen stereo speakers yearning to be free. He was one of the first of the circle. Now he's dead. And the beagle's in the middle of everything." Pawn took pawn.

"I don't understand."

"Blixen took your gambit," the old woman cackled. "What's to understand? The moon is blue tonight, did you know that? Attack with your bishop—I dare you. Attack with your bishop and you are as good as dead."

Scrbacek moved his bishop to relative safety beside his pawn. "You said I'm in the middle of everything. What is everything?"

"Keep your eye on the game," said the old woman loudly. She waved her hand over the board and continued in a soft voice. "There is a battle for control of the center. Black sees the center as a source of power, something to be controlled, bled, sucked dry like a marrowbone. White sees the center as a drag on its power, something to be obliterated as it moves to take other positions of strength."

The old woman developed her queenside knight to threaten Scrbacek's remaining center pawn. Scrbacek stared at the board and then moved his king's bishop pawn up one space. The old woman took the pawn, and Scrbacek took Blixen's pawn in turn with his queen.

"I still don't understand," said Scrbacek, softly.

Blixen shook her head sadly, moved her knight forward to attack Scrbacek's kingside position. "Blixen was born here. It was a place then. Blixen had a daughter here. 'Where are you from?' they would ask, and when Blixen told them, they'd ooh and aah. Now it is nothing except our home. And still, somehow, we're caught in the middle of their game. That is why we listened when Malloy came to us."

"Peter Malloy, the labor leader who was killed? Regina mentioned a Malloy, too. Is that the one?"

"He came. Organizing. Organizing Crapstown. What a thing to imagine. He called all the groups together, to the underworld, across the River Styx, the river of hate. The moon is blue. Make your move."

Scrbacek stared at the woman, at her wet eyes, at her wisp of beard, tried to make sense of what she was saying, and failed. He turned back to the board and moved his bishop forward one space, threatening the old woman's knight.

"In the underworld they formed the Inner Circle. A circle of hope and vengeance. Regina is our Sentinel, Donatino our Ares. And now into their house comes Caleb Breest's lawyer. With destruction behind him. You cannot stay here, not a minute more than you must. They will kill you if you don't leave before the moon has passed."

The old woman moved her queen's bishop to further protect the knight.

"Why are you telling me this?" said Scrbacek.

"Because nothing is more dangerous than a beagle with his back to the wall. Are you dangerous, beagle?"

"No," said Scrbacek. "I'm not."

"Make your move."

"I'm not dangerous. I just want to stay alive."

"Make your move."

"What do you want from me?"

"Make your move."

Scrbacek looked at the board. He thought to develop his knight to protect his bishop, but as he reached for the piece, the old woman let out a groan.

He took his hand away and studied the board anew, trying to see why the move was a mistake. He kept looking, examined his queen's position on the right side, and suddenly he saw it, clear and sweet as a knife in the heart. He wasn't much of a chess player, and he hadn't maneuvered his pieces into such a position, but still there it was. He looked into the old woman's eyes.

"Are you a dangerous man, J.D. Scrbacek, beagle-at-law with his back to the wall?"

Scrbacek moved his queen up the board, took the king's bishop's pawn, and said, "Checkmate."

"Oh my Lord," shouted out the old woman. "You beat Blixen. On a trick, a dirty trick." She laughed loudly, laughed like a maniac. "You are dangerous after all."

"It was there. I didn't know—"

The old woman suddenly grabbed at Scrbacek's extra nipple, her filthy, ragged fingernails digging sharply into his flesh. In a low voice she said, "Leave tonight. Save Blixen's home. Save Crapstown."

The old woman let go of his chest, took the top off her chessboard, dumped the pieces inside, and covered it again before hobbling out of the room, muttering to herself. Blixen was crocked, that was clear enough to Scrbacek, but her warning rang too true to ignore. How could he ever again doubt that there was someone who wanted him dead? He didn't yet have a place to run to, but he knew for sure he had to run. He swung his legs off the bed, wrapped his body as best he could in the sheet that had been covering him, and took a step forward to find a way out, before swooning backward onto the bed.

He sat for a moment, trying to shake the dizzy fatigue out of his head, when he saw a thin, handsome man in jeans come into the room, carrying a pile of folded clothes with Scrbacek's two boots on top. Scrbacek felt a wave of inexplicable relief fall upon him. Maybe it was something in the man's smile.

"Hello, Donnie," said Scrbacek.

"How you feeling there, Mr. Scrbacek?" said Donnie Guillen.

"Better, actually. That little man, what was his name? Squirrel?"

"Yeah, Squirrel knows his stuff." Donnie placed the pile of clothes on the bed and patted it. "Time to get dressed. You need any help?"

"I don't think so. The Tylenol has already kicked in."

"Good. But you have to hurry. I brought a visitor."

"Who?"

Just then, Scrbacek was hit with an overpowering scent of jasmine, followed by the vision of a woman sweeping magisterially into the room. Tall and dark, big-boned and graceful, she was dressed in a flowing purple gown, with a bright purple scarf covering her hair and jangling dollops of hammered silver hanging from her ears.

She stopped and looked around at the peeling wallpaper, the holes in the wall, the boarded-up window, the girl on the bureau with a gun. "This is dreadful," she said, her accent as thick as her perfume. "How you expect me to work in such place? It is not fit for juk. No, Donnie darling, I won't stay here one minute more. I go home."

"Please," said Donnie. "We need you desperately."

"It is impossible. I must go. You come my shop and I do what I can, but here, no."

"He'll pay you another hundred," said Donnie.

"What care I about such details?" She blew dismissively out her mouth and then turned to stare at the man covered by a sheet on the bed. "Cash?"

"Of course," said Donnie.

"This moosh, he has the money?"

"I've seen it."

"You know," she said, "for no one else would I do such a thing, but you, Donnie, are such a kushti darling. So okay. I do it. Just for you."

"Thank you," said Donnie.

She turned to Scrbacek. "I hope you are grateful of your friend. He came all the way my shop to bring me here because your trouble. If the cards they tell me you are not a grateful moosh, I will be very disappointed."

"Who are you?" said Scrbacek, still clutching the sheet to his body.

"Mr. Scrbacek," said Donnie, "I'd like you to meet the Contessa Romany."

"Charmed," said the lady.

"The Contessa Romany," said Donnie, "is going to tell you how to save your life."

14

DONNIE GUILLEN

After the Contessa swept back out of the room, Scrbacek glanced up at the girl sitting on the bureau with the gun. "Does she have to be here while I dress?"

"Reggie insists," said Donnie with a shrug.

"And if Reggie insists, then I guess there's no—"

"That's right," said Donnie with a smile.

"Okay, then," said Scrbacek as he searched the pile of clothes for his boxers. He slipped them on under the sheets before getting out of bed and starting with his pants. He tried to keep his swollen, purpled arm as still as possible. Even so, and even with the drugs, the pain at first was hard to bear, but the more he moved the arm, the less the pain restricted his movements.

"All these people," said Scrbacek, gingerly pulling on his jeans. "The old woman with the beard, Squirrel, the Lady Baltimore, Regina, that girl up there on the bureau."

Donnie looked up at her and smiled. "The Nightingale."

"Yes. Who are they?"

"Friends. We kind of live together here. Some of us, anyway. Squirrel has a rough operating room in a house on Garfield, and Elisha has a place in the Marina District, but they all help me with my work."

"What exactly is your work?"

"Same as before. I've always been good with my hands. I build stuff for people, fix stuff. Work on my projects."

"Projects?"

"Hurry up and dress, and I'll show you."

"No more guns, I hope. You're staying out of trouble, right?"

"I live in Crapstown, Mr. Scrbacek. There's only trouble here."

"So I've found." Pause. "Thank you, Donnie. For taking me in and finding me that doctor, or whatever the hell he is. I probably would have died there on your stoop if you hadn't answered the door."

Donnie looked at the floor and kicked at the splintering wood. "I don't think I'd have done too well in prison, Mr. Scrbacek. Some of the people there, man, they deserve to be there, they're, like, dangerous. You did a good thing keeping me out."

"I was just doing my job."

Donnie shrugged. "Most court-appointed lawyers wouldn't have cared like you cared, and that made all the difference. You pulled out all the stops for me. So when I saw you lying there looking half-dead on the front porch, I figured I owed you." Donnie let out a laugh. "Man, you were a mess."

Scrbacek nodded. "Someone is trying to kill me."

"I know."

"I have to get out of here, get out of Crapstown, get out of the state."

Donnie turned to look behind him and then back at Scrbacek. "That's probably a good idea. Especially the getting out of here part. Do you know where you'd go?"

"No idea." Scrbacek struggled as he slipped a white T-shirt over his lame arm and then a soft white long-sleeved shirt over that, buttoning the buttons carefully. He found he could use his left hand as long as he didn't need any strength from his arm beyond bare movement. "Thanks for the clothes."

"Elisha cleaned what we could save, but the shirt, it was totaled." Then in a hushed tone, like a conspirator, he said, "So what do you think?"

"I think I'm in serious trouble," said Scrbacek.

"No. About her."

"Who?"

"Elisha."

"Baltimore?"

"Isn't she wonderful?"

"The Lady Baltimore?"

"Yeah. I don't know. I've never met anyone quite like her. She's very spiritual."

"She's a drug-addicted stripper, Donnie."

"Well, see, that's what makes her so special. She's employed, has outside interests . . ."

"Donnie."

"She's more than just her struggle, Mr. Scrbacek. You're on the run now—you should know that as well as anyone." He reached into his pants pocket and pulled out a wad of bills. "We found the money in your boot. I had to pay Squirrel, and I used some of it to buy the medicine, the new clothes, and to pay Elisha, because, well, that's what I did with it. And then I had to give some to the Contessa to get her to come. This is what's left. Fifteen hundred or about."

"The Contessa must be expensive," said Scrbacek as he put the wadded bills in his back pocket.

"But she's worth it."

"What exactly does she do?"

"She reads the future."

"Ahh, now I recognize the name. She's the fortune-teller on the boardwalk."

"You know her?"

"I've passed her shop."

"She's got a good sign, doesn't she? 'Contessa Romany: The Mistress of Tarot.'"

"Send her home, Donnie."

"It wasn't easy to get her to come. She doesn't like it in Crapstown. I had to almost beg. Though the bills I gave her from your stash helped."

"Donnie, I don't want any help from the Contessa. One of my fondest hopes is that I go through my life never having been helped by a contessa. Send her home." He stopped dressing and looked at Donnie. "I have a lot of questions."

"I know you do."

"About the things that are happening. About Malloy. About something called the Inner Circle."

Donnie spun around and looked behind him and then back, letting out a soft "Shh."

"But most of all," said Scrbacek as he put on his socks and slipped on his boots, "I need to find out who's trying to kill me."

"That's why the Contessa is here."

"Donnie, no."

"Come on," he said. "She's setting up downstairs. But I want to show you something first."

"I'm not paying a hundred more bucks to have my fortune told by some Gypsy fraud."

Just then, the Nightingale hopped down from the bureau, moving with the athletic grace of a gymnast. She was short and lithe, pretty in a boyish way, with short dark hair, and she carried an AK-47, the trigger pointing to the sky and the barrel leaning on her shoulder. Fastened to the barrel's tip was some sort of tube, black and wider than the rest. She didn't say a word. She just stared at Scrbacek for a moment and then tilted her head toward the exit.

Scrbacek's eyes widened before he grabbed his raincoat and followed Donnie out the door.

Donnie led Scrbacek through a dark hallway, the noise of the ever-present television growing louder, and down a stairwell with a rickety handrail. The Nightingale trailed the two of them, the gun still perched on her shoulder. At the landing, they passed into a hallway to the right and came to a room at the back of the house. Donnie turned a switch, and two hanging industrial fixtures clicked and blinked and finally hummed to life, filling the room with a harsh light that forced Scrbacek to cover his eyes until they adjusted.

"This is my shop," said Donnie.

The room was large, with workbenches lining one of its walls. It smelled of oil, and solder, and burned and twisted metal. Beside one of the benches was a scatter of large metal tanks, one tank still attached to a torch, heavy goggles hanging from the tank's nozzle. Scrbacek walked slowly around the room, studying the workbenches, the tools, and the piles of material.

In the center was a table with a sheet spread over something large and irregular that sat flat on the tabletop. And in the four corners were bizarre conglomerations of twisted metal that stood tall on wooden pallets, each about seven feet in height, roughly cylindrical in shape. At first they looked like pieces of junk joined together haphazardly, possibly by chance bursts of lightning. But as Scrbacek examined them one by one, he could see coherent shapes and forms assert themselves through the jumbles, as if each contained something of great beauty struggling to pull itself out of the chaos. They reminded Scrbacek of Michelangelo's prisoners wrestling to free themselves from their cages of stone.

"I didn't know you were an artist," said Scrbacek.

"It's just something I do."

Scrbacek kept walking, slowly, as if at a gallery, examining everything, and then he stopped at one of the workbenches, where he spot-
ted a pile of steel wool, rows of narrow brake lines with holes drilled
through them, a cylinder filled with stiff metal drill rods. He picked
up a wide piece of metal tubing painted a flat black and hefted it in
his hand.

"What do you make here, Donnie?" said Scrbacek. "I mean, besides
the art."

"Stuff," said Donnie. "Little things I can sell. I learned metalwork at
vo-tech, and I've been doing it ever since, but mostly it's the sculptures.
I like it when the metal starts to heat, and then glows hot and becomes
soft enough to play with. I like cutting through steel with the torch. I
like the feeling of control it gives me."

"You know, you could get a job doing this. I bet there's a high
demand for experienced metalworkers."

"Yeah, maybe, but then there'd be some foreman with hairy knuckles telling me what to make and I'd be doing their work instead of my
own. Let me show you something else."

Donnie walked over to the table covered by the sheet.

"This is the main project I've been working on," said Donnie. He
stood there for a moment, staring down at the table, gripping the sheet
by its edges. "Something new."

When he yanked the sheet away, what lay underneath glistened
with so hard a brightness it took Scrbacek a moment to realize exactly
what it was he was seeing.

It was a model of a city—streets and houses, skyscrapers and parks,
all hammered and welded from blocks of polished steel. Breathtakingly
intricate, random and ordered, primitive and rough, it reminded
Scrbacek of the great visionary art of the American South, tinfoil palaces made by men and women who had been touched by the Lord
and thereby inspired to make their devotions substantial. And this
thing, too, formed of secondhand junk, seemed charged with a divine

electricity. It held, this vivid cityscape, a vision of hope and promise and dignity, a vision of Casinoland and Crapstown joined as brothers, a vision of a shining city by the sea. But there was also, suffused in every weld, evident in every surface, amidst all the glittering facets of metal, a sadness, because it was a silver urban paradise that never was and never would be.

Scrbacek stared at this complex metal thing, stunned by its mystery, gripped by sensations that stirred him deeper than he could understand. "This is magnificent," he said.

"You know what I call it?"

Scrbacek looked up at the grinning young man.

"New Town C-Town," said Donnie. "I like the rhythm of the words, don't you? *New Town C-Town.*"

Scrbacek looked down at the cityscape again, the familiar streets and the shining buildings formed from cast-off metal. He pointed to a large cube of polished steel. "What's that?"

"That's a community center. Next to it is a public pool. Then a school, see? Surrounded by homes. Out here is the industrial park, factories and high-rises where everyone works. And there's the music hall and the basketball arena. We're going to have a basketball team, D-League only, but still. And when they're not playing ball, there are going to be shows, rap stars from all over the country, dance concerts. You like Kanye? He'll come—I know it. And out there, in the park, they'll be playing touch football in leagues all season long. And softball. And having barbecues. And there's the playground, the kids scrambling through a fort to get to the slide. You know where I got the idea for doing this?"

Scrbacek looked up again, tilted his head without saying a word.

"From Malloy," said Donnie. "He saw some of my other stuff and suggested I make a model. So I tried it, and then the dreams started."

"Dreams?"

"That's where I got most of it. And you know what? It's more than just a sculpture, Mr. Scrbacek. It's a blueprint."

"Of what?"

"The future."

"For who?"

"For us."

"Who is us, Donnie?"

"We've got to go now, Mr. Scrbacek. The Contessa Romany, she's waiting."

"You don't want to tell me?"

"I can't. Not yet, at least."

Scrbacek looked back down at the cityscape. *New Town C-Town.* He traced a finger across the edge of one of the steel rooftops. "You ever hear of anything called the C-Town Furies?"

"It's time to go, Mr. Scrbacek," said Donnie as he tossed the sheet back over the model. "Really."

"Some gang, supposed to be nasty as all hell, out to take over all the other gangs in the city. So tough it can even challenge Caleb Breest. Is that what you're messed up in?"

"You've got it all wrong. It's nothing like that."

"Then what is it like, Donnie? Because I have the feeling my life is depending on it. Tell me what it's all about."

Donnie walked to the door and switched off the lights. Darkness fell like a blow. "We need to go, Mr. Scrbacek."

"You're not going to tell me."

"I owe you, Mr. Scrbacek. I know I do. But there are limits to everything. Come on. We don't want to keep the Contessa waiting."

15
THIS IS TAROT

"We are almost ready," said the Contessa Romany to the assembled crew, many of whom Scrbacek had never seen before. "Just one moment please and we begin."

In a dimly lit room in the front of the house, they perched on a ratty couch covered in ripped batik cloth, they leaned against water-stained walls, they sat with arms around their knees on the rough wooden floor. The Contessa herself presided at a table set in the room's middle. Behind the Contessa stood a squat young man with features remarkably similar to the Contessa's, his huge arms crossed. A chair opposite the Contessa was empty, obviously meant for Scrbacek, who leaned against the front doorframe, as far from the table as he could get, now wearing his raincoat, creased wildly from the wash and with a jagged hole in its sleeve. Atop a crimson cloth covering the table were two white candles in golden holders, an intricately worked metal egg with a stick of incense rising from its top, and a wooden box painted with a pattern of leaves and flowers.

A match flared with a hiss. Carefully the Contessa Romany lit first the candles and then the incense. A thick musk floated from the smoldering stick. The Contessa leaned down, and from beneath the table came soft music, something dusky and haunting with a woman's voice singing notes without words, rising almost loud enough to drown out the television noise from the floor above.

"If someone, please, turn off these lights," said the Contessa.

The room fell dark except for the thin flickering flames of the two candles and the glowing stick of incense.

"Thank you, darling. And now you," she said, pointing at Scrbacek. "Please. Yes, you. Come sit. It is you who has the question, am I correct?"

"I'm not sure . . ."

"If you don't want to," said Elisha, "I'll go. Contessa, I bought this stock, and I was wondering—"

"It's for the beagle, not you," snapped Blixen. "We can read your future clear enough. It's in your G-string."

"Take a seat, Stifferdeck," said Regina, the gun now in her belt. "It's time to hear some truth about you for once."

"Come now, don't be afraid, darling," said the Contessa. "I don't bite. Just a nibble now and then."

Scrbacek hesitated, and then slowly walked toward the open chair. The musk of the incense floated through him as he approached. When he sat, only the table and the Contessa were illuminated in the soft yellow light of the candles. All else was cast in a deep shadow.

"You are in middle of terrible crisis, is that correct?"

Scrbacek turned to search for Donnie, couldn't find him in the shadows, turned back, and nodded.

"Good. Now you must know the cards, they do not only read for me your future. If spirit it is with you, they can also tell what it is you must do in this terrible time. Are you ready, Mr. . . . ?"

"Scrbacek."

"Scrbacek? Strange name, Scrbacek. From where come your people?"

99

"Egypt."

"Really? From Egypt? Maybe we are somehow related. Maybe thousand years ago we had same cousins."

"And he's got a third nipple," shouted out Blixen.

The Contessa started. "Is this true, cousin?"

Scrbacek winced and then nodded.

"Show me."

Scrbacek unbuttoned his shirt and lifted up his T-shirt.

The Contessa raised a candle to Scrbacek's flesh and peered close. She rubbed a single finger gently over the small hairy protrusion below his left nipple. Her finger was cold and rough.

"The spirits truly are with you, Scrbacek."

"I told you," said Blixen.

"Let us begin," said the Contessa as Scrbacek rebuttoned his shirt. She carefully removed the lid from the wooden box and unwrapped a covering of black velvet to reveal an aged deck of cards, with moons and stars on the backs. She lifted the cards in her two open palms and raised them over her head. The candlelight flickered off her gaudy rings.

"This is tarot," she said loudly. "Its secrets have been passed in our family from mother to daughter for centuries. This very set of cards has traveled from far reaches of Transylvania, through all of Europe, over great Atlantic Ocean to this place by the sea. This is tarot."

The others in the room repeated in soft voices, *"This is tarot."*

"This is tarot," continued the Contessa. "Originated in time of Ra, it is great tradition of our people. We are not owners of tarot, we are its vessels. It is tool for those who choose to see what it can show, an aid for those who choose to believe. This is tarot."

"This is tarot."

"Good," she said as she lowered her hands and offered the cards across the table. "Take, Scrbacek."

Scrbacek took. Though there were only twenty or so of the yellow and cracked cards, he found them surprisingly heavy, as if the weight of their years had adhered to the thick paper.

"Now, shuffle cards like this, without bending." She mimed a gentle overhand shuffle. Following her movements, he gave the cards a quick shuffle and tried to hand them back.

"No," she said. "Keep shuffling. And as you shuffle, I want that you concentrate on what it is you need to know. I want that you empty your mind of everything except of your problem and you keep shuffling, shuffling."

"When do I stop?"

"The cards, they will tell you."

Scrbacek gave a snort and thought about how much of a fraud was this crazy Contessa, but he kept shuffling. He would have walked out, refused to be any part of this hoax, except that Donnie had saved his life and it would have been disrespectful just to leave. He wasn't sure, in any event, that the girl, the Nightingale, would let him walk away. Then again, if the cards were an aid for the troubled, he surely qualified. And the night before, in the casino, he had felt luck and fate intertwine with the playing of cards in his wondrous streak of blackjack. So he kept shuffling as the haunting music and incense floated about him, and slowly, as he shuffled, his mind began to consider where he was and why, and who was trying to kill him. He shuffled and thought, and suddenly a stack of cards he pulled up with his right hand wouldn't join the others, just banged against the side. Instead of forcing them, he simply put them back and stopped.

"Good," said the Contessa. "Cut cards into three piles and put together in different order."

He did as he was told.

"Now one by one, give me cards off top of deck. The first card is your problem card."

Scrbacek turned over the top card. In the candlelight he could just make out the picture. It was of a castle tower being destroyed by lightning and fire.

"Yes," she said as she put it in the middle of the table. "This is the Tower, the card of catastrophe. Unexpected reversals and upheavals. This is what you have suffered, no?"

Scrbacek nodded.

"And your question is why all this is happening. But it is not just happening to you. The tower can represent whole cities, whole civilizations. What else is being destroyed? That, too, is part of question. One and other, they are maybe related. But of course, it is also card of fate. Bad things happen. Is there always good reason? Maybe sometimes it is better not to look too hard."

"Maybe you're right," said Scrbacek. "Maybe we'll stop. Thank you for your time."

"You making joke, cousin? Don't. Now what is it you need to know most? Tell me, Scrbacek."

"I need to know who is trying to kill me."

"Of course you do. Give me next, darling."

Scrbacek turned over another card. It was a picture of a man holding a wand in one hand and a crystal ball in the other, standing behind a table filled with all manner of strange objects. She placed the card sideways over the tower to create a cross.

"This is your obstacle, what it is that is keeping you from goal. The moosh, he is the magician. A manipulator, a trickster. He controls the events. One person it is behind everything. This person who has caused the tower to fall will also do everything to make sure you fall with it. You have enemy, Scrbacek?"

"Apparently."

"Find him and you solve problem. But finding him, it will not be so easy. Next card, please."

A man caught between two very different women, trying to figure which to take, as Cupid floats above them all and aims his bow. She placed this card below and to the left of the center cross.

"This card is your past. The Lover. You would think it deals with sweet romantic love, but that is untrue. Instead it is all about choice. Somewhere in past you made choice that led you here. What was it? Something simple, like where to live? Something complex, like who to be, who to love? Who knows? But this choice, it is root of what is happening to you. Next card."

Two dogs howling at a large blue moon. She placed it directly beneath the center cross.

"This is your present. The Moon."

"I told you all," said Blixen. "The moon is blue, blue."

"Quiet, we are working here. This card, it is card of madness, of hidden truths, of confusion. Nothing can be trusted, because everything is without sanity. The choice you made in your past has led you to this craziness. Next card."

A horned and winged woman, with claws for hands and feet, flanked by two men, half-human and half-animal, chained together at the neck. The Contessa tightened her lips when she saw it and placed it to the bottom right of the cross.

"This is your future. Give me next."

"Wait," said Scrbacek. "What is that card? What does it mean?"

She looked up at him, her eyes flickering yellow from the candles. "Suddenly you're interested? Okay. This card is the Devil. It is not good card. Bondage. Bondage to what, we can't say, but it arises from choice and madness. Maybe that is all for today, maybe we stop. Maybe we should try dice instead. Sometimes . . ."

Scrbacek flipped over the next card and tossed it on the table. A spirit in the heavens blowing a great golden trumpet as naked men and women rose from graves dug into the ground. The Contessa looked at him for a long moment and then placed the card above the cross and stared at him again.

"This position represents way to solve problem. The card it is Judgment. It requires examination of self, of truth. It is difficult card. But look at way our angel, she looks downward, to other cards. The answer to what is happening to you, what is happening to all, it is in past, present, future."

"Well, that sort of narrows it down, doesn't it?" said Scrbacek.

"You misunderstand," said the Contessa Romany. "The answer to all the destruction is not just in past, present, future. It is in your past, your present, your future."

Scrbacek looked down at the cards and then back up at the woman. "I don't think so."

"So maybe it is wrong. Maybe you are not facing great upheaval. Maybe there is not some riffly moosh pulling strings. Maybe there is no choice in past, no madness in present, no bondage in future. Maybe all is well with Scrbacek."

"Is that it?" he said curtly. "Are we done now?"

"There is one more card if you are interested. It is outcome card. How it all will turn out in end."

Scrbacek stared at the woman as he turned over the final card. It was of a man, hanging upside down from a rope attached to his leg. The Contessa shook her head sadly as she put it at the top of the spread.

"The Hanged Man," she said.

"What does it mean?" said Scrbacek.

"It means you should pay me other hundred now before we leave."

"Tell me," said Scrbacek.

"This is card of self-sacrifice. To solve your problem, you must give of everything. The result must be either death or transformation. One or other, nothing in between. At the end of this struggle against magician, life for you will never be same."

"That's not what I want to hear."

"That is always problem with tarot," said the woman.

Suddenly there was a crash from the hallway and a shout, the sound of some sort of blow thudding into the soft part of a body. The next instant, the music stopped and the lights were flicked on, and in the light now appeared the man who had before been standing behind the Contessa. He was in the doorway, holding a cell phone, his head bent weirdly to the side. He took a step forward, and then Scrbacek could see that the Nightingale was behind him, one hand gripping his black hair and pulling down his head, the other holding a huge jagged knife with its point sticking into his thick neck.

The man tried to say, "I was just—"

"Shut up," said the Nightingale. "I caught him trying to make a call."

"Who to?" said Reggie.

"Don't know, but from the way he jumped when I caught him, it was about our guest."

"No, no," said the man, "I was just—"

The Nightingale twisted the knife into the neck. Blood spurted, and the man stopped talking.

"Leave him be," said the Contessa, rising from the table and grabbing the man's arm. "He is my nephew, Carlo. He did nothing wrong."

Reggie swaggered over and grabbed the phone out of the man's hand. "Who were you calling, Mustard Mouth?"

"No one. Just a woman. No one."

"Get your story straight. Was it no one, or was it a woman? My guess is you were telling someone about seeing Stifferdeck over there. How much you get for selling him out? Who'd you call?"

The man shook his head, his lips shut closed, and the Nightingale twisted the knife deeper.

"Nothing," cried the man. "No one. I called a woman only."

"Check the last number dialed," said Squirrel.

"Shut up, Squirrel," said Reggie. "I need your advice, I'll shake your tree." Then she handed the phone to Elisha. "Check the last number dialed."

"Nice phone," said Elisha, looking down at the handset. "There's just a number."

"Call it," said Reggie.

As Elisha thumbed the screen and put the phone to her ear, she said, "Too bad about the Freak. He would have paid top dollar for this baby."

"Fat chance of that now," said Reggie.

"Poor Freddie," Elisha sighed, then turned away with one hand to her free ear as someone answered the redial.

"Wait." Scrbacek stood up. "Freaky Freddie bought phones?"

Reggie gave him a look. "He was a fence, so yeah, Freddie bought everything. But especially phones. Nobody moved phones like Freaky Freddie."

"Hang up," Scrbacek barked at Elisha. "Turn the phone off."

"Since when are you giving orders, Stifferdeck?" said Reggie, but Elisha had already done what he'd said, and now both women were staring at him.

"We have to get out of here," said Scrbacek. "All of us. Right away."

And as if to prove the point, from outside the house came the sound of tires squealing madly, as first one vehicle, then many, sped around the corner and onto Ansonia Road.

16
RATS

Someone turned off the overhead light.

Someone snuffed out the two dim candles on the table.

Someone yelled, "Jesus," and started running.

"What is happening?" called out the Contessa. "What?"

Someone killed the lights in the hall as the conversation from the television continued unabated in the darkness.

Someone called out, "In here. In here," and then screamed until his voice turned into a wet gurgle.

"Carlo. Tell me what is happening. What? Carlo. Carlo?"

Outside, vehicles slammed to a stop on Ansonia Road, car doors swung open, orders were shouted.

Someone grabbed Scrbacek's arm, mercifully, his right, and dragged him across the floor.

"This way." The voice was Donnie's.

Scrbacek stumbled as he followed the pull, but he didn't fight it, wanting now to be somewhere, anywhere other than where he was.

There were footsteps accompanying them, more than two sets, more than three.

"Down here."

A door opened, and the footsteps began to tumble down a set of wooden stairs, and Scrbacek tumbled with them. He lost his balance and reached out with his free arm and grabbed hold of something, and a dagger of pain almost drove him to his knees, but he kept descending. The door behind him closed. A bolt locked. Footsteps pounded overhead. A burst of gunfire, and the television shut its fucking mouth. Scrbacek continued down until he tried to take another step and his leg locked painfully on the floor. He was in the cool of a cellar, could feel the unevenness of cracked cement beneath his boots. The hand around his arm let go, and he was adrift in the darkness, totally lost beneath the hammering of feet charging across the floor above.

A scrape and then the beam of a flashlight alighting on the red of a rat's eyes before the rodent scurried into a pile of old paint cans. Scrbacek took the moment to regain his bearings.

They were in a dank basement, overrun with rotting pieces of wood, disintegrating boxes, a bent and rusted bike, scattered acetylene tanks. There were five of them down there: Donnie, holding the flashlight; Scrbacek; Elisha; the old woman, Blixen, grasping tight to a large plastic bag full of stuff; and the Nightingale with her gun. Donnie put a finger on his lips and pointed the light to the water heater, a rusted old thing listing in the corner. The beam moved behind the water heater, alighting on a brown metal plate embedded in the rough plaster, with a small gap of blackness between its bottom rim and the wall.

Someone upstairs tried the door, found it locked, started banging on it, shouting. In the twitch of a rat's tail, the Nightingale whirled, fell to one knee, raised the gun, and braced it on her shoulder as she aimed at the door. There was more banging, the door shuddered at a heavy blow, shuddered again, and quieted.

Donnie, with the flashlight, scooted around the water heater to the rusted metal plate behind. He grabbed the edge and swung it open, revealing a great black hole in the wall. With the beam he waved the others toward it. First, Elisha stooped to enter the hole, then Blixen, groaning softly as she hobbled forward, then Donnie with the flashlight, then Scrbacek.

It was narrow and wet, this place they ducked into. It smelled of raw sewage, of foul living things huddled together. The ceiling of damp wooden planks was higher than Scrbacek expected, the ground firmer. The walls were lined with seeping cinder block.

From behind came a banging again upon the door to the basement they'd left behind and then a blast from a machine gun and then something smashing into the wood, shoulders or an ax, followed by the wood shattering. Scrbacek looked behind him and saw, in the dim light, the Nightingale climb into the hole and pull the metal plate closed behind her. Carefully she turned a latch that clicked shut. A moment later her hand was on Scrbacek's back, urging him forward.

He followed the wavering line of Donnie's flashlight through the tunnel, raising his feet high as he moved, brushing his right arm gently against the ceiling and wall to keep from banging into them, keeping his left hand close to his mouth and nose to silence his coughs and ward off the thick smell of sewage. Beyond the sound of their own progress, he could hear footsteps charging down the steps in the basement behind them, boxes being tossed and cans kicked, calls back up the stairs. There came a quick burst of gunfire and then laughter, and immediately some desperately fleeing thing scurried between Scrbacek's legs. He stood up suddenly and banged his head on the ceiling planks and barely kept from calling out.

The Nightingale's hand on his back pushed harder.

Through the tunnel, quietly following the thin beam of light, hand brushing the ceiling, Scrbacek moved ever onward. Behind him he heard the muffled voices of men in the cellar and then, suddenly, the sharp banging of metal. The men must have seen the rat dive into the gap at the bottom of the plate in the wall. They began pounding on the flat metal, pounding with the stocks of their guns, hearing the obvious reverberations of hollowness.

Scrbacek moved faster now, spurred by raw fear. He heard scraping, prying, an attempt to open the plate, more pounding.

And then it stopped, and the muffled voices faded away.

Up ahead, Elisha, illuminated by Donnie's flashlight, climbed a metal ladder. First, Elisha went, then Blixen, struggling to rise. Donnie tried to take the bag from her to make the climb easier, but Blixen clutched it to her chest. Donnie then gestured for Scrbacek to follow behind Blixen and help the old woman up.

Scrbacek grabbed hold of the damp, rusty rungs and began to hoist himself with his right hand. When he rose close to Blixen, he put his injured left arm through a rung, braced with his feet, and pushed the old woman's rear with his right hand. He climbed upward and did it again. And then one more time until the old woman and her bag disappeared through the hole above the ladder's top rung, where Elisha helped her to her feet. Scrbacek climbed after her, through the hole, onto a flat cement floor.

They were in someplace large, huge, a great cavernous space within which the slightest sounds echoed. The place smelled fresh compared to the tunnel, but after a moment he could detect the scent of dampness and sulfur. He stepped back from the hole as Donnie, with his flashlight, climbed out, and then the Nightingale.

Donnie dragged a large box over the opening in the floor and then aimed the light across the space to a set of metal stairs bolted to a wall. He started for the stairs, and the others followed. From the wavering beam of light, Scrbacek could just make out the far edges of the expanse. The walls wide and straight, boxes and debris were all pushed to the perimeter, leaving a huge emptiness, big as a basketball court, bigger.

They stepped as quietly as possible up the steel stairs, but still their footsteps reverberated. At the top was a doorway, which Donnie pushed open, and they were suddenly outside. There was more than a hint of smoke in the night air, but still Scrbacek was never so glad to see the sky over Crapstown. The moon was full and bright, casting its silver over a wide flat roof. It had to be, figured Scrbacek, the roof of the abandoned warehouse behind Donnie's house. Donnie motioned them all to be quiet and get low, and then he led them to the edge of the roof, where they scooted down and raised their heads just enough above the three-foot lip to see what lay beyond.

It was 714 Ansonia Road, and it was on fire.

They stared at the now strangely lit ramshackle building in silence. It was just starting, the fire, its flickering light barely visible through the few windows not boarded up in the rear, its smoke just leaking out through broken panes. But it would not be long before dancing shoots of flame devoured the roof and lit bright the night sky. Around the house a small army of men with guns searched the lot, waving their flashlights along the road and into the black waters of the bay, huddling in conversation as they watched the house burn. They were not in any uniform Scrbacek recognized, some in cable-knit sweaters, others wearing dark trench coats and sporting automatic weapons. A few talked on phones, apparently coordinating their murderous movements.

"I told you something was happening," said Blixen. "It's in the moon. I told you."

"I'm so sorry, Donnie," said Scrbacek, quietly. "I didn't mean to bring this down on you."

Donnie looked at him with hard eyes, and then they softened and he shrugged. "The rats were making themselves too much at home, anyways."

"Where will you go?"

"We've got places."

"But your art."

"I'll make more."

"Any idea what happened to Reggie or Squirrel?" said Elisha.

"Regina can take care of herself," said Blixen. "She's too much a hammerhead to get herself killed."

"She keeps her bike away from the house as a precaution," said Elisha.

"And that damn Squirrel," said the old woman, "is like a puff of smoke."

"There's another way out through the roof," said Donnie, "and onto the roof of that house over there and then down that tree."

Just then, the clatter of an unmuffled engine tore through the night, roaring loud in defiance before fading in the distance. The men surrounding the house turned their attention to the sound.

"Go with the wind, Regina," said Blixen.

"Who are the assholes with the guns down there?" said Elisha.

"Someone the Contessa's nephew called in," said Donnie. "What is his name? Carlo?"

"Was," said the Nightingale, looking down at the scene through a small set of binoculars.

"What do they want?" said Elisha.

"They want the beagle," said Blixen. "He's dangerous to them. Blixen told you so."

"How'd you know they were coming, Mr. Scrbacek?" said Donnie.

"My phone," said Scrbacek. "Before I got to the house, three jokers stole it. They said they were taking it to someone they called 'the Freak.' I didn't put it together with what happened to Freddie Margolis until Reggie said that Freaky Freddie specialized in phones. By the time the Freak got hold of my phone, they were out looking for me. He must have turned my phone on and brought that pack of jackals down on his skull."

"Poor bastard," said Donnie. "But that still leaves the question of who's behind them."

"You saw the cards," said the old woman. "It's the magician."

"Yeah, but who's that?" said Donnie.

"The beagle will find out."

"Let's just go down and ask the guy in charge," said the Nightingale. Slowly she put down the binoculars, raised her gun over the edge of the roof, and pointed it down at the men in the lot. "I got a bead on him." The silver moonlight glowed dully off the thick tube appended to the end of the barrel.

"Don't," said Donnie. "They get an inkling we're here, we'll be surrounded in seconds."

She looked at Donnie and then pulled the gun back.

Scrbacek stared at the thick end of the Nightingale's gun and thought of the black metal tube he had seen on the workbench inside the house. "Tell me something, Donnie," he said. "What good is a brake line with holes drilled through it?"

Donnie looked at him for a moment. "It has its uses."

"And the piles of steel wool I saw on one of your benches?"

"Cleans the pots and pans."

"Are you making silencers?"

"You asking as my lawyer?"

"I'm asking as a guy with a price on his head."

"It's a living."

"Not for the person at the other end of the muzzle. One of the things that puzzled me about getting shot was that I never heard the gun go off, just felt something slam into my arm."

"Maybe the shooter was faraway."

"Or maybe he had one of your tubes stuffed with steel wool on his gun. Who do you sell these things to, anyway?"

"People hear about it."

"You sell to anyone recently?"

"I can't talk about that, man."

"It's privileged, is that it? Lawyer-client. Priest-penitent. Munitions maker-hired assassin."

"If I want to stay alive, yeah."

"Someone is trying to kill me, Donnie. Someone tried to kill me with a silencer, and I'm guessing, since they're seriously illegal, it's safer to travel without and buy on-site. Who did you sell to?"

"Tell him," said Blixen. "He's our knight."

Donnie leaned over the wall to get a better view of his burning house. The fire had now engulfed the second floor, smoke was pouring out the windows where the plywood had burned away, and the first licks of flame were rising through the roof. The smoke brought a deep cough from Scrbacek's throat. The Nightingale slapped him hard on the back to quiet him.

"They're not just after the beagle," said Blixen. "They're gonna burn us all. Tell him."

Donnie waited a moment, watching the fire devour his house. "A guy from out of town," he said finally. "Just a few days ago. Tall, red hair."

"You get a name?"

"I don't ask names."

"Give me the glasses," he said to the Nightingale. "Where's the guy you said was leading?"

She handed over her binoculars and pointed. Scrbacek focused in. The man was standing with his back to them, wearing a long black leather coat, dancing from foot to foot with a phone to his ear, his mass of unruly red hair lit bright by the growing flames. The sight of him chilled Scrbacek's blood, as if his body could make the identification on its own.

"Turn around," Scrbacek said softly. "Turn around and let me see your face, you bastard." But the man didn't have to turn around for Scrbacek to know. Remi Bozant, not fat and happy in Las Vegas, but instead out for blood in Crapstown. "He say anything to you about me?"

Donnie shook his head. "He just said he was getting good money for the job."

"So someone else hired him, someone with resources to burn."

"He made a few lame jokes as he gave me the money."

"Well, you know what they say—comedy is hard. Did he buy anything else beside the silencers?"

"Just some guns."

"Any explosives like the stuff that blew up my car?"

"I don't mess with plastics, but they're easy enough to get hold of."

"Down," whispered the Nightingale, and everyone bent beneath the raised edge of the roof. "Someone was pointing up here."

"We have to get off the roof before this building catches too," said Donnie. "There's a fire escape on the far side."

The Nightingale grabbed her binoculars from Scrbacek and peeked over the roof's edge. "Okay, now."

Keeping as low as possible, they ran. The Nightingale, gun in hand, jumped on the fire escape and rode the ladder down as it skittered toward the asphalt. Before the ladder jammed to a stop a few feet off the ground, she was on the pavement, swinging the gun around, making a quick case of the area. After a moment she signaled for the others to follow. One by one they climbed down, dropped to the ground, and huddled in the shadow of the wall.

"What now?" said Scrbacek.

"I have to get to work," said Elisha. "I'm late already."

"You want me to walk you?" said Donnie.

She smiled. "Sure, sweetie."

"Got to find a new place," said Blixen, lifting her plastic bag. "To keep my things. Those bastards would kill to get a hold of my things."

"What about me?" said Scrbacek. "What do I do now?"

They looked at him. Donnie and Blixen, Elisha and the Nightingale, they looked at him like he was an idiot.

"The Contessa told you," said Donnie, finally. "Look to your past, your present, your future."

"That nonsense?" said Scrbacek. "Oh, come on, Donnie. Get serious."

"I am, Mr. Scrbacek."

"I really have to go," said Elisha. "Take care of yourself, J.D."

She started off and then stopped, turned around, walked right back up to Scrbacek, and whispered in his ear. "It was Dirty Dirk."

"Who?"

"The person Carlo was calling. When I redialed the phone before they came, the voice at the other end, I recognized it. It was Dirk. Be careful."

She kissed him lightly on the cheek, and then she was off, slinking quietly across the asphalt, climbing through a hole in the fence. Donnie looked at Scrbacek for a second, nodded at him, and then followed. Scrbacek watched them go until the old woman grabbed hold of his bad arm, forcing a gasp.

"Be strong," said Blixen, leaning so close that Scrbacek could smell the rot on her breath. "Be dangerous. Be warned." She blinked both eyes before she too made for the hole in the fence.

The Nightingale put a hand on Scrbacek's shoulder before following Blixen.

Scrbacek saw them stop at the fence, saw Blixen whisper something to the Nightingale, saw her look back at him and nod. Then both were through the hole and gone, and he was alone, in the shadow of that abandoned warehouse, just yards from a pack of killers hunting for him.

He waited in the shadows for a long moment, and then a moment more, paralyzed by indecision. Where should he go? What should he do? An assassin with a long leather trench coat and a personal grudge was after him, but Bozant wasn't acting alone. A call to Dirty Dirk's had set that pack of killers on his trail. So who was behind it all? Who was the magician, putting all the forces in play? Caleb Breest? Joey

Torresdale? Maybe Dirk himself? Or was it someone other, someone he couldn't even imagine?

He heard a sound. A rat rummaging through the heaps of garbage looking for a morsel? One of the killers rummaging through the warehouse looking for him? Shoved into action by a jolt of terror, he darted to the fence, climbed through the hole, and was gone again.

Lost again in the wilds of Crapstown.

17
ED'S EATS

The wash of headlights along a pitted black street. A hard bass rhythm pumping from a long brown car. Footsteps. Sirens. The crystalline crash of a glass bottle smashing on cement.

Moving through the shadows of Crapstown, chased by fear, J.D. Scrbacek felt a brutal sense of expectation in the air, darker than the night, pressing down upon the ragged buildings, the cracked asphalt, his spirit. It was the mirror image of the brilliant expectation he had felt upon entering Diamond's Mount Olympus, but both held the same total indifference to his inner nature; something would happen to him here for no reason other than his mere presence in this domain, something violent, crushing, something unspeakable, descending upon him like a plague.

A can being kicked down the street. The snarling bark of a dog. Fabric ripping. Brakes squealing. An argument in the distance growing raucous.

He didn't know where to turn, where to go, what to do. He didn't know who was after him, who could help him, what this nightmare was at root all about. He was in a situation not of his own choosing, with no answers, no shelter, only death in his future. In that way, he supposed, it was like life itself, except without sex or popcorn. And in the face of its danger, he moved on, not knowing to where, just moving and remaining unseen, unheard, his jagged, random path confined by the lights of the casinos and the limits of the bay. Moving through the shadows of Crapstown.

As a mangy dog swayed by, turning his great rabid head in Scrbacek's direction, he stopped suddenly, slinked against a street sign, and held his breath. Even after the mongrel made its way past, Scrbacek stayed there, pressed against the sign, frozen in place until the metal post marked a line down his back.

Enough of this nonsense, he told himself. Keep moving. Keep safe. He started off again, the full moon, the second of the month, keeping pace with his every step.

It was so late now the gates to the low-rise projects were shut tight, but the bars still were open, allowed to serve liquor all night to compete with the casinos. He passed one in a low gray building, its windows covered with cage wire, like the windows of the prison buses, as if installed to keep the patrons in rather than criminals out. Another was in a large brick building standing alone among a cluster of abandoned lots, its windows painted black, the outer walls still covered with the metal lath of the now-destroyed buildings on either side. Above the entrance was an intricate neon sign featuring a camel in bright yellow, a pyramid in bright blue, and two high-heeled legs—no body, just the legs—one kicking up and down, up and down, up and down. Beneath the graphic was the name **NOMAD'S**, and the motto **HOT AND COLD RUNNING STRIPPERS ALL THROUGH THE NIGHT**.

A man in a ragged coat was asleep at the curb in front of Nomad's, curled like a baby in a crib, his face covered by his arm. A survivor, no doubt, of a night of bumps and grinds, of cadged beers and bumbling passes and high-spirited fistfights. At least someone had a good time, thought Scrbacek bitterly as he stepped over the man's body.

In the desolate lot beside the club, a clutch of shadows, dimly lit by the flashing neon and the silver light of the moon, circled over some struggling supine figure in a strange ritual of barbarism. A fist was raised, then lowered, again and then again, accompanied by a sound like that of a boot slapping into a slick of mud. The beating was slow and brutal, and Scrbacek thought of intervening, rushing in to save the day. But when one of the onlooking shadows turned his way, that insanity passed quick as a shot. He buried his face into a shoulder and hurried on, and in so doing, he missed the words slipped between the blows and the muffled cries, the words soft as a whisper, the very whisper, in fact, that had descended upon Scrbacek outside his burning building.

"He's your screwup, Trent."

Smack.

"Your responsibility."

Smack.

"Find him, you fat piece of crap. And find him fast, before we do, or this will seem like nothing more than a canapé."

Pound.

"Which for you is like a whole rack of ribs."

Smack.

"Having fun yet, Trent?"

Smack.

"Because I sure as hell am. Can't you see my smile?"

Pound. Smack.

***

Blocks from the club, still frightened by the vision of the beating he had fled, Scrbacek passed a long wall with a mural painted on its brick, a rough picture of the seaside, with boats and sunbathers and gulls. He found the sight of this miserable mural, so close to and yet so distant from the actual thing, cruelly sad. A pay phone stood by the mural, its plastic covering shattered, defaced with graffiti, its only possible purpose, he thought, to place a call for help. He passed it forlornly. Who would he dial?

He was tired, he was hungry, he was feeling very, very sorry for himself, when he turned a corner and was shocked to see, halfway down the block, a glowing funnel of warm, welcoming light. His instinct was to turn from it, to run, but, with no place to run to, his feet remained planted. He waited in the shadows for a long moment and saw nothing alarming. Slowly, he made his way, along the opposite side of the street, toward the warm glow until he could see what it fell upon.

A diner. A shiny chrome thing with cement steps, two old cars parked in front of a row of newspaper boxes, and a single streetlight bathing it all in gold. A diner. In Crapstown.

Ed's Eats.

Since the bomb had blown up his car—what was it, a day ago, two days ago?—since then, all he'd had for nourishment were a couple of complimentary casino drinks and a mug of broth. The presence of that diner seemed fated for him. Weak with hunger, needing someplace to rest and think, he had turned a corner and there it stood, as if fallen out of the dark night sky like manna. Doused in light. With big plate-glass windows through which everyone inside could be seen by every passing car.

Ed's Eats.

He stared pitifully at the diner, the collar of his raincoat turned up, his hands in the pockets, and forced himself to turn and walk away. His stomach growled, loudly, as if it were a cat ready to claw whatever was in the way of its next meal. He stopped, turned around again. He actually did need to eat to keep up his strength. And a couple cups of coffee would keep him awake for the rest of the long night as he paced the streets and figured out his fate. And it was so late that there was probably nobody there who would recognize him. He stood, staring, and as he stood, he caught the drifting scent of something sweet and greasy that set again his stomach to the growl.

Ed's Eats.

A bell tinkled when he pulled open the door.

18
BLUES IN THE NIGHT

It was brightly lit inside, and warm, and Sinatra was singing from the jukebox. The ceiling was chrome, the stools were covered in washed-out green leatherette, the booths were the same wan color, with spiky coatracks fastened between each. Black-and-silver napkin dispensers, red bottles of Hunt's ketchup, cut-glass salt and pepper shakers with chrome tops, sugar dispensers filled to the brim. Beside two narrow doors leading to the kitchen, with oval windows cut in each, were shelves filled with small boxes of Kellogg's cereal and tiny cans of Campbell's soup. A blackboard with the word "Specials" painted in fancy script had one other word scrawled in chalk: "None."

A man in a bus driver's uniform huddled over a plate of eggs at the counter. A woman sitting alone in a booth dipped her tea bag, and dipped it again, and again. Another booth was filled with men, sitting shoulder to shoulder, each in a dark-red suit with narrow lapels, black shirt, yellow tie, and yellow pocket handkerchief. Red fedoras that matched the suits hung jauntily on the coatracks on either side of the booth. They talked in hushed voices over the trashed remnants of a devoured feast, a group of casino crooners after the late show.

Scrbacek looked around carefully; no one looked back. He tucked his chin into his shoulder and took a seat at the counter, away from the bus driver, his back to the plate-glass windows. Perched upon the counter, just to his side, was a chrome jukebox selector with a coin slot on top and the songs listed on a rotating menu.

When the waitress came and brought him a coffee, he avoided making eye contact by looking down at his filthy hands crossed atop the Formica.

"You need a menu, hon?" she said, her voice slack with boredom.

"No," he said. "A couple of eggs, over easy, with home fries, crispy, and rye toast."

"That it?"

"And a hamburger, scorched. And a piece of pie. Do you have pie?"

"Apple, French apple, apple crumb, blueberry, peach, lemon meringue—"

"Peach, with ice cream on top. Vanilla. And I want sausage with the eggs, burned. And extra pickles with the hamburger. Do you have pancakes?"

"Short stack or regular?"

"Short stack."

"That all?"

"No. You're right. Give me the full load. And some pudding."

"Tapioca all right?"

"Big or little tapiocas?"

"Big."

"Perfect."

"Should I set another place?"

"Nope," he said, before taking a gulp of his coffee.

She took out a pad and scratched all over it, ripped it off, placed it in front of him.

"That'll be twenty-one forty-eight with the tax."

"Thanks," he said.

She didn't move. "Twenty-one forty-eight," she said. "With the tax."

He looked up at her. She was pretty but tired, with an unfortunate set of teeth. "You want me to pay first?"

She lifted her chin toward a sign atop the wide serving window that led from the counter to the kitchen: MANAGEMENT RESERVES THE RIGHT TO HAVE PATRONS PAY BEFORE FOOD IS SERVED.

"I'm good for it," he said, taking another gulp of the coffee.

She didn't move.

"I told you I'm good for it."

She didn't move.

"I'm not going to pay first," he said. "I've never paid first in my life." He knew it was better to keep silent, but the lawyer in him couldn't help himself. It was as if the closing argument delivered itself. "I don't even think that sign is legal. Who decides who pays first, and on what basis? Have you ever heard of *Katzenbach v. McClung* and the case of Ollie's Barbecue? Have you ever heard of the Equal Protection Clause of the Fourteenth Amendment? Have you ever heard of the Constitution of the United States of America?"

"Have you ever heard," she said, still bored, "of Ed?"

She jerked her thumb over her shoulder.

There, in the kitchen, peeking through the serving window tinted devil's red by the heat lamps, standing huge and gnarled, with a scar on his lip, a filthy white apron over his T-shirt, a paper chef's hat on his head, and gripping a shotgun with his fists, stood Ed.

"Twenty-one forty-eight, was it?" said Scrbacek, reaching into his pocket.

"With the tax."

A bouquet of derisive laughter came from the booth with the red-suited men, which Scrbacek scrupulously ignored as he thumbed through his wad and dropped a bill on the counter.

"You got anything smaller?"

"Sorry."

It was one of the new hundreds he had won from the casino, a note that looked like a bad copy of Monopoly money, and the waitress held it up to the light, checking all of its myriad security features before taking it to the register, marking it with her currency-testing pen, and making his thick wad of change.

"Two over, spuds extra crisp," she called through the service window. "Sausage burnt, burger well, no cheese, stack of jacks."

On his way to the restroom at the end of the counter, Scrbacek had to pass the booth with the four red-suited crooners. Their eyes were harder than he had first thought. He suddenly sensed danger in their identical suits and black shirts, in their narrow yellow ties, in their thin-brimmed fedoras. They were crooners like he was an acrobat. He kept his head down as he passed, but he could tell they were watching him.

"I never would have imagined it," said one of the men. "Thomas Jefferson eating at Ed's."

Scrbacek ignored the laughter.

"Hey, Tom," said another. "How about an autograph, Tom?"

"Or at least," said a third in a voice as low as fate, "one of them dead presidents you tossing 'round."

"Franklin was never president," said the first. "He was too busy sticking his thang into anything that moved."

"Since when did doggin' ever stop a politician? Isn't that right, Tom?"

Scrbacek pushed open the door of the restroom without breaking stride and quickly locked it behind him. He leaned back against the door and took a deep breath before falling into a spasm of coughs. When it subsided, he pushed himself off the door and bent over the tiny sink. He unwrapped the bandage from his right hand, the gauze now black with filth. The cut on his palm was scabbed and raw, seething with infection. He turned on the water, pumped out soap from the dispenser, scrubbed his hands back and forth hard, rinsed and pumped, and scrubbed again. From his raincoat pocket he took out the pills Squirrel had prescribed. He ignored the Tylenol, fearing the drowsiness of the codeine, but shook out two of the Keflex. As he downed the antibiotic, he caught sight of his reflection in the mirror above the sink.

No wonder the waitress had demanded money up front.

His face was filthy, bruised, wet with sweat, and pale with fright. His jaw was darkly stubbled, his hair wildly unkempt and matted with dirt. He punched out more soap and washed his face, rubbing soap deep into the pores. He slapped water onto his hair and combed it back with his fingers. When he dried his face with a paper towel, the paper came up so filthy he did it all again. Then, as clean as he could get in that tiny space, he shucked off his raincoat—wrinkled, singed, streaked with dirt, a jagged hole through the left sleeve—and took a dump. Then he washed everything again.

He was in the restroom long enough that he held hopes the gang with the fedoras would have cleared out, but when he stepped back into the diner, Sinatra was still singing and the red-suits were still sprawled in their booth, as if waiting just for him.

"Hey, Tom, we thought you got lost in there."

Scrbacek ignored the laughter.

"I think I seen you before, Tom," said another. "Is that possible?"

Scrbacek kept walking.

"Yo, Tom, fuck," said a third. In that instant the Sinatra song ended and the jukebox went silent. "My man he be talking to you."

The bus driver stood, tossed a few coins on the counter, and walked out, the door tinkling behind him. The woman drinking tea buried her face in her purse.

Scrbacek stopped in front of his stool and turned around. All four red-suits were staring. The smallest of the men had twisted in the booth, leaning his face out the booth's side so his view of Scrbacek was unobstructed, his Chiclet-toothed grin in no way masking the killing hardness of his eyes. Scrbacek stared right back at him.

"I never saw you before in my life," Scrbacek said.

"You look mightily familiar."

"I have that kind of face," said Scrbacek.

"Nah, I seen you before."

"A course you done seen him before," said another of the men. "You even knowed his name."

"What the hell nonsense you spouting?"

"Tom. You called him Tom."

"Yo, Felix," said a third. "Keep your mouth shut so everyone don't know how truly ignorant you are."

"I ain't ignorant. If anyone's ignorant, it's the Worm."

"You don't even know what the word means," said the small one, the Worm, with his brutal grin.

"Sure I do. It means you got some fiercely ugly teeth."

"I seen him before. I know I have."

"Who the hell cares," said another of the men. "I've seen you before, and it's not doing Mickey a lick of good tonight. Turn around and shut up."

They laughed, and the little man with the grin stared for a moment more before turning away. Once more the red-suits were huddled over their dirty plates. Scrbacek waited a little longer, making sure they had lost all interest, before he sat down upon his stool.

It was all there in front of him, the feast he had ordered. Even with the fright from the red-suits, his hunger blossomed at the sight of it all. He mashed a yolk into the potatoes, cut a piece of sausage, scooped it all together onto his fork and into his mouth. A wave of satisfaction rushed through him. Before the fork was out of his mouth, he formed another pile with the edge of his toast. He ate like a wolf, gulping the food with barely a chew. He finished the eggs and potatoes as if in a race, and went right to the pancakes, pouring the syrup until the thick liquid lipped off the plate.

When the red-suits grabbed their fedoras and stood from their booth, Scrbacek froze, his fork stranded in midair. The men paid their bill and left, jangling out, laughing.

"Later, Tom," said one.

"I tell you, dammit to hell, I seen his ugly face before," said the Worm. "I know I seen it."

The hugest of them all grabbed a handful of toothpicks from beside the register and stuck one in his gaping mouth, sucking loudly through the teeth of his oversize jaw.

When the bell tinkled and the door closed behind them, Scrbacek let out a breath he didn't realize he had been holding and went back to his meal, eating more slowly now. Pancakes and syrup with the rest of the sausage. Hamburger, with ketchup doused atop the extra pickles. Peach pie, the ice cream melted into a creamy pool around its bottom crust. All of it washed down with his second, then his third cup of coffee.

In the middle of his meal, he leaned over to the jukebox selector on the counter and turned the song menu inside the box. Sinatra. Sinatra. All Sinatra. A hundred selections of Sinatra.

"What," said Scrbacek to the waitress, "no Elvis?"

"Ed likes Frank," she said.

Scrbacek shrugged, took a quarter of his change, slipped it in the slot, punched D7. He didn't know the song, just liked the name. First, a flute, then a clash of strings, then nothing but a simple bluesy bass line to accompany the sweet voice as it eased its way through the speakers.

As Frank sang about what his mother had told him when he was in knee pants, Scrbacek turned to the last dish of food before him, pale-yellow custard teeming with opulent beads of tapioca, glistening like pearls. There was no chance of really enjoying it—his stomach was too painfully stretched to accept another whit—but still he found himself unable to resist. He carved out a spoonful, put it in his mouth, tasted the clean burned vanilla, pressed the soft beads with his tongue.

His mother had made him tapioca pudding just like this. When he was sick in bed as a boy, she would bring it to his room on a tray, a little ramekin full, along with a mug of cocoa, and he would savor the warm vanilla custard, fresh from the pot, and the large squishy beads. He took another spoonful and tried to lose himself in a past of split-level tract homes and red bicycles, of blue station wagons and Little League baseball games and warm tapioca pudding. It had been just like that, his early youth in a suburb across the river from Philadelphia. Playing Twister with the neighbor girls, and the Game of Life, playing basketball in Kenny Park's driveway, tall glasses of lemonade, hot dogs on the grill, Saturday cartoons. The tragedy of his father's death. The triumph of an intramural championship. Springsteen concerts. Fourth of July parades. Necking at the air force base with Audrey Boccelli. He'd go there right now if he could, to the innocence of his little suburb, go there in a heartbeat if his mom was still making pudding and his dad was still alive and Kenny Park was still shooting hoops and Audrey Boccelli was still putting out and he could be seven or ten or seventeen again.

Was that the past he was supposed to examine, according to the Contessa's cards?

Or was it the blur of college when, freed from the confining definitions of the suburbs, he found himself able to explore his inner self. Drugs, sex, Kerouac and Hermann Hesse, all to the sound track of Linkin Park and the Strokes. Studying philosophy and psychology, reading Kant and Camus, Goffman and Skinner. Getting nauseated with Sartre, trembling fearfully with Kierkegaard. He had tried to open his heart to the benign indifference of the universe, but the cap wasn't a twist-off and there was no opener in sight. He toyed with being a writer, an artist, a photographer, he toyed with finding expression for all that flowed deep within him, but basically he toyed. He took his courses, wrote his papers, ingested whatever was around to be ingested, slept with whatever woman would let him slip between her sheets. He traversed the college years in a sincere haze only to discover, when the haze burned off, that he had found no inner self worth exploring.

No, the Contessa had said there was a choice in his past that had led him here, to this diner in Crapstown, hunted and in fear, with a hole shot straight through his arm. When he looked into his far past, his boyhood and his collegiate years, he saw no real choices. Whether to ask Audrey Boccelli to the prom or one of the primmer, prettier neighbor girls? Was that the choice? He had gone with pretty and prim, asked Susan Winship, who looked great but gave him nothing, not a thing. Whether to major in psychology or philosophy at college? Philosophy, because the girls in the classes were hotter. Whether to mix ecstasy with beer or with vodka? Let's try both. Whether to quit the lacrosse team after getting beat up for two straight weeks by guys a hundred pounds heavier? Quit, definitely quit. Whether to go to law school or business school? Law, because they accepted him and if he didn't go, he would have had to find himself a job.

There it was, the litany of his choices before he took his first step through the portals of the law. No, the Contessa must have gotten it wrong in telling him to look to the choices of his past, because in his past there was no choice that could have led him here. Nothing. Unless . . .

Tinkle, tinkle.

Scrbacek froze on his stool as the diner door opened. He didn't want to look, hoped it was just another lonely soul heading to a booth for a late-night breakfast. But the footsteps came right up to his stool, and then something slapped down beside his pudding on the counter.

A newspaper. With Scrbacek's picture in full color beneath a banner headline that tightened Scrbacek's throat so he could hardly breathe: MURDER SUSPECT STILL AT LARGE.

And beside the picture, in smaller type, two tombstone head-lines: SURWIN WIDENS SCRBACEK PROBE TO INCLUDE ARSON and BREEST LAWYER CONSIDERED ARMED AND DANGEROUS.

"Early edition, Tom." It was the smallest of the red-suits, the Worm, his hat tilted back on his head, his ugly grin ungainly and dangerous. "I knew I seen your face before."

Scrbacek said not a word, just stared at the paper.

"There's lots of folk looking for you," said the Worm.

"Just leave me alone," said Scrbacek.

"Offering lots of money."

"Get the hell out of here," said Scrbacek, and he said it loud enough for the waitress to take a step back. She glanced at the window to the kitchen.

There stood Ed, in the red glow of the heat lamps, looking with mute interest at the goings-on at the counter, the double barrel of his shotgun just visible in the window.

The red-suit raised his face to the window and grinned at Ed as he said, "What the hell kind of name is Scrbacek, anyway?"

"French."

"French? I never would have figured. Fucking Frogs. You know, that Jerry Lewis thing I can understand—that smile of his cracks my ass too—but Mickey Rourke? Fuck me with a crème brûlée, why don't you? We'll be outside, Tom. We'll be waiting."

And then the Worm slapped Scrbacek hard on the back and stepped out of the diner.

Tinkle, tinkle.

19
MICKEY'S HARD BOYS

He sat on his stool and closed his eyes, let the terror ratchet through him, felt it escalate until it filled every space, constricted every breath, twisted every thought. He let the terror run through him until he found an equilibrium between the terror outside and the terror in his heart, and in the center of that equilibrium he felt the first stirrings of a calm. Where it came from, he had not the vaguest idea, but with his eyes still closed he concentrated on that calm, tried to expand it as far as it would go, which wasn't much, but it was something—enough to let him take a full breath, enough to let him open his eyes, enough to let his mind turn to something other than the fear.

They were waiting for him outside, the bastards in the red fedoras, ready to turn him over to whoever would pay the most. And he held little doubt that the price had a dead-or-alive tag attached to it, maybe even more for the dead. He had to get out of this diner and past the bastards in the red fedoras and find a place to hide.

He turned around and saw the Worm grinning at him through the window. He turned around again.

The newspaper was still on the counter. He looked good in the picture, his cheek unbruised, his jaw clean-shaven, his hair coifed. The face of what he had been just two days before, when he still had an office and a career and never had to pay before being served. He pushed the pudding aside, spread the tabloid out before him, and read the article as if reading about someone else.

Noted criminal attorney J.D. Scrbacek, a named suspect in the bombing murder of Ethan Brummel, is still at large. Once considered a possible target of the bombing of his Ford Explorer behind the county courthouse, Scrbacek is now thought to have set the device himself. This comes on the heels of a fire that destroyed his office and home late last night. After putting out the blaze, firefighters discovered in the basement of his building, protected by a tarp and undestroyed by the fire, a cache of illegal weapons, along with three blocks of plastic explosives of the same type used to destroy Scrbacek's truck. Because of the weapons, Scrbacek is to be considered armed and dangerous.

A motive for the murder has only been hinted at by the County Prosecutor's Office, but one theory holds that Ethan Brummel, Scrbacek's intern, had discovered something incriminating in his boss's files and Scrbacek murdered him to stop him from talking to the police. Supporting that theory is a call from Ethan Brummel, logged the day before his death, to the State Bureau of Investigation, a record discovered only after Scrbacek came up missing. Also, in what has been described as a strange visit to the victim's family after the murder, Scrbacek allegedly sought to determine if Brummel had disclosed to his family anything he had learned about Scrbacek's practice. According to sources in the police department, the victim's mother assured Scrbacek that her son had told her nothing, which may be why her life was spared.

Caleb Breest, Scrbacek's former client, recently released from jail, issued a statement through his new attorney, Cirilio Vega, claiming that Breest knew nothing about the killing of Ethan Brummel or why his former lawyer might have turned so brutally murderous. In the statement, Breest sent his deepest, heartfelt sympathies to the murder victim's family.

Scrbacek slammed the counter with the flat of his hand and felt the delicious slap of pain within the wound on his palm. Cirilio Vega, that bastard. He had been a friend. They had shared together their dreams and aspirations. And now, the betrayal: Vega taking over Breest's representation and bad-mouthing Scrbacek to the press. How dare he? He slammed again his hand upon the counter.

Stop, he told himself. Keep calm. Cirilio was only representing his new client; Scrbacek wouldn't have done any differently. It wasn't Cirilio that was framing his ass, it was someone else. And it wasn't enough just to try to kill him, no. Now there were enough clues planted to make him the prime suspect in his own attempted murder. How insanely clever was that? And with Scrbacek considered armed and dangerous, a cop could shoot first, plant a small silver pistol in his deadened fist second, and no one would be the wiser. *A righteous shooting,* they all would say as they shook their heads over his riddled corpse. *Totally righteous.* With the magician grinning in the background.

He slammed shut the paper and turned it over to hide his picture. The back of the tabloid told him the Phillies had won. How nice for them. He turned again to look out the window. They were still out there, the red-suits, waiting with patience for their quarry, laughing and cracking wise, and perhaps not paying as close attention as before.

"Is there a way out the back of this place?" he asked the waitress.

"Not for customers, hon."

"It's a special case."

"Everyone thinks he's a special case, believe me. Every damn one."

He pulled out his wad, rolled off another hundred, slid it across the counter. "For you and Ed if I can go through the back."

She held it up to the light, checking its security features, and then leaned into the window to the kitchen. "One to go out with the garbage," she said.

Ed nodded.

"Do me a favor," said Scrbacek. "Fill up my coffee cup and then stand in the doorway to the kitchen for a moment, like you're having a deep philosophical conversation with Ed."

She cocked her head at Scrbacek as if he had just asked for ketchup with his pie. "A conversation? With Ed?"

"Give it a try. You never know. I need to hit the head."

Scrbacek stood from his stool, leaving the newspaper on the counter. Without looking to the windows, he headed for the restroom as the waitress filled his cup with coffee. He left the door slightly open as he went inside.

He immediately dropped to the floor. On his elbows and knees he slithered out the open door and scooted behind the counter where he was hidden from the windows. His left arm screamed in pain, but he ignored it as he crawled through the open door to the kitchen, brushing the waitress's legs as he crept by. The door closed shut behind him.

He crawled into something large and immovable and looked up. There stood Ed, in his dirty whites, a slab of a man with a cleaver in the tie of his apron, his heavy arms cradling a shotgun. Ed stared down at Scrbacek with disapproval.

"The back door?" said Scrbacek.

"I done heard about you," said Ed, his voice a rumble so deep it shook the pots hanging over the stove.

"Good things, I hope."

"Not necessarily." Ed frowned down a moment more before reaching out and opening the back door.

"Thanks," said Scrbacek, crawling toward the opening. "By the way, dinner was marvelous."

Then he was outside, falling down a set of cement stairs, rolling into the side of a large trash bin. Lit by a bare bulb sticking out from the back of the diner, he looked around.

Nothing.

He darted to a shadow by the edge of the Dumpster and looked around again.

Nothing.

He was in a narrow alley between the diner and the solid brick wall of a low, long building. The smell of a week's garbage caused his full stomach to churn. There was a gap at either end of the alley, and so the question was which way to run—to the right or to the left.

And then he heard a call, dark as the night, deep as his troubles, soft as a shiv in the gut.

"Oh, Tom," came a calm voice from the left. He peeked out from his shadow, peered down the length of the Dumpster, and saw the silhouette of a man in a fedora standing at the end of the alley, his legs spread. "We're waiting for you, Tom."

Not to the left, he decided quickly. Definitely not to the left.

Staying close to the brick wall, keeping the Dumpster between himself and the man, he headed to the right, skittering forward as fast as he could while still brushing his side tight against the brick. He looked behind him, saw that the sight line of the man was still blocked by the Dumpster, and then hurried on, turning forward, only to see another, bigger silhouette standing in his path.

Scrbacek froze.

"I see the sucker," said the bigger silhouette.

Before he could think it through, Scrbacek was headed back to the Dumpster, back to the yellow light of the diner. But instead of stopping and cowering, he charged forward, gaining speed, running past the Dumpster, running toward the smaller of the silhouettes, running right at the silhouette, lowering his right shoulder into a collision of pain that sent the silhouette tumbling and Scrbacek flying through the air.

He landed on his back, sprawled on the asphalt.

The moon was full in the sky overhead. The walls of the alleyway were gone. The ground felt soft on his back, soft like a feather mattress. He was sinking into the soft, lovely asphalt until he reached the bottom, which was hard and full of pain.

He shook his head to clear his brain. Slowly, painfully, he rolled onto his front and fought to climb to his feet. He rose to his hands and knees, but when he tried to rise higher something stopped him, something kept him down. His mind still fuzzy, he wondered what it could be until something hard as a boot stomped him to the ground. He rolled again onto his back and saw two faces staring down at him, their sharp-brimmed fedoras neatly in place.

"Now what have we caught ourselves here? Our own Tom Jefferson. Lift him, Luther."

The largest of the men sucked noisily on his toothpick before stepping behind Scrbacek, grabbing his torso, and effortlessly lifting him to his feet. He slipped his hands beneath Scrbacek's arms and up behind

Scrbacek's neck and kept lifting until Scrbacek's feet dangled above the asphalt.

Scrbacek's shoulder screamed in pain, or was that his mouth? He struggled to escape, and failed, miserably. The breathing of the giant was loud in his ear.

Another red-suit strode up to Scrbacek, swayed for a moment, and then flicked out his wrist. A blade appeared like magic in his hand, the metal glistening dully in the moonlight. Scrbacek stared in horror as the knife drew closer, when suddenly he heard, "Let me at the Frog bastard."

The two red-suits standing in front of Scrbacek split apart, and between them, bent at the waist, left arm tight to his side, bareheaded but still grinning, came the Worm. The small man laughed wildly before burying his right hand in Scrbacek's stomach.

Scrbacek's legs pulled up as he let out an "Oof," but Luther held him firmly in place.

"Mark him, Felix," said a red-suit with a beard.

The man with the switchblade stepped forward and placed the edge of the blade on the bridge of Scrbacek's nose. Scrbacek pulled his head away from the blade until he was stopped by a great amount of pressure from Luther's hands.

"Why?" gasped Scrbacek.

"Because we can," said the man with the beard.

"How's your breathing, Tom?" said Felix, putting pressure on the blade, letting it slide through the flesh of Scrbacek's nose. "Maybe I'll help things along."

"Not so much he can't be recognized," said the man with the beard. "Mickey already worked out a deal for the head."

"I'll be gentle-like," said Felix as he pressed the blade further into Scrbacek's flesh. The pressure was growing unbearable, the sharp edge of pain slipping deeper, when suddenly Felix flung himself back and raised his arms like a dancer.

It was a lovely bit of ballet, that move, graceful and slow and inexplicable to Scrbacek, even as the knife flew in an arc through the air, even as a darkness bled across Felix's narrow yellow tie.

Luther released his grip on Scrbacek and spun around. Scrbacek dropped to the ground and rolled away just as the huge man's knee collapsed in a mist of red and he tumbled to the ground, letting out a loud, inhuman howl.

The two red-suits still standing looked around, puzzled, amidst the huge man's cries. One of the men reached into his jacket, but before he could pull a weapon, something came out of the sky and slammed into his jaw, dropping him cold to the ground.

And now, crouched beside Scrbacek's heaped body, was the Nightingale, her gun aimed at the Worm's head.

The Worm backed away, still showing his teeth but no longer grinning.

"Say you're sorry," said the Nightingale over the huge man's shouting.

The Worm backed away farther. Scrbacek, understanding suddenly what had just happened, staggered to his feet.

"Who's looking for me?" said Scrbacek to the retreating man.

"Fuck you, Tom."

"That's no apology," said the Nightingale as she reached to her boot, pulling out her huge, jagged blade. "And his name isn't Tom."

"Whoever the hell is after me," said Scrbacek, "you tell him I'm coming."

The small man backed away even farther.

"And you tell him I'm not coming alone."

The Worm took one more step back and then turned to run. The Nightingale smoothly took hold of the blade of her knife and cocked it behind her ear like a baseball catcher about to nail a runner stealing third. Before she could spin it forward, Scrbacek placed a hand on her elbow.

"Let him go," he said.

"Why?"

"Because he's running."

"Just makes him a smaller target is all."

"Let him go," said Scrbacek. "Let him tell the bastards who are after me that I'm not defenseless."

"You looked pretty damn defenseless to me," she said.

He turned his head to look at her. She was smiling, and her smile was positively incandescent. "Who are you?" he said.

"Just a girl with a gun."

"Aren't you a little young?"

"Not too young to save your ass."

"Yeah, well, I would have muddled through on my own," said Scrbacek. He could still feel the pressure of the blade on the bridge of his nose, and his utter helplessness at that moment. But he could also feel the strange calm he had mustered just moments before at Ed's counter. He wiped at the bridge of his nose, and his hand came away slick with blood. "I was just getting ready to make my move."

"Your move?"

"My move. You know." He did a little shuffle. "My move."

"Oh, that move."

"But I guess I ought to thank you anyway. Thanks for . . ."

"For saving your ass?"

"Yeah, for that."

"Blixen asked me to look after you."

"You did the old woman proud."

"For some reason she trusts you."

"Maybe she should trust a razor."

"Wait a second," said the Nightingale, and then she went over to the huge man on the ground, still rolling, still shouting in pain. She leaned over him, put her hand gently on his forehead, and spoke to him softly. His howls quieted, and she spoke to him some more, and he listened without saying a word, and then she leaned her ear close to his mouth.

"You wanted to know who's looking for you?" she said when she returned. "Everyone. And not just because you're on the front page of the paper. The order's been passed that anyone with any word of where you are should go to Dirty Dirk's."

"Whose order?"

"He didn't know."

"Did Caleb Breest give it?"

"He didn't know. But there's money behind it. Big money."

"We have to get out of here before the reinforcements come," said Scrbacek. "Or worse, before Ed steps out the back of his diner."

"Where are you headed?"

He thought for a moment, wiping more blood from the bridge of his nose. "Remember what the Contessa said, about finding the answers in my past, my present, my future?"

"I remember."

"Maybe I'll start at the beginning."

"So, which way's that?" she said, looking around.

The night sky was changing, a grayness reaching its fingers menacingly across the black. He faced the coming dawn and pointed to his left.

"That way."

He walked along one street and then over to another and kept walking, always keeping the dawn to his right, ignoring the sirens that rose behind him. The Nightingale was walking with him, he was sure, but a hundred yards on, when he asked where she had learned to fight like that and turned around for an answer, she was gone, vanished into the thinning night. He looked along the street, swept his gaze over the rooftops, saw nothing. He rubbed more blood from the bridge of his nose and continued on his way, still hunted, still without refuge, still with less than a clue.

But no longer without hope.

THIRD NIGHT

THIRD NIGHT

20
TRENT FALLOW, PI

See him there, Trent Fallow, PI, dark stringy hair, five-day growth of beard, Buddy Holly glasses, mouth an open O through which he breathes, constantly, gulping in the liters of oxygen needed to keep his great bulk fervidly metabolizing. He is obese, Trent Fallow, PI, morbidly so, he hasn't been able to appreciate the woof of his dick for decades, but don't blame him—he's just big-boned.

Trent Fallow, PI, wears tentlike jeans, cinched at his equatorial waist, and a scabrous checked sport coat over T-shirts bearing cheap advertising slogans from down-and-out Crapstown joints, picked up on clearance for a buck and a half. And he packs licensed heat, a Colt Detective Special with six .38 cartridges and no safety device, which he harnesses in the gap between the folds of his chest and the loose fat hanging from his arm. One would never consider him quick on the draw—he's not actually quick at anything—and, in a fair fight, by the time he could lumber into position, excavate the revolver from his slabs of fat, and wrap his pudgy finger around the trigger, a quicker shot with an automatic could have riddled Fallow's stomach with lead, reloaded, and riddled it some more. In a fair fight, he wouldn't stand a chance, Trent Fallow, PI, which is why he avoids fair fights.

See him there, Trent Fallow, PI, stepping out of his office to make his way through the streets of Crapstown. His T-shirt today heralds Honest Dan's Expired Condoms at 69 West Buchanan Street, with a slogan on the back: More Bang for the Buck. It's noon, but for a guy like Fallow, who prowls for scraps in the night like a hyena, it seems ungodly early, and sleep lays crusty in his blackened eyes. He'd still be in bed nursing his wounds, but he has a job to do, a desperate job on which his very life hinges. He grabs a tabloid from the vendor on the corner.

"How you doing, Frankie?" says Trent Fallow, PI.

"Good, Mr. Fallow. Real good."

"How's the wife?"

"Still dead, Mr. Fallow."

"Attaboy, Frankie. You doing something right."

He tips Frankie the usual dime and glances at the front of the paper. His bruised and bloody face spasms with nervousness. From the wince at the newspaper and the damaged face, the inevitable assumption rises that the newspaper headlines and the brutal beating he recently suffered are somehow related. He folds the paper quickly, twists his head, flashing worried looks fore and aft, and then steps back to Frankie's shed.

"Hey, Frankie," he says, dropping a fiver and a Trent Fallow, PI, business card on a pile of papers, just atop the face of J.D. Scrbacek smiling above the fold on the front page. "Do me a favor."

"Anything, Mr. Fallow."

"You see this guy plastered on the front page, you give me a call, all right?"

"Will do, Mr. Fallow."

"You call me before you call anyone else, you got it? Even before the police. You let me take care of it, and there will be a bonus in it for you."

"I appreciate that, Mr. Fallow."

Trent Fallow, PI, pulls out more cards from his pocket and places them in a pile beside the scratched change tray. "Pass the word. Anyone finds him and calls me first gets himself a nice bonus. A nice bonus. Okay, Frankie?"

He winks, and Frankie winks back.

"Will do, Mr. Fallow."

"Good boy, Frankie," says Trent Fallow, PI, before heading off, not noticing the way Frankie, the fifty-three-year-old newsboy, still mourning the death of his life's love after a brutal six-month battle with ovarian cancer, stares after him with dark cheeks and narrowed eyes before taking the neat pile of cards and dumping them in the trash can.

Trent Fallow, PI, has himself a killer of a problem, and it isn't his fault. Ask him, he'll tell you—it isn't his fault. It all started at Dirty Dirk's one night when he was simply minding his own damn business. Dirk's, where he can't anymore show his face until the problem is solved. He was at Dirk's when Joey Torresdale called him over. What was he going to do, say no to Caleb Breest's right-hand man? Hell, the Lady Baltimore was on the stage, and what he wanted to be doing was to edge his way between the tables and flash his fivers and wait for sweet Baltimore to sashay that firm white ass of hers over to him and squat down in those strappy heels and pucker those sexy lips like she's got his schlong right there between her teeth while he snaps her thong just enough to stick the bills inside and maybe catch a whiff of her sweet sweaty scent. That's what he wanted to be doing. But when Joey Torresdale called him over, Trent Fallow, PI, came running as usual.

"Hey, Trent," said Torresdale, his big putty nose red from too much booze. "I want you to meet my dear friend J.D. Scrbacek. He's representing Caleb."

"Hey, good luck on that," said Trent Fallow. "We need the big guy out and about."

"J.D. is looking for a PI to work with him on the case. I told him you're the man."

"You got that right," said Fallow. "Anything you want, J.D., you got." Fallow pulled a card out of his jeans. "Whenever you're ready to sit down and lay out what you need, give me a call."

"I will," said J.D. Scrbacek. "Yes, I will."

And so he did, that son of a bitch, and now Trent Fallow, PI, is in the big dark deep.

21

THE MARINA DISTRICT

J.D. Scrbacek, the object of Trent Fallow's ire, had slipped unnoticed through the streets of the city while the PI was still snoring in his fetid bed like a fat boar. As the dangerous dawn reached across the whole of the night sky, and a gray light rose as if from the streets themselves, Scrbacek had hunched himself deeper within the turned-up collar of his raincoat and scurried forward as if in a race with the sun.

The landscape was different here than in the heart of Crapstown, the streets better paved, the cars better maintained, the tenements rehabbed into garden apartments and the occasional town house. The windows of the lower levels still were barred, true, but the cast iron was of a higher degree of craftsmanship. And there were no slashes of graffiti here, just flyers tacked onto posts hyping a community rally to protest Diamond's casino development plan. The trees growing from square plots in the sidewalk were alive, the flowers in the flower boxes had blooms. Coming out of Crapstown to the Marina District on the northern fringe of the city was like emerging into a fresh and fragrant dawn.

To Scrbacek the landscape here was as familiar as an old friend. He had spent his first few years after law school right here, eating in the Portuguese diner patronized by the commercial fishermen who docked their boats in the harbor, shopping in the mom-and-pop grocery, sipping cappuccino in the coffee bar that opened beside the dry cleaner, walking the dog along the still undeveloped coastline, crabbing in the bay.

It was an impossible conglomeration of ruins when they had moved there, buying and rehabbing the house because it was the only way they could afford a place of their own. But they were not alone in their industry. A whole community of pioneers worked to turn the Marina District into something other than a swath of urban blight. And, against all odds, they had succeeded. Scrbacek had always been proud of his part in the rebirth of the Marina District. He looked upon its resurgence as a personal triumph, though he had also been quick enough to leave as soon as he had freed Amber Grace from a death sentence and became a legal eagle earning enough to afford his own building in Casinoland.

But now here he was again. And this was the street on which he had lived. And this was the house.

Scrbacek stood in the shadows and searched the landscape. He had checked out the parked cars one by one, walking carefully past, peering inside to see if there was anyone sitting with a cup of coffee and the remnants of a half dozen donuts waiting for him to pop up at his old haunt. The cars had all been empty. The street was deserted. He stood a moment more and examined the town house across the way. No lights, no movement. In a lower-level window, a poster for an antidevelopment rally had been slipped behind the glass. Still the rabble-rouser. He took a step toward the house when suddenly a door opened beside him. He jumped back into the shadows.

A runner in her long-sleeved T-shirt and gloves, turning away from his position and heading off down the street, ponytail bobbing like a pony's tail.

The day was blossoming, and so was the danger. When the runner was far enough away, he left the landing, scooted across the street, and stepped up to the front door of his old house. He pressed the button of the bell that had never worked while he had lived there. It still didn't. He lifted up the knocker, with an exotic face on its handle that looked vaguely like that of the Contessa Romany, and let it drop.

A dog barked, and a long moment later a light appeared through the door's peephole, died for a few seconds, and appeared again. Then the door opened just enough for the dog to stick his black shiny muzzle through, gulping at Scrbacek's scent. Through the crack, Scrbacek saw a woman clutching at her robe.

She was beautiful still, with long black hair, high cheekbones, lovely eyes. Older now, tired, but still oh so beautiful. Behind her was a man in jeans and no shirt, with bare feet and dirty blond hair. The woman looked at Scrbacek's face for a long time without saying a word, then opened the door a bit wider to search the street behind him. Satisfied, apparently, that there was no immediate mortal threat, she opened the door wide enough for the dog, a great black monster, to leap through the opening and jump up to his chest. The dog showed his teeth and then licked Scrbacek's chin.

"You're a mess," said Jenny Ling after she had let him in, closed the door firmly behind him, and slid shut both of the locks.

"I've had a rough couple of nights," said Scrbacek, kneeling down to scratch the dog's neck as the dog flipped his hind legs back and forth like a hyperactive wind-up doll and breathed in Scrbacek's foul gaminess. "Hey, Palsgraf, how's my buddy? How you doing? You still a good dog? Yes, you are, yes. Yes, you are."

The dog thrashed his tail and washed Scrbacek's face with his great pink tongue.

"He remembers you," she said.

"It's nice to be remembered."

"What happened to your nose?"

Scrbacek stood and wiped at the wound. Still oozing. "I cut myself shaving."

"What were you using, a Bowie knife? I'm making coffee. You want coffee?"

"Not if you still make it thick as sludge and tasting of acid."

"None for you, then," she said, turning and heading for the kitchen. As she did, she passed the man with the blond hair. "This is Dan," she said without stopping. "He was just leaving. Dan, meet America's most wanted, J.D. Scrbacek."

Dan stared at Scrbacek for a moment and then turned to follow Jenny into the kitchen. "You want me to call someone?" said Dan.

She opened the refrigerator, pulled out a can of coffee, started heaping teaspoon after teaspoon into a coffeemaker. "I want you to call no one. If I thought anyone should be called, I'm perfectly capable of picking up the phone myself."

"Jen," said Dan, "it's not a good idea for you—"

"Go home, Dan. Get stoned, play guitar, watch television. Do exactly what you normally would do in your ultraproductive day."

"I think I should stay."

"What did I tell you about that?" she said, patting his cheek gently. "It's not your strong suit, is it, thinking? Get your clothes on and go home."

Dan swiveled his head to stare at Scrbacek, turned to look again at Jenny, and then strode out of the kitchen and up the stairs.

"That's Dan," she said to Scrbacek.

"So I gathered."

She filled the water reservoir of the machine and plugged it in. "What are you doing here, J.D.?"

"I'm in trouble."

"Your car's blown up, your house is burned down, your intern's dead, they think you did it, and your client, Caleb Breest, the dark lord of Crapstown, is not amused at his attorney. Yes, J.D., you're in a boatload."

"And it's following me around."

"So you bring it here. How nice for me and how typical of you. Are you clean?"

"I need a shower."

She stared at him.

"Yes, I'm clean. Forever, now. Look, I'm sorry I haven't called. But I've been thinking about you."

"How heartwarming."

"Don't act all hurt and bothered. It was you who got the restraining order."

"And you didn't deserve it?"

"It was a little harsh, don't you think?"

"You brought a gun into our house. Into our house."

"It was a client's. It wasn't loaded."

"And I was supposed to know that when you waved it in my face?"

"I was a little cranked. It was a bad time. But now I'm clean and I'm in trouble and I need your help. Can you help me, Jen?"

Steps pounded down the stairs before she could answer. Jenny bade Scrbacek to sit while she went to the entranceway to say good-bye to Dan. Scrbacek could see them there—the woman, the man, the dog—but not make out the words of their soft yet urgent conversation over the gurgling and hissing of the coffee machine. Finally, Dan leaned down to kiss her, and Jenny gave him her cheek. Dan patted Palsgraf's head and took a final glance at Scrbacek. Jenny locked the door behind him.

The thick smell of coffee permeated the kitchen. Jenny came back into the room, filled one of her huge coffee cups with the thick black slop, and sat down at the table with Scrbacek. She took her first few sips in silence. The dog raced around the room until fitting himself into a curl around her feet.

"Remember how long it took," she said, "for us to sleep together—all the hesitations and false starts? How scared I was because with you I was crossing some sort of line?"

"Yes. I remember."

"There was a Korean boy in college I never told you about, but that was just to piss off my folks. You were different."

Scrbacek smiled weakly.

"Now there's Dan. Things have a way of slipping from us, you know what I mean?"

"Tell me about it."

"What do you want, J.D.?"

"A shower and some sleep."

"And?"

"And I need some answers."

"Boy, have you come to the wrong place. I don't even know the questions anymore. Anybody know you're here?"

"Just you and Dan, and someone I trust completely."

"Is there anyplace else you can go? Think now. Anyplace?"

"No."

"And you're clean?"

"Yes."

"Then you can shower and sleep. You hungry?"

"No, thanks. I just ate at Ed's."

"Ed's?"

"Cute little bistro in the heart of Crapstown. But if you could put some bread, cheese, and fruit in a bowl outside, that would be great."

"Outside?"

"For a friend."

"What is he—a bird?"

"Close. I still don't understand what is happening to me, Jen, but a fortune-teller told me part of the answer to how I ended up in this catastrophe was somewhere in my past."

"A fortune-teller?"

"The Contessa Romany from the boardwalk."

"I've seen her sign. She has a good sign."

"So I was wondering if you had any ideas."

"On what a fortune-teller had in mind? Yeah, I have a pretty good idea."

"I came to you," he said, "because you knew me better than anyone since I entered the law. If anyone has the answer, you do. Any ideas on what it was in my past that may have brought me so much trouble."

"Isn't it obvious?"

He stared at her as she took another swallow of her coffee.

She smiled over the brim of her oversize cup. "Think, J.D. Who's been responsible for everything that's happened to you since the very first day we met?"

"I don't know. Who?"

"DeLoatch."

***

It had been almost a decade since J.D. Scrbacek, after a quick cigarette, walked with understandable nervousness into the majestic brick building that would be the center of his world for the next three years. He wore tan pants, a white shirt, suede bucks. It wasn't his normal look, the preppy-on-the-make look, but it wasn't a normal day, J.D. Scrbacek's first day of law school.

Whatever he had been in his suburban idyll of a childhood and his spent youth at college was gone, discarded now in favor of some future other. Isn't that the bedrock hope of education, to learn enough to transcend the self, to become something new and better? And where better to start then at the Gap? So he bought all new clothes for school, choosing his wardrobe carefully to match his aspirations. He added a suit, too, from an upscale clothier—a blue suit, pin-striped and double-breasted, as was the style then—bottoming out his bank account to do it. He had considered wearing the suit that first day, but instead left it hanging in the closet. The suit, he felt, would be a bit much. This was still school after all, he was still a chrysalis. The suit was for after, when the process of becoming was over, and he simply was. Was what? A mover and a shaker in the big-money world. A man to whom wearing double-breasted suits and taking for himself all that came with them was as natural as breathing. Someone of whom the mother who made him tapioca pudding and the father who died could be proud. But for now, for the first day of law school, he kept the volume low and limited himself to the tan and the white and the suede.

There were a hundred and twenty of them in the classroom that first day, nervous aspirants to the law, waiting with great expectation for their first law school professor to enter their first law school class. The hushed conversations all faded as the door opened. The man strode into the room with a proprietary air, as if he owned the room and the chairs and the very air inside. They didn't know it yet, the aspirants, but that was how a trial lawyer entered a courtroom. He was small, this man, thin, with a great shock of gray hair and lively blue eyes. He stood before them in silence, as if gathering his words from a place on high, and the students sat on the edges of their chairs. The students had already bought their hornbooks. They held visions of making law review. Their fathers were lawyers, their uncles, their best friends' mothers. They were ready, they had plans. They would be prosecutors and entertainment lawyers and public defenders. They would represent Greenpeace, they would represent Google. They would become investment bankers, divorce lawyers. But the path would be hard, they knew, and some would fail, tumbling lost into the lesser professions, like dentistry or accounting.

"What we're learning here," said the professor, "is criminal law. If you've come for contracts or civil procedure, you're in the wrong class. But stay anyway. There's no telling what you'll be missing if you leave.

Criminal law. I've been practicing it for thirty years on the defense side and still I have no idea what I'm doing. So why am I here? Because I know a hell of a lot more about it than do you. Criminal law."

He was wearing a suit, the professor, gray-checked and shabby. His tie was slightly askew, his shoes were scuffed, his eyebrows had gone decades untrimmed. His voice was prissy and precise and devoid of doubt. One and all they thought him magnificent.

"Let me see," he said, putting on his half glasses, taking a document from his case, examining it closely, turning over one page and then another. "There are so many of you. I have a question to start us off, and I need a volunteer to provide an answer." He looked around. "No volunteers? Then let me see. Ah, here's a strange conglomeration of letters. Mr. S-C-R-B—"

"Scrbacek."

"Ah, there you are. Mr. Scrbacek, yes? And are you having trouble with your legs, Mr. Scrbacek? Good. Then stand, please, when you address the class. Thank you. Scrbacek. An unusual name. Where are your ancestors from, Mr. Scrbacek?"

"Croatia."

"Good for you. Some of the greatest lawyers in this country's history have been Croatian, though I can't seem to name one off the top of my head. Let's see if you measure up. Tell me, Mr. Scrbacek, what is a crime?"

"Murder?"

"Yes, that is a crime, but let's be a little more general about it. Give me a rough definition."

"Physically hurting someone. Taking someone's property without their consent."

"Oh, very good. So if I beat you senseless, that is a crime. And if I take your car without your consent, that too is a crime."

"Yes."

"But what if I'm a police officer and you're a dangerous criminal who is resisting arrest, and in the process of subduing you, I beat you senseless. Is that then a crime?"

"In that case, it would depend on—"

"And what if I'm a banker and you've missed a year of loan payments, and I repossess your car without your consent but under authority of law. Is that a crime?"

"Well, then, I would suppose—"

"I take a gun and shoot you dead. Is that a crime?"

"Yes, of course."

"But if you're pointing a gun at me, what then? If you're pointing a gun at my child, what then? If you are my father and you've beaten me every day of my life and you're about to beat me again, what then?"

"Those are different—"

"What if you're a Jew and I'm an SS soldier and we're in Germany and the year is 1943. Is murdering you a crime?"

"Yes."

"Even if I'm ordered to shoot?"

"Still a crime."

"Careful here, Mr. Scrbacek. Even if the law of the land compels me to shoot?"

"Yes, it is still a crime."

The professor smiled, his small teeth bright and even. "I like you, Mr. Scrbacek. I admire your keen moral vision. You have a fine future ahead of you . . . in divinity school."

General laughter.

"What is a crime, people? Very simply, it is an intentional act that violates a law. What kind of law? A moral law? A natural law? No, Mr. Scrbacek. A crime is an intentional act that violates the express and clear words of a criminal statute. Nothing less and nothing more. If it is not against the penal code, it is not a crime. And thank goodness, or we'd have a pack of Mr. Scrbaceks roaming the countryside determining which of us have violated his moral code and thus are deserving of citation, or imprisonment, or even death."

"I didn't mean to say—"

"Sit down, Mr. Scrbacek. We are finished."

"But I—"

"Sit down, Mr. Scrbacek. Please. You frighten me."

And so he sat, J.D. Scrbacek, on his first day of law school, sat back down in his chair as the professor rattled on about the elements of a crime, sat in his chair and heard nothing but the voice of his own humiliation, felt nothing but the sweat rolling down his sides, soaking into the creased white of his new shirt, the tan of his new pants, running down his calf toward one of his new suede shoes.

That was Professor Drinian DeLoatch.

In the hallway, after class, Scrbacek tried to slip away unobtrusively, his head down, hoping no one would recognize him as the fool of that morning's entertainment. With his eyes to the floor, he ran right smack into a public interest claque from the class. They were in jeans, sweatshirts and T-shirts, sporting backpacks, laughing in the hallway—laughing, no doubt, at him. And in the middle of the crew, tall and thin with long black hair, shiny and straight, was a woman startlingly beautiful. She looked at him and smiled and then shyly looked away.

He just wanted to flee, to hide, to let time salve the pain of his embarrassment, but every postadolescent instinct in his body forced him to stop at the woman's smile and smile back.

And then this shy beautiful woman raised her eyes to his and said, in a voice not so soft, not so soft at all, loud enough, in fact, for all in the hallway to hear:

"It's a wonder you can still walk, Scrbacek, the way he reamed your ass in there."

And that was Jenny Ling.

22

AH, LAW SCHOOL!

Scrbacek turned the shower to very hot and the nozzle spray to very narrow and let the water needle into his back and shoulders. He had tried at the start of the shower to keep the bandage dry on his swollen and purpled arm, had failed miserably, and hadn't really cared. His hair was so filthy that he shampooed and rinsed once and then again, and still the water as it drained had been dark with soot and dirt and blood. So he shampooed and rinsed a third time and then a fourth. He scrubbed his chest, his legs, his neck, his bruise of an arm, his sliced nose. Now, when he felt almost clean, he stood still under the narrow nozzle spray and took a moment to pull himself together.

DeLoatch?

He had come to his old neighborhood, his old house, his old lover, had revisited his past to find what it was that had led him to his precarious state, and Jenny had given him one name.

DeLoatch.

She had implied that his current dire straits were his old law professor's fault, but how was that possible? The professor surely wasn't responsible for the hired assassin out to kill him, or the street gangs scouring the city for his body, or the first assistant county prosecutor seeking to indict him for murder. That was someone else, certainly. Joey Torresdale, maybe, or Caleb Breest, or someone else in the role of the magician, but not his old law professor. How could DeLoatch be responsible? How could a voice from his first year of law school have led him here, to this state of utter desperation?

DeLoatch?

***

"What is a criminal defendant?" had asked Professor Drinian DeLoatch rhetorically from his lectern. The professor's hand was slipped Napoleonically into his vest, his chin rested on his chest as an outward demonstration of deep thought. "A human being with everything at stake. Reputation, property, freedom, sometimes life itself. A human being on the edge, facing the full weight of society's damnation. Who in the whole of our legal landscape is in graver jeopardy? Who is in greater need of a champion?

"What is a prosecutor? An instrument of Draconian justice. To a prosecutor, the human being in the dock does not exist. That person is simply the manifestation of an intentional violation of the penal code. He is not a man, he is a tax evader. She is not a woman, she is a thief. He is not a child, he is a murderer. A prosecutor's universe is straight out of Dante. Violence against thy neighbor? Go to the seventh circle of hell, ring one. Forgery? The eighth circle of hell, ditch ten. For every violation, there is a punishment, and a prosecutor's job is to see it enacted with dispassion and dispatch. A job made for our Mr. Scrbacek, wouldn't you say?"

General laughter.

"And what, pray tell, is a criminal defense attorney? The judge and jury are in league with the prosecutor. They agree with his Dantean vision of the world. They're left only to determine whether a prosecutor has the evidence to enact the punishment. But the role of the defense attorney goes beyond the mere presentation or refutation of evidence. Because the defense attorney is defending more than the act. He is defending the innocent childhood of our defendant, the present conflicted soul, that soul's very future, the potential to change, to grow, to become more than could ever be imagined by the limited vision of the Mr. Scrbaceks of our world. In so doing, the criminal defense attorney is not just the defender of the accused, but the defender of the accused's humanity, and thus the humanity of us all."

***

DeLoatch?

***

"Stand up, Mr. Scrbacek. I have a question that needs your sage consideration. What is the goal of a prosecutor?"

"To convict the defendant."

"Ah, yes, to convict the defendant. You told me before, but I forget, Mr. Scrbacek, from where came your ancestors?"

"Denmark."

"Really? Denmark. Generally an enlightened people, the Danes, which surprises, since your answers are unerringly wrong."

General laughter.

"Does it seem as if I pick on you, Mr. Scrbacek?"

"With an unseemly delight, Professor."

"Well, at least something's getting through."

More general laughter.

"The goal of a prosecutor should not be to convict, although that is unfortunately too often the case. No, Mr. Scrbacek, the role of a prosecutor is to do justice within the confines of due process. That is why prosecutors must turn over to the defendant all exculpatory evidence, known as Brady evidence. That is why prosecutors must turn over all grand jury statements once a witness testifies, known as Jencks material. That is why prosecutors are not permitted to cast away jurors on the impermissible basis of race—though they do, yes, they do. The theory, Mr. Scrbacek, is that it is better that ten guilty men go free than one innocent man lands in jail. Do you agree with that sentiment, Mr. Scrbacek?"

"It depends on what the guilty did. Ten psychopathic murderers running around loose is a frightening prospect."

"And if the innocent man convicted of a crime is you, Mr. Scrbacek, and you are forced to spend the remainder of your life in a six-by-eight cell with a three-hundred-pound murdering rapist named Bubba, what then? Would that change your opinion?"

"Does he sing?"

"Oh, you'd find out, Mr. Scrbacek. Believe me, yes, you would."

***

DeLoatch?

***

"Criminal defense attorneys are always asked the eternal question," intoned DeLoatch from his lectern. "How can we defend the guilty? I can see that very same question work its way over Mr. Scrbacek's simple features. Your keen moral sense is outraged at the idea of it, is that not so, Mr. Scrbacek? What kind of morally corrupt monster can defend the guilty?"

DeLoatch ran his hand through his handsome mane of gray hair, pausing as if he had never before considered the question.

"First, I'll ask how, pray tell, Mr. Scrbacek, you are so certain of your client's guilt? What if she says she's innocent? Is it your job to prove her a liar? And even if the evidence shows her guilt beyond a reasonable doubt, how certain then is your certainty? You weren't there, things might have been rearranged, things might have been doctored. It has been known to happen, Mr. Scrbacek. Yes, indeed.

"But what if you do know for certain. Defense attorneys don't usually ask the key question—they purposely don't want to know. But what if your client blurts it out, what if he says, 'Yes, I killed that man.' What then, Mr. Scrbacek? Stand and tell us. What then?"

"You tell the client to get another lawyer."

"Well said. Sit down. Wrong again, Mr. Scrbacek, wrong again."

General laughter.

"No, still you fight. How? Why? On what moral ground? On the very foundation of this country's system of law.

"We can't determine what is truly just. That is for God, and God alone, to decide. And so we create an approximation, where no single man stands in for God. It's no damn good, our approximation, we know that. Man is lousy at approximating God's work—man's approximation of food is Spam—but this legal system is our best chance, a system of law and due process that requires all to do their part. The judge. The jury. The prosecutor. The defense attorney. One part breaks down, and the system goes awry. One actor takes the role of God for himself, and the approximation is ruined. Bad people will go free, yes. Good people will be convicted, yes. Justice will be defeated at every turn, yes, yes, yes. But the system itself will prevail. We take our solace in the system, we take our courage from our best efforts, we take our hope from the fairness and equal protection that we promise to every person in this great nation. If you believe in America, then you play your role with a song in your heart and a prayer on your lips that our approximation is close enough to find favor in God's eyes."

DeLoatch rubbed his mouth for a moment. "Well, you do," he said finally, "unless you're Mr. Scrbacek, in which case you simply throw your hands in the air and say, 'What the hell.'"

***

DeLoatch.

What a bastard he had been, the imperious Professor Drinian DeLoatch. He had mocked Scrbacek through the whole first year as an example of petty moral righteousness and had treated him with undisguised contempt. When the ethical questions in the casebook became ever so difficult—questions of cannibalism, insanity, abuse—DeLoatch regularly pulled Scrbacek to his feet and roasted his assumptions to the vocal amusement of the class. DeLoatch was like a never-satisfied father to Scrbacek's dim-witted son.

If maybe Scrbacek's own father hadn't up and croaked on him, he might have shrugged off the abuse like any other student and headed for the rich green meadows of corporate law for which he thought he was destined. But Scrbacek's father had died when Scrbacek was ten, and now DeLoatch was there, sheathed in his shabby suits and his air of authority, showering Scrbacek with not just attention, but attention of the most sarcastic and humiliating sort. For the whole of that first year, Scrbacek had hated Professor DeLoatch with an intensity that was akin to a son's hatred for his domineering father, but at the end of the year, to his strange dismay, Scrbacek found he wanted nothing so much professionally as to practice criminal law—and not as a prosecutor but as a defense attorney.

Just like DeLoatch. Just like dear old DeLoatch.

He also dreamed of fucking DeLoatch's wife till her nose bled, but then she was actually DeLoatch's third wife, blonde and bouncy, thirty years younger than her husband, and so we shouldn't read too deeply into that nasty little fantasy, should we?

Or should we?

DeLoatch.

So maybe it was DeLoatch who had sent him scurrying to the criminal bar, but was that the choice the Contessa's cards had spoken of? Was the mere practice of criminal law enough to put anyone at risk to be hunted unmercifully through the slums of Crapstown?

He was still considering it all, the water turning tepid as it pounded at his neck, when the bathroom door opened.

Scrbacek's body seized in alarm. Through the opaque curtain, he could see the bare flicker of a shadow. Visions of Janet Leigh, Anthony Perkins in a wig, black ink swirling down the drain—twisted visions flitted through his consciousness. He backed into the corner of the stall and called out, "Is that you, Jen?"

No answer.

"Jen?"

Still no answer.

Three days ago he might have stayed in the corner of the stall, cowering, but Scrbacek had learned fast and hard that cowering didn't work, that cowering only made you an easier target for the sadistic thugs bent on taking you apart. His shoulder still hurt from bounding into the Worm, but he remained alive while others were dead. So instead of cowering he tensed his body, stepped toward the opaque curtain, flexed his knees, and, in a violent thrust, twisted the curtain aside and yelled so as to get the jump on whoever the hell was coming for him.

At first he saw no one, and then he realized that his sight line was too high. He stopped his war cry and lowered his gaze. There, sitting on the toilet, with his pants down around his Velcro sneakers, facing this naked yelling man, was a boy. A young boy with shiny black hair and tawny skin, a boy with the sharp dark eyes of his mother.

The boy stared impassively up at Scrbacek from the toilet, as if finding a naked man dripping wet and shouting in the shower was nothing more unusual than finding there a bottle of shampoo.

"Who are you?" said the boy.

A fair question, thought Scrbacek, fair indeed. But also he knew, with some primordial instinct, that the bigger question in that little room foggy with steam was not who the hell was Scrbacek, but who the hell was that little boy?

23
NEWCOME

Scrbacek yanked closed the curtain, turned off the water, reached from behind the curtain for a towel, and wrapped it around his waist. When he again opened the curtain, the boy was still sitting on the pot.

"Who are you?" repeated the boy.

"A friend of your mother's."

"What kind of friend?"

Scrbacek tilted his head in bemusement at the question.

"Are you a friend friend," said the boy, "or are you a stay-over, use-the-bathroom, make-me-stupid-breakfasts-in-the-morning-while-my-mom-is-sleeping kind of friend."

"A friend friend."

"When did you come?"

"This morning."

The boy looked up and down at Scrbacek in the shower. "When are you leaving?"

"This afternoon."

"For good?"

"Yes."

The boy stared at Scrbacek for a moment more and then nodded his head as if everything now was satisfactory. Scrbacek found another towel and wiped himself dry. His heap of clothes, filthy and bloodied from his race through the tunnel and the fight behind Ed's Eats, was gone. Only the boots were standing side by side on the bathroom floor. A terrycloth robe was hanging from a hook on the door.

"What happened to your arm?" said the boy.

"I tripped on a rock," said Scrbacek, putting on the robe.

"Must have been a big rock," said the boy, still on the toilet. "Must have been like a boulder. I saw this huge flaming boulder fly through the air once. It went as high as an airplane and then came down right next to me and missed me by about an inch."

"A huge flaming boulder?"

"Well, maybe it wasn't on fire or so big, but it came down right next to me, like I said. My friend Connor from school threw it."

"What's your name?"

"Sean Ling."

"And how old are you, Sean Ling?"

"Five. Can you wipe me?"

Scrbacek took a step back.

"Sometimes," said the boy, "I don't do it so good."

"Well, first of all, you don't do it so well. And second of all, I think you should wipe yourself, Sean."

"Yeah," said Sean as he unrolled a long line of toilet paper and wadded it together into an unwieldy clump. "That's what my mommy tells me all the time."

"Where does your father live?"

"In California."

"Really? Does he visit much?"

"All the time. He comes all the time and takes me to the movies and stuff. When he can. He lives in California, and it's a long drive. And he's important there, but still he comes all the time."

"What's his name?"

"Newcome. Newcome Ling."

The boy finished wiping himself and then pulled up his pants, flushed the toilet, headed for the door.

"Bye," he said with a quick wave of his hand.

"Don't forget to wash your hands."

"My mommy says I don't have to."

"I don't think so," said Scrbacek.

The boy stopped, looked at Scrbacek for a moment, went to the sink, stood on a stool, turned on the water, pumped soap on his hands, washed until the long sleeves of his shirt were soaked, and then, without turning off the water, stepped down, touched a towel, and left, closing the door behind him.

Scrbacek had stuffed the pills Squirrel had given him and the remaining money from the casino in his boot before he showered. Now the bottles of pills stood beside the sink, their labels read and insides examined, no doubt, with utter care by Jenny. She had always been suspicious by nature, but completely honest, so there was no need to check that the money was still there.

He opened the bottles and downed the prescribed amount of antibiotics and double the prescription of pain reliever with codeine. Jenny had left a box of Band-Aids, a new toothbrush, still in its plastic box, and a disposable razor beside the sink. Carefully he gripped the tabs of a Band-Aid and pressed it over the deep slice in the bridge of his nose. He brushed his teeth long and hard, until the foam in his mouth turned pink. He lathered his face with shaving cream. One side was already clear-cut to the bruises when Jenny poked her head in the door.

"I have to go to work. You can sleep in my bed, if you want."

"Thanks," he said, still shaving, looking only at her reflection in the mirror. "And thanks for the robe and the toothbrush."

"I'm cleaning your clothes. They needed it. And I put out the food like you asked. The charges for everything will show up on your bill. Local calls are seventy-five cents."

"I'm not planning on using the phone."

"Good idea. I didn't see any cigarettes. You still don't smoke?"

"Disgusting habit."

"So at least our time together wasn't a total waste."

"No, not a total waste." He stopped shaving. "I met Sean."

"Oh, did you?"

"Good-looking kid."

"Thanks. I have to get him to school."

"How old is he?"

She waited a moment before answering. "Four."

"He said his father was in California."

"Is that what he said?"

"Said his father's name was Newcome."

"He did, did he? I have to go, or he'll be late. Sleep tight."

She closed the door, leaving Scrbacek staring at his own face—half-covered in white, with the corner of the foam mouth gaily turned up, half-clean-shaven, bruised and scowling—a face like one of those drama masks, half-comedy, half-tragedy.

24
A PATCH OF SKIN

Her bedroom was their old bedroom. Her bed was their old bed. The walls were a different color, and the duvet pattern was frillier, but the room was furnished with memories.

He needed to think about the men out to kill him and the big money behind them. He needed to think about the man out to indict him for murder and the evidence that was building against him. He needed to think about where he was and to where he ought to run. He needed to think about the boy, about the boy, oh Christ, the boy. He needed to think, but he was too tired to think. So instead he lay on her bed, still in his robe, his head resting on her pillows, surrounded by the fragrance of her shampoo, and let his mind drift to a small patch of flesh.

There was a spot on Jenny Ling's body, a small patch of skin on her side, just beside the bottom curve of her right breast, where she was extraordinarily sensitive. He had discovered the patch on their first night together, after all the hesitations and false starts, the earnest discussions in dive bars where he tried to convince her of his earnestness, the secret late-night hand-in-hand walks after study group so their friends wouldn't know. That night, when they finally grew sick of talking about it and fell into doing it, after a quick bout of pent-up screwing that was silvery and magical, he had endeavored to gently kiss his way up the lovely course of her body, starting with the curves of her feet and moving to the line of muscle on her calf, to the hollow beneath her knee, to the soft of her thigh, gently working his tongue, tugging at her skin with his teeth. He was atop her like a predatory cat, held aloft by his arms as he bowed his head to her flesh. She wrapped his body with her legs in slow constant motion, and stroked with her soft hands his neck and ears and hair, and let out light contented moans that rose and fell with every breath. He was waylaid for a time too long to remember by the richness of her scent and the very taste of her, the combination driving him to roar out loud, but then he gained control enough to continue on, to the thin and willowy stomach, the hard curves of her ribs, the taut line of skin at the base of her breasts, first one, then the other, then the ambrosial space between. He licked the flavor from her areolas, dark as cinnamon; he played her nipples, soft like taffy, between his lips. But when he reached that spot on Jenny Ling's body, that small patch of skin beside the bottom curve of her right breast, her legs squeezed his waist, her grip on his hair tightened, her back arched, and the contented moans were trapped along with her breath in the back of her throat.

***

"You want a cigarette?"

"God, no. Disgusting things."

"There's nothing better after sex than a cigarette. Try it."

"Take a look at yourself, Scrbacek. Your clothes, your aspirations, even your postcoital cigarette. You're a walking cliché."

"I thought I was profoundly original."

"Sorry."

"Even that thing with my tongue?"

"Well, maybe that. But to be frank, you have an utter lack of origi-nality. I think that's why I find you attractive. You balance out my sparkling inimitability."

"Let's not be so frank. Frankness is, frankly, overrated."

"Don't get pouty."

"I'm going to have a cigarette."

"Not in my bed you're not."

"Oh, come on."

"No, no, no. It's filthy, it smells, it leaves ashes all over the place."

"But see, if it was reefer, you'd be all for it. If it was reefer, it would be, 'Fire it up, big boy. Let's get mellow.'"

"You have reefer?"

"No. Never."

"Why not? Because it's against the law?"

"Because when I do reefer, I end up curled in the corner, thinking every person in the world is laughing at me, and that's a very hard posi-tion from which to pick up chicks. What's wrong with my aspirations, anyway?"

"'Oh, I'm going to work for some big firm and make lots of money and spend my life doing corporate debentures for really rich people so they get even richer.'"

"Yeah? So?"

"It doesn't seem to you a little . . . shallow?"

"Absolutely. But I'm a shallow guy."

"You only wish you were."

"All your public interest friends think I'm shallow. What do they call me? The Republican?"

"The Republican Asshole, to be precise."

"But you just watch. I bet all of you end up at big firms, represent-ing R.J. Reynolds and the NRA, blaming it on your student loans."

"Not me."

"We'll see."

"Go to hell."

"Okay, you won't. Instead, you'll work for legal aid and help feed the multitudes and be beatified by future generations for all your good works."

"Now you have it."

"But that's after you pay off your student loans."

"What's a corporate debenture anyway?"

"You'll be finding out soon enough."

***

He found himself consumed by that small patch of skin, entranced by the smoothness of the flesh, by the swell and sag of the breast, by the subtle striae of the ribs.

She was a hard woman to know, tight within herself, shielded by her sarcasm and mocking laughter, but he imagined somehow that by discovering that point of sensitivity he had discovered a way beneath her protections. It was a passageway, that patch of flesh, to a place secret within her, that edge of existence only reached in the richest moments, when everything held tight is thrown loose, a passageway waiting to be unlocked by his caress. He would stroke it with his hand, swirl it with his tongue. In the bath they would lie together, interlocked left legs casually resting on the edge of the tub, his arms covering her breasts, his lips on the lobe of her ear, on the hollow of her neck, and then down, down, stretching his neck as he lowered his lips to that soft plot of skin, her chin suddenly rising as if on a string.

At night, sometimes while she slept, he would lie awake and stare at that very point as it swelled and contracted with the working of her lungs.

***

"What's that, there?"

"Where?"

"There."

"Stop. It tickles. No, really. Jen. Stop."

"There."

"Nothing."

"It's not nothing. What is it?"

"My third nipple."

"God, that's disgusting."

"The Druids used to think it a mark of the anointed. They'd walk leagues and leagues just to rub one for good luck."

"Leagues?"

"And leagues. Go ahead."

"No. Please. Yuck."

"Go ahead. Don't be afraid. It doesn't have any teeth. Make a wish first."

"A wish?"

"Yes, like the Druids."

"Those wacky Druids. All right, here goes. How does that feel?"

"Fine. Really fine. You know they used to rub something else for good luck, the Druids."

"That?"

"Yes. Exactly."

"You're making it all up, about the Druids."

"Yes."

"You're a liar."

"Yes, yes."

"A big liar."

"I admit it, yes. And getting bigger all the time. No, don't stop. Don't. What happened?"

"You're nothing but a fraud."

"So?"

"I don't choose to consort with big firm frauds."

"Consort? That sounds suspiciously mercantile. Anyway, about the whole big firm thing, I've been thinking."

"Well, there you go, Scrbacek, screwing up everything."

"I'm serious."

"Roll over onto your side, and it'll pass. You were made for a big firm. You already have your white shirts and khakis for casual Fridays."

"But I think I want to do trial work."

"So you'll be a corporate litigator."

"I wasn't thinking of corporate litigation. I was thinking maybe of criminal law."

"No way."

"Hey, I need that arm. I'm thinking defense work."

"I don't believe it."

"Really."

"That son of a bitch, he got to you, didn't he?"

"No, he didn't."

"Yes, he did. He treated you like shit all year, and now you're going to be DeLoatch's bitch."

***

At the beginning, when they had finally fallen into it, they had sex constantly, obsessively—nothing new there with young lovers—their bouts interspersed with gossip and their grand hopes for their futures in the law.

But even after the beginning, when the sex was not as constant, not as obsessive, and then later, when the sex became far rarer than the arguments and when his drive was slaked by other matter, inanimate and animate both, even then the progression was always the same. Whatever the position, whatever the length of their efforts or lack of efforts, whatever their moods or their emotions or even the disdain they felt one for the other, whatever, it would always come down to his lips against that spot, her letting go of whatever was holding her back, the feel of her skin, the musk sweat beneath her arm, the taste, the rush of blood, the anger and passion and love, yes, love, spreading over everything, washing it clean.

All coming alive for the two of them from that magic patch of flesh.

***

"DeLoatch has got nothing to do with it."

"Don't be stupid, Scrbacek. He's got everything to do with it. He hooked you. The more he abused you, the more he had you hooked."

"I have a theory that he humiliated me regularly and used me as the butt of his jokes out of some fiercely sublimated homoerotic attraction."

"It sounds like you dream about him."

"Not him. His wife."

"How do you figure someone like her with someone like him?"

"The power of intellect."

"It's a good thing then, Scrbacek, that you're so good-looking. It's a tough road, criminal law. It's hard to get established."

"All it takes is one case, one great case."

"That's what we're all looking for, the holy grail, one big case to finance the rest of our careers. Maybe we can work together. Ling and Scrbacek."

"Scrbacek and Ling."

"Whatever. I'll do civil, you'll do criminal. Making gads of money in the public interest."

"All we need is one big case. DeLoatch said he'd help."

"DeLoatch?"

"I talked it over with him, the criminal law thing. He's not so fierce up close. He actually said he wasn't surprised. He said when I get out, he'll steer some work my way."

"Are you sure?"

"That's what he said."

"No, about taking his help. I mean, criminal law is cool and all, nothing hotter than a self-righteous public defender, but I've heard things about DeLoatch. How he's gotten a little too close to his clients."

"Empathy."

"How he sometimes advises as well as represents, how he becomes their friend, lives their lifestyle, arranges their deals."

"Malicious rumors."

"Shares their drugs."

"As long as he shares."

"Don't emulate too much."

"Don't worry. I know where the line is, and I won't get anywhere near it. But I like the idea of representing those in the direst circumstances, those with the biggest need."

"Now you sound like me."

"Except I'm going to get rich as sin doing it."

"Well, see, there you go. My friends are right after all. You are a Republican asshole."

***

And after the end, with all its savage hurts and bruised emotions, it wasn't the bitter aftertaste of the sarcasm or the fights that remained most deeply embedded in his memory. It was that patch of skin, and the dance of sex that it promised, a dance that seemed to transcend the physical laws that strapped them to the mattress, or the wall of the shower stall, or the dark stretch of lawn in the park at night.

Her body seemed to change in the very act, to twist and swell, to elongate and then shrink as his hand gently brushed the length from her hip to her shoulder. Her neck, her thigh, that perfect patch of skin. And from that singular touch, they would dive together, soar together, land gently or roughly, their tongues twisting like red stamens, their legs twining like hardy vines, grinding together in slow twists, banging into each other with fierce violence, oblivious to the sky, the temperature, the phone ringing in the background, the quick snapping bark of a dog, the phone, oblivious to the phone as they grew and swelled and arched, the phone, the phone . . .

***

Scrbacek woke from the ringing of the phone and the sound of footsteps up the stairs.

He was still lying on his back, in the robe, but the robe was parted and he was ludicrously erect. He sat upright and covered himself as Jenny, still in her lawyer clothes, hurried into the room and answered the phone. She smiled at him as she said hello into the receiver.

Palsgraf jumped onto the bed and started sniffing Scrbacek's crotch, as if searching for a bone to worry. Scrbacek pushed the dog away.

"No," she said. "Everything's fine . . . Still, yes, but he's just about ready to leave . . . I don't think so, no, not tonight. I'm going to spend it with Sean . . . I appreciate that, yes, but I think Sean needs some time . . . I'll call you . . . No, not tomorrow night either. I'll call you . . . Okay . . . Yes . . . Me too . . . Yes . . . Bye."

She hung up and looked at Scrbacek, sitting up in the bed in the robe, his hands crossed on his lap, still fighting to keep the dogged Palsgraf away, and she shrugged.

"Dan," she said.

"I figured. He seemed nice enough."

"He's a waste. You look rested."

"How long have I been sleeping?"

"Most of the day. I was able to get out a little early." She pointed her toes, slipped off her shoes, first one then the other, and arched her back as she took off her tight little jacket. "Your name is still all over the news. There are reports that you burned down a house on Ansonia Road."

The dog sat beside Scrbacek on the bed and let him ruffle the fur beneath his chin. "I was there," said Scrbacek, looking at the dog, "but I didn't start the fire."

She rested one knee on the bed and leaned close to Scrbacek to examine his face. The heat of her body and the scent of her perfume pressed against him. "Your face is a mess. You need someone to look at that cut on your nose."

"Eventually. Not now."

She sat down beside him, her legs stretched out in front of her.

"That boy who was killed in your car, was he your intern?"

"Ethan Brummel. Yes. He was a good kid."

"I'm sorry."

"I went to pay my respects to his parents. His mother acted like I killed him myself."

"It must be so hard. I can't even imagine it."

"I tried my best to comfort her."

"I'm sure you did fine."

"I quoted the Constitution to her."

"You didn't."

"And now they think I was planning to kill her too, if her son told her all the terrible things I was doing."

"The Constitution? Jesus."

Scrbacek leaned over to Palsgraf and grabbed the dog's face and rubbed the sides of his muzzle. The dog's head lifted, and he grimaced a smile and let out a long satisfied sigh. "I didn't realize how much I missed this guy."

"The papers say the case against you is growing stronger by the hour," she said, "and that an indictment is expected shortly."

"Surwin's indomitable."

"I've always found him pretty fair. Hard but fair."

"He wants to fry me. He'll be fair about it, sure, but still I'll fry."

"Cirilio Vega's come out saying you've come unhinged."

"Good old Cirilio. It's nice to have friends, isn't it?"

"He hit on me once toward the end of when I was still with you."

"He always had taste."

"I told him he was a smarmy piece of shit, and he laughed and thanked me."

"And then?"

"He's an asshole."

"Objection. Answer was nonresponsive. Anyway, he's representing Breest now, so whatever he says about me he's just doing his job."

"Did you do it, J.D.? Did you kill that boy?"

He stopped rubbing the dog and turned to face Jenny. "No."

"Good," she said, nodding. "I knew, I just wanted to hear it. So what are you going to do?"

"I don't know. I can't see the big picture yet, and until I do I'm running blind. Still, I have no choice but to keep running. If I don't, they'll kill me. Remember that Remi Bozant?"

"The dirty cop in the Amber Grace case?"

"He's the muscle, but somebody higher up is paying him."

"Who?"

"I don't know."

"Why?"

"I don't know."

"How long are you going to keep running?"

"Until there's no place left to go."

"You have to do something."

"I know," he said. "Something."

And as he said it, he couldn't help himself. He had to do something, and so what he did was reach out his hand and gently touch her blouse, on the side, beneath her bra, touch that small patch of skin beside the bottom curve of her breast, that magical place that lived still in the recesses of his own damaged heart, and somehow, against all odds, still represented for him the last desperate refuge of his dwindling hope.

25
Amber Grace

"What the hell are you doing?" said Jenny Ling, pulling abruptly away from his touch.

"I don't know. I've been thinking about you."

"You've been thinking about me?"

"About you, yeah, and remembering us, in this room, sitting on this bed just like this, side by side."

"You're lying on my bed in my robe with a poorly disguised hard-on, thinking about us? Are you mental? Are you a mental case?" She rapped his head hard with her knuckle. "Paging Doctor Freud."

"Jen."

He reached out again for that spot, but before he could touch her she was off the bed.

"Five years ago you stroll out of my life, and since then there's not been so much as a Christmas card."

"The restraining order."

"The order expired thirty days after issuance. You were using, you were scary, I needed you to cool off and dry out. And once you cooled off and dried out, you totally disappeared from my life. Five years. Which was fine. Your choice. Time to move on. But now, when someone's hunting to kill you and Surwin's just aching to indict your sorry butt, you show up with a bruised expression and your little hard-on to say you're thinking about us?"

"Jen."

"Where have you been for five years, J.D.? Which asylum?"

"I was lost. I came back here, and I remembered the way we were."

"Somewhere in the distance I hear Barbra Streisand singing."

"We need to talk."

"No, we don't."

"There are things we need to talk about."

"No, there are not. There is nothing we need to talk about, not a single damn thing." Her expression was as fierce as a warning. "All we need is for you to get dressed and get out. Your clothes are in the dryer downstairs. Try to keep your manhood in check while I bring them up."

"I miss you, Jen."

She stopped on her way out the door and backed up without turning. "It's been too long a time, J.D. It's not worth even saying now."

"Still, it's true. I've thought about you a lot over the years, but I've always been too afraid to do something about it."

"Sometimes it's best to listen to our fears."

"What happened to us, Jen?"

She spun around at that and spit out a derisive "Fuck you."

"Jen."

"Just fuck you. What kind of gall do you have to ask me what happened? You know what the hell happened. You won your big case, J.D., the one you were itching for since law school. You popped Amber Grace out of death row and became a star. And the clients came pouring in—the pimps and the mobsters and the big-time drug dealers with their stacks of cash and rolled-up hundred-dollar bills, like the ones in your boot. And the nights got later, and the partying got hotter, and you started taking powder in lieu of money for your fee. You lost control, with your guns and your drugs and your paranoid rants. And when I wouldn't go along on that sick little ride and told you to clean up your act or get the hell out, you left me cold without a word or a glance back and hightailed it for the greener pastures and less demanding women in Casinoland. That's what happened to us."

"It wasn't like that."

"Oh, no? You didn't start representing anyone with the cash to pay? You didn't stop coming home at night? I didn't find you sprawled unconscious on the floor of that very bathroom, lying in your own vomit, your face covered with your fine white powder, the gun you had waved in my face stuck in your belt? You didn't leave for a new office and new life in Casinoland without a single note of regret? You didn't find a string of cocktail waitresses to wet your wick without the muss or fuss of something so inconvenient as a relationship? Tell me it's not true, J.D. Tell me."

"It wasn't like you said."

"Then tell me sometime how it really was," she said. "But not now. Now just get the hell out of my house."

Before he could say anything in response, she was gone. Scrbacek watched her go and then faced the dog. The dog stared balefully at him for a moment before jumping off the bed and following his mistress out the door, leaving Scrbacek to try to remember. To remember the way it really was.

Which meant remembering Amber Grace.

***

Amber Grace.

She had been sentenced to death for the murder of a pimp named Lucius Haste, a grisly murder that had left a hole in Lucius's chest the size of a volleyball, and his face looking like half a blood orange squeezed already of its juice.

Amber and Lucius had been more than lovers, they had been business associates. Amber worked the highways and byways of the old resort town while Lucius cruised the night in his gold Lexus to keep track of her and the rest of his string. But Lucius had heard that Amber was holding some of her hard-won wages back, and he had been swearing in the Crapstown bars that she wouldn't get away with it. "I'm gonna get that bitch, you understan' what I'm sayin'? She'll earn those bills she been slippin' down her bra. You know what I'm sayin'? You understan'? You know what I'm sayin'?" And Amber, for her part, didn't like the attention Lucius was lavishing on the new girl, just off the bus, with the lank blonde hair. They had been arguing, loudly, Amber and Lucius. There were records of visits by Amber to the emergency ward, a nose broken, an eye swollen shut. And then they found Lucius Haste's body in an alley with a sawed-off shotgun by his side, the very shotgun that had put the hole in Lucius Haste's chest and afterward had battered him featureless.

The evidence showed Amber Grace's fingerprints to be on the barrel of that sawed-off shotgun, just where she would have been holding it if she'd swung it like a baseball bat against Lucius Haste's head. The evidence showed Amber Grace to be in that very neighborhood a short time before the killing. The evidence showed Lucius Haste to be no model citizen and the killing to be well deserved. But still the color photographs presented to the jury showed his face looking like half a blood orange squeezed already of its juice.

Amber Grace could have pled to a milder charge than murder one. Or she could have argued self-defense at the trial, revealing to the jury the sordid details of her relationship with Lucius Haste. Even if the twelve didn't buy that she was rightfully afraid of imminent harm and used only the force necessary to defend herself, they still wouldn't have convicted her of anything rawer than manslaughter. She would have been out in seven to ten, with a third off for good behavior.

But her defense attorney at trial had taken a different tack. He put Amber Grace on the stand to testify that she did not kill Lucius Haste, that she loved Lucius Haste, that they had intended to be married. She blamed the murder on a cop named Remi Bozant. Bozant had arrested her for prostitution a few years back, she claimed, and instead of booking her, had forced her into a sexual relationship that had continued against her will for years, with Lucius's grudging assent because of the protection it promised. She testified that Bozant eventually turned abusive, battering her eye, breaking her nose. That when Bozant sent her to the hospital the last time, Lucius Haste publicly threatened to rip for him a new asshole: "You know what I'm sayin'? You understan'? You know what I'm sayin'?" That shortly thereafter, Bozant had brought the shotgun into Amber's bedroom, told her to hold it for a second while he tied his shoes, and then taken it himself to kill Lucius Haste. All of this was what she stated, under oath, to the jury deciding her fate.

She had blamed it on a cop.

And Remi Bozant, unfortunately for Amber, was not your average potbellied nose-out-of-joint always-on-the-make beat cop. He was a member of an elite unit sent to the roughest areas of Crapstown to fight the most brutal crimes. His record was rife with citations and honors. He had a loving wife and an adoring daughter, and every year he dressed as a clown to entertain kids in the cancer ward of the hospital, dancing and singing, telling jokes in funny voices. Once, he had saved a boy on a bicycle who had been hit by a stray shot in a botched drive-by, had raced to the scene, performed CPR, and restarted a heart that had stopped. There was a picture in all the papers showing Bozant, with his bright-red hair, visiting the boy in the hospital, both of them smiling for the cameras, a picture that was passed around the jury box as Bozant sat on the stand and denied that he had ever had sex with Amber Grace, denied he had ever fought with Lucius Haste over Amber Grace, denied he had shot Lucius Haste in the chest, denied, in short, everything.

She had blamed it on a hero cop.

Let's just say the strategy didn't go over so well with the jury. Murder one. A sentence of death. Her appeals to the higher courts all denied. Case closed and locked shut. End of story. Until someone showed up at the jailhouse door.

Knock knock. Who's there? J.D. Scrbacek.

He had his own pathetic office by then, hanging out his shingle while he hung out at the courthouse, hoping for a case to be flipped his way like a loose coin. The public defender's office was underfunded and could represent only half of the indigent defendants in the system. The rest were farmed out to criminal defense attorneys willing to take the cases for the prescribed meager fees: twenty-five dollars an hour for trial prep, thirty-five dollars an hour in court. Scrbacek, still trying to make his way, still waiting for the help promised him by Professor DeLoatch, still waiting for the one big case that would make his name, was more than willing. Prostitution, drug distribution, assault with a deadly weapon, grand theft auto, DUI—Scrbacek handled them all, all but murder. You had to have experience in murder cases to be assigned a murder case, and since he had never been assigned a murder case, Scrbacek was not on that list.

And then, out of the blue, a judge sent him the Amber Grace file.

She had already lost all her appeals, the warrant for her execution had already been signed by the governor, a date certain for that execution had already been set. But in a handwritten letter, Amber Grace, seven years already on death row, had asked the judge to review her case. And the judge, so as not to be unduly burdened, had given it to a young, inexperienced lawyer who could be expected to do the minimum investigation, file his pro forma habeas motion, and, when it was denied, cash his check and move on to more promising material.

Habeas corpus, the Great Writ, a staple of Anglo-American law since the fifteenth century, explicitly guaranteed by Article I, Section 9 of our Constitution. Habeas corpus, which literally means "thou shalt have the body," and which technically demands that the state bring the prisoner to court and defend the legality of her continued detention. Habeas corpus. J.D. Scrbacek.

He was appalled at the file, not just by the full-color pictures of the pulped face of Lucius Haste, but by the strategy of Amber Grace's attorney. The case should have been pled out to a lesser charge, the lawyer should have argued self-defense, should have argued mitigation. How was it possible that a whore killing her abusive pimp could end up as capital murder?

It was as obvious a case of ineffective assistance of counsel as Scrbacek had ever seen.

***

"It wasn't my damn idea," said Bertram O'Neill, an old codger with a red-veined nose who had glad-handed his way through four decades in both the legal and corner bars. "I told her she should plead, but she said no. I told her she should tell the jury the man had beaten her, but she said no. I told her they were going to try to kill her, but she said the truth was the truth. I told her I didn't know what planet she was from, but this was state court where the truth more often than not died of starvation."

"Couldn't you at least keep her from testifying?" said Scrbacek.

"They see enough TV, they all want to take their shot on the stand. I could have sat down with the prosecutor, had a few drinks, cut a deal, and she would have been out in three. I begged her to let me, but she wanted to have her say. How long has she been in now?"

"Going on seven."

"Stupid cow. Blaming it on Bozant. Remi Bozant is one of the few cops in this town you can actually believe on the stand."

"Was there anything you found to back up her story?"

"Not a thing, though it wasn't like I had the funds to check up on everything, not at twenty-five an hour. Her alibi witness was out of town, and we had no idea where. All her corroboration turned out to be smoke and shadows. But hell, you ask me, I didn't find anything because it wasn't there to be found. She thought she could clever her way out of it, but if she was that clever, she wouldn't have been a whore in the first place."

"What do you think really happened?"

"I think she killed that man. He wasn't a good man, but she killed him and then pounded his face to mash. Sometimes, you can't say there is no justice."

***

"I don't know where she came up with that song and dance," said Lieutenant Remi Bozant, a tall, handsome man with broad shoulders and thick red hair. "All I know is she was lying. But you could tell she wasn't any genius. Closest thing she ever had to a brainstorm was a light drizzle."

"Did you ever have dealings with Lucius Haste?"

"Did you read my testimony?"

"I read it."

Big grin. "Scintillating, isn't it? Everything I had to say, I said in court. When's her date?"

"December eighth."

"It won't be the first needle stuck in her arm, but it'll damn well be the last. Though you'll probably get it delayed another couple years and feel all proud of yourself."

"I'm just trying to find out what happened."

"I'll tell you what happened. She killed him, that's what happened. She shot him through the chest and bashed in his face and tried to blame it on me. You wonder why I'm not sympathetic, Scrubmyneck?"

"Scrbacek."

"What are you, Polish?"

"Hungarian."

"The goulash, right?"

"That's right."

"Well, I'll tell you something, Mr. Goulash, whether you believe it or not. It will be best for everyone, and I mean everyone, you included, when she's put down."

"She's not a horse."

"Don't I know it. Horses I like. Murdering bitches and their lawyers, on the other hand, piss me off."

"But there's still one thing I can't figure out, Lieutenant. If you never had anything to do with her before the trial, how, when it was time for Amber Grace to invent a story, did she come up with your name?"

"You're a sharp one, aren't you? Someday you'll go far. Do us all a favor and stay there. I'm done. You want to ask me anything more, have the county prosecutor order me to talk. Until then, go fuck yourself."

"Thanks for your help."

Big grin. "Don't mention it."

***

"I said what I said because it was the truth, Mr. Scrbacek," said Amber Grace. She was tall and thin, with dark hair pulled back from a very pretty face. There was something soft to her features, something almost angelic, despite the prison garb. "I thought that was what we was supposed to do, tell the truth."

"Did Mr. O'Neill advise you what could happen if you testified like you did?"

"Yeah. But what I said about Remi and the way he treated me, I wasn't gonna lie about it."

"Lieutenant Bozant says he never saw you before you accused him."

"He's a lieutenant now? They must be hard up in that police force."

"He's a hero cop, Amber."

"Wasn't no hero when he was busting my nose."

"That wasn't Lucius?"

"Oh, Lucius was a sweetheart. He was my little man. No, it was Remi sending me to the hospital."

"Mr. O'Neill mentioned something about an alibi witness he couldn't find?"

"Loretta. When the trouble went down, she hightailed it out. Went to Vegas, I heard. Don't blame her there. She was too sweet a piece for this market."

"You have a last name for her?"

"Wayne, I think. Loretta Wayne. All blonde and skinny, driving them suburban drive-ins wild. You gonna get me out of here?"

"I don't know, Amber. It looks pretty bleak."

"I shouldn't be in here, Mr. Scrbacek. I'm no saint, I made my mistakes, but I didn't kill Lucius. You've got to get me out of here."

"I'll try."

"It's not about trying. I'm all tried out. It's about doing, Mr. Scrbacek. You do what you need to get me out of here, or they're going to kill me, they're going to kill me dead. And then no matter how hard you tried, it's not going to matter, is it?"

***

"How'd you find me?"

"The public defender's office had an address," said Scrbacek. "The woman at the apartment said you'd be here. Do you have a minute? Can we talk?"

"Talk about what, Mr. . . ." Loretta Sorenson, née Wayne, looked down at the card in her hand. "Mr. Scrbacek?"

"About Amber Grace."

The woman looked at Scrbacek for a long startled moment and then back at the card. "You came quite a ways."

"I have some questions."

She nodded and led him to a lounge in the casino, where they sat together at a table while a chanteuse sat atop a piano on the stage and sang an up-tempo jazzy version of the blues. Loretta was delicate and pretty with long blonde hair, straight and parted in the middle like a '60s teenager's, and with a teenager's desperate bands of eyeliner, but the eyes inside the liner were tired enough to give her away.

"Amber says you were with her the time of the murder," said Scrbacek after their drinks had been served—a beer for him and a double Stoli martini for her. "She says you were her alibi."

"Yeah, okay."

"But when it was time for her trial, you were nowhere to be found. Did she really have an alibi?"

"What does she say?"

"She says yes."

"Well then, yeah, sure."

"And so if I give you a subpoena and a plane ticket, you'll testify that you were with her at the time of the murder."

Loretta shrugged. "I guess so."

"Do you even remember when the murder was?"

"Not the date, but I remember. Lucius was my . . . a friend. So I remember."

"You know what time it was?"

"Yeah, sure. The time when I was with Amber. Are they really going to kill her?"

"Yes."

"Then I'll do whatever I can, Mr. Scrbacek."

"Why'd you leave before the trial?"

"It wasn't a good time."

"Why not?"

"To be truthful, Mr. Scrbacek, I don't remember much about those months. I was into shit. So was Amber."

"Shit?"

Loretta sighed and finished her drink. Scrbacek ordered her another. "Look, whatever she says, I'll say, okay? Isn't that what you want?"

"What about Remi Bozant?"

"Who?"

"You don't remember a thing, do you?"

"Some things, not much. I was using pretty heavy then. So was Amber. Who the hell knows what was happening? It was a sick time. Lucius got himself killed, and I just took the chance and left."

"What was Amber using?"

"Boat."

"PCP?"

"And some crank to keep her going. Just a little at the start, and then more. She tried to stop when she was pregnant but she didn't. Just kept at it, and kept working, too. By the time Lucius found out, it was too late to get rid of it, so she gave it away. And then it all got even messier, the using, and she was making less, and Lucius was getting antsy, putting more pressure on me. Just what I needed. So when he got killed, I left, simple as that. Thought I could get myself a do-over. Started pushing cocktails here. Got married. Got a life. It all seemed almost normal, and then it was like a switch was turned and there I was, back at work. It's in my nature, I guess. You look startled, Mr. Scrbacek. What is it? What?"

***

"Why didn't you tell Mr. O'Neill, Amber?" said Scrbacek.

"I didn't think it mattered."

"Who was the father?"

"I don't know. It was just something that happened, and I didn't take care of it in time. I tried not to think about it, and it wasn't like I was getting all huge and all."

"Where did you have the baby?"

"City Hospital. The emergency room. It fell out like a lemon drop, and then they sent me away with it, just like that."

"It?"

"A girl, I think."

"What happened to the baby, Amber?"

"Lucius took it away."

"To an adoption agency? To the Child Welfare Bureau?"

"Lucius took it away, right after I had it. That's all I know. He never told me, I never asked."

"Amber?"

"Don't look at me like that, Mr. Scrbacek. I made a mistake, I was wrong. But what was I going to do with it? Take it to the park with the other fine ladies? Find it playdates? Stay up nights singing nursery rhymes? What the hell was I going to do with it?"

"Where is she now?"

"I don't know."

"We need to find her."

"I know we do. When I was still on the street, I didn't think about her at all. It was like it never happened. But you know, in here, with nothing but time, I think about her a lot. I think about her all the time. You got to get me out, Mr. Scrbacek. You got to get me out so I can see my baby girl and hold her in my arms and tell her that her mommy loves her."

***

He traced the trail of Amber Grace's baby.

From the hospital records, he found the date of birth. Moving forward from that date, he scoured the records of the Child Welfare Bureau for any children abandoned into its care. Of the five babies whose files were opened in the operative period, two were too old and one of the others was a boy. Of the two girls remaining, one had been sent to a group foster home that would appear scandalously in the newspapers three years later upon the issuance of indictments by the County Prosecutor's Office. The girl sent there had been abused so badly that she died within days of being reclaimed by the Child Welfare Bureau, her tiny body cremated, her ashes buried in a pauper's pit.

But the second girl was not buried in a pauper's pit. Someone had taken care of her, someone had done something right. Her case had been assigned to the most conscientious social worker in the bureau, who had scheduled numerous home visits and reported directly to the bureau's director. The girl's current foster family was a model of love and concern, was considering adoption, and was terrified that Scrbacek had come to take their Maya away. That was her name, now eight years old, with buck teeth and a shy manner and ribbons in her hair.

Scrbacek felt a thrill in the pit of his stomach when first he saw her. He bought her an ice-cream soda at the local drugstore, learned that she was happy and well. And when the girl asked about her mother, Scrbacek hesitated a moment, but only a moment, before telling the girl that he was trying to help her mother and that she, Maya, might be able to help, too.

It took a full-scale hearing to get a sample of Remi Bozant's blood to compare to Maya's. Representing the state was a rising county prosecutor named Thomas Surwin, who fought bitterly against the test, but Scrbacek cross-examined Bozant for five full hours, using shards of conflicting statements from his testimony at the trial seven years before to knock the smirk off his face and impeach his credibility. Through a welter of Surwin objections, Scrbacek was able to create enough doubt for the judge, at first exasperated and then intrigued, to consider ordering the procedure. Then he put Maya on the stand, ribbons tied carefully around her pigtails. Three weeks after the judge's ruling, the results of the DNA analysis arrived.

Remi Bozant was Maya's father. He'd had a sexual relationship with Amber Grace. His entire testimony in her murder case was a lie.

A new trial for Amber Grace was ordered by the court forthwith. With seven years already served, Surwin declined to retry the case. Instead, he indicted Remi Bozant for perjury and kicked him smack off the force and into jail for eighteen months. There wasn't enough evidence to try him for murder, but everyone knew what he had done. Remi Bozant entered jail a pariah, cursing Scrbacek with every breath, and, when released, drifted into Crapstown and then out again, disappearing into the dusty reaches of the desert West.

And J.D. Scrbacek?

On an early morning in October, J.D. Scrbacek stood alone in a soft rain, bareheaded, his raincoat belted tightly around his waist, waiting outside a heavy metal door. Behind him were vans from every television station in the city. Off to the side stood a gaggle of reporters from all the local papers, from the *Philadelphia Inquirer*, the *Washington Post*, the *New York Times*. Two network newsmagazines were there to do a feature, and the *Today* show was providing a live feed to its national audience, but still Scrbacek stood alone, bareheaded, in the rain.

This was before his caseload grew, before the money started pouring in, before his dreams of success were answered and replaced with other dreams, before he found himself spending late nights with his clients, before he found his taste for cognac and cocaine and blow jobs from the sweet young things his clients so generously provided to their famous lawyer, before he fell into the dark haze of excess that swallowed him whole, just as Jenny Ling had said—though not for the reasons Jenny Ling had said, not for those reasons at all. No, this was before all of that, when Scrbacek was still a young lawyer, still struggling, yes, but about to inhabit the role that he believed then to be his destiny: savior of those in the direst circumstances, those with the gravest needs, noble defender of the beleaguered innocent.

He stood alone, in the rain, waiting for that heavy metal door to open, and for Amber Grace, two months and seven days before the scheduled date of her execution, to take that long walk from the jaws of death into the cold light of freedom, to make her awestruck way to Scrbacek, to wrap her arms around his neck with the deepest, deepest gratitude.

26
Trent Fallow, PI, Cont'd.

Trent Fallow, PI, likes his eggs runny, his home fries crisp, his bacon rare enough so that the strips of rippling fat on either side of the lean are almost clear. He likes his sausage patties sizzling, and his cinnamon buns split and grilled, and his rye toast smeared with real butter and strawberry jam. He likes his French apple pie with the icing white and thick, and he likes whipped cream on his waffles, and fresh cream in his coffee, and normally he likes two rib-eye steaks to keep it all down, but because of his problem he is off his feed this morning, so he only orders one. And when it all arrives at his booth with the chrome juke-box selector filled with nothing but Sinatra, he eats it fast, with a fork in one hand and a knife in the other, giving it only the most cursory attention from his rotting molars before it slides down his gullet and into his great, cavernous gut.

When the waitress with the teeth so crooked Trent gets piss-proud just looking at them comes to refill his coffee, he says, "Yo, Cassie, is Ed in?"

"Ed's always in," she says, bored and tired.

He grabs her wrist before she can pull the steaming pot away from the table. "Tell him I need to talk."

"Let go, or I swear I'll burn that little thing until the skin peels off."

"I love it when you talk dirty," he says without letting go.

She tilts her wrist.

Trent Fallow, PI, screams like a crazed Arkansas farmer calling for his hogs. He reflexively tries to stand and thumps his thighs into the table, rattling plates and toppling his filled coffee cup, which releases a black steaming stream that rolls right into his lap as he falls back onto the green leatherette. As the coffee soaks into his pants, he tries to stand again and fails, he slaps at his thighs and crotch, he pours his water onto his lap, his breaths come out in fast little moans.

The waitress simply watches, arms crossed now, her thin lips curved at the edges in amusement.

"What was that for?" he whines when the coffee in his pants cools enough so that it is no longer burning, just wet and warm and not entirely unpleasant. "What the hell you do that for? I didn't mean nothing. Jesus Christ, Cassie, what the hell was that all about?"

"I told you to let go."

"Ah, come on. I was just joking with you. Look at this mess. And it hurts. Ah, dammit." He grabs a fistful of napkins from the chrome dispenser and starts wiping at his jeans. Still looking down, he says, "Tell Ed I need to talk to him."

She twists in place and calls to the window behind the counter. "The private eye wants a word."

Ed peers through the red of the heat lamps and nods. He disappears a moment before swinging through the swinging chrome doors. He stands at the edge of Fallow's booth, arms like hams crossed at his chest, his chef's hat flopping to the side, a cleaver in the tie of his apron, and a sliver of wood the size of a small dagger in his teeth.

"The bitch poured coffee on my prick," says Fallow. "I think she burned me. I think she burned me bad."

"Leastways it getting some action," says Ed, in his basso profundo.

"Remember what happened with that lady at McDonald's? I ought to sue. I ought to sue your ass."

"Don't mess with the help."

Fallow watches as Ed's jaw tenses and the toothpick wiggles in his mouth. "Okay. All right. It's over. Nothing big. What's a second-degree burn among friends, hey? Listen, Ed. I heard what you had some trouble round back last night." He opens the newspaper folded on the end of the table so that Scrbacek's picture is smiling up at the two of them. "I heard this creep, he made an appearance."

Ed nods.

"He say anything about what he was doing, where he was going? Anything at all?"

Ed shakes his head.

"Nothing?"

"Nothing."

"You see what happened out back, Ed? Because I know this guy. He's a pussy. A mammy-pammy. Never been so much as in a beer brawl his entire life. So I don't get how he ended up taking out four of Mickey's hard boys behind your place. I don't get it at all."

"Had help," says Ed.

"Now we're getting somewhere. Who was with him?"

"A girl," says Ed.

"Is that all? A girl? A little-wittle girl? So what?"

"Girl had a gun."

"A little derringer or something?"

"Kalashnikov."

"Crap," says Trent Fallow, PI.

"Fitted fat with a suppressor."

"Crap, crap, crap."

"Knew how to use it, too."

"Crap in my hat. Just what I need. You recognize her?"

Ed tilts his head slightly. "Can't say."

"Ever seen her before?"

"Can't say."

"Look, Ed. I come in this dump every afternoon, right?"

"That you do."

"I got problems, man, problems you wouldn't believe."

"One look at your face," says Ed, "and I believe them all."

"They're not my fault, really, they're not. They just sprang on me. But I got them still and I really, really need your help. So do me a favor." He reaches into his pants pocket and pulls out a card, wet and stained brown with coffee.

Ed makes no move to take the card.

"You see this creep again, call me, all right? I'll take care of it. Just call me. Do me the favor, all right?"

Ed stands still, his arms crossed, the toothpick wiggling ferociously in his mouth. Fallow slips the card into a stained white pocket on Ed's stained white apron.

"That's good, Ed. Thanks. Tell your girl, too."

Ed stares a bit more and then heads back to the kitchen.

"And while you're at it," calls out Trent Fallow, PI, to Ed's retreating back, "tell Cassie that I'll be needing more of that coffee."

27
BIRDCALL

Scrbacek dressed slowly, easing his arm into his shirt, fumbling over the buttons. His arm was stronger than before, healing quickly, as if his body knew it had no choice. His muscles all were sore—he wore his pain like a tight-fitting bodysuit—but he also felt quick and lithe and ready for a physical challenge. During his short time on the run, his whole sense of self had somehow shifted. Where once he relied solely on his wiles and wits, now he also felt physically ready to protect himself, like an athlete or a bruiser. And though he was neither, he still believed that in the coming hours his muscle, his nerve, some instinctual physicality would play its part in saving him.

When he was fully dressed, he took hold of his raincoat and headed down the stairs. It was time to leave. After the fight with Jenny and her notice of eviction, there wasn't much chance of staying, but he also knew that every moment he was in that house, the danger to Jenny and the boy was growing. Still, there was one thing more to talk over with his former lover. Palsgraf ran out of the kitchen to greet him, the dog's hind legs pumping as his tail wagged eagerly, and then led Scrbacek back to where Jenny was waiting, her hand wrapped around a bottle of beer.

"That was fun," she said.

"Like old times."

She hoisted her beer. "You want one?"

He shook his head.

"I'm sorry," she said. "I was surprised how fresh the wounds still were."

"It's been good seeing you, Jen. You look great still."

"You're lying, but thanks. You do, though. Look pretty good, I mean. On TV over the years I thought you had grown heavy and self-satisfied, but now you have the same haunted look I remember from when I first met you."

"When the only enemy hunting me was Professor DeLoatch."

She laughed out of politeness and picked at the label on her beer.

"How's legal aid doing?" he said.

"The same old crap. Landlord-tenant disputes. SSI. A class action against the city now and then when things get slow. Changing the world one miserable case at a time."

"I saw the sign in your window for the rally."

"Fat lot of good that will do."

"You'll save the day. You always do."

"Not this time. Diamond's indomitable. It's like he has some deep primal wound driving him to build a casino resort that will trump even the finest in Vegas. Diamond's Fantasy Marina. I bet he'll even hire a midget to greet the guests."

"Da bus, boss, da bus."

"Once all the details are in place, he wants the state to eminent-domain us at cut-rate prices and then hand the land over to him. He's shown them he'd pay five times more in taxes than the current residents."

"What could be better than a tax base without the inconvenience of taxpayers?"

"His whole plan depends on him being able to build a highway right through Crapstown, so that's where the battle is being waged, but it seems pretty one-sided. Diamond has bought the entire city council. It's not a fair game."

"It never was."

"I used to think I could make a difference."

"I remember."

"We were so young, weren't we, J.D.? But nothing ages you like getting kicked in the face every day."

"I know what you mean."

"No, you don't. Not you. You've gotten everything you ever wanted."

"It wasn't like you said, Jen. I didn't leave here for what I thought was a better world."

"No?"

"I left because what I had become didn't belong here anymore."

"And what had you become, J.D.? A legal rock star?"

"An impostor."

She stared at him for a moment, finished her beer, picked again at the label. "Where are you going?" she said.

"I don't know."

"What are you going to do?"

"I'm going to find out who the hell did this to me and make them pay."

"How can I help?"

"You can't."

"Let me call someone for you. You can stop running, start defending yourself. How about Surwin?"

"Far as I know, Surwin's involved."

"Are you certain?"

"Certain enough not to give him the chance to prove me right. Anyway, I think it's safer if no one can link me to you and Sean."

Pause.

"Are we going to talk about him?" said Scrbacek.

"No."

"Is he mine?"

"No."

"He told me he was five."

"He's just a kid. What does he know?"

"He knows his age. You should have told me you had a son. I could have helped."

"Don't flatter yourself. When I had him, you couldn't even help yourself."

"I've cleaned up. It was hard, but I did it. If he's mine, I have a right to know."

"You have no rights when it comes to Sean."

"There are ways to be certain."

"And you're the expert on that, aren't you?"

"Five years and nine months," said Scrbacek, "that puts me here."

"You were drugged out of your skull, barely stopping in to change your clothes. I was already looking for your replacement."

"With Cirilio?"

"Go to hell."

"With Newcome?"

"Yeah, that's right. With Newcome."

"I just want to help."

"Why don't you see, J.D., if you can save your own life before you start trying to help my son."

Just that instant, Palsgraf perked up and started growling at the back door. Scrbacek froze. Jenny looked at the door, then the dog, then the door again.

A knock.

The dog was up and barking, baring his teeth. Scrbacek backed away until he was partly hidden by a series of cabinets. He nodded at Jenny to open the door.

Standing in the rear doorway was Sean, water dripping down his face. And behind Sean, a hand firm on the boy's shoulder, was a girl in cargo pants and a slick black poncho, an assault rifle hanging off her shoulder.

"Mom," said the boy.

Jenny grabbed the wet boy away from the door. "Who the hell are you?"

"What's the story?" said Scrbacek, coming out from behind the counter and taking hold of the dog's collar.

"They're coming," said the Nightingale, over the dog's barks.

"Do we have a route out?" said Scrbacek.

"Yes, but we'll need to climb," said the Nightingale.

"All right." Scrbacek, still holding the dog, looked at Jenny. "Both you and Sean need to come with us immediately."

"What is this about?" said Jenny, holding her son tight and refusing to move. "Who is this girl?"

"There's no time," said Scrbacek, surprised at his own calm. "They're coming for me."

"Then you go. We'll send them in the opposite direction."

"The last time they came for me, they came in shooting. They bring fire and they bring death, and they don't give a crap who is in the way."

"You bastard."

He pointed at the counter. "Take your phone."

"You careless bastard," said Jenny Ling as she reached for the phone and slipped it in her pocket.

"Okay, let's get out of here."

"You goddamn careless bastard," she said. But by the time she finished saying it she had already grabbed a jacket and was out the door, her son firmly in tow.

Scrbacek scooted down, roughly rubbed the dog's throat, kissed his nose. "You can't come with us. Take care of the house, old pal," he said, giving him a final hug. The dog started barking again when Scrbacek locked him inside.

Outside, Scrbacek slipped on his raincoat and then headed after the two women and the boy, the wild woofs of the dog chasing after them all.

28
ON THE ROOF

They rushed through Jenny's soggy yard, over a fence, and across two others before the Nightingale led them to a sturdy metal ladder leaning against the roof of one of the row houses. It was raining softly but steadily as the Nightingale scampered up first, and then Sean, and then his mother, her foot slipping off a wet rung, and then Scrbacek. When Scrbacek dragged himself onto the slanted asphalt, the Nightingale pulled the ladder to the roof and, bending at the waist, carried it off with her.

The roof was wet, but not slick, and the others followed the girl with the ladder, Jenny holding tight to Sean's wrist as they passed over a series of rooftops with differing surfaces, the route curving as the road curved.

"Where are we going, Mommy?"

"I don't know, sweetie."

"I'm cold. I'm wet."

"Quiet, Sean. It's okay. Just be quiet and very careful. Do you know where we're going?" she said to the Nightingale.

The girl turned back and smiled. "I do," she said. "And thanks for breakfast."

Beyond that roof was a gap before the next elevated surface. The Nightingale put down the ladder. "We have to get over."

"How?" said Jenny.

The girl smiled and, with a great leap, jumped the gap, barely reaching the other roof's edge, water splashing as she landed.

"I can't jump that," said Jenny, but the Nightingale motioned for Scrbacek to push the ladder across, making a bridge. The girl anchored one end, Scrbacek the other.

"Go ahead, Sean," said Scrbacek.

The boy looked at his mother. "I can't. It's too high."

"Does he have to?" said Jenny. "Can't we just go down and up again?"

Scrbacek looked at the Nightingale, who gestured at him to hurry. In the distance now, above the steady patter of the soft rain, they could hear the roar of cars, brakes squealing, doors opening and slamming shut.

"There's no time," said Scrbacek.

"Go ahead, sweetie," said Jenny, with a false cheeriness in her voice. "Just go on your knees and don't look down. You want me to go first?"

The boy nodded.

Jenny gave the boy a nervous smile before turning and crawling slowly across, the metal ladder bowing as she went.

"Your turn, Sean," said Scrbacek when Jenny was across.

"I can't," he said.

"You can," said his mother.

"Go ahead, Sean," said Scrbacek. "Pretend it's the playground and you're on top of the jungle gym, and Connor has already made it to the other side."

"I'm a gooder climber than Connor."

"Better, Sean," said Jenny. "You're better than Connor."

"He repeats my sentences, too," said Sean to his mother, motioning toward Scrbacek with his chin.

Jenny gave Scrbacek a stare. He shrugged back.

"I'm a better climber than Connor," said the boy.

"That's the ticket," said Scrbacek. "If you're better than Connor, you've got it licked. Go on ahead."

The boy hesitated, looked at his mother, hesitated, and then, arms shaking, began to make his way across. It was slow, his trek across the ladder, careful, rung by painstaking rung, until, finally, he made it to the end, jumping into his mother's arms and laughing loudly as Scrbacek scurried across.

The Nightingale pulled the ladder over, left it on the other side of the gap, and led them to an area behind a double chimney where they could stay hidden even as they were able to see the street in front of Jenny Ling's house.

It was lousy with police cars, sirens off but lights flashing, sending arcs of red across the entire neighborhood. The cars formed a semicircle with officers behind, some in yellow rain gear, rifles out as if expecting a shoot-out with Ma Barker and the gang. On the edges of roofs around Jenny's house, they could now see more officers, prone in their dark ponchos, their rifles trained on the front and rear entrances.

Jenny, hugging her son close, sighed in relief. "It's just the police," she said, but Scrbacek quickly quieted her.

"How'd they know about me?" whispered Scrbacek.

"Did you tell anyone about my visitor?" Jenny asked Sean.

The boy shook his head.

"Who else knew?"

"No one but . . ." said Jenny, and then she stopped, shaking her head. "Dan. That fool."

"What are they waiting for?" whispered the Nightingale.

"I suppose we'll find out," said Scrbacek.

The four huddled behind the chimney in the rain and watched as the police held their ground until an unmarked brown sedan pulled onto the scene and the doors on either side opened.

Scrbacek could just make out the figure coming out of the driver's side—blocky, with a yellow slicker and a rifle in her hand—and he let out a breath in relief.

"It's okay," said Scrbacek softly. "I know her. She's an agent of the State Bureau of Investigation named Dyer, and I think she's pretty straight with—"

Scrbacek stopped speaking as the passenger door opened and a tall man with unruly red hair, a full-length leather coat, and a shotgun in his hand stepped out of the car.

"Son of a bitch," he whispered.

29
PALSGRAF

"He looks familiar," said the Nightingale.

She reached into the side pocket of her pants, pulled out her small set of binoculars, and trained them on the man as he loaded his shotgun. Then both the man and Dyer started, side by side, through the rain toward Jenny Ling's front door.

"He was at Donnie's," said the Nightingale. "The one shouting orders into the phone."

"Goddamn son of a bitch," said Scrbacek.

"What?" said Jenny. "Who is it?"

"Remi Bozant."

"My God," said Jenny, who had been with Scrbacek through the whole of the Amber Grace case.

The Nightingale handed the binoculars to Scrbacek. He wiped them dry, put them to his eyes, moved them about until Bozant came into view. He watched as Bozant kicked in Jenny Ling's front door. Scrbacek could hear the wild barking of the dog as Bozant waited at the doorway, crouched, now holding the shotgun by its double barrel.

Then suddenly he took a step forward and swung his gun like a baseball bat. The barking turned into a squeal, stopped for a moment, and then started again. Stephanie Dyer followed Bozant into the house.

"Call your house, Jen," said Scrbacek, "and then give me the phone."

He listened to it ring—once, twice, three times—and then a voice answered, a woman's voice feigning unconcern even as a dog growled and barked hysterically in the background. "Hello. Who is this, please?"

"Stephanie, it's me," said Scrbacek.

"Scrbacek. Where are you? We're looking for you everywhere. Tell me where you are."

"I don't think so."

"My God, let me help you. Let me bring you in. It's your only chance. I can guarantee your safety."

"You and Bozant?"

Pause. "I'm the only one keeping him under control. He wants to rip out your heart. I can control him, but barely. Let me bring you in. Where are you?"

"Someplace safe. Who's behind all this, Stephanie?"

"We don't know yet. Come in and we can figure it out together."

"Let's figure it out now. Let's start with who paid you off. Who bought your soul?"

"It's not like that at all. You have to trust me. I'm trying to help."

"Like you were trying to help when you falsified the Bureau phone logs to make it seem like Ethan tried to call you. Like you were trying to help when you stayed outside my house to make sure I didn't leave while Bozant set about turning me into a cinder. You've been dirty from the start."

Pause. "Not from the start."

"Then why?"

"It may pay to be honest, but it's a long time collecting."

"I have a message for whoever it is who bought you. Tell him to watch his back."

"What are you going to do, Scrbacek?"

"I'm going to find out who's behind all this and crush him beneath my shoe like a cockroach."

"You don't know what you're up against, Tenderfoot."

"Not yet, but I will. Someone's going to pay for Ethan Brummel."

"You don't have the stones for it," she said. And then, over the phone he heard a gunshot from inside the house, which echoed outside it. The wild barking of the dog suddenly died.

Scrbacek's teeth ground together at the sound. Sean shouted out a "Mommy" before Jenny hugged him close to her chest and quieted his cry.

"I could hear the report over the phone," said Dyer. "You're somewhere close. Buckle up, Tenderfoot. Here we come."

On the street, Dyer, still in her yellow slicker, rushed out of the house and began looking around, raising her sights to examine the rooftops nearby.

"Who was inside?" said the Nightingale quietly.

"Just the dog," said Scrbacek.

Jenny hugged her son more tightly.

The Nightingale shook her head as she unslung her rifle. "Bitch wants to play nasty."

"Don't even think it," said Scrbacek, disconnecting the call.

"I have the suppressor," said the Nightingale. "They won't hear it through the rain, and the yellow lady will be dead before she hits the asphalt."

Scrbacek looked at the Nightingale and then at the boy, whose mouth was crushed into his mother's shoulder but whose eyes were open wide and staring at him. "Put it away."

The Nightingale shrugged and slung the rifle back upon her shoulder.

Dyer continued her examination of the rooftops until her gaze fell on the double chimney. The four on the roof pressed themselves against the brick, but Dyer kept staring and then she began to lift her arm to point. At that instant a car appeared, a small blue economy piece-of-garbage kind of car, and as soon as Dyer saw it she retreated back inside the house. A moment later, out of the back of the house darted Remi Bozant. His long leather coat flapped as he jumped a fence, water spraying when he landed, and disappeared through a gap between two houses.

The blue car stopped behind the semicircle of cops. Out of the driver's side doorway climbed a man in a pale-tan raincoat with a pinched face and flattop haircut. Scrbacek aimed the binoculars at the man.

"Son of a bitch," said Scrbacek.

"Who is it?" said Jenny.

"Surwin."

"I don't believe it."

"Look."

Jenny Ling took the glasses and focused on the man. "You're right."

"Son of a bitch," said Sean.

"Sean," Jenny whispered too loudly before staring angrily at Scrbacek.

Scrbacek took back the glasses, wiped them dry once again, and watched as the police, at Surwin's urging, suddenly rushed, one after the other, guns drawn, into the house. A moment later, out the front, her rifle pointing down, came Special Agent Dyer.

Surwin stormed up to his special agent. From Scrbacek's viewpoint, it was as if he were in the bleachers watching as an irate baseball manager let an umpire have it for a blown call.

"What just happened?" said Jenny.

Scrbacek waited a moment, thinking it through. Finally, he said, "You and Sean can go back to the house now."

"I don't understand what just happened."

"And when you go back, I want you to talk only to Surwin."

"You thought he was in on it."

"Not anymore. Dyer and Bozant went in to wipe me out—and, I assume, any witnesses, which would have meant you and Sean. But Surwin got the call, too, and showed up in enough of a hurry to ruin everything."

"Are you sure?"

"As sure as I can be of anything anymore. Take Sean back to your house now. The cops there will take care of you. Speak to no one but Surwin, and do it in private. Can I keep your phone?"

Jenny nodded. "Just don't call France."

Scrbacek turned the phone off and stuffed it in his pocket. "There's a pay phone in Crapstown by the mural of the seaside. Surwin will know it. Tell Surwin to show up there at midnight and I'll contact him. Tell him to come alone."

"The mural of the seaside," said Jenny. "Alone."

"Tell him everything. You did nothing wrong."

"What should I say if he asks where you are?"

Scrbacek looked at the boy who was wet and shivering and taking in every word. "Tell him everything and tell him the truth. Only the truth. The truth matters. And then you should get out of here. Is your mother still in Philadelphia?"

"Yes."

"Take Sean and visit for a few days. You're linked to me now, and that's a dangerous thing to be."

"What about you?"

"Go on. You need to get there before Surwin leaves. The Nightingale will help you off the roof. Be careful climbing down."

"J.D. . . ."

"Thanks for taking me in," said Scrbacek.

"J.D. . . ." She came over and gave him a tight hug.

"I'll be all right. We'll talk when this is over."

She nodded and backed away.

Scrbacek went down on a knee and faced Sean. "Take care of your mother, all right, Sean?"

"Okay."

"And be a good boy."

"I am."

"I know." Scrbacek reached out his arms. "You want to give me a hug, too?"

The boy shrank away and gripped his mother's leg.

"That's all right," said Scrbacek with a smile.

"What happened to Palsgraf?" said the boy. "Will he be all right?"

"I don't think so," said Scrbacek. "But you'll be all right, Sean. And your mother."

"Come on," said the Nightingale as she started toward the edge of the roof and the ladder.

"Be careful, J.D.," said Jenny Ling. Her lips pressed together, and rainwater dripped down her pretty cheeks. She took Sean's hand and headed after the Nightingale. Then she stopped and turned to face Scrbacek one last time. "And when this is over, can you do me a favor. One favor? Please?"

"Anything."

"Stay the hell out of our lives."

The boy, pulled along by his mother, took a final glance at Scrbacek before turning away.

Later, with the Nightingale behind him, Scrbacek stooped in the rain behind the double chimney and watched as Jenny and Sean Ling made their careful way down the street to the front of the house. Sean's head kept moving back and forth, taking in all the sights, every now and then looking back at Scrbacek's position behind the chimneys, but Jenny made a beeline for Surwin. When she reached him, she took hold of his arm and pulled him out and away so she could talk with him in private. Scrbacek couldn't read their lips, but he could tell by her body language, and by Surwin's, that the message had gotten through.

And then Surwin asked a question.

And Sean Ling pointed up to the very roof where Scrbacek and the Nightingale stooped.

Surwin barked out orders. A group of cops tore down the street toward the house Sean had pointed to. The snipers, contacted through their radios, started running across the roofs, bent at the waist like soldiers, toward the double chimney.

It was only fractions of a minute before one of the snipers had leaped across the gap, but by then the space behind the double chimney was deserted and Scrbacek was gone.

30
TRENT FALLOW, PI, CONT'D.

The investigative work on the Caleb Breest murder case had been a solid gig for Trent Fallow, PI, despite the usual kickbacks he had to slip to Torresdale on the side. The retainer was higher than his normal three hundred, he could puff up his time sheets without anyone giving him shit, and the tasks themselves were a nice diversion from the usual husband-with-a-whore routines. And he actually liked working with Scrbacek. The man was smart and funny and treated him with more respect than his usual clientele. Sure, before Fallow did anything that Scrbacek asked or turned over anything that he found, he had to pass it first through Joey Torresdale, but still, he developed a sort of relationship with Scrbacek. They had some laughs. They bantered. So it was only natural that after Fallow put that little Mexican creep Mendoza in the hospital because he wouldn't leave the building after Fallow had asked three times, and Mendoza talked to the cops, and the cops laid that assault rap on Fallow, it was only natural that he decided on J.D. Scrbacek to represent him.

And why not? Scrbacek was representing Caleb Breest. He had to be safe. Who would have thought different?

"Why were you talking to this Mendoza in the first place?" said Scrbacek.

"I was trying to get him to move the hell out of the building."

"Why?"

"I was doing the guy a favor. He could have gotten hurt staying there. The building had become unsafe."

"Unsafe? How?"

"Hey, I don't know. I'm no building inspector. All I know is I was told it was unsafe and to clear it. That was the job. Routine landlord-tenant stuff. The papers were in the file."

"What file?"

"The one she gave me."

"Who?"

"My client. I got clients other than you, you know. I'm running a successful business here."

"I'm sure you are, Trent. Look, you're going to have to get me the file and all the paperwork you have on that building and any other landlord-tenant work you did for the client."

"Why?"

"Because I'm telling you that's what I need. If you want me to represent you, get that stuff over to my office. I'll look through it, and then we'll talk. ¿Comprende?"

"Say what?"

"Okay?"

"Yeah, sure. Whatever you say. You're the lawyer."

Scrbacek was representing Caleb Breest. He had to be safe. Who would have thought different? Certainly not Trent Fallow, PI. Which is why Fallow's face is a bruised mess and he now spends the whole of his day walking the streets of Crapstown, talking to whomever the hell he can talk to, passing out his coffee-stained cards, flashing the picture of J.D. Scrbacek in the paper. He stops in clammy corner taverns. He chats with the lunks huddled on stoops. Knowing of Scrbacek's once-upon-a-time bad habit, he talks to drug dealers and waves down cars cruising for opportunity.

"If you see him, Luke, call me first, all right? There'll be a bonus in it for you if you do."

"Remember that thing I did for you, Sanford, with that girl from Texas? You owe me, right? You see him, you call me. Got it? Me. I'll take care of it."

"Take some extra cards for your girlfriends, Tina. Maybe earn yourself a referral fee."

It is late afternoon when Trent Fallow, PI, breathing heavily now and sweating like a fat glass of lemonade, knocks on the door of Nomad's nightclub. The neon sign advertising **HOT AND COLD RUNNING STRIPPERS ALL THROUGH THE NIGHT** is off, and the door is locked—Nomad's doesn't come alive until nightfall—but Fallow knows the place isn't empty. He bangs hard on the door, waits a moment, bangs hard again. He waits a moment more and gives it a solid kick.

The door opens a crack. The insane Russian with the hairless head gapes out the narrow opening.

"We closed," the Russian says.

"Hey, Sergei. It's me. I need to talk to Aboud."

"He's sleeping."

"I didn't know lizards slept. I thought they rested on logs with one set of eyelids shut and waited for a fly to happen by."

"He's sleeping, and you no fly. We closed. What you want?"

"Open the door."

"What you want, fat boy?"

Trent Fallow tries to peer past Sergei into the crack, tries to see if that little creep Aboud is standing there behind the Russian, but Sergei steps sideways until all Fallow can see are the Russian's white shirt and plaid pants. Fallow shows the newspaper picture to Sergei.

"You seen this creep?"

Sergei shrugs. "We get lots creeps this place."

"But this creep. I'm asking about this creep. Be a good little Russky and take a closer look. Two nights ago he blew up a car and burned down his own building in Casinoland. Last night he burned down a house on Ansonia Road and a few hours later got into a fight with some of Mickey's boys behind Ed's. He's got a crazed girl assassin working for him. Together they killed one and sent two to the hospital. The guy's a bad guy, the guy's a killer. Take a look, Sergei. You seen this creep?"

Sergei shrugs. "I can't tell one creep from next. You Americans all look same."

Trent Fallow pulls a card from his front pocket and hands it to Sergei. "You see him, you call me, understand? You call me first."

Sergei pops his bridge off his lower teeth with his tongue, flips it in his mouth, fits it back in place before taking the card.

"You tell Aboud if he gives me this creep, I'll take care of his tax for the next twelve months, and he knows I can do it, too. You tell him that. Twelve months."

"I tell him."

"He doesn't even have to give me the whole guy. Just the head is enough."

Fallow rises on his tiptoes and shouts over Sergei's shoulder, "Hey, Aboud, you hear that?"

From behind Sergei comes a voice. "Yeah, I heard that. Now get your fat ass off my walk before you dent the cement."

Fallow nods and turns to leave and then turns around again. He leans in close to the door. "Hey, Aboud," he says softly. "Is Shelly on tonight?"

"Maybe," says Aboud, still behind Sergei.

"I'm a little tense right now. She got any openings?"

"Not for you. Not after last time."

"It was an accident."

"I don't want to hear about no accident. You stunk the place up so bad I had to get it fumigated."

"It was that thing she did, what with the rubber and the ice. It was too much."

"Get out of here."

"She does things like that, what does she expect?"

"Get lost."

"Come on, Aboud. She can do anything she wants. Even that thing again. Especially that thing again. I been having dreams about it. I'll be good. I promise. It won't happen again. I'm all cleared out. Give me a break. I'm begging here."

"Beg somewhere else."

"Hey, fuck you, Aboud. I got my ass kicked outside your place last night. I tell the right cops, they'll close this dump down. You see the creep, you tell me, dammit. And if you're caught helping him, so help me, I'll make sure they stuff you feetfirst down a garbage disposal. Stuff you alive, you understand? There'll be nothing left but your head, screaming and screaming and screaming."

Sergei growls before he slams the door.

Fallow slaps the newspaper on his thigh once, twice, kicks at the door, and then continues on his way.

***

When Trent Fallow, PI, realized his mistake, when the order came down to get that file back, an order relayed by that asshole Remi Bozant, Fallow had called his lawyer, with Bozant on the extension. He was told not to make a big deal out of it, not to create suspicions, just to inquire.

"Hey, J.D. How's it going?"

"I'm busy, Trent. I'm in the middle of a trial, in case you haven't heard. What's up?"

"You ever get a chance to eyeball that file I sent?"

"Yeah. Sure. Interesting stuff. What about it?"

"I was just wondering whether you still need it. I might want it . . ."

"Look, Trent. I got your court date delayed until after the Breest trial. We'll talk about it then, all right? But I just don't have the time now. Caleb's case is swamping me, and all I have helping is an intern. We'll talk after, all right?"

"Sure, J.D. Sure. No problem."

No problem. Sure. No problem. And fucking isn't fun, and Diamond isn't rich, and Bozant isn't a sadistic son of a bitch who will fillet him alive if he doesn't make it right.

The shadows grow longer hour by hour until all of Crapstown is covered in darkness and only the thin drizzle of the streetlights falls upon the asphalt along with a soft rain. Trent Fallow, PI, has passed out all the cards he had available, has spoken to everyone he could collar, and he has come up empty. But while he gained no information as to Scrbacek's whereabouts, he had learned disturbing information about the girl.

"Yeah, I knowed who you be talking about, I knowed that number," had said a junkie named Tic-Tac-Toe. "Short little thing with broad shoulders and a luscious smile. Carries that AK when she working. Sweet little bird without an ounce of fear. Not an ounce."

"Who is she?"

"Daughter of some special-ops vet that taught her all the dark arts so she'd be prepared for the end times. She learned to take apart a Glock while she was still on the bottle. Name is Nightingale."

"Where does she live?"

Tic-Tac-Toe did something strange then. He looked up at the roofs, like someone was up there, and then shrugged his shoulders.

"Who does she hang with? Who does she work for?"

"Free agent, from what I hear. Though she's tight, they say, tight with the F's."

Trent Fallow spun around at that. He didn't want to hear Scrbacek was in any way mixed up with the Furies. He didn't want to have to tell that to Remi Bozant, no way, no how. If Bozant found out that Fallow had brought together, however inadvertently, Scrbacek and the Furies, Bozant would slice his cock off with that knife, toss it in a freezer to stiffen, and then stick it up his ass.

"She tough, this Nightingale?" said Fallow.

"She is stone-cold, man," said Tic-Tac-Toe, in a voice that sent a shiver up the squashed amorphous blob that was Trent Fallow's neck. "Stone-cold."

31
THE MAD RUSSIAN

Scrbacek hid behind a bruised metal trash can in a dank alley at a forlorn crossroads in Crapstown. The alley smelled of rot and burning rubber. An inexplicable hissing spurted from the dismal darkness behind him. The rain had halted for the moment, and the street was now a shiny black, catching the harsh city light and reworking it into a smeared pastiche of color, soft and lovely. Beyond the mouth of the alley were two abandoned lots with a single black building standing between them. Above the closed entryway was a camel, a pyramid, a pair of high-kicking legs, a motto, and a name—all lit in neon that twittered and spit into the night.

Nomad's.

It was 12:23 in the morning.

The door swung open, and a man staggered out, singing. The man reached in front of him for something to grab, found nothing, and fell like felled timber, smack into a puddle. He rose, dripping, to his hands and knees, and started crawling across the street, as if toward Scrbacek, still singing. A woman in a short fur jacket and long heels stumbled out after the man, shouted out what might have been the chorus of the man's song, swayed over, and dragged him to his feet. After she wiped the smeared blood from his chin, she let him put his arm over her shoulder, her back bending from the weight, and together they made their way down the middle of the street, singing now a plaintive duet.

Nomad's.

It was 12:24 in the morning.

Scrbacek had watched with the Nightingale from a rooftop facing that mural of the seaside as he placed the call to Surwin at midnight. The first assistant county prosecutor had followed instructions, arriving at the phone booth by the mural alone. The conversation had been short and to the point. Scrbacek wanted to meet. He wanted Surwin to tell no one about the meeting and to come alone. He wanted Surwin to promise not to arrest or detain him. He wanted Surwin to agree to all of these conditions before he told him where.

"Let me take you in," had said Surwin. "I'll put you in protective custody."

"And who's going to protect me?" said Scrbacek. "Dyer?"

Pause. "Point taken. But even if I don't take you in, I'll need to ask again about the murder."

"Understood."

"And about the fire at your building."

"Of course."

"And there have been reports about an attack on a fence named Freddie Margolis, and another fire that destroyed a house on Ansonia Road, and a gang fight behind some diner with one dead and two seriously injured. Apparently, all these things are connected to you."

"Apparently."

"And you'll talk about all that, too?"

"I'm willing to answer your questions if you're willing to answer mine."

"And what is it you want to know, Scrbacek?"

"You'll find out," he said. "Nomad's. Have you heard of it?"

"Twisted little dive."

"Twelve thirty."

He waited for Surwin to hang up, swing his head to either side, walk alone back to his car. And then Scrbacek had made his way the half dozen blocks to this spot, intermittently turning on the phone to check the time, waiting to see if any surprise showed up for the meeting. Nomad's.

It was 12:28 in the morning.

Slowly, from down the street, a spreading double fan of headlights approached. Scrbacek pulled himself further behind the trash can. The car drove up to the entrance to Nomad's and then slid past. It was small, blue, cheap. Scrbacek watched as it continued on its way, turning the corner. A few moments later, from the same direction, a man walked quickly down the street, leaning forward, one hand in his pocket, the other shielding the side of his face, his heavy-soled shoes dropping flat on the street with each step. Scrbacek watched as he stopped at the entrance to Nomad's, looked quickly around, pulled open the door, and disappeared inside.

It was 12:30 in the morning.

Scrbacek waited a moment, and then a moment more, before emerging from the protection of the alley. He walked up the street, on the opposite side of that which Surwin had taken, crossing only when he came to the intersection. A few feet down was parked Surwin's crappy little car, the one Scrbacek had seen pull up in front of Jenny's, a Hyundai, further proof that Surwin was not on the take. Scrbacek approached it carefully, slowly, and peered inside. Nothing, just a bright-red Club fastened to the steering wheel. It seemed a comical, almost innocent gesture, that Club fastened to that cheap little car in that neighborhood. If anyone here wanted the Hyundai, Surwin would find the car gone and only the Club, still locked, sitting in the parking spot. But then again, even in Crapstown there were standards.

Satisfied, Scrbacek turned to the rooftop, waved at a silhouette just visible against the night sky, and then followed Surwin's route to the club.

Inside the front door was a small alcove, with a beaded curtain, through which Scrbacek could glimpse the outlines of a narrow red-tinged bar with stools on one side, ratty booths on the other, and a little stage in the center, fronted by a pool of round tables, mostly empty. On the stage a woman, old and thick, in loose pants and veils, snapped finger cymbals and shook her ample belly in an exhibition Scrbacek found only mildly less erotic than watching his mother take a sitz bath. Beside the beaded curtain, a large man, bald, with hands like bricks and green plaid pants, sat on a stool.

Scrbacek eyed the man warily before stepping forward to pass through the beads. The man's arm shot out and barred his way.

"Ten-dollar cover for you," growled the man in a heavy Russian accent.

"Is there a band?" said Scrbacek.

"No band."

"A singer? A piano player?"

"No singer. No piano. Nothing but girl and cover," said the man.

"I don't think she's been a girl for a number of decades."

"She hot to trot, I promise you. Ten-dollar cover."

Scrbacek thought a moment and then reached into his pants and pulled out the small bills he had folded into a roll. He slipped out a tenner and handed it to the man, smiled, and started again through the curtain, but the man's arm didn't drop.

"You the one we looking for?"

Scrbacek froze and turned his head slowly to stare at the man. "No. No, I'm not."

"Yes. Yes, you are. I recognize you face from picture in paper."

"You're wrong."

"Mebbe. But even so, I still take you to boss."

Scrbacek took a step back and braced himself. "You're not taking me anywhere."

Like the attacking head of a cobra, the man's hand darted forward and grabbed the collar of Scrbacek's raincoat, winching both lapel ends together tight to the neck. The man jerked Scrbacek close to his huge glabrous head and said, slow enough and close enough so that Scrbacek could smell the cumin on his breath, "No offense, mister, but I take you to boss."

Scrbacek tried to pull away, but the grip on his collar was a vise. The man rose from his stool until he towered over Scrbacek, who felt himself being lifted off the ground.

"No offense," repeated the man.

"And none taken," said Scrbacek cheerily.

The man in the green plaid pants opened a door hidden in the wall to the right and, with his grip still firm on the raincoat's collar, pulled Scrbacek through the door, closing it softly behind them both.

32

Nomad Aboud

The Russian dragged Scrbacek down a steep set of stairs, along a narrow hallway, and into a basement office, windowless, ruthlessly plain, with a metal desk and a few folding chairs. A number of closed doors led out from the office. Behind a sign on the desk that read **BOSS** sat a little man with a porkpie hat, counting money, licking his thumb as he went through the bills.

In a chair in front of the desk sat another man, leaning back casually, skinny legs crossed, hands folded atop his potbelly, as if all were as normal as could be even though he was sheathed crown to toe in thick brown leather, with brown gloves, brown booties, a brown mask with holes for his eyes, a leather thimble for his nose, and a slit for his mouth, the edges of the slit sewed almost together with leather straps.

"I told him I can't do it," said the boss as he continued to count. "It's too much. But the bastard told me I had no choice."

The man in brown leather replied with evident sympathy, his voice muffled by the mask, "It's getting crazier out there, everyone's telling me."

"So now I got to find an extra two thou a month," said the boss. "Every month. It's gotten so bad, I have to charge a cover even though all I can afford to put onstage is my aunt Gethsemane, and believe me, she wasn't so hot even before the menopause. It's killing my business."

"We could sell some of your mutual funds," said the leather man.

"Not when the market's down."

"What about your insurance annuity?"

"Maybe. With Blaze leaving me for that trucker asshole, what's the point?"

"Plus, your returns have been disappointing."

"Excuse me, boss," said the bald Russian, hand still gripping Scrbacek's collar. "Remember guy fat private eye with busted face he said we should be looking for?"

The boss stopped his counting and glanced up at Scrbacek and then turned back to his money. "That's not him. The guy we're looking for is bigger, and there was nothing about no bandage on his nose."

"Still, boss, this is guy."

"And he was supposed to have some class. This guy's a bum. Look at that schmatta he's wearing. Forget about it, Sergei."

"I'm not the guy," said Scrbacek.

"See," said the boss. "He's not the guy. Let him go."

"Fat private eye showed picture in paper, boss. Picture had beady eyes of chicken thief. See this guy? In Russia, he would have feathers in his teeth."

The boss stopped counting and turned his attention to Scrbacek. "Remember what I heard about him?"

"Yah, boss. I remember."

"So show me."

The bald man spun Scrbacek until he was facing the front of the desk. With one hand firmly on Scrbacek's shoulder, he pulled apart Scrbacek's coat, and jerked up his still-buttoned shirt along with the T-shirt underneath, exposing his chest.

The boss put down his money and leaned forward. "That's something you don't see every day."

The man in leather twisted stiffly to get a view. "Talk about odd."

"Just like we was told," said the boss. "J.D. Scrbacek, the man with three nipples."

Just then, one of the doors opened, and a tall, drawn man in a suit walked slowly out, a fedora tilted forward to cover his face. The man took small pained steps, ignoring everyone as he made his way to the stairs. A tiny drop of blood fell from one of his cuffs.

"Hey, Mr. Posey," said the boss, "you're dripping."

The man started, looked down at his wrist, and clasped it tightly with his other hand. Then he smiled meekly and said, "Sorry, Mr. Aboud."

"Just be more careful next time, all right? I'm running a business here."

"Yes, Mr. Aboud."

In the lull, Scrbacek made his run for it. He twisted out of Sergei's grip, brushed by Mr. Posey, headed for the stairs. He was just hitting the hallway when he felt a hand clamp around his neck, pulling him back. Scrbacek kept churning his legs, but he wasn't any longer getting anywhere.

Suddenly a loud crack shot through the room.

Scrbacek, sure he had been shot, winced so violently he almost fell to the ground, despite Sergei's grip on his neck. When he recovered enough to look up, he saw a woman leaning against the frame of the doorway out of which the sanguinary Mr. Posey had just departed, and the sight of her froze him in place.

She was big, with piles of blonde hair and breasts like great mounds of saltwater taffy. She stood with a whip in one hand and a cigarette in the other, her right leg propped against the opposite doorjamb. It was hard to tell if she was pretty, because she wore a black leather mask, which matched her black leather bustier and long black boots. It was hard to tell if she was pretty, but she sure as hell was something.

"Himmelfarb," she sneered.

"Yes, Mistress Brewster," said the man in leather, dropping to his knees.

"Have you been a bad little accountant?"

"Yes, Mistress Brewster."

"Well then," she said as she casually snapped her whip, loosing another loud crack. "It's time for your punishment."

"Yes, Mistress Brewster," he said before scurrying, still on his knees, to the doorway and crawling under Mistress Brewster's outstretched leg.

Mistress Brewster inhaled deeply from her cigarette, winked at Scrbacek, pushed herself off the doorframe, neck arching back, and closed the door behind her.

"Believe it or not," said the boss, shaking his head, "he's a godsend on April fifteenth." The little man leaned back in his chair. "Have a seat, Scrbacek. Make yourself comfortable."

Sergei dragged Scrbacek to the front of the desk and threw him into a chair before letting go of his neck. Scrbacek rubbed at the bruises.

"The name's Aboud. Nomad Aboud. So, Scrbacek, can I get you anything? Something to eat? Something to drink? Cash?"

Scrbacek just stared at him.

"Take this." Aboud took a pile of bills bound with a rubber band from his desktop and tossed them to Scrbacek. "It'll come in handy."

"I don't need your money," said Scrbacek.

"You don't need my money? That's a new one. Hey, Sergei, in all the years you been with me, you ever hear that from anyone before?"

"No, boss."

"You're an interesting guy, Scrbacek. Scrbacek, huh? What kind of name is Scrbacek?"

"Lebanese."

"Really? So was my mother. I got family still up the coast from Beirut. Uncle Yassir. He sends me oranges every Christmas. 'Uncle Yassir,' I tell him, 'it's nice you sending me oranges all the way from Lebanon, but haven't you ever heard of Florida?' So what's your game, Scrbacek? We're having a hard time figuring you out. You still working for Breest?"

"Not anymore. Now I'm just trying to stay alive."

"That's a good plan. That's my plan, too. Well, listen, take the money or don't take the money, it's up to you. But anything you need, you let me know. I want to help. Here." Aboud opened a desk drawer, reached his hand in, and plopped a large black gun onto his desk. Scrbacek flinched at the sight of it. "It's a Zastava. Those Serbs might be bastards, but they know their guns. Unloads like so." He hit the catch at the heel of the butt and pulled out the magazine. "Holds nine rounds with one in the chamber. Nine millimeter. Sweet." He slapped the magazine back in place. "Untraceable, but it's got a kick, so watch out." He slid the gun along the desktop toward Scrbacek.

Scrbacek picked up the gun. It was heavier than he'd imagined, and it exuded the rich slick scent of machine oil. As he eased his finger into the trigger guard, his heart began to race with an excitement that was almost sexual. He could escape now, blast his way past Sergei and out of this basement. Nomad Aboud had just punched his ticket to freedom.

His hand tightened on the grip for just a moment and then loosened. "I don't want a gun."

"The way I hear, you're going to need it. You know, my daddy, he taught me a lesson early. 'Nomad,' he said. 'A man without a gun, he's just a man. A man with a gun, now that's a man to be reckoned with.'"

"What happened to your father?"

"Ran his car into a train. Never was the best driver, Dad, but he knew his way around a pistol. Look, Scrbacek, the old lady told me to look out for you, so that's what I'm doing."

"The old lady? Blixen?"

"I've known her forever. Most around here think she's a crazy old loon, but I grew up with her daughter. Una Blixen. Nice girl, Una. She died in the ocean, surfing around the pylons of the pier. Wave caught her wrong, and she banged her head on a wooden post. She drowned not twenty yards from where the Mount Olympus now sits. The old lady's never been the same, but I remember what she was before. Used to be some tony professor over at the university, though you wouldn't know it to smell her nowadays."

"That's a sad story."

"This town's got a million of them. So what are you really after?"

"Answers."

"And what are you going to do when you get them?"

"Damage."

Aboud chuckled. "Then keep the gun. But you better do your damage fast before they do it to you."

"Who is 'they'?" Scrbacek leaned forward. "Who's after me?"

"Good question," said Aboud. "Some fat asshole PI was here this afternoon asking about you, an idiot named Trent Fallow. You know Fallow?"

Scrbacek's shoulders stiffened. "Yeah, I know Fallow."

"You know who he's working for?"

"I thought I did, but not anymore. Could be anyone waving a turkey leg in the air."

"So you do know him. Look, there are hoods who ain't pleased with what's happened in the last few days, and he might be shilling for them, but they're not the ones who started it all. That car bomb thing and the fire in your building, if you didn't do it, then we don't know who did."

"I didn't do it."

"Of course you didn't. If you did, the gun would already be pointed at my face. Too bad about that kid in the car, though. Was he a friend?"

"Yes."

"This is a bad business all around."

"Tell me about Malloy."

"Malloy," said Aboud, shaking his head sadly. "Now there was a man to be reckoned with. You got to understand how bad things have gotten. You have Breest on the one hand squeezing everything to death. And on the other hand, you got the state coming in on behalf of the casinos, trying to sweep us out because we"—making quotation marks with his fingers—"'adversely affect their resort image.' The state's trying to buy us out, the carrot, and kick us out, the stick. Speaking of sticks, you'll never guess who's in my club tonight."

"The first assistant county prosecutor?"

A chuckle. "You're an impressive guy, aren't you?"

"He's waiting for me. I asked him to come."

"Next time pick some other joint. It makes me nervous him sitting in my shop. He's been fighting for years to clean Crapstown of its vices on his way to the governorship. But what's the point? I mean, let's be honest, without the vices there's nothing left in this whole damn town."

"About Malloy."

"Malloy. Malloy." Aboud propped his shiny brown loafers on the desktop. "We couldn't figure out whose side to be on—Breest's, who at least wants us to stick around, or the state's, which pretends to be on our side even though they'd be happier if we just disappeared. It was always one way or the other. Malloy was telling us about a different route."

"Different how?"

Aboud looked at Scrbacek for a long moment. "The Inner Circle's split on you. Some think you're nothing but trouble. I figure the way things are going, trouble's an improvement. Anyway, take this at least." He took a card out of his pocket, flipped it over, started writing. "I'll give you the private number."

"Tell me about the C-Town Furies."

"Sorry, pal, there's only so much I'm allowed to say. You were Caleb Breest's attorney, after all. But at least you're asking all the right questions." Aboud passed the card to Scrbacek. "You need anything, anything at all, give me a call."

Scrbacek took the card and stared at it for a moment before sticking it in his shirt pocket. Then he slid the Zastava back across the desk. "I don't want the gun. I'm liable to kill somebody with it."

"That's the point. It's like in that gangster movie. Someone comes at you with a fist, you bring a knife. Someone comes with a knife, you grab a gun."

"They're coming at me with guns. What do I bring, a bazooka?"

"You interested?" said Nomad Aboud, smiling. "Because if you're interested, I know a guy who knows a guy."

"Yeah," said Scrbacek, "I just bet you do."

33
GETHSEMANE'S TEETH

Upstairs at Nomad's.

Scrbacek slipped through the beaded curtain, under Sergei's stern gaze, and headed into the red-tinged darkness. On the stage, Aunt Gethsemane's belly shook to some brassy song piped through the speakers. Scrbacek winced at the sight as he passed a sad and thin assortment of bored drinkers, two men with hats at the bar, a lady with a bag on her lap. A pretty young thing who was neither pretty nor young reached out a claw for him as he walked by. He stopped, finally, at a booth that had a view of the stage. The prosecutor eyed him severely as Scrbacek slid into the bench opposite him. There were two beers on the table and a bowl of peanuts.

"What is happening to my town?" said Surwin, rage clenching his teeth.

"That's what I'm trying to find out."

"That's what you're trying to find out? Who the hell elected you to save the city?"

"Let's say I was drafted."

"And who's your supervisor, Scrbacek? Who makes sure half the city doesn't burn down as you conduct your little search? Who protects the innocent citizen who gets in your way, like Ethan Brummel? Who protects the Constitution? What is going through your head? Are you insane?"

"Insanely pissed."

Surwin's jaw locked, and his neck flared. He tried to speak, but only a growl came out before he closed his eyes. When he opened them again, he was under control. "You look like hell," he said.

"Rough couple of nights."

"What happened to your nose?"

"Some hood tried a little nip and tuck in the alley behind Ed's."

"The gangbang I heard about. How'd you survive?"

"I've got skills," said Scrbacek.

"Not those skills. And what's with the sleeve of your raincoat?"

Scrbacek looked at the loose flap of material. "A sniper, sitting outside as my building burned to the ground. He took a shot at me when I fled the flames."

"A sniper?"

"With a silencer. Went right through my arm. An unlicensed sawbones patched me up."

"So you didn't blow up your own car or burn down your own building?"

"Does that even make sense?"

"I could make it make sense in court. But I'll probably never get the chance, since half the force thinks you're guilty as hell and wants to shoot you dead to spare the citizenry the expense of a trial."

"Is that the half of the force that showed up at Jenny Ling's house ready to kill me on sight?"

Surwin took a handful of peanuts. "I always liked Jenny." He shook the peanuts in his hand. "She seeing anyone now?"

"Me."

"Funny, I didn't get that impression."

"Why, what did she say?"

Surwin smiled and popped some of the peanuts into his mouth. "Tell me about Freaky Freddie Margolis."

"Someone stole my phone and fenced it through him. When he turned it on, the people after me traced its location."

"What happened on Ansonia Road?"

"Someone called Dirty Dirk to tell him of my presence there."

"Dirk?"

"That's right, and a few moments later a hit squad came after me. You want to know who was leading the squad?"

Surwin just stared.

"Remi Bozant," said Scrbacek.

Surwin's eyes widened.

"And you want to know who was with Dyer when she stomped into Jenny Ling's house looking for me, and who ghosted out the back door just as you rolled up?"

"Remi Bozant?" said Surwin.

"You're catching on."

"Let's go back to the office. I'll take your statement. We'll get a task force grinding on the problem."

"Forget it."

"You just can't run around my town, Scrbacek, like a woodchuck with his tail on fire."

"A woodchuck? With his tail on fire?"

"That's right."

"How does that happen, his tail catching on fire?"

"Maybe like an idiot, he ran through a campfire, or maybe it wasn't his fault at all. Maybe it was an act of God. See, that's the thing. It doesn't matter how the fire started. Running around like a woodchuck with his tail on fire as the city burns down behind you is a guaranteed way to lose your popularity. But we'll protect you. We'll find the answers. Come on in."

"I appreciate the offer, but I don't think you guys could protect a tennis ball."

Surwin leaned back and took a long pull from his beer. "I could arrest you on the murder and arson charges right now."

"But you won't."

"How are you so sure?"

"Because you said you wouldn't, and because you know I'm being set up."

"I do?"

"Let me guess. All those weapons found in the basement, all that plastic explosive. Not a fingerprint."

"You were careful."

"Careful enough to leave no fingerprints but sloppy enough to leave the weapons in my basement so they could be discovered after the fire? I was set up. By Bozant and Dyer. The phone message, the visit to the Brummels, it was a setup from the start."

"Who's behind it?"

"I don't know, but I'm going to find out."

Surwin took another pull from his beer and looked around at the desolate surroundings. "The dancers here used to be younger."

"So I heard."

"I must say, it was a little livelier when the dancers were younger."

"Why, Prosecutor Surwin, you should be ashamed of yourself."

Scrbacek looked up at Aunt Gethsemane going at it onstage. She shook her belly, grinned madly, and her teeth fell out.

"Let's get the hell out of here," said Scrbacek as he stood.

Surwin watched him for a moment and then stood himself, dropping some bills on the table.

"I've got more questions," said Surwin as they walked side by side through the bar, past the beaded curtain, past Sergei on his little stool, into the cool night air. "I need details."

"Uh-uh. It's my turn," said Scrbacek. "Last night, in that house they burned down on Ansonia Road, I had my fortune read by the Contessa Romany."

"The Contessa Romany? From the boardwalk? With the sign?"

"The same."

"I've had a few chats with her myself."

"Tarot?"

"Bunco."

"Well, the Contessa, she said the answer to who is trying to kill me is in my past, my present, and my future. I've already checked out my past. You're going to show me my present."

"And how do I do that?"

"I'm haunted, it seems, by the ghost of one man, still very much alive, whom I served, for good or ill, to the best of my abilities."

"And who would that be?"

"Caleb Breest," said Scrbacek. "It's time I learned who my client truly is."

34

SHADOW OF THE BREEST

"Caleb Breest's boyhood home," said Thomas Surwin, nodding to a brightly lit house, its brick scrubbed and repointed, its siding painted, the little patch of lawn neatly edged. On the porch, a beefy lug in a white cable-knit sweater and a black beret swiveled his head as Surwin and Scrbacek drove slowly past and then stopped half a block down the street. "His mother still lives there, with twenty-four-hour sides of beef to chase the door-to-door salesmen away."

"During the trial she seemed in perpetual fright."

"It's sometimes hard to tell if the guards are keeping criminals out or her in."

"Nice neighborhood," said Scrbacek. "Like Berlin after the war."

Every other building on the block was rubble, as if a B-52 had indeed dropped a full load on the neighborhood. Walls without windows, fronts without walls, not a pane of glass that hadn't been shattered, not a door that hadn't been forced open so that the copper pipe could be stripped, not a floor that hadn't been covered to the height of a rat's ass with debris. Every building but one had lost its roof. Every building but one had been covered with foul graffiti. Every building but one. That one, that house, stood brightly lit and perfectly maintained, as if it had fallen into that tragic urban landscape like Dorothy's house into a firebombed Oz.

"Are you sure you really want to learn exactly who it is you defended?" said Surwin.

"Last thing I did before the hammer came down was represent Caleb Breest. For me, he's the present I need to discover."

"You might not like what you find."

"I didn't find much to like in my past, either."

"This used to be a nice neighborhood," said Surwin. "Fourth of July barbecues at the fire station, pickup basketball in the park. Breest's father worked at a metal-pressing factory, half a mile down, that used to employ a hundred men and women manufacturing rain gutters and spouts from great rolls of sheet metal. Ever-Dry. Ever-Dry products were shipped all over the eastern United States. Breest's father worked at Ever-Dry from the time he left high school. He rose to shop foreman and helped build Ever-Dry into one of the largest employers in the city."

"An American success story."

"He was supposed to have been a hell of a guy, Caleb Breest's father, until the tragedy."

"Tragedy?"

"He had a son."

Scrbacek sat silent for a moment. In the side mirror, he could see the brightly lit house. The guard was still on the porch, but no longer seated. He was standing at the rail, looking at their car.

"I've heard the rumors of the father's bones being buried in the basement of his house," said Scrbacek.

"He disappeared when Breest was fourteen. I'd love to go into that house with a pick and shovel, but it's hard to get a warrant to dig up a basement floor based on hearsay rumors of legendary crimes."

"What kind of kid was he?"

"Your client? The kind that put firecrackers down the throats of hamsters. The kind that was suspended from kindergarten for biting."

"A lot of kids that age bite."

"Not an ear off a little girl. And that's not rumor, that's in the record."

"The permanent record. What else does it show?"

"Emotional outbursts in the classroom, brutalizing students half his size, threatening teachers. He was such a problem he was put into a special-ed class with kids in wheelchairs, which he knocked over regularly, kids with Down syndrome that he egged on to do horrible things. He was already big, as big as some of his teachers even in elementary school, and he became as wild and as uncontrollable as his size allowed."

"Why didn't they do something for him?"

"The high school football coach came to the elementary school to get a look at this huge aggressive kid he had heard so much about, and after that the coach pulled every string he could to keep Breest from being expelled or sent away. They gave him special programs, tutors, psychological testing and counseling. Nothing did any good. And then, in his physical for the junior high football team, the doctor found Breest's heart to be grossly oversize. He would never play football. The coach lost interest, the district threw up its hands, and that was the end of Breest in school."

"Sounds like a kid desperate for help and not finding any."

"You don't have any children, do you, Scrbacek?"

Scrbacek shrugged.

"I have two sons. They live with their mother now in Delaware. They're both great kids and both completely different—one loud and physical, one quiet. We didn't form them as if out of clay. They simply came out the way they are. Mozart came out with the ability to be a great musician. Caleb Breest came out a monster. You can't blame the parents or society all the time. Sometimes out pops Mozart, sometimes out pops Breest."

"And who judges which is which?"

"You don't have to judge. They let you know. Some kids you can chart a slide from a specific point—the death of a father at an early age, say, or a period of abuse. But with Breest there was no slide. At six he was biting off a little girl's ear, and then he turned nasty."

Scrbacek looked up again at the house. The guard, while still staring at their car, was walking down the steps, his hand reaching into his belt. A second man, also in cable-knit and beret, was now standing in the doorway.

"The guy on the porch is coming for us," said Scrbacek.

Surwin checked out the rearview mirror without noticeable alarm. "Like I said, this used to be a nice neighborhood. But then a swarm of cutthroats and thieves descended like a plague. Burglaries. Arsons. It didn't take long. Within a few months the whole thing was a ghost town, except for Mrs. Breest's house. One rumor had it that Breest decided to clear the whole block, even though families had lived here for generations. The neighbors hadn't been nice enough to him as a boy."

Surwin took a final glance at the man coming toward them before putting the Hyundai in gear and slowly pulling away. Scrbacek eyed the expanse of ruin and rubble as it slid past his window.

"All the abandoned properties on the block," Surwin continued, "were bought for pennies by a developer named Frances Galloway."

"Galloway?"

"You know her?"

Scrbacek shrugged. "Not personally. I've read her name in the papers."

"She keeps a low profile, but she's the biggest slumlord in the city. Inherited great swaths of real estate from the husband she married when he was eighty-four and she was thirty-one, with two failed marriages already behind her. She hasn't done a thing to these houses. She's let them fester and crumble. Word is, she's afraid of what Breest will do if she rebuilds. In effect, the garden of ruins that surrounds the house is now a permanent fixture of Mrs. Breest's landscape. A fitting tribute, I figure, to the blessings she has bestowed upon all of us through her son."

***

"The corner plot of land used to be the seat of power in this town," said Surwin as they drove toward a high wooden fence, covered in posters advertising this angry new rap band or that high-octane new movie. "The place where those who wanted to do business had to come and get their permits."

"A government office?"

"A restaurant. Migello's. They made a cioppino that was legendary. Fresh clams, mussels, vermouth, enough cracked peppercorn to light your mouth on fire. Migello's was where three generations of the Puchesi family did business."

Immediately surrounding the fence, buildings that had once been fine, grand, with facades of cut stone, lay abandoned, boarded up, crumbling one into the other. The whole neighborhood appeared abandoned as if in a hurry. Something terrible had happened here, something long ago, from which the neighborhood had never recovered. Surwin parked the little blue Hyundai beside the high wooden fence at the corner of Ninth and Polk.

"They had carved this niche out for themselves, the Puchesis, controlling crime in this city even as they ruthlessly kept the bigger families in New York and Philadelphia from moving in. This was before the casinos, when gambling meant the numbers, and the Puchesi syndicate kept strict control of prostitution, loan sharking, extortion, and a minimal amount of drug trafficking. In the old days they said the Puchesis were the biggest problem facing the city. Now they seem like kindly old caretakers who were keeping the city together."

"What happened to them?"

"They made a mistake in personnel."

Scrbacek simply looked at Surwin and waited.

"Caleb Breest was fifteen when he was sent to reform school for assault. It seemed a high school football player made a snide comment about Breest's weak heart, and in response Caleb Breest repeatedly slammed his fist into the kid's face until it fell apart. Breest, being only fifteen, was locked away in reform school for the last three years of his minority. It was in reform school that he met Joey Torresdale."

"I wondered when Torresdale entered the picture."

"After Breest turned eighteen and was released, Joey brought him in to meet Luigi Puchesi. Torresdale was just a hanger-on with the Puchesi syndicate, but Luigi was always in the market for big amoral thugs who liked pounding flesh, and he immediately hired Caleb Breest as one of his collection agents. Breest proved himself to the bosses in his very first week by taking care of a deadbeat debtor with six kids who couldn't come up with the three hundred he owed. He killed him with his bare hands, in front of three witnesses from the syndicate. Breest's evident enthusiasm for his work earned for himself and for Joey enough promotions so that after only a few short years of mayhem, Breest was making loans himself, using his boss's money, while Joey had become one of Luigi Puchesi's captains. Breest wasn't Sicilian, so there was only so far he could rise in the family, but he was rising, gaining more responsibility, garnering more fear. Then the inevitable happened. A Puchesi lieutenant accused Breest of shorting the family on profits."

"Was he?"

"Probably. It was a criminal organization, and Breest is a criminal. But the truth of it didn't matter. A week later they found the lieutenant stuffed shoulders-first into a trash can, his legs sticking out and his head missing. Not so earth-shattering a move except this lieutenant was married to a granddaughter of the old man himself. The feds had a bug in Migello's, and they caught Luigi Puchesi in a meeting with his top men. 'There's a cancer in the family,' he said in a hoarse Old World voice. 'You don't negotiate with a cancer, you don't make deals with a cancer, you don't sign treaties with a cancer. What you do with a cancer is you cut it out and stamp it dead and then feed it to the rats. There's a cancer in the family, and it's time to feed the rats.' It was a declaration of war, and the outcome is all there on the tape. Luigi's declaration, a discussion of strategy, Joey Torresdale leaving the restaurant to relay orders to the troops, and then, exactly thirty-seven minutes after Luigi Puchesi said it was time to feed the rats, there is a dark rumble of sound before the tape goes dead."

"What happened?"

Surwin leaned over to his glove compartment and pulled out a flashlight, which he handed to Scrbacek. He nodded at the fence surrounding the corner lot. "Go see for yourself."

Scrbacek approached the wooden wall with trepidation, keeping the flashlight off as he moved closer. A moist rot seeped through the edges of the posts. The fence was over six feet high, too tall for him to see over, and the top was jagged and full of splinters, so pulling himself up with his hands was not an attractive possibility. He tramped up and down the edge, looking for something to stand upon, and found, finally, a piece of cinder block with one edge flat enough to serve as a stoop. He hoisted the block close to the wall and stepped up onto it, pressing one hand on the wall for balance. The scent of rot grew stronger. Slowly he rose on tiptoes to peer over the jagged top.

Nothing.

Not a building, not a sidewalk, not a light, not even a vacant lot. Instead there was a great hole in the surface of the earth, a massive crater, as if something supernatural had reached down and grabbed a handful out of Crapstown, leaving nothing but the nauseating scent of ruin and death.

In the thin glimmer bleeding over the fence from the streetlights, Scrbacek could barely make out the edge of the crater, but not its depth. He switched on Surwin's flashlight, lifted it over his head, and focused it on the center of the crater's darkness.

It was impossibly deep, the crater. The flashlight's uneven circular light was too weak to light up the entire pit, so Scrbacek could not immediately get a clear view of what was inside, but he could tell, even in the uneven light, that it was fearsome and deep. And, somehow, in motion.

He shifted the beam back and forth to get a better view, and suddenly he realized what he was seeing, and from the sight and the smell he gagged loudly and gagged again. The puddled bottom of the pit was alive with a scavenging army of rats, huge angry rats, scores of them, their fur slick, tumbling one over the other, gnawing at an oily pile of fat and bone. As the beam moved among the plague, their eyes, caught in the light, glowed red.

"The lot is now owned by Galloway," said Surwin after Scrbacek retreated back into the car. "The husband tried to build on it once, but someone burned down his mobile construction office before he could start, and that was the end of that. Since his death, the wife's done nothing to fill in the hole, despite orders by the city to clean it up. She owns so much of the city's ruins, and has so many orders to clean up so many properties, that the city can't afford to enforce any of them."

"That's as ugly a spot as I've ever seen," said Scrbacek.

"Every once in a while, to great fanfare among his goons, Caleb Breest sponsors a dog shooting contest. Whoever brings to Dirty Dirk's the bodies of the most strays gets a thousand-dollar bonus."

"I heard about that," said Scrbacek. "Joey Torresdale made it seem like good-natured civic-minded fun."

"I bet he did. It's illegal as hell, and the night is a terror for civilians in the worst parts of town, but the cops let it happen. Wild dogs are a problem in those neighborhoods, they figure, and the less roaming the streets, the better. And then, after all the beer, the boasting, the shots fired in celebration, after roasted pig is sliced and digested by all the hunters, they pile the stiff bodies of dogs and the pig carcass into a pickup truck, take them here, and toss them over the fence into the pit that was Migello's. Twenty years after he packed enough dynamite in the sewer beneath Migello's to level a small town, twenty years after he destroyed the Puchesi family and took control of the city's criminal organization, Caleb Breest is still feeding the rats."

***

Surwin parked the car across the street from a nicely maintained row of houses on a block with living trees and streetlights that glowed brightly.

"It's a brothel, one of his better ones. You go in the door as if you're heading into a simple narrow row house, but four of them have been gutted and combined into one grand sex palace. Many of the high rollers from the casinos end up here for a couple of frolics, and to get their pictures snapped."

"Sounds kinky."

"Oh, they don't know about the pictures until they get an envelope in the mail."

"How come it's still there?"

"It's licensed as an oriental massage parlor. But we're getting ready to close it. We've closed others, we'll close more. Even now he's setting up another site for when this one shuts down. The girls get out of jail on bail, and he sends them to the new house. He keeps the younger ones, boys and girls, in a separate house we haven't yet been able to find."

"Maybe it's just a rumor, then."

"What I've found in investigating your client, Scrbacek, is that behind every rumor is a reality that is far, far darker."

***

Surwin and Scrbacek were parked a hundred yards away from a street corner alive with lights and trucks and hordes of people, despite the late hour and the wet streets. Cars lined up to be greeted one at a time by a young runner, as if at a McDonald's drive-thru.

Scrbacek didn't have to get too close to recognize what he was seeing. He had spent enough nights waiting in line in his car—not at this corner, maybe, but others just like it—waiting in line with a desperate joyful anticipation, pulling up to the curb, the brief conversation with the young runner, the bills given, the runner strolling off to the stash beneath a stoop or under a rock, coming back without even a hint of concern and bringing with him the sweet little vials with their brightly colored caps.

"He runs corners all over the city," said Surwin. "The price is low enough that he gets customers from four different states. You can see it in the license plates. He hires the youngest to deal with the customers—you've surely defended some of them—but he has put in place an astounding number of levels between himself and the street. Less profit for himself, but more safety and more control. We've run up the chain a number of times, but it always stops one or two levels below the big man."

"Are you sure then that he's behind it all?"

"Not sure enough to get an indictment, but still pretty damn sure. Lately he's been expanding—setting up new corners, lowering the price, as if he's trying to hook the entire city. Whenever he sets up a new distribution center, the neighborhood in which he situates it goes straight to hell. It's as if he's purposely turning the city into one huge crack corner."

***

"The story you've heard," said Surwin, "of the guy with the Mercedes who won money off of Breest in a poker game and who was later steamrolled in his car?"

"I thought that was just an urban legend."

"Well, there's the lot where they found him," said Surwin, "flat as a playing card."

***

"This used to be one of the city's prime employers," said Surwin, in front of a burned-out hulk of a building, sitting low and squat, its edges black, its sign charred and crumbling. The air around the building still smelled of carbon, the ashes still sifted in the night breeze. "Like every place else, it was paying its city tax, its state tax, its federal tax, and its street tax. It had been paying the street tax, actually, for decades, from back when Luigi Puchesi was still running the show, but it was always a reasonable amount and the owners simply expensed it above the line. Except this year, suddenly, the tax was raised precipitously. It was like Breest was trying to ruin them. They argued and pled and tried to meet with the big man himself, but he refused to see them, and no one else could lower the demand. They had no choice but to come to us. We asked the owners to set up meetings, and they bravely agreed to let us wire them for sound. On the recordings we can clearly hear the threats and their pleas, and then fists smashing bone. The assault was so sudden it came before we could rush in and save them."

"What happened to the enforcers?"

"They're out on bail, waiting for the trial. Cirilio Vega's representing them. They've said nothing about who they were talking for. It's clearly Breest, but I don't know how to connect the dots for a jury unless the enforcers talk, and they're simply not talking. And the day after the arrest, before the enforcers were back on the street, despite the guards we had stationed around the building, the fire started. There was nothing left of the inventory, of the machinery, of the records. Nothing but rubble."

"Are the owners rebuilding?"

"Not here. They sold the property to Galloway, took the insurance money, bought a plant in South Carolina with the promise of all kinds of tax breaks. There's no employment left in the city except in the casinos. And the dealers and bartenders and cocktail waitresses, they either live in Casinoland or outside the city. Crapstown is dying, fast, and for some reason your client wants to speed up the process."

Surwin slowly pulled the car away from the burned-out factory, and as he did, Scrbacek turned to take one last look. From this angle, he could see the charred sign and just make out the letters burned like a negative into the wood:

KEEPING THE RAIN OFF YOUR PARADE.

EVER-DRY.

35
CALVARY

"I should have my head examined," said Surwin, driving slowly through the misty Crapstown night. "We're preparing a racketeering indictment against the whole organization, top to bottom, and here I am spilling what we know to Caleb Breest's attorney."

"Former attorney. Apparently, I've been replaced by Cirilio Vega."

"On a temporary basis, so they say. Vega came in the day after the acquittal and the bombing, his briefcase stuffed with motions and legal authority. We offered to continue the probation revocation hearing until you showed, or until Cirilio could bring himself up to speed, but he wanted none of it. Filed his notice of appearance, sat right down in your seat, handled himself like he had been there all along."

"He's crackerjack, Vega. And he's Breest's attorney now, not me."

"Still, if the Bureau knew what I was doing with you, it would mean my job."

"Then why are you doing it?"

Surwin looked at Scrbacek for a moment and then back through the windshield. After a moment, as if in response, he parked the car on a deserted street and killed the engine. "Let's take a walk."

Surwin led Scrbacek down the street and then into an alleyway, dank, stinking of garbage and piss, wet with rain, infested by rodents, inhabited by one person, of indeterminate sex and age, curled inside a cardboard box.

"Help for the homeless?" said the person in the box.

"Not tonight," said Surwin. "You recognize this place, Scrbacek?"

Scrbacek looked around and shook his head. "Should I?"

"I expect you were here once, just to case it out, but I'm not surprised you don't remember it. It's not very memorable without the blood and shattered brain on the walls, or the chalk outline of a figure drawn on the asphalt, but still I thought this an important stop on our tour. This is where your client beat the life out of Peter Malloy."

Scrbacek didn't say anything, just kicked at the wet blackness at his feet.

"Malloy's wife is doing as well as could be expected, in case you're interested," said Surwin. "I suppose she doesn't have much choice but to keep going, what with four daughters. I talk to her regularly, and the sadness is overwhelming. It seems to run in a current over the wires, from her house to my office, bleeding through the phone into my gut. She still asks one question over and over again: *Why?* I don't have an answer."

Scrbacek turned to stare at Surwin. "That was why I was able to get Breest off."

"I gave the jury the best motive I had."

"But it wasn't the right one. The crap about Malloy trying to clean up the labor union never rang true."

"You have a better one?"

"Not yet," said Scrbacek. "But it's out there. You shouldn't have brought the case before you found it."

"I had the DNA. I had the fingerprint."

"But it wasn't enough, was it? You've been giving me nothing but shit for winning my client an acquittal—the underlying theme of the whole night has been 'See what you've done, asshole'—but you were the prosecutor who lost the case. You were the prosecutor without all the answers. You were the man who was so certain about everything but couldn't prove out his case. All I did was widen the hole in your proof and lead my client through it as the Sixth Amendment requires."

"Is that what the Sixth Amendment requires, that you spread lies and falsehoods to get a criminal off?"

"Absolutely."

"I don't think so."

"It's easy enough to sit back in the County Prosecutor's Office with an untroubled heart because you decide who to investigate, who to indict, who to try to kill. But it's not so simple on the other side of the bar. Not everyone you accuse is guilty. Not everyone you want to kill deserves to die. Someone has to represent the human being in the dock."

"But it wasn't Amber Grace this time, was it?" said Surwin. "This time you were representing Caleb Breest."

"You think I should stand in judgment of my client?"

"Yes."

"You think I have a responsibility to society beyond doing whatever the hell I can to get my client off?"

"As an officer of the court, you have a responsibility to see justice done."

"My old law professor would disagree," said Scrbacek. "He would say that since we are merely human, we can't know what true justice would really entail. He would say that only God can make that determination. All we can do is perform our roles and hope for the best. I did my job. If you have a problem with what happened in that courtroom, look in the mirror."

"But what happened wasn't justice—you know it as well as I do—and leaving the determination to a higher authority is a cop-out. Do you know what medicine Caleb Breest takes for his oversize heart? Digitoxin, nitroglycerin, and Lasix. Digitoxin keeps his heart beating like a machine, nitroglycerin is an explosive, and Lasix is what they give to racehorses to make them run faster. Caleb Breest is an inhuman predator and you were his knight-errant."

Surwin backed up, took a deep breath, and turned away, as if he couldn't bear to look at Scrbacek.

"Get in the car," he said. "I have one more place to show you."

***

"I could take you to Dirty Dirk's," said Surwin. "Show you your client in his natural cesspool, but I don't suppose that would be the healthiest spot for you to show your face. So I'm taking you somewhere else instead."

"Dirk is in league with the guys who are after me," said Scrbacek. "But what I still can't figure is why the hell they want me dead in the first place."

"It's not too hard to puzzle out."

Scrbacek didn't say anything, just turned his head and stared at Surwin.

"We went into your office after the fire. All your files had been burned beyond recognition."

"My file cabinets were supposed to be fireproof."

"They forced the locks, pulled out the drawers, spread a homemade napalm over everything. They did the same to your computers. There wasn't a piece of data remaining in your whole building. And they would have burned the files even if the car bomb had killed you as planned. They need you dead, because in the course of your representation of Caleb Breest you learned something they can't afford to have revealed. There's something going down in Crapstown, and you know what it is."

"But I don't know anything. They're wrong."

"They're not wrong. You learned something—you just don't know its importance yet. What you need to do is tell me everything you learned while representing Breest, and we'll figure it out together."

"You know I can't do that."

"They're trying to kill you, Scrbacek."

"But I don't know who *they* are. And I won't violate the attorney-client privilege just because you have a theory."

Surwin sighed with disgust. "Only conversations between you and your client are covered by privilege. From what I understand, most of your meetings were with Joey Torresdale."

"That's right."

"Anything Torresdale told you is fair game."

"Don't you think I'm in enough trouble?"

"I'm trying to help here, Scrbacek, but you need to throw me a bone."

Surwin pulled the car to a stop at the edge of a seedy business district, with a dusty old grocery, a fishmonger's storefront, a clothier with yellow and brown suits in the window. In front of the stores was a shuttered newspaper shack, and from behind it came a woman, ratty and thin, hunched over, black scraps of wet cloth hanging from her limbs.

She stepped closer to the car and swayed on her heels. "Are you two boys looking for—?"

Surwin pulled out his credentials and flashed his badge. The woman stepped back unsteadily and then slinked behind the shack.

Surwin pointed to a row of windows on the second floor above the clothier. Painted across two of the windows were the words:

TRENT FALLOW INVESTIGATIONS

"Trent Fallow, PI," said Surwin. "That's his office and, as best we can tell, his living space, though it's not zoned residential."

Scrbacek looked up at the filthy office windows. "Doesn't say much for his lifestyle."

"He was your investigator on the Breest case."

"That's right."

"How'd you meet?"

"Joey Torresdale introduced us one night at Dirty Dirk's. Why?"

"Fallow is one of Breest's primary errand boys. Those pictures from the whorehouse sent to powerful high rollers? It's Fallow who sends them and works out the payment. The young kids who fill the secret brothels? It's Trent Fallow who hangs out at the bus stations and kiddie parks, recruiting the loners who wander free. Word is, if there's a scut job that Breest needs doing on the sly, he sends Fallow. What did you and Fallow talk about?"

"When we first met, it was just small talk. You know, 'Hi, how you doing? Let me buy you a drink.'"

"And then what?"

Scrbacek shook his head. "I can't."

"What do you mean you can't?"

"Why do you care, anyway?"

"Because he's just the kind of low-life, low-level fixer who ends up knowing more than he should about everything. And then ends up dead. I've been sort of expecting him to bite the dust for a while now, but it turns out that it's you, not him, who's getting chased all through Crapstown. He might be the connection."

"I don't see how," said Scrbacek.

"That's because you're not looking."

Scrbacek lowered his head and closed one eye in thought. Aboud had told him Fallow was looking for him. He had thought the PI was just after the reward, like everyone else in Crapstown. But maybe it was something else. He peered again at the windows, thought about their meager interactions. "Son of a bitch."

"What?"

"Son of a bitch."

"What's going on, Scrbacek?"

"I'm not sure."

"Tell me what you think."

"I can't."

"What the hell do you mean, you can't?"

"First, because I honestly don't know anything yet. And second, because I can't tell you anything he told me. Half our conversations were about his work on the Breest case, which makes it attorney work product. I'm not allowed to disclose that."

"And the other half?"

"Well, I can't reveal anything about those discussions either."

"Why the hell not?"

"Because it turns out that Trent Fallow, that son of a bitch, is a client of mine, too."

36
TRENT FALLOW, PI, CONT'D.

Finished with his rounds, Trent Fallow, PI, now heads home to reap the fruits of his sowing. His answering machine, he hopes, is full of answers. It would have been better, on a day like this, to have a cell phone bought cheap from Freaky Freddie, but at forty bucks a month for service, fuggetaboutit. It's cheaper to pay to hijack a line off the fish store downstairs. Zero a month. Now that is a calling plan he can live with.

The street outside his office building is deserted, except for the girl who stations herself nightly outside Frankie's shed, thin and skanky, with her hair lying flat and greasy on her pimply shoulders. It's not the best or most energetic spot to hustle, the desultory corner outside Trent Fallow's office, but then she's not the best or most energetic whore. Though she does have, as Fallow has discovered on many a lazy night, a certain pleasant passivity and an indisputable talent with her tongue. As he wheezes toward his building, she edges toward him, her black rags still soaked from the rain. He waves her away. He's got work to do, does Trent Fallow, PI. There's no time to mess about with that mess of bones.

Slowly, and with great effort, he pushes his bulk up the stairs and into his office.

It's not much, his office, just a room with a desk, a phone, file cabinets, and a large map of the city taped to the wall. Off to the side sits a storage room with a bed and a heating plate, and off the storage room sits a small bathroom with a toilet that overflows once a week and a sink in which he washes out his T-shirts and sponges himself every other morning or so. Hygiene, Trent Fallow, PI, has found, is overrated. Even before he checks his machine, he strips off his jacket, drops his pants, and plops onto the toilet, groaning out loud like a gut-shot bear. It streams out soft and burning. A stress shot. What could he expect? And the stink, oh, the stink. He can measure his level of stress from the stink, and this, oh my, this is off the scale. What is he going to do? What the hell is he going to do? What he is going to do is wipe his ass until it is raw and then check his machine.

There are six messages. He readies a pen and pad before he presses the button. All six messages tell him the same story. Scrbacek was in the Marina District, the cops came flying in, shots were fired, the only corpse was a dog. Scrbacek, that son of a bitch, got away. Trent Fallow, PI, listens with dread, relieved that no one else has yet found the lawyer, that he still has a hero's shot to save his own life and collect the bounty, but scared, too, terrified that if everything goes right he'll have to face all by his lonesome Scrbacek and that girl, that stone-cold girl.

Trent Fallow, PI, sits at his desk, waiting for the phone to ring. One hour. Two hours. He falls asleep in the chair, his fitful dreams full of sex and violence, sexy violence, violent sex, and wakes with a start, sweating and shivering, wakes to silence. Someone has to have seen something. Someone has to have a lead on where Scrbacek is now. Someone. He tells himself to calm down, but he can't stop shivering. He's too tense, he's too scared, he's useless. He needs something to regain his nerve.

He finds her at her usual spot, under the streetlamp beside the shuttered newspaper shack. She stands before him, her eyes dark sockets, her collarbone protruding.

"Five dollars," he says.

"Twenty-five."

"Now you're being silly."

"Get lost, then, you cheap smelly bastard."

"And who am I bidding against, Mia?" he says, waving his arm to take in the whole of the empty street.

"I've got standards."

"You've got nothing but me."

"You're a pig."

"A pig with a fiver, what needs a blow job."

"He'll beat me if I settle for that."

"What do I care what the likes of him does to the likes of you? Come on up or not—it's your decision."

She hesitates a moment, looks around, and then begins to follow him to the building, saying under her breath, "You walking fart."

He stops, turns around, takes a step toward her. "What did you say, you whore?"

"I said you're a walking fart."

He looks at her for a moment, at the defiant hatred in her eyes, and feels himself grow hard. He takes another step forward, slaps her across the face, and then grabs her hand and rubs it across his swelling crotch. "Be sure to take it all in. It's pure protein, baby, and you could use some meat on those bones."

Up the stairs, he opens the door for her. She walks, hunched over, through the doorway and stops suddenly.

"My Lord," she says. "What died?"

He locks the door behind him and opens his belt.

It is dark in the office, only a crack of light slipping from the barely open door of the lit bathroom and the dim glow of the streetlight bathing everything in a tarnished silver. He lets his jeans fall, and his boxers; they pool around his ankles like a Great Lake. He stands in front of her wearing only his T-shirt and holster and boots.

The bottom of his stomach glistens with sweat in the narrow light as it sags below the shirt, his thighs are huge and lumpy as if injected with great mounds of curdled lard, his knees are grossly dimpled, his calves are overstuffed sausages erupting from his boots, and his ass, his ass is as big as all creation. From the matted, twisted hair of his crotch protrudes his skinny uncircumcised dick, like the probing proboscis of an anteater.

"God, you're ugly," she says.

"You better believe it, baby. Now on your knees. And if you want to dig your nails into my ass while you're at it, feel free."

She's a few minutes in, squatting on her haunches, gagging at the gamy, coffee-flavored taste of him, thinking of the glamorous life of the call girl for which she left the secretarial pool. Her mouth feels to him like a sink of warm soapy water. He grips her head with both hands and jams it back and forth, into and away from his crotch, back and forth, back and forth—baby, yes, baby—back and forth, and forth, and fucking forth, when he glances up and sees a shadow slip through the darkness of the storage room.

"What the—?" is all he can get out before the shadow splits into two.

He can see only silhouettes, one taller, in a long coat, the other shorter, thin, a girl with broad shoulders and an assault rifle held at the ready. He pushes the whore away, starts to run to his right. His feet tangle in the clothes at his ankles and he falls so hard the room shakes.

On the floor he rolls onto his back and is reaching for the Colt Detective Special still holstered in his armpit when the girl with the gun says, "Don't," and he freezes.

"Hey, Trent," says the second silhouette, stepping forward until it stands over his half-naked, supine figure. In the thin silver light, Trent Fallow, PI, can detect the silhouette's features. J.D. Scrbacek, as if he didn't already know. "How's it going, buddy? Sorry about barging in like this. Am I interrupting something?"

"Well, you know, I was—"

"Good. I'm glad it was nothing important. Word I got is you've been looking for me."

"You know, J.D., as a matter of fact, with all this stuff happening I was concerned about—"

"You were concerned? Really?"

"Yeah, sure."

"I'm touched, Trent, touched."

Scrbacek kneels down over Trent Fallow's torso, swats Fallow's hand away from the holster beneath Fallow's armpit, and himself pulls out the Colt Detective Special, hefting it in his hand.

"Nice piece."

"Thanks."

Scrbacek takes hold of the gun by the grip, his finger on the trigger, and starts aiming it around the room. "You could do some damage with this baby."

"Careful with that. It's loaded."

"Is it?" says Scrbacek, waving it loosely now back and forth between Fallow's head, eyes bulging, and his bulging stomach. "But I'm sure the safety's on."

"There is no safety."

"No safety? That could be dangerous."

"Yo, J.D., what are you doing here?"

"Trent, buddy, remember that time when you called and asked about the file you had given me about your case, that Mendoza matter, where you were just helping the man vacate unsafe premises, and I told you we'd talk about it after the Breest trial was finished?"

"Yeah, I remember. So?"

"Well, good news, you fat fuck. Trial's over. Time to talk."

37
MONEY AND HAPPINESS

Trent Fallow, PI, sat behind his desk, pants back up, thank God, ankles and hands bound with duct tape, his torso and legs taped tightly to the chair, trussed like a well-stuffed turkey ready for roasting. Feed a family of forty with plenty left over for sandwiches the next day.

Mia the whore was back on the street, three Ben Franklins warming her breasts in exchange for her promise to tell no one what she had seen, wondering at the price of a bus ticket to Chicago. The Nightingale was perched atop the roof of Fallow's building, scanning the streets below. And J.D. Scrbacek, on the loose again after being allowed by Surwin to just walk away, was searching through Trent Fallow's files, one by one, as he spoke to the man in the chair. "Mendoza," he said. "Let's start with Mendoza."

"I got nothing to say," said Trent Fallow.

Scrbacek stopped, lifted the Colt Detective Special from the top of the cabinet, aimed it at Fallow's face.

Fallow winced.

"Who painted your face bruise?"

"Bozant."

"He did such a nice job it would be a shame to ruin it." Scrbacek lowered the muzzle until it was approximately in line with Fallow's crotch. "Mendoza," said Scrbacek.

"You wouldn't," said Fallow. "Your balls aren't big enough."

Scrbacek cocked the gun and waited for a moment. Then he gently pulled the hammer and let it slide harmlessly back into place. "You're right," he said.

A broad smile broke out on Fallow's swollen face. "I knew it. You're too pussy to pull this off. Just let me go, J.D. I won't tell a soul where you are. I promise. You have my word."

"Your word? Please. I don't have what it takes to shoot off your nuts, true, but the Nightingale does. Wait just a minute while I get her."

"No, don't," he said, his face red from the pressure of the tape with which she had so tightly bound him. "She's cold, that bitch. Stone-cold."

"So they say."

"She'll do it."

"Not only that," said Scrbacek. "She'll do it well, and she'll like it. Mendoza."

"You read the file."

"But it's gone. They burned it. I need the original."

"I gave the original to you."

"Then where are the copies?"

"I didn't make any copies."

"What kind of idiot doesn't make any copies?" Scrbacek looked up and down at Fallow, taped to the chair, and shrugged. "All right, you'll just have to tell it to me. Mendoza."

"I thought you read the file."

"I lied. I was too busy with the Breest case to look over your crappy file. Whenever a lawyer says he looked at the file, it means he intends to, sometime in the future, probably on the way to court."

"So you could have given it back to me when I asked and never known what was inside?"

"That's right."

"But you had to lie." Fallow laughed. "You're a lawyer. You couldn't help yourself." He laughed harder. "And none of this would have happened. None of it." He laughed until his body convulsed with laughter. "Who's the idiot now, Scrbacek?"

Scrbacek let him laugh, let the hysteria build until tears streamed down as Fallow fought for breath, waited without a trace of amusement for the guffaws to devolve into chuckles, and the chuckles to peter out like a choked outboard until the jag ended with a high-pitched sigh.

"Tell me about Mendoza," said Scrbacek when it was over.

"I can't," said Fallow, laughter tears drying on his cheek, the afterburn of a smile still on his face. "Bozant will kill me. He'll fillet my ass off the bone with his knife."

"Must be a hell of a knife. Who's he working for?"

"Does it matter? He'll kill me."

Scrbacek took some crumpled bills out of his pocket, sorted them out, tossed several onto the desktop. "Five hundred dollars. You can get out of town as soon as we're through here. Burrow in someplace, hide so he'll never find you. Start over. A new job, a new life. Maybe find an all-you-can-eat buffet that doesn't have your photo posted."

"He won't stop until he finds me."

"The Nightingale doesn't even have to search."

Trent Fallow stared at the five bills on the desk.

"I'll go get her," said Scrbacek.

"No. Don't." Fallow eyed the bills on his desk. "You got any more to add to that pile?"

Scrbacek took out another hundred and tossed it atop the others.

Fallow stared.

Scrbacek took out another. "That's it."

"A man's got to eat."

"Mendoza," said Scrbacek.

Fallow looked at him, down at the seven hundred dollars on the desk, back up at Scrbacek.

Scrbacek waited a moment more. He was just reaching to take the money back when Fallow said, "Mendoza was nothing."

"Tell it."

"He was just a guy who wouldn't leave. I lost control, and when the doctor saw what he looked like, she called in the cops and the loser talked. That's all Mendoza was, one of hundreds. The job was to clear them out. A sharp lawyer got some judge named Dick or something to declare the buildings unsafe so I could clear them legally."

"Judge Dickerson?"

"Yeah, that's the one."

"Chief Judge Dickerson?"

"I suppose. He was the one what signed the orders."

"Condemnation orders?"

"Fuck if I know."

"How many buildings did Judge Dickerson condemn?"

"Dozens. I hated that job, tramping door to door to give the bad news, roaches falling on my head. It's not like these places were palaces. 63 West Polk. 694 Fillmore. 38 North Taft—that was Mendoza's building. The vultures in the city had already pretty much taken these places apart. It was like they had been squeezed already for anything of any worth. My job was to evict the hangers-on, the ones like Mendoza who stayed only because they had no place left to go."

"Who was the client?"

"Galloway."

"The developer?"

"Yeah, sure, if that's what you want to call her, though all she develops is slums. She owns half the city, Frances Galloway, and still she's the cheapest bitch I ever met. Said she'd take me to lunch to set the thing up. Dragged me to some hot dog vendor. And then after she took her dog, she turned her back. I had to pay. Woman's worth fucking millions and can't even buy herself a hot dog. So there we were, this millionaire slut, all dressed to the nines, and me, eating hot dogs on the street as she told me the plan. She wanted to redo the buildings, she said, make them shiny and nice. But to do that, she needed them cleared, so she got her lawyer to do the legal work and wanted me to make sure of the evictions. I was going to be her Sherman, she said, which I understood completely. She wanted me to be strong like a Sherman tank, to roll over obstacles and blow away anything got in my way. That's what I did with Mendoza, just like she said."

"How'd a loser like you end up with a big-time operator like Frances Galloway?"

"Torresdale set it up. I mean, not for free. Not out of the goodness of his heart, you know what I mean? He got his twenty percent just like when I worked for you. But he set it up, and Galloway's got pockets, know what I mean?"

"So Joey Torresdale and Frances Galloway are somehow linked. That means Breest is involved." Scrbacek sidled over to the map of the city hanging on one of the dingy office walls. "Any idea who brought Caleb Breest and Frances Galloway together?"

"They tell me nothing but what to do and when to do it. I'd love to get inside one of them deals, take some points, make some real money, but I'm just a drone to them."

"You're breaking my heart, Trent," said Scrbacek, staring now at the map. "What were those addresses again?"

"63 West Polk."

He searched for the location on the map. The map had street numbers indicated, and he quickly found the spot. "All right. Next."

"694 Fillmore."

"Okay. Next."

"There was one at 79 West Polk."

"Go ahead."

"And 223 Harrison."

"Right. And you said something about North Taft?"

"Thirty-eight."

"Son of a bitch. Hey, Fallow, give me a pen."

"Fuck you. I look like I'm in any condition to play your butler?"

Scrbacek turned to look at Trent Fallow, trussed in his chair, and shrugged out a "Sorry" before darting to the desk, searching through the junk on top to find a pen, and then heading back to the map to mark the locations. "Give me some more addresses."

"I don't remember them all."

"Just give me what you know, all right?"

Trent Fallow let loose a string of numbers linked to names: Pierce, Hayes, Van Buren, Tyler, Taylor, Arthur, Cleveland, Harding, the whole gamut of undistinguished presidents after whom many of the streets in Crapstown were named. The greater presidential names—Washington, Jefferson, Lincoln, and Kennedy—were reserved for the boulevards of Casinoland. One by one Scrbacek marked the locations on the map, and when it was over it looked like he had drawn a graph, something like a supply curve in an economics textbook or a well-correlated example of money and happiness, not a bell-shaped curve but something straight and wide, moving upward to the right.

Scrbacek took a step back from the map and stared at it for a moment. "You remember the Ever-Dry factory?"

"Sure," said Trent Fallow. "'Keeping the rain off your parade.' What they needed was a little more rain to put out that fire."

"What was the address of that place, do you remember?"

"I don't know. Something like Ninth and Garfield."

Scrbacek stepped slowly to the map, made another mark, and then stepped back again, shaking his head and sucking his teeth, staring and staring.

"You got it wrong, Trent," Scrbacek said, finally, "the remark about Sherman."

"What do you mean?"

"Galloway wasn't talking about the tank, she was talking about William Tecumseh and his march from Atlanta to the sea. Look what you've done here. You've cleared out a direct path from Diamond's Mount Olympus to the Marina District, where James E. Diamond plans to build his new casino resort. Galloway and Caleb Breest have somehow gotten together to buy up and clear the land for Diamond's highway straight through the heart of Crapstown. Breest ruins the properties with crime, Galloway buys them cheap, and Chief Judge Dickerson signs the orders that lets you clear them of tenants so they can be knocked down with no fuss, no muss. It's like a highway through the heart of the city to Diamond's new casino has already been built."

"I thought the politicians hadn't yet given the Marina District plan the okay."

"Well, Breest and Galloway have sort of preempted City Council, wouldn't you say? Either they figure it's a done deal and are working together to make a killing when they sell out to Diamond, or . . ."

"Or what?"

Scrbacek stared for a moment more at the map.

"Who's Bozant working for?" Scrbacek said.

"Breest, I thought. Or maybe Galloway. While he was beating the shit out of me he wasn't, like, into answering my questions. He told me what to do, and I did it."

"Galloway ever mention Diamond?"

"Never."

"Never mentioned some business partner or some big megaplan?"

"It's not like she confided in me."

"How often did you guys meet?"

"That one time, with the hot dogs, was all. After that she told me I should deal with her lawyer, the one that was getting all those orders from that Judge Dick."

"Chief Judge Dickerson. Who was the lawyer?"

"A cocky little Cuban asshole. Treated me like shit."

"What was his name, Trent?"

"Vega. Yeah. Like the car. Something something Vega."

38
CIRILIO VEGA

Cirilio Vega, Esquire, looks left, then right upon climbing from his BMW and scans the landscape once more when hitting the street out of the lot. His caution is understandable, what with the craziness that has infected the city in the last three days. The courthouse is to his right, but he ignores it. His office is behind him, but it will have to wait. He needs to make his regular morning stop before he starts his day, he needs to hear the early morning word, and the best place for hearing the early morning word is at Sweeney's Sunrise Club.

He picks up his pace, knowing he is later than usual, thinking of the sweet burn at the back of the throat, of the calm that settles like an alighting butterfly with the very first taste. And today, with a madman on the loose, his need for the calm is greater than usual.

He is handsome and dark, Cirilio Vega, with sharp feral features. He wears a double-breasted suit, small shiny shoes, a bright tie tied into a tight Windsor knot. Cirilio Vega. Cirilio. Not Cy, like some fat gym teacher. Not Cyrus, like some cabin boy on a Greek freighter. Not Cyril, like some poofy British writer. Not Rilio, not Leo, not Cirry, like some diseased drunk. Cirilio. Cirilio Vega, a Cuban fire-eater on the rise, you better believe it. They can't keep him down, no matter how they try, and oh, how they try. On the rise, headed to the top, if he can just make it through all this craziness without losing his ticket or his mind.

The sign outside Sweeney's is unlit, the neon in the windows is off, the place looks deserted, but that's how it looks every morning. Sweeney opens the door just for them, the Sunrise Club, so they can have their morning pick-me-ups without a load of gawkers, so they can talk over the morning's news without the gossip spreading beyond their narrow corps, so they can strategize their way through the minefields set for them by the County Prosecutor's Office. They are criminal defense attorneys all, the Sunrise Club, men and women, defenders of the dispossessed, part of an elite club that went into law for all the right reasons, no matter how it has turned out. There are some in the defense bar who started out as prosecutors before falling into the private sector to earn more money, but those are not welcome in the Sunrise Club. Former prosecutors tend to maintain allegiance to the enemy. They tend to make deals, to convince their clients to flip and rat out former compatriots. The Sunrise Club frowns on such behavior. The names of its members—Vega, Gray, Pomerantz, Broida, Cannoni, Gonzalez, Scrbacek—read like an honor roll of the hard-core.

They'll all be there, thinks Vega. All but Scrbacek, of course, though J.D. will undoubtedly continue to be the main subject of discussion. It is only rumors that are spreading through the Sunrise Club—rumors the lawyers have learned from their clients or overheard in the cells below the courthouse—but rumors that have the ring of authenticity. Scrbacek burned down his own building to destroy his records; Scrbacek burned down a house on Ansonia Road; Scrbacek stole a red Cadillac convertible and was on his way to Vegas; Scrbacek single-handedly battled four gang members in the heart of Crapstown; Scrbacek embezzled millions from a trust fund and was already in Rio; Scrbacek was dead, his corpse buried so deep in the wetlands that it would never,

ever be found. It is to this last rumor that Cirilio Vega gives the most credence. It is always that way, hope driving belief, but in this case Vega has a valid basis for so believing. He knows better than anyone what Scrbacek is actually up against.

Cirilio Vega pulls open the door and steps into Sweeney's. It is cool inside, and dark, the morning light slatted dim by dusty venetian blinds, and it smells of camphor and spilled beer. It is not much of place, Sweeney's—a long bar on the left, booths on the right, a jukebox, a pay phone, a video poker game—it is not much of a place, especially when it's empty. Vega is running late, and he would have expected the whole of the Sunrise Club to have been there already, huddling at the bar, swapping rumors and stories, but all he sees is Sweeney, standing by the sink, polishing.

"Morning, Sweeney," says Vega, bellying the bar, looking around. "Where is everybody?"

"I told 'em not to show," says Sweeney, his voice a harsh Irish whisper. "I told them I'd be staying shut this morning. I told 'em I had a funeral to be going to."

"Yeah? Then what are you doing here?"

"I couldn't find meself a corpse to drink over," says Sweeney before taking down a bottle, lifting up a glass, and pouring a double shot of vodka for Cirilio Vega. Vega likes vodka in the morning so his early appointments can't detect from his breath that he'd treated himself to a dawn breaker.

Vega lifts the glass to Sweeney and takes a gulp, his eyes closing reflexively as he feels the burn and the calm. "You lose my number or something?"

"I was asked not to be calling you away."

"Oh? Is that so? So who's the practical joker? I'll be sure to pay him back in triplicate."

Sweeney nods to the back of the bar. Vega turns to see a hunched figure in a ratty raincoat sitting in a booth, his back to Vega.

And then the figure twists around in his seat.

And then fear ripples through Vega's blood, and his lower lip begins to shake.

"Scrbacek."

"Hello, Cirilio," says J.D. Scrbacek, his normally booming voice soft and hoarse. "How's tricks?"

Cirilio Vega spins to stare at Sweeney behind the bar. Sweeney looks at him with a hard, level gaze. Vega downs the rest of his vodka in a quick snatch. When he turns back to face Scrbacek, the shake in his lower lip is gone, willed to still. On his face now is the unctuous feigned concern of a trial lawyer.

"Scrbacek, my God. How are you? We've been so worried about you. Let me get you something. Your normal scotch and soda? Anything."

"Club soda will be fine," says Scrbacek.

"No scotch? No nothing?"

"Not this morning, Cirilio."

Cirilio Vega turns and gestures for Sweeney to make up the club soda for Scrbacek and another double vodka for himself, and while he waits, he thinks desperately about what he should do.

He has the urge to run, but he fights it and holds his ground. Scrbacek doesn't intend to kill him, Vega figures, or he'd already be dead. And Scrbacek wouldn't try to start anything here, in the tavern, not with Sweeney and his shotgun behind the bar. No, Cirilio Vega figures he's not in danger from Scrbacek, so long, he's certain, as he doesn't try to make a call. So he'll act calm, make no urgent gestures, retain his normal cheerful manner. Scrbacek is there to talk, that is all, and so Vega will listen. He'll hear what Scrbacek has to say, learn what he knows, promise to help, and then, when Scrbacek leaves, then and only then, he'll let out his breath and take out his phone.

Cirilio Vega is smiling when he brings the vodka and the club soda to the booth. "Here," says Vega as he sits across from Scrbacek and slides the club soda toward him.

Scrbacek's face is misshapen with bruises, a filthy bandage spans the ridge of his nose, his five-o'clock shadow is well past midnight. Vega squints to get a look into his eyes and stiffens slightly at what he sees. There's something fearsome and keen about the man across the table from him, something dangerous. Whatever blows he has taken, Vega imagines Scrbacek has given worse. Vega tells himself to be careful before he says, "My God, J.D., what happened to you? You look like you've been caught in a washing machine."

"And then tumbled dry."

"Are you all right?"

"For the time being."

"We've been worried, so worried. Can I help? Do you need anything?"

"I could use some money," says Scrbacek flatly.

"Sure, J.D. Yes, of course." Vega digs out his wallet, pulls out a stack of bills, counts them quickly. "Two hundred? Two fifty?"

"As much as you can spare."

"Here, take it all. I can get more at the bank if you want to wait."

Scrbacek stuffs the money into his pocket and smiles. "No, I don't want to wait. This is enough, thanks."

"What are you going to do?"

"I'm going to get the hell out of here. I've been hiding, running, but they're getting closer."

"Who?"

"I don't know, Cirilio. For a few hours I was hiding out at Jenny's. Remember her? Jenny Ling."

"Yeah, sure. Nice girl."

"She speaks highly of you, too. She says you helped her out when we were going through our rough patch."

"I try to be helpful."

"And I can't tell you how much I appreciate it. Well, I went to our old place in the Marina District, tried to get just a few hours' rest, but somehow they found out and came for me there. At Jenny's house. With their guns. They killed her dog, our dog. They killed my dog, Cirilio. It's that bad. All I know is that I have to lose myself. You want to get lost, the best way is to hunker down on a bus heading nowhere. It can take a week to get to California by Greyhound if you go first through Austin and then through Jackson Hole. Now I have enough for the ticket." Scrbacek glances at the clock above the bar. "My ride leaves in an hour."

"This is crazy, J.D. You can't just run away. Go to the cops. Get yourself some real protection."

"We never trusted the cops before, so what makes you think we can trust them now? No, it's just you and me. That's why I asked Sweeney to set up this meeting on the sly. I knew you carried enough money for me to get out, and I wanted to give you a chance to come with me."

"What? Why would I want to come with you?"

"Because they're after you too, Cirilio."

"Me?"

"You."

"No. They're not. You're crazy. No one wants to kill me. What are you talking about, J.D.?" He blows air out of his mouth. "You're talking crazy."

"That's exactly what I said after they blew up Ethan Brummel. Surwin suggested they were trying to blow me up instead, and I used the exact same words. But, Cirilio, since then, as best I can count, there have been four more attempts on my life. They're getting closer each time. Next time they win, I lose, game over."

"Who's trying to kill you? Kill me? Why? None of this makes any sense."

Scrbacek leans toward Vega and lowers his voice. "They think I know something. When they burned down my building, they napalmed my files. There was something in my files they wanted to keep a secret, and I have no idea what it is. But it's something brutal enough for them to kill me simply because I might have seen it. And, Cirilio, they're going to kill you, too."

"You keep saying that. Why, J.D.? Why me?"

"Because you're Caleb's lawyer now."

"I was just trying to help you out. After you disappeared, Joey Torresdale called me to see if—"

"Somehow this thing I'm supposed to know involves Breest. You took over the case, so you're involved, too. Do you have any idea what it is they're trying to hide? Do you have any idea what was in my files?"

Scrbacek looks searchingly into the eyes of Cirilio Vega, and Vega knows better than to give in to his instincts and let his gaze fall away. You do that with a jury, let your gaze waver in the crucial moment of an argument, and all twelve know right away. What you do, instead, in the crux of the argument, is pin your eyes to the juror you know is most against you—the old man with the jowls and the American flag pinned to his lapel, or the woman with the pursed mouth and the hair done up church-tight—you keep your eyes right smack on that juror as you emphatically make the point until the doubts begin to dissolve under the shining light of your certainty. So that's what he does, Cirilio Vega, well-trained trial lawyer that he is, keeps his gaze bolted on Scrbacek's eyes as he says, "No, J.D. I don't. I have no idea."

Scrbacek's eyes narrow, as if in pain. "I'm sorry to hear that," he says. "I was counting on you for answers."

"I wish I had them. Believe me."

Scrbacek sticks out his jaw, nods, and takes a gulp from his club soda. "Do you remember Remi Bozant?"

"The cop in the clown suit?"

"The bastard I got kicked off the force and into jail."

"He left town, I heard, years ago."

"He's back, and he's the one leading the hunt for me. When I was running through the depths of Crapstown, I met someone who heard him shooting his mouth off in a bar. He said Scrbacek was only the first, some fat shit was second, a crooked judge was third, and then the Cuban lawyer. This is what he was supposed to have said, Cirilio. He's working for someone, I don't know who, but someone who wants to wipe out anyone who might know anything he needs to keep secret."

Cirilio Vega's dark feral face turns two shades paler. His tongue licks his mustache nervously. He takes a sip of his vodka and then another. "I don't know what to say. I don't know anything."

"It doesn't matter what you know, it only matters what they think you know." Scrbacek checks the clock once more, finishes what is in his glass, stands. "I have to go. I have to catch a bus. Thanks for the money. You've always been a friend, Cirilio. Remember what I said and take care of yourself."

"Wait, J.D. Wait. Where are you going? Where can I get in touch with you?"

"Santa Monica Pier, one week from today," says Scrbacek. "Good luck, Cirilio." And then he leaves, does J.D. Scrbacek, turns and walks out of the bar with only a quick nod toward Sweeney before closing the door behind him.

Cirilio Vega stares at Scrbacek's back as it disappears through the door before violently throwing the rest of his vodka down his throat, coughing as it tumbles its way into his stomach.

Did Scrbacek see the panic in his face? Probably, yes, but it was understandable, considering. How else should he have reacted to being told someone was trying to kill him? No, he did fine, played the part of the unknowing friend to perfection. It was Scrbacek whose behavior was strange, no anger or fear twisting his features. His whole being was suffused with serenity, a dangerous serenity, something slow and suppressed and ready to erupt. Vesuvius the day before.

For the first time in all the years he had known him, Cirilio Vega had been afraid of Scrbacek, as if he had underestimated him from the first. It's a good thing Scrbacek doesn't know about that night with Jenny, a very good thing. Vega wouldn't want to go head-to-head with that violently serene J.D. Scrbacek, and now, thankfully, with one call, he won't have to. He grabs his cell, flicks through his contacts, and darkens it before he can dial. He can't use his own phone, can't have the call on his records. He heads to the pay phone on the wall to make the call, lifts the receiver, hesitates.

What about Bozant? Vega doesn't put it past Bozant, that animal, to blab with pride over beers in some ragged Crapstown joint about who he was going to kill. First, Scrbacek. Then the fat slob Trent Fallow, for sure, the idiot who had given Scrbacek the file in the first place. Then the crooked judge, Dickerson. And then the Cuban lawyer, Vega. Why him? Because he's Cuban, which makes him expendable. It's always been that way; when things turn bad, turn on the Cuban. Was it all a lie, what Scrbacek had said? If it was, then Scrbacek had indeed read the file and put it all together and knew everything. But Scrbacek was clearly a man who knew nothing, desperate to figure it out but even more desperate to get out of town. No, the way Vega figured it, Scrbacek had never read the file, or had not put the disparate facts together. And if Scrbacek doesn't know, then Bozant must have said exactly what Scrbacek said he said. Bozant had a list, was checking it twice, and Vega was on it.

Jesus. This has turned worse than he ever could have imagined. Jesus, Jesus, Jesus. The telephone handset is still in his hand, and he bangs it against the wall. Dammit. And then, suddenly, he is seized by terror.

He looks around, first slowly, with a dawning awareness, and then desperately. Someone is there, he is certain, watching him, readying to off him right where he stands. Maybe aiming at him right now from the other side of the window, through the space made by that weirdly bent venetian blind. He doesn't want to die, and he especially doesn't want to die in this shabby place, amidst the numbers scrawled beside the pay phone, the stains on the walls rubbed there by pathetic slatterns giving up an end-of-the-night screw, the uneven browned ceiling tiles loosed helter-skelter from their places in the grid. Not here, not here, not now.

Bit by bit he gains a grip on his calm. No one is here. The venetian blind has always been bent that way. He is safe for the moment, reassured finally by the broad hunched figure of Sweeney still behind the bar. He is safe here, but he has to do something, and fast, and he knows exactly what it is he needs to do. He isn't some tragic refugee right off the raft, wading onto a Florida beach. He is Cirilio Vega, the Cuban fire-eater on the rise, a man not to be trifled with. A man who has already taken the necessary precautions. He'll have a busy morning, for sure, but he'll pull himself out of this mess. First, he'll make the call, take care of Scrbacek once and for all. Then he'll have another double vodka to fire up his courage. Then he'll pay a visit of his own, right away—go straight to the man and make sure that bastard understands the price they all will pay if something untoward comes to pass.

He turns to the phone, punches in the numbers, waits for the ringing to stop.

"Let me talk to Dirk."

39
MAI TAI

Scrbacek peered over the lip of the wall surrounding the flat roof of the building across the street from Sweeney's. He watched as Cirilio Vega, that bastard, slipped out of the front of the tavern and looked first right, then left, like a little thief, before heading away from his office, away from the courthouse, heading toward, Scrbacek was certain, a confrontation with the man behind everything, the man pulling the strings.

The magician.

Scrbacek had scared him, he could tell, forcing a doubt into those arrogant lying eyes. And now Vega, that bastard, would take that doubt to the person who was giving him his orders. Who was it? Breest? Galloway? Torresdale? The great James E. Diamond himself? Scrbacek slipped across the roof to the corner to get a better view of Vega, that bastard, making his way down the sidewalk.

As Scrbacek watched, a dark presence alighted beside him.

"Did you catch it?" he said without looking around.

"He called Dirk's," said the Nightingale. "The view was clear as day through the venetian blind you bent."

"That bastard. I need to find out where he's going, but I can't be seen on the street. Can you tail him?"

"Sure." She slipped off her rifle and laid it by the side of the roof. "Keep your eye on baby."

She skipped across the roof, jumped the gap to the roof next door, and kept moving. Scrbacek watched as she moved, lithe and quick, like a cheetah on the prowl. When she finally disappeared, he was left alone, on the roof, with her gun and his emotions.

Cirilio Vega had sold him out, that bastard, had sold him to those who would build a trench through the heart of Crapstown. First, Vega had fucked Jenny, of that he now was certain, and then he had fucked Scrbacek. Scrbacek would be having a postcoital cigarette if his lungs could bear it. He had seen it all in Vega's eyes when Scrbacek asked him if he knew what was in the file. Vega knew, that bastard, and the fear in Vega's eyes was the fear that maybe they wouldn't get to Scrbacek in time.

He took Jenny's phone from his raincoat pocket, powered it up, and made a call.

"I'm surprised you're still alive," said Surwin.

"I'm surprised myself. You sound beat."

"Late night."

"Want to have some fun?"

"Always."

"Show up at the bus terminal in about half an hour. They're going to come in full force to find me. There's a bus leaving for Austin that they think I'll be on."

"And how'd they get that idea?"

"A rat in a double-breasted suit whispered the word in Dirty Dirk's ear."

"You want to come in? I could have a squad anywhere in the city in fifteen minutes to give you full protection. You ready?"

"Not yet. I'm getting closer."

"To what, Scrbacek? To you finding an answer or to us finding your corpse?"

Scrbacek didn't respond. Instead he pressed the "End Call" button and kept it pressed hard, as if he were choking the damn thing until the good-bye screen died. Scrbacek was scared, no doubt about it, but he felt the fear giving way to something else, something dark and sharp and vicious. It took a moment for him to recognize it.

Anger. Ruthless and predatory and breathtakingly familiar.

It had been in him from the start, from the moment someone blew up Ethan Brummel. It had been superseded by fear and then confusion and then the raw purpose of survival, but now it burst from its hiding place and spread its wings like a huge hideous raven. Its great black shadow covered at first only Cirilio Vega, that bastard, but then spread to everyone who was behind what had happened to him, and then spread even farther, to anyone who had stood by untouched as it all rocked out of control, until it encompassed the whole of humanity. The muscles in Scrbacek's jaw tensed, his fists balled, blood reddened his sight. He called out in frustration, and the sound from his throat was like a great angry caw. He flailed his arms about and slapped his fist into the barrel of the Nightingale's Kalashnikov.

He picked it up and felt its heft, its brilliant sense of direction. He snapped the gun into firing position just over the edge of the roof. He could stay atop here and pick them off, one after the other, keep firing until he shot a hole in the center of the universe. He could feel the anger drag him up to the bell tower of the University of Texas, or through the halls of Columbine, gripping his shoulders in its claws as it swept him away from his life. His life.

He turned onto his back and tossed the gun away, the stock skittering loudly on the roof.

His life. It was gone, torn apart as surely as his cherished Ford Explorer, and the building he owned, and the law practice that had defined him now for too many years. His life was like Crapstown—abandoned, lost, left to rot and ruin. And who could he go to for help? Donnie and Elisha Baltimore? Blixen and the Nightingale? Nomad Aboud? That a bunch of Crapstown freaks were all that he could rely on anymore seemed unbelievably sad to him. A rush of loneliness rose to choke his throat. He wiped at something wet running down his cheeks and was embarrassed at his weakness. He moved across the roof, picked up the Nightingale's gun, and squeezed it tight to his chest as he swallowed down the tears.

Scrbacek was a hard guy. Scrbacek could take whatever the hell they dished out. He had built his practice from nothing, had faced down the toughest prosecutors the state could throw at him, had whipped Thomas Sour-Wine in the biggest case of his career. Scrbacek could lick what ailed him, just like he licked his little addiction, all by his lonesome, cold turkey. He had taken off in the middle of winter for some seaside place where he could drink himself silly out of coconut halves, screw divorcées, and let the poison drip out of his system. That was his twelve-step program, three piña coladas, four mai tais, a double hurricane, a pack of Marlboros, a night with Val from Toledo, a night with Glynna from Santa Fe, a night with Charlotte from Savannah, who wasn't technically divorced but had a husband who didn't understand her. Scrbacek wasn't the kind of guy to cry about his loneliness. They could blow up his car, burn down his home, send their hit squads through the city hunting for him, and still here he was, ready and willing and able to bring the fight to them. He was so tough he thought about himself in the third person. Scrbacek was a hard guy.

He wiped again at his face, suppressing a sob.

Suddenly the sun burst over the edge of the taller roof to the east, shooting flares into his eyes, forcing a squint. It felt good, the sun. He had been running for so long now. How many nights? Three, heading into his fourth. And in all that time, this was the first he had seen of the sun. And before he was on the run he had been on trial, working nights and mornings, glimpsing the sky only as he grabbed a quick lunch from a vendor before rushing back to the courtroom to prepare for the afternoon session. The kiss of the sun on his face felt lovely and loving. Maybe that was what was wrong with him, maybe all he had was a seasonal affective disorder, maybe all he needed was a tan. He stood on his knees, took off his coat, balled it up, put it on the black tar of the roof, laid his head upon it. When had last he slept? At Jenny's, yesterday. In her bed. With her scent.

The sun lapped at his face, and he fell asleep hard, as if he were dropped from a great height into the flat black earth east of Eden in the Land of Nod.

The story he dreamed had the sort of deep strangeness characteristic of dreams, with switches of setting and plot that had no internal coherence. But there was running in it, and a gun that wouldn't go off, and a woman with long dark hair, and a boy who watched him and followed him and tugged at his shirt. Tugged at his shirt. And in the dream there was something drifting between the three of them, around Scrbacek and the woman and the boy, a purple haze floating through all the shifts of place and incident.

When he did wake, finally, when the Nightingale pulled at his shirt and woke him and told him the exact room in Casinoland where Cirilio Vega had run off to, Scrbacek would forget all the settings of his dream, all the incidents, he would forget even the woman and the boy, forget everything except that which had swirled around him. It was like smoke, this swirling thing. It rose and fell with the ebbs and flows of the ocean. It snaked its way into his throat and down until it pierced his heart. And it stayed with him after he awoke, and it followed him through the rest of that day and the night to come, a night full of discovery and terror and violence, a night that would change a thousand lives and end more than a few of them.

And this is what he felt from the swirling thing in his dream, each component keen as the blade of a freshly whetted knife: he felt regret, desperation, confusion, need, fear, desire, hope. It was a potent cocktail, though he couldn't recognize the combination, because he had never felt it before. He didn't know where it came from, and thought, maybe, the flutter in his stomach was merely adrenaline pumping through his veins. But he was wrong. It was the purple haze he had felt in his dream. Regret, desperation, confusion, need, fear, desire, hope. Take dark rum, curaçao, lime juice, sugar, a splash of grenadine, shake it with ice, serve it with a lime wheel, and what you get is a mai tai. Take regret, desperation, confusion, need, a splash of fear, shake it with desire, serve it with hope, and what you get, pure and simple, is love.

And from where the hell in a place like Crapstown did ever he find that?

FOURTH NIGHT

40
DOLORES ROSAS

Dolores Rosas, the former Dolores Jepsen, the former Dolores Delossantos, though only for six months before that louse slinked out and knocked up her best friend Jeannie, the former Dolores Macklin of West Orange High School in West Orange, New Jersey—*Field Hockey 9; Best Buddies 9, 10; Library Aide 10; Affiliation Club 10, 11; Italian Club, 11; Joseph Delossantos 11, 12*—Dolores Rosas waits beneath a flashing sign with an arrow pointing straight down at her head.

PARK HERE. PARK HERE. PARK HERE.

She holds a brown paper bag to her chest and taps a shoe nervously upon the cement as she waits. The doubts about what she is doing whisper madly in her ear. She tries to banish the voices but fails.

PARK HERE. PARK HERE.

If the tragic patterns of her adult life could be distilled into one moment, it would be this: standing outside a run-down pile of cement, holding a brown paper bag filled with false hope, ignoring the doubts as she waits for a man to ask too much of her while he brings nothing but trouble.

PARK HERE.

By the time Dolores had finished her shift at the casino and reached J.D. Scrbacek's office apartment three nights before, the fire trucks were already there, the ambulance and police, a small crowd of gawkers that had seen the flames or heard the news on their police scanners. She had rushed under the yellow tape, past a police officer, to a firefighter with the clean shape of a mask on his otherwise filthy face, and asked if anyone had come out of the building.

The firefighter shook his head.

"There was someone inside. J.D. Scrbacek. The lawyer. He was inside, waiting for me."

"I'm sorry, ma'am. We didn't find no one. Let's hope he left before it started. Why don't you talk to Captain Beckman over there and tell him what you know. He's the one writing up the report."

But she didn't talk to Captain Beckman over there, sensed somehow that it wouldn't be wise to officially connect her name to Scrbacek's. Instead, she took a last lingering look at the fire, clutched her arms around her chest, and walked slowly back to the casino, where she caught a bus to the employee parking lot, climbed into her wreck of a car, and drove back to her small apartment to confront another night of nothing. The papers all said J.D. was missing, and she knew what that meant. It meant that her last hope for something different than her past was missing, too, and, like J.D. Scrbacek, presumed dead.

She was aware how sad a case she was, resting any hopes on the likes of J.D. Scrbacek, whose deadened eyes seemed to fire only as they scanned the exaggerated curves of her body. There was something curiously empty about him, as if nothing inside was firm enough to hold an imprint. The moment she left his bed at dawn, dipped down to slip on her heels, quietly climbed down the circular stairway and out of his building, that moment any impression of her similarly slipped out of his life. And, in fairness to J.D., he never pretended it was anything more. He didn't ask about her day. He didn't ask about her daughter. He would see her and pounce, and after, amidst the tossed sweat-sodden sheets, when she tried to raise their talk to something more than ordinary chitchat, she found his concentration faltering as he slipped into sleep. He longed only for her body, she knew, not her immortal soul.

But could she ever expect anything different? Who knew better than Dolores that there was nothing the least bit extraordinary about her immortal soul? And to have a body men longed for, wasn't that, after all, why she had suffered all the operations?

She was married to Sammy at the time. "What about looking like that?" he'd say, holding up the foldout of one of his magazines. "I know a guy who owes me a favor." Or he'd say, "You know, your thighs, they're getting a little chunky. I heard it don't even hardly hurt." Or he'd say, "And tell the doc with what I'm paying for them injections, he ought not to be scrimping on the collagen." She hadn't wanted the operations, had been scared of the knife and of that little vile vacuum, but when Sammy Rosas asked, she had silenced the doubts that were whispering like a chorus of madwomen in her ear and said yes. Anything to keep him happy and home, even as she knew he was cheating all the time, even as she knew he was soon to be out the door.

When she had looked at herself in the mirror after the surgeries, she wasn't sure who was looking back. Is that you, Dolores Macklin, or is that someone else, some Sammy Rosas sex-fantasy blow-up doll come to life? She should have listened to the mad whispering doubts that were not so mad after all, but what could she have done then? Reduce the tits? Enlarge the nose? Thin the lips? Thicken the thighs? And, of course, it had its uses, this new and improved thing that stared back at her from the mirror. Every night she served her drinks to gray-haired men with too much money. They would notice the improvements, and it might spark something, anything. Everyone could use a little insurance.

And then along came J.D. Scrbacek.

At first, it suited her fine that he was only after her new body, because, to be frank, after Sammy Rosas, with his bad knees and forty-five-inch waist and soft dick, it was nice to be with someone younger, harder, who didn't make her do all the work. But then she began thinking of J.D. at off moments, looking for him her entire shift on the floor, feeling disappointed the nights he didn't show, which was most nights. The gray-haired men still made their passes while their wives were off at the slots, but she wasn't interested anymore. She had a man on her mind.

When she was with J.D. Scrbacek, somehow she felt full of possibilities. It wasn't money she was after—the gray-haired men had enough if that was all she wanted. And it wasn't to snare herself a lawyer husband and to thereby rise, somehow, into a higher level of status—because, honey, after all she'd been through, she could care less about either status or a husband. No, it was something far richer than riches: the hope that a relationship with a man could be other than domination and casual cruelty, punctuated by bad sex. And somehow, in J.D. Scrbacek, she had seen that possibility.

He was gentle, except in bed, which suited her fine. And he didn't carry the same controlling arrogance of her other men, even Bert Jepsen, Charlene's father, who had seemed so nice and steady after the disaster of Joey Delossantos, but who had turned out to be the most viciously controlling of them all. Somewhere beneath the hardness he feigned, Dolores could see in J.D. Scrbacek the necessary kindness of a nurturer. He'd be a good daddy, J.D. would, someday, and maybe that was what she was looking for—someone to support her emotionally even as he threw her ankles over his shoulders and kept her bouncing deep into the night. Someone who would allow the Dolores Macklin of West Orange

High to step out of the false shell that had been constructed around her and maybe make something new of her life. That was the possibility she felt when she was with J.D. Scrbacek, a last chance, burned all to hell in the fire.

Until he called, just this afternoon. J.D. Scrbacek had called and asked her to meet him here with the stuff in the bag. The whispering doubts told her it could only mean disaster, and yet how could she refuse? She had a man on her mind, and, as history had proven, when the former Dolores Macklin had a man on her mind, she was lost.

PARK HERE.

She is waiting, beneath the flashing sign, wondering if he will really show, and then there he is, turning the corner and walking down the sidewalk toward her, a ragged figure, body hunched, face tilted down, hands jammed in jean pockets, torn and ratty raincoat trailing behind.

She drops the bag, runs up to him, says in a rush of words, "J.D., J.D., my God, it's so good to see you, J.D.," tries to throw her arms around his neck, but he dodges away and moves on past.

"Follow me" is all he says, without lifting his face, before he turns beneath the neon arrow and disappears into the garage.

She is stunned for a moment, dumbfounded, and then she does what J.D. had scrupulously not done, she twists her head from side to side to be sure no one is watching. When she turns her attention back to the garage's entrance, it is empty, as if J.D. had been merely a mirage. But he hadn't been a mirage. She walks back to the bag, stoops to pick it up, enters the cement structure beneath the neon arrow. Beyond the ticket machines she sees the door of the stairwell slowly shut.

He is waiting for her inside the doorway, smiling. "Hello, Dolores."

"J.D.?" It is clearly J.D. Scrbacek staring at her from the stairs, one foot higher than the other, but there is something different, too. He is unshaven, his hair is greasy and mussed, his cheeks are red from sun and dark in patches from bruising, there is a dirty bandage over his nose. She has never seen him so unkempt, but that is not what is different. It is something in his eyes. They hold a purposefulness she has never noticed in him before. He doesn't let his gaze perform his typical rove over her body, despite the time she spent before the meeting opening the top of her jacket to reveal her revealing work halter. Instead he looks into her eyes, as if, for the first time, he is actually looking at her, not at what the surgeons have done to her.

"Did you bring what I needed?"

"Yes. I did, yes. The razor I already had, and I went to the mall at the LondonTown Pier for the other stuff, but I had a devil of a time finding someone who would let me—"

"Good," he says, cutting her off and beginning to climb the stairs. "There's a bathroom up here on the fourth floor. We can get ready there."

"J.D.? What's happening here? Tell me what's going on. I need to know what you are getting me—"

He turns around and puts his fingers to his lips, and she quiets. "Fourth floor," he says softly.

When she reaches the bathroom door, he pulls her inside, closes the door behind her. The room is cramped and desolate, thick with stink, the toilet stuffed with gobs of toilet paper, a bare roll of brown paper standing on the edge of the filthy sink. She cringes from the smell and holds her arms tight to her body, making herself as small as possible in that fetid space. He takes the bag from her and rummages inside.

"Let's see what goodies you brought." He pulls out the pair of reading glasses she picked up for him at the bookstore in the mall. The rims of the glasses are dark, the lenses thick. A large tag still hangs down from the bridge.

He puts the glasses on and blinks wildly. "I can't see a thing."

"You said as powerful as they make."

"So I did. How do I look?"

"Like a nearsighted computer geek who still lives with his mother."

"Perfect."

"What's going on, J.D.?"

"I'm getting ready for Halloween."

"Take off the damn glasses and talk to me."

He slips the glasses off his nose, carefully folds them, and returns them to the bag. "I'm in serious trouble, Dolores, and the man responsible is in room 2402 of Diamond's Mount Olympus. I have to get inside that room, find out who is behind what's happened to me, and figure out a way to turn the tide. The problem is, I'm being hunted like a cougar, so I can't just stroll in on my own. I need your help."

"How serious are they about finding you?"

"Serious as a bullet in the head."

"And so naturally, you thought of me."

"I finally realized that in the whole of Casinoland, you're the only one I can trust."

She tilts her head at that and can't suppress the smile. It's the nicest thing he's ever said to her. For a moment a rush of emotion silences the whispering, and she takes a hesitant step forward, another, and then wraps her arms around his neck.

"Oh, J.D. I was so worried. When I saw the fire. And then you came up missing. And there was talk of you being a murderer, which I knew was a lie. And I thought I'd never see you again. J.D." The tears come. She wipes her nose on his filthy jacket, hugs him tighter. "If anything happened to you, J.D., I don't know what I'd do. I missed you so much, I was so worried, I . . . I . . . ."

She stops speaking when she realizes that he is not hugging back. By now, the old J.D., the two of them alone in a sordid little room like this, would already have his teeth in her neck as he dry humped her against the door. But this J.D. is doing nothing. She lets go of him, takes a step back, and wipes her face, smearing mascara on the back of her hand.

He is staring at her, right into her eyes, like before. "Stop it," she says. "Stop looking at me."

"You normally like it when I look at you."

"Not like that, like you're looking into me or something."

"It's just you're a very sweet woman, Dolores, and I feel bad about how it has been between us."

She wipes beneath her eye with a thumb. "And how has it been between us?"

"I don't know. You know."

"Tell me, J.D. Tell me what you feel bad about. No, forget it. Please don't. Just tell me how it's going to be after all this crap is over. Tell me that."

"Not like it was."

"Does that mean better, J.D.? Are you going to take me out to dinner some night, maybe a show? Are you going to take Charlene and me to an amusement park come Sunday? Are you going to maybe stay awake until I show up one night? Tell me how it's going to be."

"While on the run, I . . . I . . ."

"Go ahead, spit it out."

"I saw an old girlfriend."

"Oh . . . my . . . God."

"What?"

"He's going to give me the old-girlfriend speech. Please, dear God, anything but that."

"And I think I have a son."

"A son. And he thinks he has a goddamn son." She stops her performance, wipes her nose with her palm, looks up to J.D. "A son?"

"I think."

"You're not certain?"

"I don't know. All I know is that I saw her and the boy, and I started feeling things I haven't felt in a while, or ever."

"And so you and this old girlfriend, you just hit it right off again? The two of you are smack back into the swing of things?"

"She hates me. She told me to stay the hell out of her life."

Dolores wipes at her nose again and looks down at the black smear on her hand. "I'm a mess."

"No, you're not."

"Is she pretty, this old girlfriend?"

"Yes, but not like you."

"So let me get this straight. You roped me into getting you all this stuff, endangered my life and my job, brought me to this shithole, all just to break up with me?"

"I need your help, but I wanted you to know."

"Next time, use the phone." She spins around and opens the door. "I need some air." The door slams shut behind her.

At first, she is bent with disappointment, overwhelmed with frustration, crying and banging her fist on the cement walls outside the bathroom. But the former Dolores Macklin, while quick to lose her head over a man, is also quick to recover after it all goes bad, has always been tougher than anyone had ever credited her for, has grown even tougher doing the single-mom bit. And so by the time J.D. Scrbacek comes out of the bathroom, bag in hand, she is able to stare at him for a long moment, her arms crossed and eyes dry, before breaking into laughter.

"You should see yourself," she says.

"I told you, I can't see a thing with these glasses."

"Well, that's too bad, J.D., because you are quite a sight."

He has shaved off his beard into a goatee, enhanced by the hair-in-a-can she found that he has carefully sprayed atop it. With the fake teeth she bought, he looks like a bad Jerry Lewis movie. And then, of course, he wears the dealer's outfit she scrounged for him, the crucial thing that was so difficult for her to find. The shirt and pants are so big they blossom out of the fancy vest he wears. With his glasses and his hair hacked short and blackened he appears so hapless that the sight of him eases whatever pain she is feeling at being unceremoniously dumped just a few moments before.

"You look like the most pathetic dealer on the boardwalk," she says.

"But do I look like me?"

"No," she says with utter honesty. "You don't." She steps forward and taps the name tag fastened to his vest. "But then again, you don't look like Lee either."

He reads the name off the tag. "Lee Chon Yang?"

"He played football in high school," she says. "Here, let me."

She takes the safety pins from the bag, puts them in her teeth, removes his vest, and works, pin by pin, to cinch up the pants and corset the back of his shirt. When he puts the vest back on she walks around him, checking her work. "Not bad," she says. "Just don't breathe too deeply or it will all go kablooey."

"All right, picture time." He hands her the purple Polaroid camera she picked up in the mall. "Here, this wall should do."

He stands in front of a light cement wall, glasses on, as she aims the camera at him. Flash. With a hum, the undeveloped photograph shoots out. They wait a moment as the picture develops, then compare it to Lee Chon Yang's photo on his ID tag.

"Too big," he says. "You have to get farther away."

Two more attempts—flash flash—and they have a photograph the exact right size, which they cut out and place over Lee's photograph on his Casino Control Commission tag, before slipping the tag back into its plastic case and clipping it to his vest.

"Now you at least match the photograph," she says, "if not the name."

"It will have to do. Anyone looks close enough, they'll see through it anyway. How do I get in? Through the front door?"

"There's a back entrance for employees," she says. "We'll wait for a bus from the parking lot to arrive and then slip in with the others. They won't even check."

"Sounds like a plan. And once you get me inside, I have another favor."

"Don't. Don't even."

"Just one more thing."

***

Dolores hates this.

It isn't bad enough that she sneaked Scrbacek into the casino, the place where she has worked steadily for five years and made what she's needed to support herself and her daughter. It isn't bad enough that she now has a seriously wanted man stashed in a storage closet beside the boiler room in the casino's basement. It isn't bad enough that she has done all this for a man who no longer wants her because of some old girlfriend and a boy who may or may not be his son. Now she has to do this one thing more, and the whispering doubts chatter monstrously, and she hates it.

Even as she walks to the front desk, she wonders why she is sticking her neck out so far for a now-ex-boyfriend, why she is willing to endanger and humiliate herself simply because he asked her. Isn't it just another piece of deference toward another abusive man? Sure, Joe, I'll have the abortion. No, Marty, my poor baby, I know you didn't meant it, and it will heal, and yes I still love you. Sure, Sammy, I'd like my boobs to be bigger too, and you're right, I hear they hardly ever leak anymore.

And now: Sure, J.D., I'll risk everything and make myself out to be a whore to my friend if that's what you need, you asshole.

Each time before, she ignored her doubts and lived to regret it. She wants to listen this time, to turn around and tell Scrbacek no, no, she is done tying herself in knots to please another faithless man, no. But she keeps moving forward. He's in trouble, he needs help, he has come to her. There is some weakness in her character that compels her to ignore her doubts, to do everything she can for the man in her life. She hates this, what she is about to do, but she feels helpless to stop it.

Stacey is at the desk, former cocktail waitress, current clerk trainee, typing something into the computer, wearing her white shirt and blazer, her long nails clicking on the plastic keyboard keys, the tight rolls of hair beaded and piled high. It is slow at the front desk, and the three couples checking into the hotel are already being helped by others. Stacey smiles when she lifts her head and sees Dolores.

"Look at you," says Dolores.

Stacey can't stop herself from beaming.

"Moving up in the world like a rocket ship," says Dolores.

"It's not so grand as it seems," says Stacey. "And I sure miss those tips."

"I bet you miss the hands on your butt as you sashay by with a full tray, too."

"Those you can keep. How's the floor?"

"Lonely without you."

"Give Pederson my regards."

"The old dog." Pause. "Stace. I need a favor, Stace."

Stacey looks at Dolores for a moment before turning to a man working beside her, motioning that she'll be a minute, and then taking Dolores around the desk and into a back room where they can be alone. Stacey closes the door behind them and leans against it.

"What you got?" says Stacey.

"Something stupid."

"Go ahead."

"Really stupid."

Stacey just waits.

"I was at a party in one of the rooms last night," says Dolores. "Just a quick invite that I accepted. It turned pretty . . . well, whatever. I somehow left my rings and a bracelet in there, beside one of the beds. It was stupid, and it ended badly, and I don't want to go back, but it was my rings."

"What room?" asks Stacey.

"Twenty-four-oh-two. I was just up there with Tamara's elevator pass and knocked on the door, but there was like no answer. I waited for a while, really, and nothing. If I could just get into the room and get my rings and get out, it would be so great. I am so stupid, but it's my rings, Stacey."

"The Sammy diamond?"

"Uh-huh. It's about all that asshole left me with after the divorce. And if Pederson ever found out, he'd . . ."

"You know what you are, Dolores? You're a crazy lady. What are you doing up there in the first place?"

"I don't know. Some gray-hair with too much money said there was a party. Charlene was with her father. I was bored. It was something to do."

"And you were probably too polite to blow the guy off. You know your problem, Dolores? You don't know how to say no. Repeat after me. No."

"No," says Dolores softly.

"Say it again, girl."

"No."

"Say it loud."

"NO."

"Say it proud."

"NO, YOU ASSHOLE, NO."

"There you go. Now you got it. I'm sorry, but our time's up. We'll begin again next week. Twenty-four-oh-two?" Stacey winks and pushes herself off the door. "Let me program a key card. Be back in a jiff."

While Stacey is gone, Dolores winces at what she has just done—told a lie that could cost a good friend her fancy new job. Why is the equation so instinctual? Ignore the doubts, help the man, screw the woman. Why is this pattern so ingrained, even when the woman getting screwed is herself?

Generally, she can't see it so clearly. Generally, there is some desperation that compels her to comply with what is asked of her. I want the man to still love me, and so I'll do whatever he says because that will make him still love me. I want the man to stay because I don't want to be alone. I want . . . I need . . . I'm afraid . . . But here, now, Scrbacek has already exploded those excuses. Scrbacek needs the help—truly, she can tell—but he isn't playing on her emotions to get it. He's not promising anything, or threatening anything, or twanging her false hopes. And somehow, because of his honesty, she finds herself somehow freed to make an actual decision.

There is J.D. on the one side, in deep, deep trouble, desperate for her help. And there is Stacey on the other side, trying to help a friend and hoping not to get screwed in the process. Dolores is confused, unable to balance the two, overwhelmed with the sound of the doubts she is fighting to ignore. And then, with a sudden start, she realizes she doesn't have to.

When Stacey comes back into the room, looking nervously behind her, she has a key card in her hand. "Got it," she says.

"Are you allowed to do this?" asks Dolores.

"Not really," says Stacey.

"And if they find out?"

"Back to the floor for me, if I'm lucky. But you're a friend, Dolores. I trust you."

Dolores steps over to her and gives her a hug. "Thank you, Stacey. Thank you so much," she says before she leaves.

"Hey, girlfriend," says Stacey, waving the key card. "You forgot this."

"It's not worth it," says Dolores, her chest swelling with a strange elation. "I'll find some other way."

41
ROOM 2402

Room 2402.

From the crack of a stairwell door, Scrbacek could see the entrance to the room. The twenty-fourth floor was not your usual stack-them-into-the-casino-like-Japanese-salarymen type of floor. When Scrbacek had first stepped out of the elevator, he had walked the corridor, back and forth. As best he could tell, there were only seven numbered rooms on a floor that would usually have forty, and the room he was looking at, 2402, was the grandest, at least by size. It must be some hell of a room, 2402, the Bridal Suite, or the Syndicate Suite, or maybe, in keeping with the city's presidential motif, the Nixon Suite. It was a room for oil-mad sheiks, for tycoons from Macau, for Panamanian middlemen.

A room fit for a magician.

Scrbacek eyed the door from within the stairwell and tried to figure out how to get inside. He could knock, of course—that was always the polite way—but polite didn't cut it when you were on the run and the bastard inside was leading the effort to kill you. *Excuse me, could I have a word? No? Oh, in that case, sorry to bother you. Enjoy the rest of your hunt.*

He stared at the door and felt helpless. He had thought he would have the key. Why was he up there if he didn't have the key? If he had the key, he could just slip in, hide here or there, reconnoiter. The whole plan had depended on Dolores getting him the key.

She had hesitated when he asked, stepped from one foot to the other and back again, tensed her face in frustration. She hadn't wanted to get him the key in the worst way, but he had been certain in the end that she would. Dolores was one of those people who could be moved easily enough with the right kind of pressure. He didn't know what it would cost her to get him the key, hadn't really cared. He was fighting for his life here, dammit. Dolores would simply have to take some risks, that was all there was to it. And he had been dead certain that in the end she would do as he bid, until she came back to the storage closet, where he had been sitting in the dark upon a great tub of cleaning fluid, leaning against a phalanx of mops, his foot resting on a rolling bucket with a wringer attached, came back to tell him that getting the key was out of the question.

"But, Dolores, it's life or death."

"Whose?"

"Mine."

"Then, no."

"No? What do you mean, no?"

"I'm sorry, but no." She stopped. "Actually, I'm not sorry. I'm not sorry at all. And it feels pretty damn good to say no. No."

"Dolores?"

"No." She exaggerated the roundness of her pronunciation. "No."

"What's going on, Dolores?"

"I won't get you the key card. It's too risky for a friend of mine. You'll have to get in the room on your own."

"How am I going to do something like—?"

Dolores put up a hand. "You'll figure it out. But the twenty-fourth floor requires special access. I've arranged to get you up there. That, at least, won't cost anyone her job. Let's go."

She walked quickly down the basement corridor, and he stared at her for a moment before struggling to catch up. They caught the elevator from the basement. The buttons only went up to twenty. After that, you had to access the floors with a key card. Dolores pushed the buttons for the fifteenth and nineteenth floors and then stepped back. "There's a camera on," she said quietly, without turning to him.

At the casino level the doors opened upon the glittery chop-chop-slash of coin and bell. Two old ladies stepped on with them before the doors closed again. They rode with Scrbacek and Dolores, laughing to each other about some cousin named Treat, who was drunk as a snake and losing his shirt at craps, until they stepped off at twelve. On the fifteenth floor, as soon as the door opened, Dolores stuck her head out for a moment. Quickly, a maid pulled her cart into the elevator.

"I'm sorry," said the maid, tall and pretty, with the name Tamara on her tag, "but the service elevator is busy and I needed to get up one flight." She pushed the button for the sixteenth floor and then, almost too quickly to catch, slid a card in and out of the slot for the twenty-fourth floor. At the sixteenth she backed out with her cart and smiled at Scrbacek.

When the door closed, Dolores, without looking at him, slipped a key card into his palm. "This will get you back to the basement. Good luck up there. I appreciate your honesty this afternoon, and I really hope everything turns out for you. Good-bye."

The elevator slowed, the light stopped at nineteen, the doors opened.

"Oh, and J.D. One favor, please?"

"Sure," said Scrbacek.

She stepped out onto the nineteenth floor and turned around to look him square in the face. "Here on in," she said just before the doors closed in his face, "stay the hell out of my life, too."

All of which left him alone and keyless on the twenty-fourth floor. He stood now in the stairwell, staring out from the crack of the barely opened stairwell door, waiting. Waiting for what? Who the hell knew?

If Scrbacek's guess was right, inside that room was the Contessa's magician, who had orchestrated the campaign to destroy J.D. Scrbacek. Which was why Scrbacek was desperate to know who the hell was behind that door. Once he found out, he could begin to plot his next couple of moves. All he needed was a glimpse. But there was another reason, too, for getting himself into room 2402. His past, his present, his future. He had revisited the lost opportunities of his past with Jenny Ling; he had seen the desolation of his present with Thomas Surwin, and now he couldn't shake the strange suspicion that the person inside that room was the designated spirit to show to Scrbacek the shade of his future.

The elevator opened. Slowly something moved closer—surface metal groaning, wheels squeaking—moved closer and closer until it came within the narrow ambit of Scrbacek's sight.

A room service cart. The obligatory room service cart.

In the back of his mind, Scrbacek had known it would arrive. The room service cart always arrives at the Nixon Suite. The crisp white linen, the bud vase with a bright-red flower, the food staying fresh under two gleaming silver domes, the twin bottles of champagne on ice. The room service guy knocked and, when there was no immediate answer, knocked again. The room service guy always knocks twice.

The door was pulled open by a beautiful young woman with a weary smile, clutching a toweled robe at her throat, strands of dark-blonde hair falling wetly on the white terrycloth. From the bottom of the robe, the bright pink of her toenails glittered on the carpet like tiny jewels.

"That's fine," said the woman as the man and the cart brushed by her. "Leave that here. The old cart's in the back. You can take it down now."

The door began to drift closed.

"That was quick," said the room service guy.

"We were thirsty," she said as she snatched one of the bottles out of the bucket with a swift rustle of ice and led the room service guy away to another room.

As the closing door picked up speed, Scrbacek stopped its progress with his shoe, gently pressed it open, and slipped inside.

42
SWEET SUITE

Scrbacek stood alone in the entrance of a suite furnished in astonishingly bad taste. The foyer held a painting that looked to be done on a spinning table at a kid's fair, and a gold table on which stood a plaster sculpture of a naked woman, legs spread, as if modeled straight from the pages of *Hustler*. A few steps beyond the food cart was a massive living room with a wall of windows overlooking the ocean, which was catching the last bits of the late-afternoon sun. A huge flat-screen faced a large wraparound leather couch, a wet bar with high stools, and a great black sculpture of a horse rearing on its hind legs, its prick oversize even for a horse. In the distance he could hear soft music, laughter.

The sound froze Scrbacek for a moment before he scrambled around the cart and dived behind the living room's leather couch. He could hear them coming toward him now, the man pushing the other cart, the woman in her bare feet walking beside him.

"Looks like you're having fun back there," said the man.

"He's having fun," she said, her voice tired.

The door opened, the cart wheeled out, the door closed again. Scrbacek could hear the woman rustle her way to the cart, lift one of the lids, then another, snatch a piece of something between her teeth. She let out a weary sigh, something slumped to the floor, and her bare feet brushed the carpet as she made her way back toward the music.

Scrbacek waited a moment and then a moment more before slowly raising his head above the edge of the couch. The living room was empty of all but its gaudy furniture. On the cart, a silver dome had been moved to the side, revealing a bounteous plate of cocktail shrimp. On the floor, in a heap, was the woman's terrycloth robe.

He made a quick reconnaissance. There was a kitchen, a small dining room, and two bedrooms branching off to the left, all empty. To the right was a hallway that led toward the music and the voices.

Before heading any farther, Scrbacek approached the cart to see if there was any bill or receipt that would give him a name. As he looked around, he absently took a shrimp, dipped it in the sauce, bit it off at the shell. He immediately spit his fake teeth into his palm and gagged at the sensation of biting with the plastic in his mouth. Then he finished the shrimp. It was firm and cool, tangy with iodine, the sauce saucy-hot.

When he found no slip on the cart, he stooped down to see if one had fallen to the floor. Nothing. He scarfed two more shrimp. Really, he thought, standing over the cart, is there anything better than good cocktail shrimp? He chomped on three more while he tried to figure out when he had eaten last. It was a while, longer than he should have let himself go without fueling. In the middle of the plate was a bouquet of lemon wedges, and he took a few and squeezed them over the plate. Yes, he thought, jamming more shrimp into his mouth, the necessary touch of lemon.

In the distance he could still hear the music, the talk and laughter, the quiet clink of glasses. Carefully he lifted the other silver dome.

Caviar. Lovely.

He reached with two fingers and let the salty black pearls slip down his throat, then went back and snapped off another shrimp. The combination was brilliant, like swimming with his mouth open in fresh seawater. More caviar dripped down his throat, more shrimp. He looked around for something to drink. There was only the champagne bottle, and he couldn't open that without the telltale POP! giving him away. He took the ice bucket and, wincing at the noise of shifting ice, poured out what water he could into a champagne goblet and drank that.

He put down the glass and decided it was time to check out the party. But first he took a final scoop of caviar and a final shrimp, took another final shrimp, and then another, until the once-bounteous plate held nothing but squeezed lemon wedges and discarded shells. Within the small caviar bowl was only a black smear. He looked at the desolation queasily before sticking his teeth back in his mouth and making his way, at long last, toward the music.

He kept close to the wall, moving carefully, until he could peek around the corner. His eyes widened at the sight.

The wide room had a mirrored ceiling and a huge hot tub roiling in the center. The space was lit by two lamps, the base of each a plaster cast: one of a naked couple sensuously entwined, the other of a single huge phallus. Baldly pornographic paintings hung on the dark walls. But it wasn't the decor that caught his attention and held it rapt. He had expected to find a brutal, pragmatic killer in that room. He had expected to find a criminal mastermind, a magician. He had expected, somehow, to find his future. But what he found instead was a breathtaking assortment of breasts and thighs, calves and lips, finely shaped asses.

Naked women, four of them, three in the tub, one bending over the edge, all with champagne glasses in their lovely hands, were moving languorously. They were laughing and talking and ministering, it seemed, to a figure in the middle. Without thinking, Scrbacek took a step forward. One of the women in the tub turned around, startled for an instant, and then smiled.

"There you are," she said.

They were beautiful, these women, young, like sirens, smiling at him and calling him forth. The girl who had answered the door, now leaning over the rim of the tub, stood up straight in her nakedness and stepped toward him. Her breasts were like . . . Her lips were red as . . . She had legs long as . . . And an ass like . . . like . . . And she came unabashedly up to him and smiled and reached out a filled champagne glass for him to take.

He was so entranced that he didn't notice the three women in the tub moving to the sides, stepping out, wrapping themselves in towels, and leaving the room, so that when he glanced back at the water now, in the middle of the roiling white, he could finally see the old man they had been ministering to. He lolled in the tub, the old man, his head back, a champagne goblet in his hand, his narrow shoulders, his thin chest, his face falling apart from age and something more ravaging than age. The old man lolled and smiled a dreamy I've-just-been-sucked-off smile, and Scrbacek gasped audibly when he saw him.

"So what have we here?" said the man in the tub. "A casino dealer? His face black with my caviar and his vest stained with my shrimp sauce. Come forward. What is your name, boy? Can someone read his name tag?"

"Lee Chon Yang," said the naked woman standing beside Scrbacek, still offering him the champagne.

"Funny," said the man in the tub. "You don't look like a Lee Chon Yang. In fact, if it weren't for those glasses, that ridiculous goatee and, what is that, fake teeth? Marvelous. If it wasn't for all of that, I would have sworn that you look just like a student I once had."

Scrbacek took a step forward.

"His name was J.D. Scrbacek," said the man in the tub, "and last I heard, he'd been very naughty and was in way too much trouble for his own good."

Scrbacek's jaw hung loose in shock as he stared at the man in the tub. The fake teeth tumbled from his mouth.

"Welcome, Mr. Scrbacek," said Professor Drinian DeLoatch from the depths of the roiling hot water. "We've been wondering when you would come and join our party."

43
A SIMPLE TOAST

Have a drink with me, Mr. Scrbacek. Join me in a toast. Come now, don't be shy. Take the glass from Sheena.

Your name is Sheena, isn't it, my sweet? Oh, close enough.

In fact, Mr. Scrbacek, I ordered this champagne just for you. A nice vintage, too, if I say so myself. It should be, it cost enough. Your friend Vega came running this morning, and I knew you'd follow. Funny how obvious you all can be. Take the glass, Mr. Scrbacek, and raise it with mine in a simple toast. Ready?

To the criminal law.

Hear, hear, no? What a marvelous guide for us all. How else can we know how we're doing? Oh, of course, money can tell us, or our surroundings, or the number of naked women who share our hot tub, but really, what tells us more clearly of our status in the world than the criminal law?

There are only two classes of people, the innocent and the guilty, and all of us are among the innocent until the bastards have proven otherwise. And they have to go through us to do it, right, Mr. Scrbacek, we great defenders of the despised? Innocent until proven guilty in a court of law with a defense lawyer snarling down the prosecutor's throat. Now that is an innocence worth defending. Quite the opposite of the catechism drilled into me as a child. Guilty, guilty, guilty before I even breathed my first. How Draconian is that? If that is God's law, then I'd far sooner put my faith in the penal code. I've spent my life pursuing innocence, Mr. Scrbacek. It is my calling. Along with pursuing the occasional whore.

Join me, Mr. Scrbacek. Join me in my toast. Join me in my hot tub. Join me in tasting all the delicacies this town can offer. I need a junior partner, someone to carry my briefcase and arrange for my entertainments. I need someone I can piss on for a price. We'll be DeLoatch and Scrbacek, PC.

DeLoatch and Scrbacek. It doesn't have much of a ring to it, does it? How about DeLoatch and Associates? Much better, no? You'd be one of the associates. Sheena here would be the other, wouldn't you, sweetheart?

Yes, I know, you already told me.

You have objections, Mr. Scrbacek. You've seen through the mists, latched onto the truth of things. But what have I done that you wouldn't have done in my place? Joseph Torresdale entered my office with a pending racketeering indictment that I successfully thwarted. Frances Galloway hired me to defend her against attacks by the city over real-estate properties her husband had saved from the wrecking ball. And then serious questions were being raised by the Casino Control Commission about Mr. Diamond's silent partners, questions that Mr. Diamond believed needed to be addressed by a criminal law attorney. That these three citizens should turn to me was no surprise. Who better to help them maintain their status as innocents in this world?

What was it I told you was the most crucial characteristic of a great trial lawyer? Do you remember, Mr. Scrbacek, or were you too busy making eyes at the beauteous Ms. Ling? Imagination. How often did I stress that in class? Gather the facts you are given, the facts you can't avoid, and use your imagination to weave a story that will capture the jury. You know of what I speak, you've done it yourself. With my help, of course.

Oh, I had my eye on you, Mr. Scrbacek, all through law school. You were dead in my sights from the first. Day in and day out I worked on you, and it was sweet vindication when you came to me and declared your interest in the criminal law. You asked for my help, and I promised to give it. And I did, yes, I did, in the worst way. It was I who directed this small case and that small case to your office, all surreptitiously. No need for you to know you had a secret benefactor. It was I who whispered in old Judge Newsom's ear that he might give the Amber Grace defense to you. Your first death penalty case, and you shocked me, boy, by not screwing it up. Tracking down that child was lovely, simply lovely. The first of many surprises you gave me. And after, when you had become famous, it was I who told the drug lords of Crapstown that you were the perfect lawyer for their particular legal problems. I knew the very moment you began to take product in lieu of fees. It seemed so out of character at first, but then I supposed your character was changing under my influence, even from afar. And so, naturally, it was in your talented hands that I entrusted Caleb Breest.

It was more than an inconvenience to us all when Mr. Breest was arrested. We were delighted when he went after that fool Malloy, but to do it with his bare hands, to leave so much evidence, that was more than we expected. He deserved to languish on death row for his stupidity. But still, we needed him out of jail, where he could be disposed of properly. No sense waiting with bated breath to see if Caleb Breest ever found his singing voice. We were relying on you to do your job, and then for Mr. Bozant, from Nevada, to do his.

You were marvelous, I must say, better than ever I expected. All that dramatic finger-pointing at prosecutor Surwin. I was in control throughout, of course, through my intermediary Mr. Torresdale. I handed you the case, spoon-fed you the strategy, ensured through my contacts that there were enough flaws in police procedure for you to create a compelling case for our Mr. Breest. But still, Mr. Scrbacek, bravo. Bravo. After your brilliant performance, you were bound to rise to great heights in this town. I would see to it. You had quite the future ahead of you.

Pity then about Trent Fallow and his foolish file. But there was nothing to be done. So we added your name to Mr. Bozant's to-do list. I must tell you, he was quite thrilled with the assignment. For some reason he desperately wants to kill you. Have you any idea why? Hmm?

Imagination. We were talking of imagination. There come to me three businesspersons. One has dreams of moving out of crime, of partnering with an established legal business. One learned from her husband to buy and sell slum real estate, looking only for the gross profit. One seeks to expand his empire across the wasteland of a ruined city. It took a lawyer of imagination to see how all three desires could be met in one masterstroke. Let's have the crime lord create a wave of terror across the whole swath of desired land to lower drastically the value of the real estate. Let's have the slumlord buy up the necessary properties and hide them among her other myriad of ruins. Let's have the casino mogul pave over everything, creating by fiat his highway to a new megaresort in the Marina District.

Oh, please, don't talk to me of costs. Don't talk to me of communities devastated, neighborhoods lost, of families thrown from their homes. Don't talk to me of Crapstown. What did Robert Moses care of long-lived communities when building the modern megalopolis that is New York? What did our own city fathers care when they let the casinos usurp the boardwalk, leaving the rest of the city to rot? For every plus there is a minus. Such is life in the real world. Try asking the lion to weep for the gazelle. Don't talk to me of morality, talk to me only of innocence and guilt.

Answer me this, Mr. Scrbacek. I slit your throat, leave no evidence, the police are dumbfounded. Am I a criminal? Is the perfect crime a crime at all? Didn't we discuss this already, lo those many years ago? Whatever we do, my associates and I, we do as innocents, because we have not yet been proven guilty. Only when we are proven guilty have we committed a crime. Isn't that the logical conclusion of all you have learned in the law? In the eyes of the law, nothing matters until the jury returns and the gavel is slammed. And if there is no jury verdict, and if there is no gavel, and if there is no evidence, then there is no guilt.

Whatever we are, our little group, we are not criminals. There is no evidence. There has been no trial, no verdict from a jury of our peers, if such a jury could ever be found. In the eyes of the law, we are as innocent as a newborn pup. And, trust me when I tell you this, Mr. Scrbacek, we will maintain that status. Whatever we must do we will do. We honor the law too much to bar any action that will keep us on its right side.

Which brings us to your friend Vega. I had much faith in Cirilio, but he lost his nerve. He threatened me, Mr. Scrbacek, can you imagine? I once thought it would be DeLoatch and Vega. A nicer sound, don't you think, the symmetry of an iamb and a trochee? DeLoatch and Vega. Too bad. So now, Vega—dead. He thinks the documents he stashed away are his protection, but we have them already. I expect he'll prove easier to kill than you. But we won't stop there. Fallow—dead. He's more of a fool than we can afford. Breest—dead. He has proven too brutally unpredictable to be trusted. And as for you, Mr. Scrbacek? As for you? You, too, are as good as dead. I can already smell the sweet rot of your corpse. Dead, dead, dead.

Unless . . .

You have impressed us, Mr. Scrbacek. Your exploits in your current travails have interested even Mr. Diamond in his Far Eastern fortress. You have demonstrated a wiliness that has been nothing less than shocking. And, just as important, you show a taste for the finer things in life. The caviar stains on your lips prove that, as did your messy little habit of not so long ago, one that I still favor. Tell me, Mr. Scrbacek, wouldn't you like a little taste? Just ask, and it is yours. Or maybe you would like to take sweet Sheena into the bedroom. Of course you would. Look at her. How lovely. I wouldn't want to work with a man who didn't know the meaning of such pleasures. Where does the root of ambition lie, after all, if not in the deep-seated desire to wrap Sheena's legs around our necks?

We need someone like you, now that Vega will no longer be available. Join me. We'll be DeLoatch and Associates. We can send word that you are no longer to be hunted, yea, that you are now to be protected. Bozant will be disappointed, but he knows how to obey. And the unpleasant murder charge, the mysterious phone message and convenient cache of guns and explosives in your basement, they can all be cleared up, explained. With one call your travails can disappear. We can give you back your life and more, more than you ever imagined. Sheena, dear, turn around and bend over. Provide Mr. Scrbacek a preview of coming attractions.

What, not in the mood? Sheena is quite the talent, I assure you. Oh, don't mind me, Mr. Scrbacek, please. Go right ahead. Frankly, I like to watch.

No? Oh, all right, if you insist, I'll put your name on the door. I can get used to it, I suppose. One can get used to anything.

DeLoatch and Scrbacek, PC.

I made you what you are. Think of all you owe me. And now I offer you this, more than most men can dream of in a lifetime.

Join with me, Mr. Scrbacek. Raise your glass. A toast to the good life. A toast to life itself, which is far preferable to toasting death. To DeLoatch and Scrbacek, PC. To the grand practice of the criminal law. Are we to traverse this landscape of work and pleasure together, arm in arm?

What say ye, partner?

What say ye?

44
CHINA, MY CHINA

"You almost had me," said Scrbacek.

"Only almost?" said DeLoatch. He sipped his champagne and leaned back in the hot tub, steam weaving a pattern before his ruined face. "What was it that caught your interest most? Lovely Sheena? The cocaine? That's it, yes. The blithe white powder. What if I promise you oceans?"

"It wasn't the drug. You almost had me with that 'defender of humanity' patter you laid on us in our very first class in law school. That 'champion of those most in need' crap. You remember, don't you?"

"Of course I do. A staple of my first-year criminal law course. 'What is a criminal defendant?' 'What is a prosecutor?' Sometimes I am too precious for words."

"I bought into it. All of it. The romance, the stirring image of the defense attorney holding back the mob at the prison gates. I wanted to be young Abe Lincoln with his almanac. I wanted to be Atticus Finch. I wanted to be the great defender of humanity you told us about. God help me, Professor, but I wanted to be you."

"Good choice."

"And then the world shifted, and suddenly I knew what it was to be you, knew it with a certainty that stunned. And I didn't know what else to do but embrace it."

"And wasn't it wonderful?"

"No, it truly wasn't. I dived into cocaine because I could forget what I had become for small periods of time. But never for long enough. And the women, well, I dived into them too, yes, but in the end, when it's one after the other, it's a sad, empty exercise. True, seeing their breasts come loose from their shirts and dropping each into its own lovely pattern was, I have to say, glorious. But, frankly, and no offense, Sheena—"

"China. My name's China."

"No offense, but all the loose sex with high-priced women was never as good as it sounded. I gave up what I had for what I was getting, and the trade was the worst of my life. Only love lives up to its billing."

"Oh, please," said DeLoatch, "you'll make me puke."

"And the nights, the dangerous nights with the dangerous men, riding around in their big black cars, meeting and plotting, eating big meals and drinking magnums of champagne and making crude jokes at others' expense."

"The best part, if you ask me."

"I lived it, and hated it, and hated myself as I lived it, and still I felt I deserved every stinking inch of it. As punishment."

"So what was it, Mr. Scrbacek? What pushed you over the edge?"

"Amber Grace," said Scrbacek.

"Your big success. It went to your head, of course."

"No, it wasn't the success. It was the failure. It was after I pinned the murder of that pimp on Remi Bozant. It was after I reversed her conviction and released her from death row and picked her up in the rain outside the jailhouse when they let her go free. It was after all the interviews on national television and the interviews for the national press. It was after all of that, as I was driving her back into the world.

She talked about seeing her daughter again, and starting over, and I said that sounded like a fine idea. And then she turned to me and smiled and said, in the sweetest voice, 'You know, he had it coming, Mr. Scrbacek. Lucius, I mean. I loved the man, I did, but he hurt me once too often, and I had no choice. I want you to know that. I want you to know that whatever happened, he had it coming.'"

DeLoatch stared at Scrbacek from out of the swirling steam of the hot tub, his eyes wide with amusement. "Is that all?"

"Not just that," said Scrbacek. "There was also what happened to Maya, Amber Grace's daughter, after Amber's new lawyer got the court to order her surrendered back into Amber's custody."

"Yes," said DeLoatch, not so amused anymore. "I remember. It's always the boyfriend, isn't it? And you, precious boy, felt responsible for everything. You know what you should have become? A bankruptcy lawyer. At least then you would have held some certainty about your clients. They all would have been broke."

"Do you know the Contessa Romany?" said Scrbacek.

"From the boardwalk? With the sign?"

"Exactly. She read my cards, told me that I would find all the answers to my predicament in my past, my present, my future. I found guides for the first two, but I never imagined it would be you who would show me the last."

"Yes, well, death is such a brutal way to end things," said DeLoatch, sipping again from his champagne, "but in your case, if you decide poorly, inevitable."

"No, you didn't show me death, you showed me with utter clarity my life. My life as it has become. A life where the criminal and the lawyer join and become one. A life where anything goes as long as it avoids a conviction. Blame him, blame her, blame the victim, blame the cops, blame anyone, say anything, do what must be done, no matter the price, to squeeze out that victory. We're not defenders of anything, you and I, we're coconspirators."

"Well, as my dear mother always said, 'If you're going to be a coconspirator, you might as well coconspire with the best.'"

"Here I stand in the middle of the path. At one end, the beginning, is the idealistic student you mocked that first day of class. At the other end, in this very room, surrounded by prostitutes of a lesser scale, rotting of disease both physical and moral, is you. You have shown me the pot of gold at the end of my path, and all I want to do is flee."

"Does that mean your answer is no?"

"My answer for you is to go to hell."

"Then you should. Run, I mean. Back away, please, darling Sheena."

"China, China, dammit. Can't either of you get it straight?"

"Please."

The woman took a step back, her breasts quivering, then took another, before spinning and hurrying from the room. As Scrbacek watched her leave, DeLoatch casually turned his body to place his champagne glass upon the table behind him. When he turned around again, he was holding a telephone in one hand and a gun in the other.

He aimed the gun at Scrbacek's heart.

"Forgive me," said DeLoatch, waving the gun, "but I need to make a call. Security, please," he said into the phone. He winked as he waited to be transferred. "Hello. This is Dr. DeLoatch in room 2402. There is an intruder. He is dressed like a dealer, with a false beard and glasses and a fake name on his tag, but his real name is Scrbacek. Yes, that J.D. Scrbacek. He has a gun. He is threatening to kill me and Mr. Diamond. I have him now at my advantage, but he is wily beyond belief and I am terrified. Please block the exits and send some men at once. And notify Mr. Bozant. Yes. Thank you. Oh, one more thing. Could you please tell room service to send more shrimp and caviar. I'm afraid the intruder helped himself to my original order. Perfect."

Scrbacek looked around as raw terror tightened his throat. He had come for just a glimpse of a face, the final piece of the puzzle, had planned to surreptitiously enter and surreptitiously leave, but that plan had been blown straight to hell. Now there was a gun, silver and sleek, aimed at his heart. If he turned around to escape, DeLoatch would drill him in the back. If he waited too long, frozen in position, DeLoatch would drill him in his chest. He needed to attack before he could run.

"Ever hear, Professor," he said, trying to stall the inevitable, "of the Furies?"

"You are getting desperate, aren't you, calling forth a myth."

"A myth?" Scrbacek looked about himself, looked for something, anything, even as the terror descended from his throat, leaked through his whole body, turned his muscles frigid with fear.

"In the ancient world," said DeLoatch, "the Furies were the wild, vengeful spirits of retribution unleashed against the unpunished guilty. Strange female wraiths, they were. Snakes writhed from their heads, and blood dripped from their eyes. Though their tits, so goes the tale, were marvelous."

Scrbacek was puzzled at the answer even as he continued his desperate search to find the way out, somewhere, somehow. And then he saw it, there, in plain sight, the answer.

"This is not like you, placing your hope in myth," said DeLoatch. "The Furies didn't exist then and, despite the rumors that rise like smoke from the slums, they don't exist now. You're very much on your own, Mr. Scrbacek, and I'm the one with the gun."

Scrbacek tensed for an instant, watched as DeLoatch's squinty eyes squinted, and then he dived to the left, just as the shattering report of the gun sounded and the lamp with the plaster sculpture of entwined lovers in midhump exploded into dust.

Scrbacek rolled on the floor until he sprawled flat. Staying low, beneath the level of the hot tub's rim, he scooted around the tub toward a side table up against the far wall.

"Security's coming, Mr. Scrbacek," said DeLoatch.

The professor squeezed off another brutal report, and a hole blossomed in the wall directly above Scrbacek, who kept scooting.

"It matters not if I get you or another gets you, only that you're gotten," said DeLoatch, a certain glee in his voice. "You should have joined me. Oh, what fun we would have had."

Another shot, another roar, and this time plastic shards bit into Scrbacek's face as a stream of water began to flow out the side of the tub just in front of him. How did the bastard know where he was? Scrbacek looked up at the ceiling and saw DeLoatch grinning insanely at him from the ceiling mirror.

His ears ringing from the fusillade, Scrbacek backed up quickly, on elbows and knees, reached up to the table, and grabbed hold of the shaft of the second lamp, the huge white plaster phallus base that had been his target from his first leap. He jerked his arm down and to the right so that the top of the lamp smashed against the side of the hot tub, the bulb shattering and the light dying with a pop. Quickly he scooted away from the table.

"I can still see," said DeLoatch, loosing another shot, another roar, another stream flowing, this time directly upon Scrbacek's back. The old man's aim was getting truer, the bullet missing him by only inches. The next shot would be on target. "Foolish boy," said DeLoatch. "Trying to lose the light. It's not even dark outside. Maybe I overestimated you after all."

"Hey, Professor," said Scrbacek, still below the level of the hot tub. "You know what you need?"

"What is that, Mr. Scrbacek?"

"A good prick up the ass," he said as he tossed the huge white cock, cord still attached, over and into the tub.

Along with the sizzle and dimming light came a quick and awesome scream. Scrbacek was immediately on his feet, racing through the hallway, past the decimated tray of food, out the door of room 2402.

Without slowing, Scrbacek slammed open the emergency stairwell door and leaped down one flight and then the next and then the next, holding onto the rail for balance, one foot barely landing on the cement step before it was pushing off to send him leaping down further. He kept jumping down until he stopped, suddenly, by one of the exit doors.

There were harsh sounds rising in the stairwell, a door banging open, footsteps shuddering upward.

Quietly, Scrbacek opened the exit door, slipped out, pushed it shut behind him. The elevator door down the hall was just opening for a couple, she in a bright-orange chiffon, he in a sport coat tight around his heavy shoulders. As they entered the elevator, Scrbacek straightened his glasses and hurried toward them.

"Hold, please," he said as calmly as he could manage, still gasping for air. Inside, he turned around just as the door closed. He glimpsed, through the vanishing crack, a bulky man in a cable-knit sweater lunging through the stairwell door.

45
A TASTY CUT OF MEAT

The jazzy, sweeping clinka-dink of insincere elevator music played, appropriately enough, in the elevator, giving the same sense of dead space as in a capsule tumbling helplessly past Mars.

Scrbacek wiped his face with his hand as they started to fall and the lights atop the doors moved to the left. Eighteen, seventeen. Along with smeared hair-in-a-can, blood came away on his palm. The sight of its rich crimson shocked him. Had DeLoatch hit him? Was he somehow shot? But he remembered the plastic shards flying into his face when that crazy bastard first shot a hole through the hot tub. That must have been it. Scrbacek wiped his face again, checked the elevator's progress. *Fifteen, fourteen.* He slipped the key card Dolores had given him into the bottom slot, and the basement indicator switched on.

Suddenly worried about what the couple standing behind him thought of a dealer rushing for their elevator, his vest filthy with shrimp sauce, his face bleeding, he said, "How you folks doing today? You having much luck?"

"I'm getting killed at blackjack," said the man.

"You play like an idiot," said the woman.

"What are you talking about? I play."

"You hit on a seventeen."

"I felt something."

Eleven, ten. "The whole table groaned."

"What do I care they groan? I was a loser anyway. The dealer drew to twenty-one."

"He would have drawn your queen and busted if you had stayed pat."

"I felt something."

"What you felt, Jack dear, was the lunch buffet. What you felt was your third helping of prime rib."

"It was a very tasty cut of meat."

Seven, six. "Hey, Jack," said Scrbacek. "You come to my table, I'll find you some luck."

"Really?"

"I've been cold as ice. People have been making a fortune off me all day. I'll save a seat."

"Well, that would be great," said the man, leaning forward to get a look at his tag. "That would be great . . . Lee. Lee? Lee Chon Yang?"

Three, two. "My mother's Swedish."

"Ahh," said the man, "that explains it."

The elevator opened suddenly onto the wild razz-jazz-a-ma-tazz of the casino level, the ring-a-ding of the slots, the desperate cheers from the craps table, the thirsty calls to the cocktail tail, the ring-a-ding-ding. Scrbacek watched two bruisers in cable-knit sweaters sweep by as Jack and his wife stepped around him and off the elevator.

"I'm on shift in another twenty minutes, Jack," called out Scrbacek.

"I'll be looking for you," said Jack, "you bet."

"I'll save the seat."

Scrbacek smiled and waved as the bruisers glanced his way, saw the friendly conversation, kept on moving.

The elevator doors closed.

Scrbacek let out a breath.

He waited tensely for the elevator to descend two more levels, to the basement. Before the doors were fully open, he was out of the elevator, ducking into a doorway, listening.

Nothing.

The elevator door closed again and left him in silence.

He was in a fluorescent-lit hallway filled with the spoils of abundance, trolleys heaping with soiled sheets, carts loaded with room service trays, massive rubbish containers brimming with rotting food. Carefully, quickly, scooting from doorway to doorway, he made his way through the basement level, trying to retrace the path he had taken with Dolores.

At one point he turned down a hallway, realized it was the wrong way, and as he turned back he heard something coming along his original path. He ducked behind a maid's trolley and peered out. An electric golf cart, driven by a maintenance worker, with a man in the ubiquitous cable-knit sweater and beret standing on the back, gripping a rifle, searching. Scrbacek waited for it to pass and turn down another route before he continued on his way.

Finally, after testing two, three, four doors, he found the unlocked maintenance closet, in which he had stashed his clothes, and shut the door quietly behind him. He took off his vest and shirt and jammed them against the bottom crack of the door before he pulled the cord on the overhead bulb. A fierce yellow light crashed down upon him.

He tried to lock the door from inside, but found there was no button or slide. He jammed a folded **WET FLOOR** sign under the knob to keep the door shut. From one pocket he took out a card. From another he pulled out Jenny's phone. He turned the phone on, checked the reception—one bar would have to do—and dialed.

"Do you know who this is?" said Scrbacek when the call was answered.

"Don't tell me, let me guess," said Nomad Aboud. "It's that donkey, isn't it, the one running around like a crazy Indian."

"That's right."

"How you doing out there? Dead yet?"

"Close, but not yet. You said for me to call you if I needed something. Well, I need something."

"Go ahead."

"I'm hidden in the bowels of Diamond's Mount Olympus. They're looking for me up and down, guarding all the exits. I need to get out."

"And you want for me to come and get you?"

"That would be great. Just great."

"How'd you get in there in the first place?"

"A long story."

"And what was the purpose of your visit? A little relaxation at the tables? A quick hit at the Elysian Buffet?"

"It was business, not buffet—though I heard the prime rib was mighty tasty."

"Where are you now?"

"In desperate straits."

"Where in the hotel, numchuck?"

"The basement."

"Okay, I know that basement. I've hijacked enough sheets from that joint to sail to Cuba. In the southwest corner of the basement level is an emergency exit that leaves you at a stairwell that climbs out onto Jefferson. The alarm goes off as soon as you open the door, so you got to hustle once you bust through. Twenty minutes, exactly from the time I hang up, we'll be outside that exit, in a maroon Lincoln Town Car."

"Nice."

"You bust out the door, we'll be there. Five seconds early, they catch you before we arrive. Five seconds late, we'll be gone."

"I got you," said Scrbacek, checking quickly on the phone's menu for the tools page and finding the timer. "Okay."

"You ready?"

"Ready."

"Twenty minutes from now." Click.

Scrbacek pressed the button. The time started counting down. Okay, nineteen minutes and fifty-nine seconds to find the doors and burst through them to meet the Lincoln. Nineteen minutes and fifty-eight. And fifty-seven.

He slid off his boots and stripped off the rest of his dealer's costume, including the Lee Chon Yang name tag, of which he had grown quite fond. He didn't rush, he had plenty of time. Six or seven minutes would be enough to find the exit. Anything longer would increase his chances of getting caught. He grabbed the paper bag he had stashed on the upper shelf and pulled out his old clothes, dirty and smelly, and now creased beyond belief from being jammed into so small a package. He put on his jeans and white shirt, replaced the boots. He was a target in his old clothes, but he was a bigger target, in that casino, fitting the description DeLoatch had given over the phone. They were searching for a man dressed as a dealer; he needed to look like anything but. He replaced the vest and dealer's shirt with the raincoat to keep light inside from drifting out, and wiped his face as best as he could with the shirt, taking off blood, shrimp sauce, more hair-in-a-can. He lathered up his beard with the shaving cream Dolores had brought him and shaved by feel, slicing off the goatee along with strips of skin. He gave a final wipe to his face before stuffing the dealer's uniform and tag into the bag. He returned the bag to the high shelf for Dolores to retrieve.

He checked the stopwatch on the phone: Seven minutes and twelve seconds. And eleven seconds. And ten seconds. It was time to get moving.

He turned off the light, shucked on his raincoat, put his ear to the door, and froze.

Footsteps.

46
COUNTDOWN

The footsteps Scrbacek heard were coming down the hall, two sets of them, coming down the hall, doorknobs rattling as they moved ever closer, coming down the hall.

Maybe he should burst out, surprise the hell out of them, jump one, beat him into submission, jump the other, and drag their unconscious bodies into the closet before making his getaway. That plan had a certain *Die Hard* derring-do, and it fit his new attack-first strategy, but there were obvious downsides, not the least of which was that they might just shoot him the moment he leaped like an idiot out of the closet.

The footsteps were coming nearer, the rattling doorknobs coming closer. His would be soon, next. He opted to remain in hiding. By the light of the phone, and carefully, so as not to make a sound, he leaned his weight against the sign that was jammed against the doorknob, pressed his shoulder to the door's metal, and pushed with his legs until his full strength was mustered against the door.

The footsteps came right up to the doorway and stopped. Scrbacek held his breath. The doorknob jiggled. There was pressure on the door from the outside, but it refused to budge.

"It's locked," came one voice. "What is this?"

"It says it's a janitor's closet," said a second voice over the rustle of paper. "Big hey."

"Who has the key?"

"Duh. The janitor?"

"Mark it with the others."

"He's not in there. He's not down here. He's probably somewheres eating dinner, which is what we would be doing if they hadn't called us out."

"We need the key." The knob shook again. "It feels soft somehow."

"They have pills for that."

Scrbacek could feel the pressure. He gritted his teeth and pushed with his legs, and the door refused to budge.

"Something's wrong," said the first voice. "Help me shove."

"I'd rather you use the pills."

"Shut up and help me push."

More pressure. Scrbacek's legs began to ache, his shoulder burned. He exhaled and took a slow deep breath.

"I'm getting the key to this room."

One set of footsteps hurried away and turned down a corridor.

"I'm getting the key to this room," mimicked the second voice before it called out, "You know, they could have at least let us finish our steaks."

The second set of footsteps slowly followed the first. When he thought he heard the second set turn down the corridor, Scrbacek carefully pulled the sign away from the door. As he moved it, the metal frame clanked. An army of mites crawled beneath his skin. He spent another moment listening.

Nothing.

He checked the phone. Four minutes and fifty-four seconds. Fifty-three seconds. Fifty-two seconds. It was getting late. He was running out of time. With no choice, he carefully pulled open the door and stuck out his head.

The hallway was empty. Scrbacek crept out of the doorway, closing it silently behind him. To the right, the way the footsteps had gone, was the casino and the boardwalk and the sea. East. He turned to his left, kept close to the wall, and began his way to the exit.

"Hey, you," he heard being called from behind him. "You the janitor?"

Scrbacek turned around but kept walking, backward. A short chubby man in a cable-knit sweater stood at where the hallway turned a corner, a badly folded blueprint in his hand. "Yeah," said Scrbacek. "But I'm just off shift."

"We're looking for some keys," called the man, taking a step forward, his round buttery face tilted now at an angle.

"You got to find the supervisor," said Scrbacek, still walking backward, his arms wide. "I can't help you. Sorry. I'm off shift."

The man took another step forward.

Scrbacek checked the phone in his hand. Four minutes and twenty-three seconds. Twenty-two seconds.

"You in a hurry for some reason?" said the man as he began walking toward Scrbacek, matching Scrbacek's pace. "Can I talk to you for a minute?"

"Actually, I got a hot date waiting on me. Maybe later."

"Not later. Now. Stop," said the man, speeding up into a slow run, throwing down the blueprint, hopping awkwardly on one foot for a moment as he pulled a silver revolver from beneath the cuff of his pants.

"No time," shouted Scrbacek, and then he was off, sprinting down the hall, away.

"Hey, Bert," shouted the man as he pursued. "We got him. We got the bastard."

Scrbacek heard the pounding of footsteps behind him and then the brutal shout of the pistol. On the wall to Scrbacek's left, an explosive puff of powder.

Southwest corner, southwest. That's what Aboud had said. At the far end of the hallway was a T. Scrbacek knew he had to go left, and fast. He sprinted toward it, madly, his boots slipping on the smooth linoleum. He faked a move to the right and then dived left, sliding on the floor for a moment before he picked himself up. As he was diving, he glanced down the hallway he had come from and could see the short pudgy man running, his butter face red with effort, and behind him a taller man rushing forward, hauling an absurdly large rifle.

The hallway before him was long, with doors on either side. At the far end, it turned to the right with a sign on the wall, pointing in that direction, saying **EMERGENCY EXIT**. He didn't think he could make it to the exit before the men chasing him turned the corner, and there were almost three minutes left now, too much time for him to risk a mad dash to the door. He'd set off the alarm, be too early for his ride, they'd come crawling out of the casino, bullets would fly.

There was a door on his right. He stopped to try it. Locked. There was a door on his left. He dashed to it and spun the knob. His hand slipped. The charging footsteps grew closer. He spun the knob again, and the door opened and he jumped inside, shutting the door behind him.

He was on a large iron grate, part of a catwalk that surrounded the upper third of a cavernous room suffused with an unnatural heat. From the grate, a set of metal stairs led to the floor twenty feet below, where four massive boilers, like four huge insects, squatted, each boiler fitted with valves and controls, wide tubes snaking from their bodies and shooting into the walls. It was as if whatever power drove the casino was supplied by these giant insects, burning oil, money, and hope as they maintained the building's gross bodily functions.

He had no time to explore the lower depths of this room. A glance at the timer on the phone showed he had about two minutes left to catch his ride. Outside the door, he could hear his pursuers pass by. They would go to the exit, see that it hadn't been opened, then come back checking each of the doors, looking for him.

There was a wooden wedge, to keep the door open, hanging from the inside doorknob. Three hard hats hung on a rack behind the door, along with a clipboard. A large sign held a cartoon of a man smacking his bare head against a metal beam with the words writ large: **SAFETY FIRST!**

He took the wedge off the knob and placed it on the floor just a few feet from the back wall, securing it with his foot. He grabbed one of the hats off the rack and spun it like a wobbly Frisbee. It clattered off the top of a boiler and clanked down onto the floor.

They had to have heard that.

He took another and did the same, throwing this one farther, and then grabbed the third hard hat before scooting to the wall, behind the door, which banged open suddenly, jamming into the wedge, and missing his nose by half an inch. The second hard hat was still rattling in the far corner of the room.

"We got him," said one of the men as he charged down the stairs. "You stay up here on the walk, go around the other side and sight him out."

"He's our meat, Bert," said the other man. "Meat."

Scrbacek could hear their footsteps, one moving down the stairs, the other circling the room on the catwalk. He peeked his head out from behind the door, saw the chubby man with the butter face slide across the catwalk, his gun held in two hands, pointed down toward the far corner of the room. The other man, the man with the rifle, was somewhere on the floor, out of Scrbacek's sight.

It wasn't quite right, they weren't in perfect position, but Scrbacek didn't have any more time. He glanced at the phone, took a breath, and then spun the last of the hard hats toward the back wall.

It flew through the air like an ungainly bird, tipping to the right and then diving behind one of the great insectival boilers. The instant it hit, there was a barrage of explosions, from the catwalk and the floor, accompanied by the singing of lead bouncing off concrete.

Subsumed by the repeated roar of gunfire was a set of quick, stealthy footsteps fleeing the room.

Down the hall, he turned the corner, stopping at the emergency exit with the large red panel spanned by white letters proclaiming **ALARM WILL SOUND.**

He checked the phone. Nine seconds. Eight seconds. Seven seconds. He took a deep breath. Six seconds. Five seconds. He heard something furious charge behind him, but by now he didn't care.

He crashed through the door, sounding the alarm, felt the slap of the fresh evening air upon his face, bounded up the stairs, four steps at a time, spun around a landing, more bounding.

The sound of shouting, the report of a gun.

At street level there was the cacophonous rush of running from all about him, but he didn't look fore and aft. Instead, he darted directly toward the large maroon Lincoln Town Car that was cruising along slowly, just in front of the exit, the car's rear door open.

He dived through the car's open door. The hump of the floor slammed into his side as the car door shut. From the floor he could feel the car accelerating smoothly into the stream of traffic, before taking a hard left, which meant it was now speeding west, heading for the heart of Crapstown.

"Thanks for stopping by," said Scrbacek as he pulled himself up and onto the car's large bench seat.

"It's good to see you so prompt," said Aboud from the front passenger seat.

Scrbacek sat back in the leather, closed his eyes, felt the great clench of his muscles ease.

"You said you was at that casino on business," said Aboud. "What kind of business?"

"Let's get someplace quiet, away from everything," said Scrbacek, his eyes still closed, "and I'll tell you all about it."

"Good idea. Someplace away from everything. That's just where we're going."

There was something in Aboud's voice, a catch of anger. Scrbacek opened his eyes, and his heart stopped. The little man was turned in his seat, pointing the large black Zastava at Scrbacek's ribs.

"What the hell?"

"I got to tell you, I'm sorry about this, Scrbacek. I like you, I do. You got pluck."

"Like chicken," said Sergei from behind the wheel.

"No, Sergei," said Aboud. "You pluck chickens, chickens don't have pluck."

"This English is like bad puzzle."

"And you don't have no nuns smacking your knuckles when you get it wrong. So, Scrbacek, like I said, I'm sorry about this, but there's a load of unhappiness about what is happening. You know, for a lot of us, the only way out was the bus terminal, and now it's gone."

"The terminal?"

"Gone, poof. Burned to the ground, and six dead besides. Mostly hoods, granted, but still. Word is you set the whole thing up, called in the police, everything."

"I didn't realize . . . I didn't . . ."

"You see, Scrbacek, some of us don't know how long we can survive with you running around like you are."

"What is expression?" said Sergei. "A chicken running like man with nothing on his head?"

"What's this with you and chickens all of a sudden?" said Aboud. "If you're hungry or something, we'll stop at a Popeyes."

"I okay, boss."

"What are you going to do to me?" said Scrbacek.

"If it was my decision," said Aboud, "I'd drive you up to Newark myself, put you on a plane to like Rio or something. They got some nice-looking broads in Rio. I had a Brazilian girl dancing at the club once. Pretty girl. Black teeth, which was a shame, but pretty girl."

"The Brazilian Firecracker," said Sergei.

"But, see, it's not up to me."

"Who's it up to? DeLoatch? You in with DeLoatch, you bastard?"

"What, the criminal attorney? Why would I be in with him? No, I have orders from the Inner Circle. I got to take you in."

"Where?"

"To the underworld, pal. The Inner Circle, it needs to figure whether it's better for everyone if you live or you die."

"And how are they going to decide that?"

"How the hell do you think?" said Aboud. "They're putting you on trial."

47
OYEZ, OYEZ

A great cavern deep underground, a space long forgotten, damp, foul, surviving from a time of cold war, when signs in every school taught children to duck and cover at first glimpse of the white-hot light, when good honest folk stocked their basements with canned goods and vats of Coca-Cola, when great thinkers in the Pentagon believed battalions could be saved by burying themselves in bunkers far beneath the surface of the earth, awaiting only the all clear to rise from the depths and beat back the communist hordes. But now capitalism worldwide reigns triumphant, the Russian bear has collapsed, the battalions have been sent to a division in the south, the entrances to the nuclear bunkers have all been sealed with cement, and what is left of the hysteria and fear is this great cavern deep underground, a space long forgotten, damp, foul.

The air is fetid and warm, the stench of sewage a marker of the huge leaking pipes that run above the cavern's roof on their path to the sea. At the edges of the vast cement floor, now cracked and uneven, lie remnants of supplies brought here long ago to feed and tend an army as it awaited its moment of glory: metal barrels, cabinets rusted shut, vermin-infested mattresses, the scraps of ruined cots. At the floor's center, forming a large circle, candles burn. The candlelight reveals shadowy figures seated outside the flickering ring, their faces hidden in darkness, a score or more of hellish silhouettes, seated on discarded pallets, on halved oil canisters, on tilting piles of obsolete army manuals. Cigarette embers glow and sputter like the eyes of Cyclopean demons.

Suddenly, from overhead, powered by pirated current, a narrow beam of light falls within the center of the circle, illuminating a large wooden crate with one word printed on its side:

FLAMMABLE

Atop the crate, within the cylinder of spinning motes and shifting smoke, stands a demented master of ceremonies. The man is short and hunched, diffident, his ears huge, his teeth bucked, his thick spectacles hiding the tenor of his eyes. His face is rent by shadow, and his hands are clasped tightly one in the other. This man is known to all those present as Squirrel. He inhales loudly, the wet rush of breath echoing through the cavernous darkness, and whatever sounds that had been filling the chamber die.

"The Court of the Furies," says Squirrel, "is now in session."

A loud murmur rises from outside the circle. Squirrel stands motionless on the crate until silence again fills the cavern.

"Will the defendant rise?"

From overhead, a second beam of light falls upon a broken man. He sits also within the circle of flame, in a chair, alone, behind a ragged metal table of military issue. The man's face is bruised and swollen. A filthy bandage spans the bridge of his nose. His hands are cuffed in front of him, his calves tied tight to the chair with thick army-surplus rope. He wears torn jeans, a filthy shirt that had once been white, a raincoat, singed and torn. He looks as if he had been formed from the very grime of Crapstown. Pressing his hands upon the table, the man leverages himself to standing.

He had been dragged down to this great hole in the earth by a small Arab man with a big gun, pulled through a manhole, led with a flashlight along the great rivers of sewage, while a huge bald Russian shoved him from behind.

"The old woman calls this the River Styx," the Arab told him as they passed along the vile stream—a thousand flushes, one atop the other, in a never-ending flow out to the sea. "More like the River Stinks, if you ask me."

At one point the Arab's flashlight hit upon a lump in the middle of the sewer, which on further examination proved to be a huge frog, its eyes wide with delight, its mouth open to catch the morsels drifting by. "That's the life, hey, Sergei," said the Arab.

"You make joke," said the Russian in his dark accent, "but in Moscow now is every night fight for best spot in sewer."

Prodded by the Arab and the Russian, the defendant had leaped a gap that seemed to have no bottom, had crawled through a rat-infested tunnel built originally to circulate air, and had climbed down a ladder of steel inserted long ago deep into the rock by the Army Corps of Engineers, climbed down to this cavern, where a circle of fire and dark justice awaited him.

"J.D. Scrbacek," says Squirrel, "you have been brought before the Court of the Furies on trial for your life. The Sentinel has brought this charge and will now relate to the Court the accusations leveled upon your head."

From behind the circle of light comes a woman, huge and angry, with dreadlocks thick and a vest of black leather. She had come to the seaside a decade ago from a southern city sinking into the sea, looking for something better, and found instead Crapstown. More stubborn perhaps than smart, she made her life here among the ruins. Her name is Regina. She walks to the defendant until she is inches away from the broken man's face and says softly, "You're getting it now, Stifferdeck." She smiles darkly before spinning to address the circle.

"J.D. Scrbacek, you are charged with being a spy for Caleb Breest, the murderer of Malloy. You are charged with being in league with them casino interests that seek to destroy us all. You are charged with bringing to Crapstown violence and destruction and death. You are charged with placing the fate of all Crapstown in violent jeopardy to save your own miserable skin."

"The penalty of all these crimes," squeals Squirrel atop his crate, "is death by"—Squirrel pauses for a moment and rubs his hands together—"dissection."

A soft murmur from the circle, followed by distinct lines of laughter.

"J.D. Scrbacek," says Squirrel, "how do you plead?"

"Not guilty," says the defendant in a hoarse, defeated tone.

"Figures he'd start off by lying," says Regina. "Why don't we just do it now and get it over with? Why waste everybody's time?"

A voice from the edge of the circle, a deep bass: "We doing this right."

The light veers from Squirrel to seek the source of the voice. It is a large man wearing cook's white, with a chef's hat tilted on his melon head and a stained apron splattered with rendered fat. He sits on a high metal box, his figure rising above the others. In his right hand he holds a giant cleaver, which gleams in the spotlight. "We doing this by the book. Ain't no railroad here."

The others of the circle murmur their assent. The light moves from the huge man in white back to Squirrel.

"After a summation of the evidence by the Sentinel," says Squirrel, "and a plea by the defense, the Inner Circle, as the elected representatives of the entire Fury membership, will vote on the defendant's fate."

"What about witnesses?" says the defendant.

There is a loud, wet intake of breath from atop the crate. "The accused has asked for witnesses," says Squirrel. He takes off his spectacles, his tiny eyes blinking into the light as he examines the lenses before he bows his head to wipe them clean. "That seems a fair request. We'll put it to a vote." He replaces his spectacles and raises his voice. "Who among us thinks we need witnesses?"

There is a dark silence.

"Who thinks," shouts Regina, "we know what the hell happened to our town the last four days and we don't need no fool to tell us lies?"

First, one voice from the circle says, "No witnesses," and then another, and then a third, until it is a chorus of denial that surrounds the defendant in a rising pitch of hatred.

When it quiets, Squirrel says, "The Court of the Furies has decided. We don't need no stinking witnesses."

"What about due process?" asks the defendant.

"I promise you, Stifferdeck," says Regina, "all the process you're due."

"What about the right to a lawyer?" says the defendant. "My Sixth Amendment right to counsel."

"The accused wants a lawyer," says Squirrel. "We see no reason to deny him this privilege." Squirrel breathes in loudly and laughs. "We are short bar-certified attorneys here, but the Court has chosen the next best thing for the accused. At least we got the bar part right."

From outside the ambit of candlelight steps a shadow, hesitantly, awkwardly, one painful step after another, until the shadow steps slowly into the light. An old woman, hiking up her filthy rags and hobbling slowly, her body stiffened like a single rheumatic joint. Her face is sunburned and lined and whiskered; the harshness of the streets covers her like a cloak. A few more painful steps and she is standing next to the defendant. She lifts her swollen hand to place it on the defendant's shoulder.

The defendant smiles at the old woman. "Hello, Blixen. We meet again."

"I'll take care of you," croaks the old woman. "I will. Like my own child, I will. Count on it. Yes, I will."

"Enough of this crap," shouts Regina. "Let's get it on."

48
IN THE DOCK

J.D. Scrbacek, exhausted and in pain, knowing himself innocent yet burdened with a despair that had burrowed so deep into his bones it seemed a part of him, felt, more than saw, the anger aimed at him from the circle of shadows. The fatalism that coursed through him was like a paralytic agent, stilling every muscle in his body while driving his brain into a frenzy.

So this is what it is to be reviled, he thought as the Inner Circle prepared to decide whether he live or die. This is what it is to be hated, feared, to be deemed worthy of exclusion and death. In all my time as a criminal lawyer, I had never truly imagined the torment of being on this side of the line. And yet along with the anguish and fear, I can't help a thrilling sense of justification. Despite every perversion of justice taught me by DeLoatch, better a life on the side of the despised than to be an instrument of hatred, a reaper of the persecution.

For who are they who claim the right to judge me? Squirrel, the failed medical student who saved my life only so he could preside over my death? And Regina, relishing with an unseemly glee her role of prosecutor? And big Ed from the eponymous diner, acting as the foreman of this jury of the damned? A man of few words, Ed, but enough, I'm sure, to say "Guilty" and join the others in sentencing me to die. I see the stunted silhouette of Aboud, with a huge shadow standing behind him, Sergei, that wild and crazy Russian, ready to dance like a Cossack on my grave. And sitting on that crate, over there? Et tu Donnie? And beside Donnie, the woman with the glowing cigarette, must be Elisha Baltimore. And there, in the deep shadows, high on a tower of boxes, the squatting silhouette of the Nightingale, once my protector, now my prison guard. This then is the different route preached by Malloy. To form a vicious gang of vigilantes, taking no sides but their own in the great battle over the future of Crapstown. To use any means necessary to protect the interests of the unprotected against their most hardened of adversaries, among whom they count one J.D. Scrbacek.

And on my side, who do they present as my one lifeline, my last hope, my lawyer? Blixen says she will defend me like her own child, and we know how well that turned out. They'll probably dump my body off the very same pier that claimed her daughter, dump my body after Squirrel has taken all he wants from it, unless I can figure out a way to rebut every one of their charges.

The lights from above narrowed onto the figure of Regina, who stood alone now in the center of the circle, her dreads a wild mane about her angry face.

"Y'all know I didn't think much of Malloy when first he showed his face in these parts," she said, with the artifice of a natural dramatist. "I didn't trust that Malloy wasn't just out for his lonesome like ever'one else in this town. It was only after all of what he said came true that I started listening to the man some say is our prophet. And this is what he told us. That we could be more than we were. That our dreams for our home could be made true through the workings of our collective wills. That apart we are but feeble excuses for life, but that together we are near unstoppable. And he told us from the fire a leader would rise to turn dream into reality and we need to wait for such a time. And so that is our lot. To play off our enemies one against the other, to survive and wait for our day. And he also said beware the dancing fool, for he will wreak havoc and change everything. I point to J.D. Scrbacek, and I say to y'all, beware. What is he doing here? What is his purpose? We can't just up and ask him—he's a lawyer, every word from his lips is lies—but I tell you this: he ain't here to help. He's here to destroy. He is a fool for stepping into our world. Beware the dancing fool."

Is that what I am, a dancing fool? I didn't bring this on myself; it came to me and I've reacted as best I could. From inside the tumult, it seems I've done pretty damn well with what I've been handed. I'm still alive, I found some answers, I even found something I lost long ago, something that might be love. From inside it all, I'm a goddamn hero. But here I am being called a fool and, somehow, I can't help the suspicion that it's not so far from the truth. What is life but something brought to us, an obstacle course in which every decision, even the most disastrous, makes perfect sense at the moment we make it? Every man is the hero of his own life, but what man, from a distance, can't be painted the fool?

"What do we know of this here man? That he's a lawyer. Isn't that enough? That he was lawyering for Caleb Breest, who has been torturing us slow all these years. Isn't that too much? That wherever he has gone, ruin and death, they've followed. Back home in New Orleans, the rules was same as here: one strike, two strikes, three strikes, you're out. I say this fool, he is out."

Is that why I'm going to die, condemned for the destruction that followed me like a plague? Might as well condemn Surwin's woodchuck for running through the woods with his tail on fire. Is that justice, to shoot the innocent woodchuck? And when did being a lawyer become a capital offense? What about the great lawyers of our age: Lincoln, Cardozo, Holmes, Darrow, Marshall? I'll hitch my star to theirs. Kill me, I'll say, only if you would kill again the noble Lincoln. Just be sure to leave out DeLoatch. But mark, if I am to die as a lawyer, I'll fight like one, too. My only chance is to listen to what she says—Regina, my persecutor in her black leather vest, like one of DeLoatch's vengeful wraiths with bleeding eyes and snakes writhing from her head—hear her words and out of them use DeLoatch's precious imagination to craft a lie I can sell to this jury, a lie big enough to save my life.

"But what he'll say is he is no longer Caleb Breest's tool. What he'll say is he himself is on the run. And he knows good well not a one of us wouldn't lend a fugitive a helping hand. But is he really running? Where is his proof? His car, it blew up, but he wasn't sitting in it when it did. Inside instead was a boy named Ethan Brummel. And his house and office burned to the ground. How convenient for him, all his records gone, any chance of digging through his papers to find his true purpose destroyed. And surprise, surprise, what do they find in the basement? Guns. Explosives. Whatever he is, he ain't no innocent. Finally, he was shot, running. Was he shot in the kidney? In the heart? No. Shot in the fleshy part of the arm. Squirrel will tell you it was a miracle that no serious damage was done. A miracle, or else a carefully aimed self-inflicted wound whose purpose was to do no serious damage except to us. Is he a spy? He says no, but what can we trust from a lawyer?"

Lies, lies, planted evidence, false innuendos, and lies. Oh, how bitter to be at the mercy of such lies. That I would blow up my own truck, kill a young man with the world ahead of him, burn down my house, shoot through my arm, all to insinuate myself with a bunch of ragged Crapstown losers. How can she get away with such lies? I should stand and object. Your Honor, she's lying through her yellow teeth. Overruled, Mr. Scrbacek, overruled. This is argument and she is interpreting the evidence, as you very well know. If I remember correctly, Mr. Scrbacek, you yourself are the master of twisting the evidence to fit the lie. But that was my job, Judge. That is what defense attorneys do. It's right there in the Constitution, spelled out in black and white: any lie in defense of the client. It's the Sixth Amendment, or the Fourth, or the Twenty-Third—somewhere in there, I know it.

"So he says he is a man racing for his life. And where does he run? To a hospital, to fix his wound? To the police, to help the hunting of poor Ethan Brummel's murderer? To the bright lights of Casinoland, where he had lived and plied his deceitful trade? No. He runs to Crapstown. To us. And in all of Crapstown, he just so happens to run straight to Donnie Guillen. Why Donnie? Is it because, as he said, he just happened to remember an address? Or is it because Donnie Guillen had created the blueprint of our transformation?"

From outside the circle came a sound, a creaky rolling sound. The spotlight shifted until it was dead on Squirrel, pushing a rusted metal cart toward the center of the circle. Atop that cart was Donnie's cityscape, the great metal relief of Crapstown's future that Scrbacek had seen in the house on Ansonia Road. But the sculpture was no longer glossy with shine. It no longer sparkled along its sharp and precise edges. It was blackened and twisted and defaced. It had survived the fire, but barely, and if it now served as a vision of the future, that vision was apocalyptic.

"This is what we've been dreaming of, ever'one of us, a new place, a place of our own, shiny and bright, sturdy and stainless. This was the vision we protected and intended to make real. Malloy told Donnie to build the story of our liberation, and this is what he gave us. Hope. So answer me this, if Scrbacek is not a spy seeking our ruin, not out to destroy our dreams, why, when he runs into Crapstown, does this fool head straight to Donnie Guillen? Why, by the time he leaves Ansonia Road, has our vision of the future turned to this?"

It was not like she's making it out to be. How can she twist my truth to serve some evil end of her own? I am not a spy, I know it. But to hear her tell it, I can't help but doubt myself. Was I an unwitting spy? Was I duped by DeLoatch to smoke out the opposition so they could be destroyed? Maybe DeLoatch let me escape to follow me here. Maybe, at this very moment, they are on their way, Bozant and his killers, dashing through the sewers to destroy us all. Stop. If I doubt myself, I am lost. But what does that mean, to be lost? Wasn't I lost before ever I stepped into Crapstown? Wasn't I lost before ever I lay eyes upon Caleb Breest?

"Need I trace the destruction that has followed in his path? Freaky Freddie Margolis, a founding member of the Furies, burned to death along with his business. The home of Donnie Guillen, burned to the ground, Donnie's great blueprint blackened and defaced. A swoop of violence into the Marina District, with even a dog being shot to death. A dog. Beware the dancing fool who endangers even dogs. And finally, just this afternoon, the bus terminal, refuge and home, our bus terminal burned to the ground. More dead bodies, more destruction, a fire that he himself set with his devious lies and a borrowed cell phone. How much more of this fool can we survive? And is he doing this on purpose? I hope to God yes. Heaven help us if it is all an accident."

But it was an accident, all of it, or, if part of a design, not my design. What she says is true, yes, I grant her that, but to blame it on me is obscene. What about mens rea, the cornerstone of criminal law? See the woodchuck with his tail on fire, running through the forest, setting fires in a blazing path behind him. Does the poor woodchuck deserve to die because his tail caught flame? Isn't his state of mind pure of evil? But is that my justification, that I have the innocent consciousness of a woodchuck? He runs, feeling the pain of his burning tail, a burning inescapable no matter how fast he races. He gives into the fear, running for safety, seeing only the narrow path before him, one tree at a time, while acres disappear behind him.

"He was Caleb Breest's lawyer. He met late at night with Thomas Surwin, the first assistant county prosecutor. He rousted that fat fart Trent Fallow, PI, and met with Cirilio Vega in the early morning hours, both on the payroll of Frances Galloway, who has done as much as Caleb Breest to step on our hopes. And moments before Aboud brought him here, he was meeting with a muck-a-muck high in one of Diamond's towers in Casinoland. How is it possible for him to argue that he is not a spy? Tell me, which of our enemies is he not working for?"

Oh, I know it looks bad. Oh, how could it look any worse? And from their point of view, maybe my death is justified. How to stop the destruction, the death, the despair? Kill the woodchuck before the forest is utterly destroyed. Kill the woodchuck, save the world. So how do I escape? What lie can I use to turn them around? But isn't that what got me here in the first place, lies? The lies that acquitted Caleb Breest. The lie I told Trent Fallow about having already looked at his file. And any lie I hand them, my judges, isn't that further justification for my death? But how desperate can I be if all I have is the truth? And what truth could possibly be powerful enough to reach into this cave of darkness and save my life?

"Malloy told us to hang on, to survive, and that is damn well what we're going to do. Scrbacek's death for us has become a matter of survival. It is him or us. Beware the dancing fool, for he will wreak havoc. And this fool, he is dancing like mad. Freaky Freddie Margolis would tell you, so would Ethan Brummel, so would those lying dead in the bus terminal. So would Malloy. When Scrbacek stood beside Caleb Breest, murderer of Malloy, he gave up any hopes for our sympathy. We can't afford to let him leave here alive. Him or us? I say us. Kill him. Kill him. Do your duty. Kill him, and when he's gone, lift up your heads and holler with joy."

Regina raised her arms and let out a howl that careened around the contours of the cavern. A stomping joined it, just one foot at first, one stomping foot, then another, then a third, until it seemed that the entire circle was stomping feet in a rhythmic dance of accusation. The sound closed in on Scrbacek, the stomping, the stomping. He hunched over from the force of it, as if they were stomping on his back, on his neck, on his very spirit. The tempo increased, the noise grew louder, the floor itself shook with the fury.

Squirrel waited on his crate for the cavern to quiet. Waited and waited, standing still, doing nothing to stop the stomping. It slowed of its own accord, weakened by its own spiraling hatred, and then silenced as Squirrel finally raised his head to speak. He took in a wet breath as loud as a snore. "Time now to hear from the defense. Blixen, stand and do your worst."

The light from above shifted to the old woman who stood beside the seated Scrbacek. She turned around slowly, hobbling even as she turned, and croaked out, "Our fate. What to do? Can the fool help? Is the fool for us or against us? Three nipples. Show them."

The old woman's hand, swollen knuckles, nails lined and cracked, her hand reached out and pulled open the front of Scrbacek's shirt, baring his chest.

"Three. Don't you see? Ignore the portents at your peril. It was in the moon, and I knew. Never go against the moon. You heard the Contessa? The fate of the world in his cards."

She stopped. The stomping began again until Blixen silenced it with the anger of her stare.

"Speeches are crap. Four score or something something. Speeches are crap, but I heard it from the moon."

Someone from the circle yelled, "Then tell it to the moon, old woman," the remark followed by laughter.

"Trust him," she said. "Trust the fool. My daughter died for all the fools. Three things I learned in this miserable world. Two I forget, the third I don't believe anymore. Where else are we going? Hell. Trust the fool. My daughter is dead, but the moon told me to trust the fool."

The laughter that rose from the circle was thick with derision. Blixen opened her mouth to say more and left it open even as she remained silent in the face of the laughter and the scorn. She turned and mouthed to Scrbacek, "I'm sorry."

Scrbacek looked at the old woman's rheumy eyes, saw the mark of defeat in them, the sadness of having lost a child. Scrbacek stood and reached his cuffed hands to grab the lapels of the old woman's ragged coat and shook them gently. The circle silenced at the gesture.

"It's okay," said Scrbacek. "It will be okay. Thank you." Scrbacek watched as the words pulled tears out of the watery eyes.

Then Scrbacek turned to Squirrel. "I have something to say."

A loud catcall came from the circle, then a flock of hoots.

"Your counsel has spoken for you," said Squirrel.

"I have something to say," said Scrbacek, hopping to the side of the table. The chair, still attached to his legs, bounced loudly across the floor with him. "But first I need my legs untied."

Squirrel stared at Scrbacek without saying a word. The stomping began again. The floor shook again. And then, suddenly, silence.

From out of the circle, his white cook's outfit glowing in the darkness, Ed stepped toward Scrbacek. His cleaver, the size of a sheep's head, lay in his hand. He approached the standing defendant. His jaw was clenched, his eyes were dark in the shadow of the overhead light. He stopped right in front of Scrbacek and raised the cleaver.

With a quick stoop and a slash of steel, the ropes tying Scrbacek to the chair fell limply to the ground.

Scrbacek nodded to Ed, stood on his chair, climbed onto the table, raised his still-cuffed hands high over his head, as if forming a steeple of the self, and then proclaimed, in a voice suddenly grown strong, a voice that washed over the circle of judgment, a voice that filled every corner of the huge dark space:

"I confess."

49
SCRBACEK'S CONFESSION

I confess.

I confess that I am a lawyer. I planned to stand here and present myself as another Lincoln, but I am no Lincoln. I am a scum-sucking parasite, the lowest of the low, worthy of whatever contempt you can muster for my miserable professional life. And however low you think I've stooped, trust me, you don't know the half of it.

I confess that I was Caleb Breest's lawyer, that I defended him against the charge of murdering Peter Malloy, father, husband, leader of the dispossessed, that I spread lies and false accusations in order to gain Breest an acquittal. This is a strategy permissible under the law no matter how despicable in practice. A strategy that was clearly in my best interests but maybe not in my client's. A strategy in which I am particularly deft, so believe anything I say at your peril.

I confess that my SUV was blown to smithereens and that Ethan Brummel, a good boy who had done nothing wrong in the entirety of his life other than wanting to learn the law from me, was likewise blown high to heaven. If Ethan Brummel had never met me, he would be alive today, sharing a malt with a pretty blonde, staring deeply into the blue-eyed face of bliss instead of being buried in a coffin that was never opened for his mother to view, because what was left of the corpse was in pieces, and the pieces looked like nothing more than chunks of mutton charred.

I confess that my office and home were burned to ash and with them all the records of all my trials from my very first day after passing the bar. My professional history was wiped out with a single match, and I confess not a single regret.

I confess that my cell phone was stolen by a man named Jorge, and fenced with Freaky Freddie Margolis, and as soon as he turned it on, the phone's location was located, and Freaky Freddie was wiped out in a firebomb of anger. If I had never become a lawyer, Freaky Freddie would still be around to turn your stolen cell phones into cash.

I confess to running in blind panic to Donnie for help. And I confess that Donnie's attempt to help me turned to death and ruin, torching his house, warping and blackening his three-dimensional blueprint for the future of this city. All because I brought my problems to him instead of dealing with them on my own.

I confess to running through Crapstown like a woodchuck with his tail on fire, leaving a trail of destruction and death, my own life saved only by the oft-applied sweet violence of a nightingale. Yes, there was a fight behind Ed's Eats that left three in the hospital and one in the morgue. Yes, I was hiding in the Marina District until they found and shot my old dog Palsgraf, a far nobler figure than I could ever hope to be. Yes, I misdirected my attackers to the bus station, clued in the state to the deception with a borrowed cell phone, and incited a conflagration that devastated much of what was vital to you all, an event which I did not foresee but which I should have foreseen and for which I take full responsibility.

And I confess, finally, to knowing something that they don't want me to know, to knowing something the price of knowing is my life, to knowing a secret for which they will burn down all of Crapstown to stop me from revealing. It was a piece of knowledge I didn't even know I held, something consigned to my forgotten files before ever I glanced upon it. But the reason I met with Surwin, with Trent Fallow, with Cirilio Vega, and with Drinian DeLoatch, high in Diamond's Mount Olympus, was to find out what it was they thought I knew and why it was important. And this I did.

I confess to learning what it is that is truly going on beneath the cracked surface of Crapstown, and it is a knowledge that can shake this world. So long as only I know it, only I am at risk. Anyone I pass it to will be as endangered as I. I have told no one. The knowledge resides only with me. With this secret, I am a woodchuck with his tail on fire, destroying any wood through which I pass. If I survive and continue to run, the destruction will continue to follow.

What do you do to a woodchuck with his tail on fire? You shoot him, you shoot him dead, and hope to contain the damage.

So that is what you must do. I stand before you after my full and honest confession and give you no choice but to kill me. But as you sing your executioner's song and lower your pistol to my head, I ask only that you don't pretend you are gaining some sort of sweet revenge. I am not a spy, I am not a plant set amongst you by your enemies. I am no innocent, true, but I had no intent to do you harm. The bomb that destroyed Ethan Brummel, the fire that destroyed my office and home, the war that engulfed 714 Ansonia Road were not my doing. If you wonder at the cache of weapons found in my basement, ask Donnie from where they came, for I have no doubt they were among the weapons he sold to a tall red-haired man named Remi Bozant, who for reasons personal to himself wants nothing more than for me to die. Be assured that I am not a conspirator in your ongoing tragedy. All I wanted was to survive. All I wanted was what all of you want: to be left alone to screw up my own life, and maybe to find some semblance of redemption in the end. How pathetic that even such a meager hope is now impossible for me.

I know a secret. So kill me, kill me now, but not out of hatred or disgust or anger, no. Kill me now so that the secret will die with me and they won't be chasing me still and endangering your cozy homes. Give them my corpse so that you can go back to where you were before ever I showed my face in Crapstown, so that you can continue to wait and hope for something to come and turn the promise of Malloy's fine speeches into your reality.

At root I am a timid man. If I had the choice, I would never have learned the secret that curses now my life. The Gospel says, "Ye shall know the truth, and the truth shall make you free," but don't you believe it. Nothing imprisons like the truth. The path my knowledge has set me upon has been hard and brutal, and I blame you not for killing me to avoid it. If I passed my secret to you, I know who you would be matched against and what you would be forced to do. I now know all it would compel of you, and I say better to let it die with me. For listen when I tell you that once you learn what I know, all of you will be at risk, all of you will be forced into the battle of your lives, all of you will be confronted with what it truly means to pit your collective will against the massive might of your enemies.

So kill me, as you must. Listen to your dread and kill me. Think of yourselves as realists, not as cowards, as artful tacticians who bow to discretion, not to valor. Think of yourselves wiser than the foolish brave. You heard Regina. Your fate is to wait for a savior to save you, and I am not he. All I have is a secret and a chance for you to save yourselves. So kill me and kill the secret, take yourselves out of the battle, survive within the narrow limits of your constricted lives, and wait and wait and wait for your future. For that is your destiny.

Unless . . .

50
RICO

-Hello, Mrs. Ling?

-Who's calling?

-I'm looking for your daughter, Jenny.

-She's not here. Who's calling and how you get her phone?

-This is J.D. Scrbacek.

-She's not here, especially for you, mister. She's never here no more for you.

-It's very important, Mrs. Ling. I desperately need to talk to your daughter. Can you tell me where she is?

-You did not hear me? Something wrong, mister, with that phone you stole? She's not here for you. She's wasted enough on you. How many years thrown out the back door like yesterday's cabbage. Go away and leave her alone, and don't call here again. We don't want to hear from you no more. Disappear like smoke.

-Mrs. Ling, please . . .

-What do you need? Money? You need money for your drugs and your girls to shack you with? That is why you ran away, no? You ran away for your drugs and your girls, leaving her alone. You have done enough to her already. Rob a bank if you need money, but don't call here again. You ran away once, now you stay away.

-How's that crab soup you make, Mrs. Ling?

-Magnificent, what you think? Way too good for you.

-I miss it. I dream about it sometimes.

-Shame for you then. Never no more crab soup for you.

-Don't count on it. Stock up on hard-shells and corn, Mrs. Ling, because I'm hungry as a bear, and I am back.

<Connection Terminated>

-Stop calling, you.

-I need to talk to Jenny.

-I tell you once already, she's not here for you.

-Is Sean there? Are they safe?

-Don't call here again, or I'll tell police. They lock you up a hundred years for what you did. I promise what I say. I know people. The sergeant Chen Zong, big man on force, he is my cousin. Don't call here again.

<Connection Terminated>

-Please, don't hang up again, Mrs. Ling. Please. I'm desperate.

-Tell me about it.

-Jenny? Jenny. You're there. Good, great. Are you safe? Is everything okay? What's it like in Philly?

-Smothering.

-I don't think your mother likes me very much.

-She never did, as she takes time to remind me each and every day. It's why her phone's unlisted. In case you want to call.

-It was on your speed dial, right after the pizza place. How's Sean? Does he ask about me?

-No.

-Did you tell him anything? Did he ask you any questions?

-He hasn't mentioned you. But he does talk about that girl—what was her name, Nightingale?

-He's got a good eye.

-Are you two, kind of, like, an item or something?

-What? No, Jen, no, no. You're the only one for me.

-Please.

-I've been thinking about you. I'm serious.

-No, you're not. You're scared and in trouble, and the danger has made you delirious. Where are you?

-In the sewer.

-And I'm back with my mother. It's funny how we always end up right where we belong.

-I was caught in some strange trial for my life in this huge cavern beneath the sewers with some self-appointed vigilantes as my jury. I had to climb up a hundred feet just to get a signal.

-What drug are you on?

-Nothing, I swear.

-J.D.?

-It's true, it happened. It was like *The People's Court*.

-But you're still talking.

-Well, you know, if there's one realm in which I'm competent, it's the courtroom.

-Bamboozled them with lies, I assume.

-I developed a new strategy. I bamboozled them with the absolute truth. It was all very dramatic and satisfying. Except now comes the hard part.

-Are you still being chased?

-Yes, though the tables are about to be turned. But first I have to go into the lion's den. Tonight. I have to have a final talk with my client.

-Caleb Breest?

-Yes, I owe it to him.

-You owe him nothing.

-No, I do. It's like I've woken up from a dream and realized all I've done wrong in the past decade. Not everything can be corrected, but there's still time to right some of the mistakes. Caleb Breest is one of them. I wasn't looking out for him like I should have been, Jenny. All I was doing was trying to get him out of jail, but he needed more than that from me. I have to see him tonight and deal with him once and for all, and I don't know if I'm going to come out of it alive. Which is why I needed to talk with you now. Remember when we used to dream about opening a practice of our own, doing good and making pots of money while we did it? Remember how we said all we needed was one big case?

-The holy grail.

-I have it for you, Jenny. Your one big case, and it is huge. A class action that will save Crapstown, save the Marina District, that will finance the rebuilding of the entire city. And it will make any lawyer who touches it as rich as Midas.

-Why are you giving it to me? Why don't you keep it for yourself?

-Because I had a dream about us.

-Please. There aren't enough violins in the world.

-And because if I don't survive the night, which is highly likely, I want to leave something behind that will take care of my son into the future.

-Don't be so damn dramatic. He's not your . . . He's not . . . Crap. Do the defendants have deep pockets?

-The deepest. James E. Diamond is one of them.

-Jesus . . .

-Do you have a pad? Are you getting this down?

-Hold on, hold on. Okay. James E. Diamond. Go ahead.

-Francis Galloway. Joey Torresdale. Remi Bozant. Cirilio Vega. The Right Honorable Chief Judge Jonathan Dickerson.

-Get out of here.

-And Drinian DeLoatch.

-DeLoatch?

- You were so right about him. You were so right about everything. He's rotten at the core. Or was. I think I might have killed him.

-With a gun?

-With a prick the size of a baseball bat.

-Now you're boasting.

-I want to try again. Me and you. A full shot. And Sean. What do you say?

-Shut up with that already. Survive the night and we'll talk about it.

-Really?

-What's the designated class for the suit?

-The residents of Crapstown, the residents of the Marina District, the estate of Ethan Brummel, the estate of one Freaky Freddie Margolis, all parties who were in any way damaged by a conspiracy among the defendants to bulldoze a path through the heart of Crapstown and make Diamond's dream of a marina gambling resort a de facto reality. File it in federal court. Make it a racketeering case seeking treble damages, with predicate offenses of arson, extortion, murder.

-Who are the named plaintiffs?

-Well, for starters, me. Title it *Scrbacek v. Diamond*. Or *The Estate of Scrbacek v. Diamond*, depending on what happens tonight. Before I head out, I'll scratch up a will giving you power of attorney for my estate and leaving everything I own to Sean.

-J.D., don't.

-I'll mail it to your house. I dreamed about you, Jen. And in the dream I loved you.

-Shut up with that, J.D. It's not fair, it's not right. You just can't come back into my life and start spraying your bullshit again.

-And when I woke up, I realized it wasn't just a dream. Losing you is another of the mistakes I might have time to right.

-Stop. Please.

-But you have to file the complaint tomorrow.

-What? No. It's impossible.

-Listen to what I say. File it tomorrow. It's okay if it's rough—you'll amend it when you can, after discovery—but file it tomorrow, and notify the press. As soon as you file it, the story will be in the open, the arena will change from the streets to the courtroom, the big boys will back away. If you file it tomorrow, you'll save lives.

-I'll file it tomorrow. But why don't you just come in now and we'll draft the complaint together.

-Because it's not over. This is a conspiracy of money and violence. You can fight money with the law, but violence only responds to one thing.

-J.D.

-And my client is in the way. Standard complaint. Plaintiff Scrbacek is a resident of bla bla. Defendant Diamond is a resident of bla bla bla. Jurisdiction in the federal courts is predicated on RICO, eighteen U.S.C., bla bla bla bla bla. You got that?

-Yes.

-If I make it through, you'll give me a chance?

-No, J.D., no. I can't.

-You won't forgive me? Ever? I forgive you that thing with Vega.

-Go to hell.

-I do. I forgive you, just like that, and it feels good, too. You should try it.

-Kumbaya.

-Just a chance?

-We'll see.

-That means yes?

-That means we'll see. You hurt me, J.D. I'm barely recovered. You just can't snap your fingers and make it go away.

-What will it take?

-More than you have.

-Don't bet against me.

-No, I would never do that, J.D. You can go broke doing that. Tell me the story.

-Okay.

-From the beginning.

-Okay. It all starts with DeLoatch.

51
Dirty Dirk's

Dirty Dirk's.

It appeared to be just another warehouse. It crouched by the bay on the western edge of town, a ragged commercial area that shut down dead for the night, a landscape of dark shadows and darker schemes, of rats licking dry the bloodstained drains behind Nate's Processed Meats. You climbed out of your Porsche, you crawled out of your pickup, you emerged like a walking shadow from the buckling black streets. You came quiet, you came with war whoops, you followed the steady rhythmic bass, like the heartbeat of some great Cyclops buried deep underground, to what at first glance appeared to be just another warehouse.

You told the beef in front that you knew someone who knew someone, somebody sent you, you were in with Mickey or with Johnny Mac. And if the bald guy with the nose ring gave the nod, the door was opened and they let you pass through to a night filled with the raw violence of pure possibility. There was a band behind cage wire, there was a poker room with armed guards, there was an unending stream of draft beer and watered whiskey. And there were girls, oh yes, girls, of every race, creed, political affiliation—even one member of the ACLU, bless her bleeding heart—girls with legs like sprinters, wearing nothing but glitter, who would writhe on your lap till the sweat from their breasts drenched your shirt, and tell me true, friend, does it get any better than that?

You came for the action, you came for the booze, you came to do business because it was the place to do business when other businesses closed, you came for the show, for the fights, for the pungent scent of danger, you came for the girls, you came for the girls, my God, you came for the girls, but whatever it was, you sure as hell came.

Guaranteed.

Scrbacek waited in the shadows, watching the comings and goings at the ungainly old building, trying to pick out escape routes if he needed to run, though he knew if it came to running he was as good as lost. The rain fell in a shifting rhythm, spitting against the turned-up collar of his raincoat before soaking his back. The raincoat no longer kept him dry; it only hid how wet his shirt had become.

There were guards in the front, he remembered, though possibly more this night than he remembered, but he had no intention of strolling through the front door. There was a loading dock in the rear, where cases of liquor, cases of beer, dull metal kegs, pallets of frozen chicken wings, dog-size bottles of Tabasco, where all of the necessities were brought into the building, and it too would be guarded. There were most likely spotters on the long flat roof, maybe a few hiding in the cars parked in the lot. He had no doubt the place was being tightly watched, and that the watchers were watching for him.

Scrbacek circled the building, keeping a careful distance, until he reached the bay, the black water pocked by rain. He stooped over and followed the coastline until he faced a long stretch of wall with a wide-open doorway gleaming in its middle. A man in a cable-knit sweater and black beret sat in a chair and leaned back against the wall right beside the doorway.

This is where she'd said to come, this is where she'd said to wait, so he had come and now he would wait.

Through the doorway he could see women with bare legs and flannel shirts passing back and forth, stepping outside for a smoke, talking with each other. One woman was crying, her back bent with a weary sadness, and two other women were comforting her. He saw a blonde, holding a pocketbook, take a step out the door and stand beside the man in the sweater. She peered into the darkness toward the bay. Elisha Baltimore. As she looked out, she spoke to the man in the sweater. He puffed out his chest and turned his full attention to her.

Scrbacek stood and waved his arm slowly. She kept peering as if she didn't see a thing, and then she stepped out into the rain, outside the man's hearing distance, and pulled a cellular phone out of her pocketbook before putting the pocketbook over her head to protect her hair from the rain. A few seconds later, Scrbacek's phone rang.

"We've been having power problems," she said. "One or two a night, something about a balky transformer sending surges through the system. We're due for another in a few minutes. Remember the map I drew for you? You'll have about thirty seconds to get in the door and through the hallway to the bar before they reset the circuit breaker."

"What about the guard?"

"Just before it goes dark, he'll be off searching for a mouse."

"He'll leave his post for a mouse?"

"It'll be in the dressing room. Pete never fails to come up with excuses to find his way to the dressing room. More tits than a dairy barn in there. You see him leave, get ready. Lights out, you go."

"Will do."

"I can't help you once you're inside."

"I know that. But once I am inside, you get the hell out of there. It could get bad."

"Don't worry about me."

"You going to meet the others?"

"Yes, of course. I have a weakness for romantic shipwrecks. I saw *Titanic* four times."

"You're a hell of a woman, Elisha Baltimore, with strange masochistic tendencies."

"I hope you realize they're going to kill you."

"I have a card to play, and I think it's an ace."

"Scrbacek, you're a sweet guy and all, but what you know about playing poker with these guys wouldn't fill the inside of a matchbook."

The line went dead. Scrbacek watched as Elisha hustled back into the building, patting Pete on the beret as she passed by. Pete's head whiplashed.

Scrbacek bent low and scooted closer to the building until he was directly in front of the door. He kneeled down and waited. And waited. The rain battered his shoulders. The bass lines from the band rose from the ground like drummed messages of war. Scrbacek waited. And then Pete in the sweater swung out of his chair and rushed inside and Scrbacek readied himself like a sprinter for the lights to go out.

And they did.

And Scrbacek was off.

Running through the dim skittering emergency lights flickering from the rooftop, running for the outline of the entrance, hearing the groan of exasperated patrons from inside. Up the steps, to the right, past trim shadows in their flannel shirts, brushing past swatches of soft skin.

Hearing the women's shouts and curses, and a male voice going, "Where's that rat? Where's that damn rat?" Another yelling, "Get the goddamn breaker, goddamn it."

Pushing his way through a swinging door into a place of absolute blackness, sliding forward until he was enveloped in the luscious thickness of velvet curtains. Finding the opening, pushing through the curtains into a vague stroboscopic light, like the light of a local subway station pulsing through the windows of a dark express train as the crowd hooted and yelled obscenities at the darkness. Rushing across a flat open surface, slamming into something so hard he fell back onto his tailbone.

A pole? What the hell is a pole doing there?

Oh yeah.

Grabbing hold of the pole, pulling himself up, spying a row of faces lining the front of the stage, the faces blinking on and off with the strobe, eyes following his rushing shadow with the hope it might be something worth seeing. Scampering to the left, jumping off the edge of the stage, twisting his ankle and crying out even as he popped once again to his feet.

Limping his way along the wall to the bar, past one stool, past another, some stools open, some with asses firmly in place, a scattering of curses, a hand slapping him away. Still moving, finding an empty series of stools and hopping on one, taking a deep breath, crossing his hands in front of him, another deep breath, calming his breathing a few seconds, a few seconds more.

The lights blinked on, dim and red, true, but on. A cheer rose, a trumpet blasted, the crowd laughed and high-fived one another. The bartender, a tall, droopy man who looked like he himself had been poured, made his way along the length of the bar, barely noticing Scrbacek sitting on a stool all by his lonesome.

"Rolling Rock and a tequila," said Scrbacek.

The bartender, without eyeing his new customer, reached behind for a bottle, popped off the top, poured a sloppy shot of house tequila, and slammed bottle and shot glass in front of Scrbacek.

Scrbacek pulled a bill out of his pocket and handed it to the man.

A very wet hundred.

The bartender looked at the bill, looked at Scrbacek for the first time, cocked his head like the face was familiar for some reason, and said, "It better be good," before heading to the register to make change.

Scrbacek lifted the beer and took a long swig. As he drank, bottle tilted in front of his face, he spun around on his stool and took in the scene.

Dirty Dirk's.

52
THE BARKEEP

It was like a temple to the goddess Aphrodite, if the Greeks had gone for navy-blue velvet instead of white marble, if the high priests played live blues, and if Aphrodite herself wore high heels and a G-string, and called herself Sunny DeLight.

The stage at Dirty Dirk's snaked across the front of the huge room, with walkways leading directly into the crowd. And there was a crowd, believe it, jammed up against the edges of the stage, frenzied in the red-tinged light, men drinking and laughing and reaching out with bills in their hands. They were shouting at Sunny, loudly, if you could tell anything from the straining of the tendons in their necks, and Sunny was hearing it, the way she stared into the crowd and shook whatever could be shaken. But the men's voices were lost to Scrbacek beneath the loud batterings of the band, trumpet and bass, two electric guitars, a saxophone.

Waitresses dressed like underdressed Catholic schoolgirls weaved in and out of the clots of men, trays loaded with beer and bourbon. Naked women walked among the tables, pulling up chairs, sitting on laps, rubbing hard with the palms of their hands, letting the customers do everything but touch between their legs or unzip themselves. Weightlifters with pinched faces looked on and kept the peace.

Behind the general crowd was a higher tier of tables, where the better-dressed men sat, where the band was not so loud, where the women were not so strict about the rules and were more than willing to diddle you under the table. And behind that, on the highest tier, was a rail with two guards and a single table, flanked by large red panels, each imprinted with a dragon rearing back and shooting flame. This was Caleb Breest's personal table, where Scrbacek himself had sat with Joey Torresdale on his visits to Dirk's. Scrbacek's stomach sank when he saw that the table was empty.

Scrbacek turned around and waited for the bartender to come back with his change.

"You want to keep that?" he said.

The bartender shrugged, the long, droopy face evidencing distinct disinterest even as he slipped the wad of change smoothly into his pocket.

"Is the big man in tonight?" said Scrbacek.

"Who?"

"Don't play cute. You don't have the face for it."

The bartender glanced behind Scrbacek and lowered his voice. "I don't know who you're talking about, mister, and neither do you if you know what's good for you."

"I want advice, I'll write Dear Abby."

A hint of a smile attached itself to one droopy lid. "Do I know you? I think I know you."

"When Mr. Breest finds out I was asking for him, he won't be happy that I was ignored."

The smiling eyelid quieted. "Still don't know who you're talking about." The bartender backed away before turning to acknowledge a thirsty call a few seats down.

Scrbacek shrugged, took another swig of the beer, sucked the top off the tequila. He twisted once again to check out Breest's table. Still empty. When he turned back, there was a different bartender behind the bar.

He was into his second beer and shot when a woman stepped right beside him. He tried not to pay her too much notice, but it was hard, seeing as she was wearing a G-string and nothing else, and seeing as her breasts were positively Germanic and worthy of baring on some sun-slopped Spanish beach.

"I'm Sandy," she said.

"Not from what I can tell," said Scrbacek.

"You want to buy me a drink?"

"How much are champagne cocktails going for these days?"

"Mine cost twenty-five," she said, "but buy me two and I'll dance on the bar and stick my ass in your face."

"You're easy. With my usual dates it takes at least five."

"So we're on?"

"Thank you, Sandy, and it's quite an attractive offer, but I'm here on business."

"Why the hell do you think I do this?"

And then, from behind them both, a voice like a metal blade grinding on a stone wheel: "Beat it, Sandy."

Sandy startled at the sound and stared behind Scrbacek, who didn't turn around. "I was just—"

"Get lost."

Sandy backed away, spun around, ran.

"You got nerve coming here," said the voice, "and less than half a brain, if you think you're getting out alive."

"Just in for a quick pop," said Scrbacek, still without turning. "I hear you've been looking for me, Dirk."

"Was. Don't have to anymore. How'd the hell you get in here anyways?"

"I followed the rats."

"Funny. Now, nice and easy, get your ass in gear and come with me."

"I don't think so," said Scrbacek, finally turning around and leaning back with both elbows on the bar, bottle in his hand just in case.

In front of him was a refugee from the WWE, tall, bald, with a great gold ring through his nose and a black T-shirt showing off his body, huge and cut and grotesquely steroidal.

"I'd go if it was Sandy asking," said Scrbacek, "follow her to a back room, sure. Those breasts. Gesundheit. But, frankly, Dirk, I never swung your way."

"You're not man enough," said Dirk.

"That might be it, but for now, I think I'll wait for Caleb. He told me to meet him here."

"And you wonder why everyone hates lawyers. We're here talking not one minute and already you're lying to my face."

"Ask him."

"Don't need to."

"Tell him his attorney is here."

"Last I heard his attorney was dead. A hit-and-run accident right in the middle of Jefferson. Splat, like a possum on the road. Too bad, too. Vega was a good customer. In fact, Sandy was one of his favorites."

"Who you answering to these days, Dirk?" said Scrbacek. "Who's got your balls in his fist now?"

From behind Dirk came a soft voice, "Do we have a problem here, Dirk?"

Scrbacek leaned to the side to get a view of the man behind Dirk, a small man in a gold jacket, fuchsia shirt, black tie, his hair slicked back tight to his skull. The nose on his face was a misshapen blob of putty.

"Well," said Scrbacek, "that answers that."

"J.D. Scrbacek," said Joseph Torresdale. "It's so good to see you again. And still alive, too. Wonderful. I was never able to congratulate you on your courtroom victory. Thrilling, just thrilling. You and I, working together as we did, it made me feel like I had a hand in it all."

"We had a little help, I gather, from my old law professor."

"I consulted DeLoatch, yes. Too bad about him—have you heard? He had a heart attack in a hot tub. They say people with heart conditions should avoid excessive heat. His pacemaker shorted on him, imagine that. Critical condition."

"It's a dangerous night for lawyers."

"Oh, Dirk told you about Vega, did he? We just heard. He was a nice boy. Handsome too. Why are you here, J.D.?"

"To talk to Caleb."

"He's indisposed, I'm afraid. He had another episode with his heart. He took his pills, thank God—where would we be without the nitro— but we have no idea when he'll be up and about. It's such a dangerous thing to have an oversize heart."

"I'll wait."

"Well, no reason to sit like a lump at the bar. Come join me at the table."

"I like it here," said Scrbacek.

"Come now, J.D. This is a respectable business, and you are our friend. You have nothing to fear here."

"That's probably what Luigi Puchesi thought about Migello's before it blew all to hell around him."

"Ah, suddenly a student of history. Next you'll be lecturing me on the Defenestration of Prague."

"As far as defenestrations go, that's the tops."

"The night is still young. Come, join me at the table. A bottle of cabernet for our guest, all right, Dirk? One of the good ones. Who are we saving it for? I don't think the queen is coming, though I must say those pale-blue dress suits of hers are smashing."

"Let me waste him," said Dirk. "Let me pull his liver out his throat."

"Patience. What have I been teaching you? Patience. Come, J.D., be a dear and don't be afraid. Let's chat."

53
JOEY TORRESDALE

"Have you ever wanted to reinvent yourself, J.D.? Have you ever considered the joy of becoming something completely new? Take your experiences, your learning, your view of the world, your joie de vivre, take everything you care about, everything that makes you J.D. Scrbacek, yet leave behind that useless encrusted matter that traps you within other's expectations. Your race, your profession, your class. I walk the streets, and mothers pull their children away. I open a club, and it is immediately a mob club. I give away turkeys to the poor on Christmas Day, and I'm laughed at as a hood trying to burnish his image. And they're right. That's why I give away turkeys on Christmas Day. What do you think, I care?"

Scrbacek leaned on the table, before him an untouched wineglass filled with a liquid the color of blood. He was watching a woman on the stage do things to the pole that he had never before imagined but that he never again would forget. How did she get that one leg behind her head? he wondered. Joey Torresdale, beside him, was talking about something or other, trying to get whatever was aching him off his narrow chest, but Scrbacek was too tired and too afraid to listen very carefully. He was beginning to think coming here was a mistake.

"When I was growing up, there wasn't any choice," continued Torresdale. "You either slaved in some factory or became a hood, working for the Puchesi family. I could never waste my life in a factory, J.D. Look at me. I'm not the type. I need more snap and jive, I need more excitement and adventure. I would have joined the marines, but I was too small, so I joined the mob. I was young, angry, I became a hood, and now I don't want to be one anymore."

"Has Caleb recovered yet?" said Scrbacek, his gaze skittering around the club. "I need to talk to Caleb."

"Are you listening, J.D.? I'm pouring out my heart to you, not to mention the house's finest wine, and I don't even think you're listening."

"It's been a long night, Joey, and already I've heard enough speeches and monologues, enough solipsistic self-satisfied confessions, including my own, enough bullshit to make me want to puke right here on this table. Right here. On this table. The one thing I always admired about you was that you gave so little of yourself. Joseph Torresdale, man of mystery. Do I really need to listen to your confession too?"

"Yes, you do."

"I guess it's my night to be disillusioned about everything." Dramatic sigh. "All right, go on, make me more nauseous than I already am. Tell me how you want to reinvent yourself."

"That's it. Exactly. And how does one do that? Reinvent himself. Is it enough just to run away, change your name, steal some dead slob's social security number, and start over? That's a way, yes, but so unsatisfying, don't you think? Working as a short-order chef to make the weekly rent on your motel room. I deserve better than that, J.D. And you do, too. So how do we go about it? Tell me. How?"

"You turn Crapstown into a parking lot," said Scrbacek, still scouring the club with his gaze. "Where is he? Caleb, I mean. Maybe I could go to wherever he's resting and talk to him there?"

"I would think reinvention of the self would be foremost on your mind these days, J.D. Who needs a new identity more than you? What with some mysterious force out to slit your throat. And even if you survive the assassin's knife, the county prosecutor is ready to indict you for murder. But don't worry, they love lawyers in jail. You'll be writing habeas petitions for every two-bit con in your block, at least those nights when you're not on a date."

"I like being busy."

"But you could be someone else, J.D. Someone anonymous, someone rich enough to be left alone."

"I'll stay just who I am."

"Whatever the cost?"

"Are you offering something, Joey? Is that what this is all about? All right, let's cut to the chase. What's the deal?"

"We'll give you a piece, J.D. We'll give you enough to change your life. I know what your life is like now: alone, lonely, hunted, no one to love and no one to love you."

"Old data."

"You can start anew or return to the old, whatever you choose. It's your opportunity, J.D. I can even arrange to fake your death, to make you completely free to reinvent yourself as anyone you want, live anywhere you want, experience any adventure you want."

"And how do I earn my new life?"

"Tell me who you told."

"So that's what you want, more names for Bozant's list."

Joey's eyes narrowed above his putty nose. "Who did you tell?"

"The whole of the Furies."

Joey's eyes widened with surprise.

"I told them everything. They dragged me into some cavern deep within the bowels of the city and put a spotlight on me. I started with a few jokes, did some soft-shoe, recommended the veal, and then I told them everything. They were pretty angry. They seemed to take it more violently than I expected. Last I heard they were getting up a mob to tear down this place and rip your careful plan to shreds. You know, the old rush the ramparts, storm the Bastille, burn down the feudal lord's manor in order to free the serfs. They seemed particularly angry at you. Was it something I said, you think? And I also told a sharp lawyer who tomorrow, right after she delivers the complaint to the press, is filing a racketeering suit against Diamond and DeLoatch and Galloway and someone else . . ." Dramatic finger snapping. "Oh yeah, you. So you see, Joey, you're not going to reinvent yourself after all. Once a hood, always a hood. I'll be sure to send you a Christmas turkey in jail."

"Pity."

"All that scheming for naught."

"No, not that. We're too strong to lose." Torresdale reached his hand beneath the table. "It's a pity, because, believe it or not, J.D., I actually liked you."

Immediately the table was surrounded by three men: one of them was Dirk; two others were large with cable-knit sweaters and toughed-up expressions, designed to let Scrbacek know just how hard they thought they were.

"What's with all the cable-knit sweaters and berets?" said Scrbacek. "Everyone looks like a beat poet on steroids."

"My design," said Torresdale. "A little more bohemian than the usual trench coat, don't you think? Even in my business it helps to have a sense of style."

"I came here to speak to Caleb," Scrbacek said in a slow, careful voice, enunciating each syllable. "He will be very unhappy if he doesn't get to speak to me."

"Frankly, J.D., I don't give a shit. I think you know Stephanie."

Two of the men stepped away, and behind, in her suit jacket and sturdy shoes, her lips pursed in perturbation, stood Stephanie Dyer. Coming here was a bad mistake, thought Scrbacek upon seeing her angry pocked face, a very bad mistake. What had he been thinking? He had come to talk to Caleb, and now it looked like he would be dead before Breest knew he had come at all. A very, very bad mistake. He tried to calm his nerves and sound hard by saying, "Look what the tide flushed in," but he failed on both counts.

"You and I, we've got ourselves a date, Scrbacek," said Dyer. "You and I, we're going dancing."

"You killed my dog."

"We're going to dance slow, and hard. I'm going to slap you bloody, and I'm going to enjoy every minute of it."

"It's not bad enough that you sold your soul for a small piece of change from the turkey man here, but then you went and killed my dog. You'll pay for that. But just now I came to speak to Caleb. He'll be very—"

Scrbacek didn't finish his sentence because Dyer stepped forward and punched him in the face, splitting a gash in his cheek just below his left eye and sending him sprawling on the floor. He was enveloped in pain. His arm, his ankle, his cheek, every part of him screamed silently. He rolled over to face his attacker.

"What were you before you became a law enforcement agent?" he gasped. "A gym teacher?"

Dyer kicked him in the side. Scrbacek's ribs dented with pain, he writhed on the floor like a beached fish. Dyer leaned over his twisting body. "Yes, actually."

"Pick him up," said Joey, pouring himself another glass of wine, sniffing its scent, holding it to the light.

The two beefy men grabbed Scrbacek from the floor, each taking hold of an arm, raising him to his tiptoes. The salt of his own blood dripped into Scrbacek's mouth. His ribs felt smashed to pieces. He looked groggily around the room, wondering when someone was going to come and stop this. A few faces stared at the scene before turning away. The others were too enraptured by the entertainment. The men who were holding him pulled his arms behind him. The blues band blew louder, the girl on the stage did a split, hands beneath her breasts, lifting them high, and the crowd went wild.

"You're looking for help?" said Joey. "Here? Charming, really, but believe me, J.D., they don't care. It's my club, I only let my people inside. And it's a special night tonight. I brought everyone in. Big doings tonight, oh yes." He reached into his jacket pocket and tossed a set of keys to Dirk. "After Stephanie's finished, take him to Nate's, put him in the grinder, feed him to the rats."

"Won't that be fun," said Dirk.

"And hose it down but good when you're done. I don't want Nate chewing my ass. Sorry about this, J.D. Anything you want to say to me, before you go?"

The two men turned Scrbacek toward Torresdale, and Scrbacek said, between gasps of pain, "I came to see—"

But that was as far as he got, because before he could continue Dyer slammed a fist into his stomach, expelling whatever air he'd had in his lungs.

"Are you done?" said Torresdale. "Any other bons mots to toss my way? You were a big man, weren't you, running around, figuring things out. Now look at yourself. What made you think you could stand up to us? You're just another goddamn lawyer. One thing we're not afraid of is lawyers. That's what Vega learned, too. And what your friend Jenny Ling will learn before she ever gets a chance to bring that suit."

"How did you . . . How?"

"Who else would you give it to? We're not idiots. You thought we didn't keep track of where she went after our little misadventure at her house in the Marina District? After they finish with you, Stephanie and Dirk will be taking a ride to Philadelphia. On the expressway it won't take them but an hour. You'll use the Camaro."

"Got it," said Dirk.

"Take care of her, and her little boy too. Oh dear me, now I sound like the Wicked Witch of the West. But what's that you said, J.D.—once a hood, always a hood. At least it's not your worry anymore. You'll be reinvented just like we talked about. Reinvented as ground chuck."

"You touch her, so help me, I'll—"

"You'll what, J.D.? Sue me? Bore me to death with some constitutional argument? You're a lawyer, not a warrior. Forget about Ms. Ling. Help yourself first. That's always been my motto. Help yourself first. And I do. Take him away."

The men holding him turned Scrbacek around and started dragging him from the table, behind one of the dragon screens, down a short flight of steps, into a darkened tunnel smelling of oil and piss. The bass rhythms of the blues band drilled into his head.

He had to get away, get out, get to Philadelphia before Dyer, that bitch, and Dirk. How had he been so stupid as to mention the lawsuit, to bring Jenny into it, and Sean. How had he been so arrogant? He couldn't leave it alone, had to push the lawsuit into Torresdale's face. Why was he still such a jerk?

He tried to shrug his way out of the hold of the two men, but they tightened their grips and kept dragging. He tried again, and something from behind smashed into his head, dazing him.

At the end of the tunnel were two lights, and as he was dragged toward the lights, Scrbacek had to fight the thought that he was already dead, in the tunnel, reaching for the heavenly glow. Walking behind him still were Dyer and Dirk, laughing about something. Ahead were those two lights. He struggled again, futilely, halfheartedly, but it was hopeless, and he knew it was hopeless.

And then the lights went out—first one, then the other, eclipsed as if by a giant moon.

But not a moon, no, a silhouette that had stepped directly in front of him. A huge figure, tall and massive, with shoulders so wide they brushed either side of the hallway. The figure took a step toward him. The men who were carrying Scrbacek halted. The footsteps behind him stopped. The music suddenly died, and in the corridor now there fell not a sound, except a deep wet breathing and the little moans that Scrbacek hadn't even realized he was making.

The voice, when it came, was a soft, cracked whisper.

"Leave him to me," said Caleb Breest.

54
LAWYER-CLIENT

"I came here to talk to you as your lawyer," said Scrbacek, sitting awkwardly now, his abdomen bent from his beating, a wad of bloodied tissue pressed to his split cheek.

He and Caleb Breest were alone in a bleak back office, a single light dangling above the oversize oak desk that squatted between them. Breest had sent away Dyer, Dirk, and the two goons with a jerk of his head, placing two men of his own choosing outside the office. One was a squat fireplug, the other a monster almost as big as Breest himself, and he told them in his cracked whisper to let no one in. No one.

"Since I have not heard specifically from you that I have been dismissed," continued Scrbacek, "I will continue to assume the role of your attorney, though after tonight I am resigning. I came to tell you about what has happened, to warn you about what is going to happen, and to discuss with you, as your lawyer, your options going forward. This is something I never did during my representation of you, and which was a failure on my part that I needed to rectify."

Scrbacek looked at the great unmoving figure of Caleb Breest and wondered if the man had understood a word.

"What I mean, Caleb, is that I'm still your lawyer and I've come to help."

Caleb Breest, sitting stiffly behind the desk, failed to smile at the last line, which others could have construed as a joke. His hands, clasped tight one in the other, rested heavily on the raw wooden surface. His huge head tilted forward, and in the overhead light the shadows of his brow formed deep black blotches that ran down either side of his face. The blotches lent his appearance a ferocious sadness, like Oedipus after he had plucked out his own eyes, dimly aware of where he was, of what he had done, of what terrors the future held. But then again, the depth of emotion in Breest's shadowy appearance could all have been a mirage. Scrbacek had represented this man on a capital murder charge, had defended him before the world and a jury, was aware of all this man was accused of having committed but still held not the first hint of what lay beneath the fearsome facade.

"For the past four days, someone has been trying to kill me," said Scrbacek. "It started when they blew up my car. I told you about that in the courthouse holding cell after the acquittal. At the time we didn't know whether the blast was intended for me or for you, but now I know it was intended for you and me, both. It has been decided that both of us need to die."

Caleb Breest remained still as a statue, a larger-than-life hulking figure of menace, formed by Rodin, cast in bronze. What Scrbacek could see of the face surrounding the deep shadows did not flinch. Did he know? Was all this old news? After what DeLoatch had told Scrbacek, he'd assumed that Caleb Breest had been aware of the casino deal but not that Breest himself had been marked for death. In coming here he had assumed that he would be giving Breest new information, information that would be of great interest to his client, information that would save his client's life and induce his client to save Scrbacek's in turn. But Breest was not reacting. Was everything that happened a piece of his design? Was Caleb Breest clever beyond imagining, a master manipulator, sitting back and watching his own schemes come to glorious fruition? If so, then Scrbacek was now just a minor obstacle to be swept away, like Malloy before him. A shiv of fear inserted itself between Scrbacek's shoulder blades. He closed his eyes, steeled himself, continued.

"Me they wanted to kill because they thought I had learned the truth behind the casino deal. In fact, I had learned nothing. The details were in a file given me by accident, a file I had not yet looked at. But still, they burned the file and my office with it, and they tried to kill me, all because I might have known what you were up to, and that couldn't be allowed."

Caleb Breest remained perfectly still, emitting not a sound except for the roilings of his breath.

"You they intended to kill because you don't fit into their future plans. After the car bomb failed, they were waiting for me to be killed before they went after you. While I was on the run, they still had use for you. But that use, I think, is over."

Scrbacek flinched as soon as he said it, certain he had gone too far. He stared at the statue across the desk from him, his fear ratcheting higher with each moment of silence. And then, from out of this still mass of bronze came a single word:

"Who?"

Scrbacek thrilled at the one word, grabbed at it like a lifeline. He spoke now in a quiet gush. "It was the rest of the group, the casino group. You know about the casino plan, don't you? I thought for sure you knew."

Scrbacek waited a moment, but there was no response. Was it possible he knew nothing of the broader scheme? No, that couldn't be possible. But still . . .

"It's a group, put together by a lawyer named DeLoatch, who was acting as a sort of promoter, with the intent of forcing through the construction of and access to a casino resort in the Marina District. The group includes James E. Diamond, the casino owner. It includes Frances Galloway, the real-estate developer."

Scrbacek stared at the unmoving figure before him, the reaction of the huge man's eyes hidden in the blotches of shadow. He was impossible to read, it was impossible to know what he was thinking, but still, Scrbacek couldn't help but feel that the next sentence would come to the figure before him as a total surprise.

"It includes," said Scrbacek, "Joey Torresdale."

Breest said nothing, but there was a slight flutter of the neck, like a flinch from a blow. Scrbacek felt it more than saw it, but it was there, and with it came a strange sensation, as if the silent man were somehow speaking to him without saying a word, as if he could hear Breest whispering in his ear. And what he was whispering to Scrbacek, this huge figure in shadow before him, was, *No. Not Joey. No.*

"It's true. You have to trust me. DeLoatch told me everything, and Joey as good as admitted it to me."

Was there a flexing of the forearms? Were Breest's hands tightening one against the other as if readying to destroy Scrbacek with a single blow? Breest remained still and silent, but Scrbacek could still hear the whispering. *Not Joey. No.* Scrbacek stared at the blotches of shadows that made up Breest's face. Was it possible that Caleb Breest knew nothing of the scheming behind the great gouts of violence he had perpetrated upon the city? His oldest, probably his only friend, moving him, year upon bloody year, like some death-dealing chess piece? No, it did not seem possible that Breest wouldn't know, and yet with a certainty he didn't understand, Scrbacek believed now exactly that. How could Scrbacek one moment think this man before him a mastermind of crime and the next see him as nothing more than a dupe?

"Were you aware that they were trying to kill me?" said Scrbacek. "Did you give the order?"

No answer, only a dark silence in response. A silence that told Scrbacek that no, this man before him had not given the order.

"Were you aware that your organization was working alongside Diamond and Galloway to build a corridor of ruin running from Diamond's Mount Olympus through Crapstown to the Marina District, where a billion-dollar casino resort was to be built?"

Still no answer. Still only the dark silence.

"The Ever-Dry factory was in the way of that path. That's why you torched it."

Breest said nothing, but his great head tilted to the side, and at the sight of it a chill ripped down Scrbacek's spine. Scrbacek remembered the great angry tale spun to him by Thomas Surwin: Breest had done this, had done that, had killed this, had burned that, had raped the city for his own vile ends. Scrbacek had believed every word; now he wondered if Breest was left not only out of the scheme but also out of all that was being done in his name.

"Do you remember Ever-Dry, where your father worked?"

No movement, no reply. But of course he did, this man before him. He remembered the company picnics, the shirts with logos, the way his father talked of the plant at night. Whatever he had done to his father, Caleb Breest would have remembered where his father worked for all those years, whether with hatred or respect. However he felt about it, he would feel something.

"Did you know that the business had been destroyed, Caleb? Did you know that Ever-Dry balked at paying an increased level of protection, and that as a result the factory was burned to the ground?"

No response.

"Didn't Joey tell you?"

No response.

"Caleb, did you give the order to burn down your father's old factory, the place where he became a foreman before he disappeared? Did you give that order?"

Still no response, and Scrbacek could detect no movement in the still body. But he knew the answer. It had been relayed to him clear as pain in the way Breest's head had tilted, questioningly, when Scrbacek spoke of the fire. No, Caleb Breest had not known what had happened to the plant, had not burned it down in revenge.

Silent as Breest now, Scrbacek sat dumbfounded, feeling a peculiar heat rise from his gut to his ears. How had he missed all this? How could he have taken step one as a defense attorney without knowing even the least thing about his client? If he had learned all that was happening in Breest's name, would he have done anything differently? Had he acted in his client's interests in gaining the acquittal, or in the interests of Joey Torresdale, James E. Diamond, Frances Galloway, that bastard DeLoatch? In the interests of J.D. Scrbacek? Yes, certainly in the interests of J.D. Scrbacek—another pressworthy acquittal for his record—but what about the interests of Caleb Breest? Would it have been better to cooperate with Surwin, turn state's evidence? Would it have been better to plead insanity? Would it have been better to spare his client's life, some way, any way, without bringing him back to this? It had to be, in the end, Breest's decision, but had Breest indeed made the decision, and if so, was it fully informed? Was this man in front of him, silent, still, seemingly oblivious to all that had happened around him, was this man even capable of deciding?

"Caleb, I have some questions that you need to answer. Everything you say to me is confidential, but I need to know. Who makes the decisions for your organization?"

No answer, but still, somehow Scrbacek knew the answer. He felt strangely linked to this hulk of a man before him now, as if the hidden emotions coursing through the silent man's blood were somehow pouring directly into Scrbacek's heart, and the words behind his dark silences were being hissed like the most secret of messages into Scrbacek's ear.

"It's Joey, isn't it? He runs the drug operations. He runs the extortion, the prostitution. He oversees the flow of the money through the entire organization, isn't that right?"

No answer.

"It's Joey who picks your lawyers, isn't it? It was Joey who brought me in, wasn't it, Caleb?"

No answer, but there was no answer necessary.

"And it's Joey who tells you what needs to be done, what you yourself need to do. Including who to kill. It was Joey who told you to kill Malloy, wasn't it? You can tell me, I'm your lawyer, this is all privileged. Who told you to kill Malloy?"

No answer, still no answer, but Scrbacek knew.

"Caleb, I want you to think back now. Caleb, whose idea was it to blow up the restaurant Migello's and destroy the Puchesi family? Was that your plan, or was it Joey's?"

No answer, not a breath of movement, but still Scrbacek knew.

"And it was Joey who killed the Puchesi granddaughter's husband and stuffed him in a garbage can."

Silence, stillness from across the table, but now Scrbacek sensed something else, sensed somehow that he had gotten it wrong.

"No, it was you who did it, isn't that right, Caleb? You killed him because Joey told you to do it. Because the kid had accused you of stealing from the family. But you hadn't been stealing, had you, Caleb? Joey had. Joey. It was Joey who brought you into the family and used you to destroy it. You were his tool from the start."

No response.

"You met Joey in reform school, didn't you?"

No response.

"Before that, you were just a big scared kid, a bully because no one understood you. A bully because it's easy for a big kid to be a bully, easier than being the lonely one at the end of the schoolyard that everyone makes fun of. The big kid in the special-ed class. And you ended up in reform school because that football player did something to you that made you mad, that made you lose control, and you hit him and hit him and hit him. What was it, Caleb? What had the kid done to you?"

There was no response, no movement, until, slowly, the huge man leaned forward, and his head tilted up, and the great shadows on his face retreated until Scrbacek could see the huge man's eyes, one looking straight at him, one looking over his shoulder. And the eyes were crazed, and Scrbacek knew suddenly everything.

"Because he laughed at you? That was why?"

Breest's face tensed, the thick, ropy muscles beneath his jaw dancing with anger.

"And that's what Joey told you about the Puchesi kid. That he had laughed at you."

Breest's eyes narrowed. He breathed in deeply. It was as if he was getting ready to rise and smite someone with all his horrible strength.

"And that's what Joey told you about Malloy."

No movement, not a stir. Just that one eye staring at him as the other stared over his shoulder, both creased in some strange pain.

"What happened to your father, Caleb?"

No answer.

"Some people say you killed him, that he is buried in your basement. But it's not true, is it?"

No answer, but even so, Scrbacek knew. "He left, didn't he? He left your mother and you. Simply gave it up, all the work, the responsibilities, the hardships—gave it up and went away. And you spread the word that you killed him, didn't you? Because then he wouldn't have left, he never could have left."

Scrbacek stared at the huge boy-man before him with the mutant oversize heart. He's on Lasix, like a racehorse, Surwin had said. A huge racehorse, with blinders, seeing nothing to either side, nothing but the object placed in front of him by Joey Torresdale. He had been lost as a boy and left to rot by the system and used like a rented mule by Joey Torresdale, and no one had stepped in to help, least of all his lawyer.

"Caleb, my God, I'm sorry. Caleb, let me help. I can help."

Slowly the huge man leaned away from Scrbacek. The shadows from his brow lengthened, his eyes hid again in the blackness. As if a cord had been yanked free, the whispering silenced and whatever connection Scrbacek had felt disappeared. The man in front of him was again a bronze cipher, and Scrbacek was left to wonder if the certain knowledge that had flowed from Breest to him had all been mirage, a figment of his own fear and exhaustion.

"Caleb, I had a meeting with Thomas Surwin, the man who indicted you for Malloy's murder. He is planning to indict you again for racketeering and drug dealing. The penalty is life imprisonment without parole. But, Caleb, if we leave here right now and go talk to him, if we tell him what you know about Joey, if you are prepared to testify, if you let me talk with him, I'm sure he'll help you. Caleb, I can make a deal."

And then, from this huge hulking man of brass came the first word in minutes. "No."

"You have to. Caleb. I can save your life."

"No."

"Joey is going to kill you."

"No."

"Caleb, he used you from day one. You were his front man. His tool. Caleb."

"No."

"And he is going to kill you, Caleb."

"No."

"Like he is going to kill me, and my son, and my son's mother. He is going to kill us all and then he is going to kill you."

"No."

"And if he fails, others will succeed. There is going to be a war tonight, Caleb. Everything is converging—here, tonight. The Furies are coming. Your only chance of surviving is to come with me. Come with me. We'll go to Surwin together."

"No."

"Caleb."

"No."

"Let me help you. I can help you. Caleb."

"No," said Caleb Breest, the arc of his shaking head growing longer and faster as he repeated the word "no," his voice growing louder each time he said it. "No. No. No." Slowly his great interlocked hands rose high over his head and, with a sudden snap, were brought down like a sledge onto the surface of the great oak desk.

The desktop splintered in two like a cracker.

The goons stationed outside banged through the door, the fireplug and the monster, short-barreled semiautomatics waving forward as they rushed in. When they saw Breest sitting before the shattered desk, they halted and coolly pointed their guns at Scrbacek.

"Trust me, Caleb," said Scrbacek. "I'm your lawyer."

Breest stared at Scrbacek, and Scrbacek imagined he saw the faintest hint of a smile, as if Breest had finally gotten the joke.

"What's up, boss?" said the fireplug.

"Caleb, I can help," said Scrbacek. "We'll go together. Out that door. To safety. Let me help you. I can help you. Please."

"You want us to drill him, boss?"

"Go," said Caleb Breest to J.D. Scrbacek. "Now."

One of the men pulled back a lever on his gun with a distinct grinding click. Breest, without rising, turned and reached into a cabinet behind him, bringing out a huge shotgun, which he pumped once and then twice.

Scrbacek's client, now fully informed of his options and perils, had made his decision.

"They're going to kill my son and his mother," said Scrbacek. "Dirk and Dyer. Joey gave the order. If they get out of here, they're going to go to Philadelphia. They have to be stopped."

"Go," said Breest.

"I have to be sure that nothing—"

"Go," said Caleb Breest.

"Caleb . . ."

"Go."

Scrbacek went.

55
LESS THAN A WHISPER

The fireplug escorted Scrbacek through the building, leading him down the long dark hallway with the two lights, turning left and right, and then into a huge storage area with a loading platform at the far end. One of the bay doors was open. When one of the goons who had taken him from Torresdale's table tried to stop them at the open bay door, the fireplug, still with the gun in his hand, simply shook his head and the goon slipped away.

"Don't come back," said the fireplug as Scrbacek jumped down from the platform and into the soft rain.

"No chance of that," said Scrbacek.

He was running through a maze of cars when he heard a twang of metal and then a shot. He didn't stop to turn around and search through the rain for the gunman on the roof. Instead he kept moving, zigzagging now, still conveniently bent at the waist from his beating, heading for the safety of a squat brick building about fifty yards away. Another shot, no sound of a ricochet this time. Where was the ricochet?

A shout, another shot, and then he reached the brick and spun around the corner so that he had fully disappeared from the roof shooter's view.

He stopped for a moment, wiped the blood from his cheek, the rain out of his eyes, took a deep painful breath, grabbed hold of his side. He was north of Dirk's. He needed to get east, but he couldn't go there directly. He had to weave from building to building to keep the safety of mortar and block between himself and Dirk's. He took another deep breath and started again.

No longer running now, in too much pain to run, moving in a steady skip-jog through the wet streets, left then right then right, traversing the byways and alleyways, keeping as close to the safety of the walls as possible, pausing a moment here or there before sprinting through the rain across open streets. They couldn't get to him from Dirk's anymore, but who knew how many were following him, trying to catch a glimpse.

He scurried like an insect through the wet streets, making snap judgments—left here, right here. He saw a faint glow in the distance, heard shots. Was that it, what he was looking for? Carefully he made his way toward the light and sound, keeping tight to a wall, moving more slowly now, stepping along a pitted, pebble-strewn alleyway with care, the sporadic shooting in front of him growing louder all the while. Back pressed against the wall, he shifted slowly toward the source of the light, craning his neck to get a view.

Dirty Dirk's.

Crap. He had moved in a circle, a useless loop, right back to where they were looking to kill him. But he hadn't come out by the loading platform. Instead he could see the long empty wall, the eastern edge of the building. And there was shooting going on, louder now, clearer, like a pitched battle was raging inside that very building. Men ran from the exits, some bloodied. Others ran toward the doors, itching to get into the fight.

So it was going down, the inevitable war between Caleb Breest and Joey Torresdale. He wondered who had fired the first shot, wondered who would end up still on his feet when the last shot was sounded. Torresdale was wily beyond belief, and apparently had more men, but Torresdale himself had turned Breest into an awesome killing machine. Whatever the result, Scrbacek was glad as hell to be out of it.

Now that Scrbacek knew he was east of Dirk's, he understood where he needed to go. He backed away, slowly, carefully, so as not to be seen, backed away until Dirk's disappeared once more from his view. Just as he was about to turn around and run, through the delicate patter of the rain, he heard it:

"Scrbacek."

It was less than a whisper, as soft as a thought, and terrifyingly familiar, like an old bad dream that keeps haunting. He froze.

"Scrbacek."

56
RIMSHOT

"Scrbacek."

From where had it come, this soft yet pernicious whisper, this familiar taunt? In front of him? Behind him? Was it only his imagination?

He spun around, his back to Dirk's. Nothing. The gunfire continued behind him, an aural spur, reminding him he had to get away. He took a step forward, pebbles shifting beneath his feet. He looked around.

Nothing.

Another step.

Nothing.

Another step.

"Scrbacek."

He didn't wait now. He just started running, his boot soles slipping at first on the wet, and then gripping the pebbly surface as he picked up speed, fists pumping, running.

A dark shadow stepped out from a wrecked building just ahead of him, a large piece of scrap wood in its grasp, the wood catching a gleam of light.

"Here's the windup," said the shadow.

And then the wood swung, like a Louisville Slugger, landing flush on Scrbacek's bad arm, slamming him into the wet ground with an explosion of pain and surprise that forced out an inhuman howl. As Scrbacek writhed on the pitted asphalt, the shadow stepped toward him.

Scrbacek rolled slowly, painfully, and then backed away, crab-like, hands scrabbling through puddles and pebbles. Backed away as fast as his wounded left arm would let him, which wasn't very fast at all. From his low angle, he could only see his attacker's silhouette against the dim glow of the rain-sodden sky: a man with broad shoulders and unruly hair, his long leather coat sweeping low to the ground as he stepped calmly toward the retreating Scrbacek. But even with only a silhouette to judge, and even with rain falling into his eyes and blurring his sight, Scrbacek knew.

Bozant.

"I've been looking high and low for you," said Bozant as he took a quick hop forward, planted his left foot, and swung his right foot hard into Scrbacek's crotch. The kick thudded solidly. The pain of it, more than the blow, spun Scrbacek onto his face. He let out a groan, his body contracted into a ball.

"I guess I just wasn't looking low enough," said Bozant.

Almost unconscious from the impossible pain that rose in thick waves from his abdomen, Scrbacek stretched out and started crawling away, pebbles and stones pressing into his forearms. He was moving by instinct, driven by fear, moving as fast from this demented madman as he was able, which was only as fast as a slug.

"What, no clever comeback? You always had a ready wit. Let me know when it's ready."

Bozant started toward the crawling Scrbacek, leaped into the air, and landed one foot on Scrbacek's back, flattening him on the pitted asphalt.

"I'll never forget the first time I saw you," said Bozant. "And don't think I haven't tried. There's always been something about your face that puts me in the mood for violence."

Scrbacek's face was pressed into a pebble-strewn puddle, his cheek pouring blood into the water. He had to turn his head to breathe. When Bozant removed his shoe from his back, Scrbacek slowly rolled until he was lying faceup on the ground. Bozant squatted over his limp body, and Scrbacek, totally exposed, could do nothing except let the wet and the pain flow through him. Resignation overwhelmed his fear.

"Just . . . tell me," said Scrbacek, gasping for air, "what the hell do you want?"

"I want to kill you."

Scrbacek was too dazed to even react. Bozant grabbed Scrbacek's head with both hands and slammed it into the street so hard Scrbacek felt his consciousness slip wholly into the pain and disappear.

When Scrbacek opened his eyes again, he was lying faceup in the gutter. Bozant sat beside him, atop an overturned trash can, picking at his palm. Scrbacek attempted to slide away as stealthily as possible. Bozant lifted his head and smiled. Scrbacek stopped.

"I used to dress up like a clown for kids in the hospital," said Bozant. "I loved that, and I was good at it. Some clowns couldn't make a hyena laugh, but I had a talent. They don't let me do it anymore. Felons aren't welcome in the children's ward. What is a clown when he can't clown anymore?"

Bozant reached down and flicked a finger into Scrbacek's eye. Scrbacek screamed and clutched his left hand to his socket.

"At wit's end," said Bozant.

"You're insane," shouted Scrbacek, the sharp pain wakening him out of the daze.

"So they tell me. I'm actually in court-ordered therapy, but it hasn't much helped. My doctor's an ambivalence chaser. I take so many different-colored pills I dream in Technicolor."

Scrbacek pressed down on his right hand until he was sitting up slightly. "You're getting paid to kill me, not to torture me with bad jokes. If you're going to do it, just do it."

"You shouldn't think I'm just killing you for the money. Well, not only for the money. I'm not a total mercenary."

Scrbacek spit blood, his hand still to his eye. He couldn't help notice Bozant's ease of manner as he sat on the trash can, chatting. "You killed Ethan Brummel," said Scrbacek, "you killed Freaky Freddie Margolis."

"They just got in the way of what you had coming."

"Go to hell. Stop blaming me for your getting kicked off the force and into jail—you did that to yourself. You were the one who corrupted your badge, you were the one who lied on the stand, you were the one sleeping with the whore."

"Well, you know what they say—nothing risqué, nothing gained." Bozant's foot shot out and caught Scrbacek in the stomach. "Still, I owe you some of the credit."

Scrbacek groaned as he rolled onto his side, curled like a fetus. "I was just doing my job," he managed to get out.

"Your job. You've always had the Midas touch, Scrbacek. Everything you touch turns into a muffler. Well, I'm just doing my job, too. But you're right—I'm as much at fault as you. I loved her from the start. Amber, I mean. She was crazier than I was. First time I took her in, she kicked me in the nuts, I smacked her in the jaw, she smiled and spit out a tooth. I couldn't help myself. I always wanted a girl just like the girl that Dad had on the side, and she was it."

Scrbacek pushed himself again to sitting. He rubbed at his eye. "So if it's not the money, and not because I proved you a liar, then why are you still after me?"

"You thought you were on the side of the angels getting Amber off, didn't you?"

"You gave me the key, I just turned it."

"I know. And don't think I don't beat myself up over what happened, too." Bozant slammed his fist into his own face.

"What are you talking about?"

Bozant leaned over and rapped his knuckles on Scrbacek's head. Tap tap. "Hello?" Tap tap tap. "If ignorance is bliss, why aren't you happier? I'm talking about Maya. My daughter, Maya. Remember her?"

Scrbacek stared at Bozant for a long moment as the rain poured like tears off the both of them. He felt something slide through him that was different now than the fear and the pain.

"It was one thing to release that psycho-bunny into the world," said Bozant. "It was quite another to deliver my daughter into her grasp."

Scrbacek closed his eyes and felt that thing slip through him and knew now what it was, exactly what it was. "How could I know what would happen?" he pleaded, as if to a judge and not some homicidal maniac.

"You found her. It was your job to know."

"It was another lawyer who brought her back."

"But you didn't stand up and fight it. You knew it was happening, and you let it."

"What could I do?"

"Tell the court the truth."

"I couldn't. I couldn't. Everything I knew was privileged. But it wasn't even Amber who ended up killing her. It was the boyfriend."

"Who did you think she was going to end up with after Lucius and me? Pop Warner? Did you have any expectation that crazy Amber would protect her daughter?"

"What could I have done?" moaned Scrbacek, even as he knew he could have done more, even as he knew that the thing slipping through him was the keen blade of shame for all that he didn't do to protect that girl, that young, pretty girl with the ribbons in her pigtails.

"You found her, you dragged her back to Amber's attention, it was your responsibility to do something to protect her. I convinced Amber—with much difficulty and violence, I might add—to give her away. And I made sure Maya had the best care the foster system could deliver. She was out of the life, into something better, and then you dragged her back. I was never much of a father to Maya, but I figure I owe her one last thing. So get up, Scrbacek. Get the hell up."

Bozant rose from the trash-can seat, grabbed Scrbacek's collar, and pulled him to standing. Scrbacek staggered onto his feet, weak with the brutal cocktail of pain and shame.

"Get up so I can give my little baby one last gift." Bozant reached into his coat and pulled out a huge fillet knife. "Today, on *The American Sportsman*, catching and cleaning the North American largemouth bass."

Bozant shoved Scrbacek away. Scrbacek staggered back, unsure of what to do, still filled with a paralyzing shame. Bozant was going to kill him. He was going to kill him, dammit, and Scrbacek wasn't sure he didn't deserve it. Bozant took a step forward and gave Scrbacek another shove. Scrbacek fell back onto the ground. Bozant stood over him, waving the knife.

"We're playing *The American Sportsman*, so I'm going to be sporting. I'm going to give you to five before I chase you down and gut you with this knife. I like this knife, because if I stab you in the chest it's flexible enough to slip around a rib and still dive into your heart. I finished off that dog with this knife."

Something came loose in Scrbacek. He shook his head to alertness and, for a moment, the shame abated, overcome by anger. "You killed my dog."

"Was that yours? If I had known, I would have enjoyed it more."

"You shouldn't have killed my dog."

"One."

Scrbacek scrabbled to his feet, grabbing a handful of pebbles and stones in his right hand as he did.

"Two."

Scrbacek turned as if to flee and then whipped around again, tossing the pebble mixture into Bozant's face. As Bozant reeled back, arm to his face, Scrbacek began to run.

From behind, he heard Bozant scream out, his voice still in good humor, "Three, four, five. Ready or not, here I come."

Scrbacek gripped his left arm as he lurched forward, step by step, gripped the arm that Bozant had first crippled with a bullet and then slammed with the wooden board and was now aching and useless. He leaned forward to keep up his speed, fighting to ignore the pain spinning like a cyclone through his body. He could hear Bozant's footsteps gaining on him at an alarming rate. He only had a few dozen seconds before the maniac would overtake him. He darted right, along a building's edge, darted left at its corner, staggered down a narrow street.

He felt flooded with a strange sensation that he had done this already. And he had, the night his building burned down and Bozant had called out his name and then shot a bullet through his arm. How long ago had that been? A lifetime? He tried to count the passing of the days, fought to separate what had become a blur. One two three four nights. Four nights that changed everything. And now, still gripping his arm, the very same killer in mad pursuit, he was running out of Crapstown, out of the darkness that had once promised safety, toward the corrupt yellow glow of Casinoland. But he wouldn't get there, he couldn't, Bozant would catch him first, he wouldn't get there, unless . . .

He cut right again, running as fast as his weary legs and the pain still pooling in his abdomen would let him, zigged left once more, the footsteps gaining on him, the knife growing ever closer. And then, to his right, he saw the flickering glow of fire reflect off the top of a building.

He dived right, into an alley, Bozant behind him, so close now that Bozant could almost grab at the trailing edge of Scrbacek's raincoat.

When they burst out of the alleyway, they ran smack into the center of a great crowd, a strange army of men and women packed together, torches held high, standing shoulder to shoulder, facing away from the sea, a wild shifting regiment that filled the streets and spilled over onto the sidewalks. The two lurched together into the middle of the crowd just as Bozant dived at Scrbacek with his knife.

Scrbacek jumped back as the knife sliced the front of his shirt. He turned to run and felt hands grab at him. He swatted them away, but others grabbed at him as well, more than he could fend off, gripping him around his chest, his biceps. Dozens more, grabbing his legs, his neck, lifting him off the ground, immobilizing him totally, halting his escape from the knife. As he struggled, he noticed that Bozant was being similarly embraced, lifted, held in check.

But for how long? Bozant was fighting furiously, knife still in hand. How long until he slashed himself free and lunged at Scrbacek's chest with his blade? He was close, so close, less than an arm's length away. Scrbacek struggled to get free, to continue his flight. "Stop it," he yelled. "Let me go!" But his screams were useless, caught as he was, imprisoned, clutched into helplessness, at the mercy of the mob.

And then Bozant seemed to pull away from Scrbacek, as if atop a cloud, magically floating away into the sea of arms and faces, shoulders and necks. Bozant reached out a hand, grabbing hold of Scrbacek's raincoat. Scrbacek felt the tug, but he was held too firmly himself by the mob, and Bozant's grip faltered and then failed. And he floated away alone, floated farther and farther away, until slowly, as if in a dream, the mob closed in around him and he disappeared from view, except for the one arm that had gripped Scrbacek's coat. That arm now stretched high, over the heads of the crowd, as if seeking to grip the heavens themselves and drag them down with him. There came a scream, something dark and inhuman, fierce and strangely empty, and slowly the hand fell until it vanished from Scrbacek's sight, along with the rest of Remi Bozant, disappeared into the mob, vanished as if from the face of the globe.

Scrbacek was stunned at what he had witnessed, didn't understand what had happened, why or how he had been saved. And then the part of the crowd that had swallowed Bozant whole split in two, and through the opening roared a motorcycle, huge as a horse, encrusted in chrome, its handlebars reaching high to the sky. Straddling the great machine was a huge woman in a black leather vest, with a gun in her belt and thick reddish dreads coiled about her face.

"What have we here?" said Regina. "Why, bless my heart, it's J.D. Stifferdeck, bloodied but still alive, come to join the party."

57
THE FURIES

They had come from the crumbling buildings of west Crapstown, from the tenements in the south, gangbangers and schoolteachers, weight lifters carrying the lame and the halt. They had come from church shelters and from squatters' dens and from town houses in the Marina District. Shopkeepers, shoplifters, the guys who sell vegetables from their trucks. One by one and in clumps and in streams, they had joined together, turning themselves into the Crapstown Furies, feared avengers seeking justice for all. Waitresses and drug dealers, taxi drivers and bicycle messengers, blind men clutching their tin cups, sunburned women walking in packs, talking to themselves as if talking to each other, together approaching normal. There had come pimps in business suits, there had come women in whorescloth, there had come kids with skateboards, wizened old women, bookish men with wire spectacles. They had come from the basements of shattered buildings, they had come from the cardboard boxes under the colonnades on West Harrison. Girls with guns, guys with cell phones, old men with tattered clothes falling like stripped skin off their backs. There were bookies taking bets, and gamblers searching for better odds, and men and women both who had found the one true God and were exclaiming to the world at the glory of His word. They had emptied out the crack houses on Coolidge. They had emptied out the mission centers on Pierce. Hoops players and craps players, rappers and twelve-steppers and addicts who hadn't yet stepped, the coughing, the limping, predators and prey. They had come from west, north, south, from even within the penumbra of Casinoland's neon glow. They hugged and laughed and fought as they marched together in the rain, ready to violently assert their collective will against that which had torn apart their home.

Scrbacek stood in the middle of the advancing army, amidst a group with which he had become strangely familiar in the past four nights. Regina, still on her Harley, and Ed, shotgun in his arms and cleaver in his apron, and Aboud with his Zastava, and Sergei the Russian, brandishing a tommy gun, and Blixen, a ragged old rifle leaning on her shoulder, and Elisha Baltimore, holding on to Donnie's arm as he pulled a heavy wooden crate on a dolly. Scrbacek felt a surprising fondness for them all as marchers streamed by on either side. If he had friends outside this ragtag crew, he couldn't bring them to mind just then.

"Well, we're doing it, Stifferdeck," said Regina. "Just like we told you we would. Don't you be trying to stop us."

"If you wait a bit," said Scrbacek, "they'll do your work for you. When I left there was a war going on inside of Dirk's."

"That don't matter none," said Regina. "We're wet to the bone and tired of waiting. If it's only mopping up, all the better."

"Suit yourselves," said Scrbacek. "Did you get me what I asked for?"

"Behind us, Mr. Scrbacek," said Donnie. "Waiting for you."

Scrbacek glanced at the crate Donnie was dragging. "What's in there?"

"Just a few little treats," said Donnie, grinning. "Homemade."

"You're a damn good artist, Donnie. Too good to waste your talent on guns. After this, no more silencers, all right? No more grenades. You can make a fine living from your artwork."

"I'd like to believe that."

"You fix up that model, someday it will be on a postcard. You saved my life, Donnie. All of you did. Thank you."

"You're the one we owe."

"Malloy maybe, but not me. I'm just the fool. Ed, when this is over, you'll keep the grill warm for me, make me some of those special home fries?"

"On the house, Mr. Scrbacek. And from now on, you'll never have to pay afore you eat, only after."

"Then all this hasn't been for naught. You've got the common touch, Ed. You ever think of politics?"

"Hell no. I'm an honest man."

"Well, be careful. All of you. Sergei, take care of Aboud."

"He safe as puppy with me."

"That's good to know."

"Of course, in Russia now they eat puppy like chicken."

"Aw, I can take care of myself," said Aboud, casually waving the Zastava. "You come to the club when this is over, Scrbacek. With Dirk's gone, business will improve. We'll be able to hire us some of our girls back, have a whale of a time."

"I wouldn't miss it."

"Maybe I'll even have the great Elisha Baltimore dancing for me."

"Dream on," said Elisha. "I've got plans. That lawsuit thing you were talking about, J.D., am I going to get a piece?"

"I expect so," said Scrbacek. "You all should, though I can't say when anyone would see the money."

"Well, maybe when I get my share, I can sort of try this thing I've been wanting to try. A dance school."

"Exotic?" said Aboud.

"No, silly. Ballet. For kids. I took ballet as a girl and loved the twirling. I'd like to pass something on."

"There was a dance school in my model," said Donnie. "Right next to the West Side Community Center."

"That's what got me to thinking about it."

"I put it in just for you," said Donnie.

"Donnie," said Elisha, beaming, "that is so sweet."

"It's going to be good, Mr. Scrbacek," said Donnie, a wide smile. "The whole thing. I know it is."

"I believe it," said Scrbacek. "I actually do. Hey, Blixen?"

"Yes, sir," said the old woman, raising her poor old bones into some semblance of attention.

"What about you? Are you going to hang around?"

"I'm sticking by the sea," said the old woman. "With my daughter."

"I'm glad. When I get back, I expect I'll start lawyering again. Maybe represent kids in trouble, start making up for past mistakes. I'll need someone to work in the office, keep track of files and motions. You looking for a job?"

"What do you think, I'm crazy? Wear a dress? Go to work? Shave? What do you think, I'm insane?"

"Well, maybe then you'll just hang around the office and play chess."

"You can't keep up with me."

"I beat you once already."

"I let you."

"I know."

"I told them you were our knight."

"I'm not. I never was."

"You've got the nipples for it, though, don't you? Our home is your home now. Just stay away from the piers. Don't swim near the piers. The pylons are murder."

"I won't, Blixen. I promise." Scrbacek looked around. "Where's the Nightingale?"

Blixen pointed into the air. Through the rain, Scrbacek could just make out a shadow standing tall on a rooftop, hip cocked, gun in hand. Scrbacek waved, and the shadow waved back.

"This is touching as two humping hummingbirds," said Regina, "but we're getting soaked just standing here."

"Caleb Breest wasn't part of it," said Scrbacek.

"He tell you that?"

"Not in so many words, but it's true. It was all Torresdale."

"It don't matter. Breest killed Malloy, didn't he?"

"Whatever he did, it was because of Torresdale."

"What are you, still his lawyer?"

"I'm just telling you the truth."

"The truth is, Stifferdeck, it's time for you to clear out and for us to do our damage."

"There's another way."

"Maybe," said Regina. "But this is our way." She revved her engine and shouted to the passing crowd: "Let's kick some ass and make it happen."

There was a huge cheer as she rumbled forward into the guts of the moving mob. Torches were raised high, the flames burning wildly, sizzling in the rain. Guns were held aloft, blades waved, invectives shouted. The whole scene grew ever more medieval as the grand army of the Crapstown Furies moved west, through the rain, marching toward the stronghold of the enemy. Scrbacek held his ground as his friends rejoined the march and the remainder of this ragtag people's militia surged past.

He had told their Inner Circle, deep in the cavern, that there would be a lawsuit, that the killing would stop, that if they had the strength of purpose to hold their ground, they could do it without the war, do it within the system, and everyone would be better off. But Regina, converted to action, had led the battle cry and the others had followed. The word had been spread, this army had been raised, there was no turning back. They wouldn't wait for the system to take the boot off their necks, they wouldn't wait for a deliverer, they would do it themselves, now, and Scrbacek couldn't blame them. He couldn't join them, because it was not his way, but he couldn't blame them. Hit first—that was part of what he had learned in his four nights in Crapstown. Jump on them before they jump on you. And so they would.

At the tail of the mob, he could hear the creak of wheels and a bumping, rolling noise. It was a metal cart, like a room service cart, its top and sides covered by a white oilcloth, except that room service carts don't have a big red cross painted on the cloth and a black medicine bag sitting in the center. The cart was being pushed by a small man, his head down, straining to keep up with the crowd.

"What do you have there, Squirrel?" said Scrbacek.

Squirrel stopped suddenly and lifted his head. Rain poured down his face as he squinted behind his big round glasses. "Oh, Scrbacek. It's only you. Just a little first-aid station. We each must do our part."

"I bet." Scrbacek leaned toward the cart and lifted the oilcloth. The stink of formaldehyde washed over him. Rows of large glass bottles sat on the two wide shelves beneath the cloth, all but one empty except for a clear fluid sloshing back and forth. All but one. This last held some large obscure mass, and the fluid in the jar was dark, and all that gave away what once the mass had been was the great clot of red hair that floated about it.

"Everyone needs a hobby," said Squirrel as he jerked the cloth out of Scrbacek's hand and let it fall to cover the spectacle.

"So you've said."

"He won't miss it, I promise you."

"No," said Scrbacek, "I suppose he won't. You got a bandage for my cut?"

The little man examined Scrbacek's split cheek before rummaging in his bag. "You need stitches," he said as he pulled out gauze, tape, a gleaming pair of scissors, "but I don't have time for niceties."

When Squirrel was finished, the wound closed with tape, covered with gauze and more tape, he put everything back in his bag, bent low, and without a word began again to push his cart forward, the creak of the wheels following like a warning.

Later, much later, after the lawsuit was settled for an astonishing amount of money and after Ed was elected mayor, astounding the pundits, and after the first of the new community centers was erected, its stainless steel surfaces echoing the hammered sheen of Donnie's model city, Scrbacek would handle a delicate legal matter for one Octavio Shlemnick. In gratitude, Shlemnick would invite Scrbacek into his private den on Garfield Street, lead him through the secret doorway, and then down the long dark steps to the basement, where rows and rows of large glass jars were each brilliantly illuminated. Inside the jars floated Octavio Shlemnick's grand collection. Hands, eyes, livers, the twisted lines of aborted Siamese twins. A foot, with its toenails needing trimming. A bottle of spleens. A penis that, by God, must have been Dillinger's. The long loops of a gastrointestinal tract. Remi Bozant's smiling face.

Scrbacek would gasp when he saw it all, and then feel the fascination rise within him. Rubbing his chronically sore arm, itself once destined for the jars, he would walk among the samples, examining each. And he would stop in front of one bottle, larger than the others, and stare for a long time. Even after examining the rest, he would return to this selfsame bottle. Inside, so big that the oversize bottle could barely contain it, would be a huge pink thing, flabby and soft, the consistency of a rotting sponge, with clogged white things swooping up and out on either side. There would be no labels, but no labels would be needed, for Scrbacek would know exactly what it was inside that gaol of glass.

And whenever the old stories again were raised, the litany of horrors, whenever the legend of Caleb Breest was told and told again, Scrbacek would tamp down the talk and tell one and all, with complete conviction, "Say what you will about Caleb Breest, but I represented him, I understood him better than anyone alive, and I can tell you, unequivocally, that he had the biggest heart of any man I've ever known."

When Squirrel had caught up to the mob, Scrbacek turned away and began again walking east. He could see now, behind the sallow glow of Casinoland, the brightness of something rising above it, promising to turn the neon insignificant. He kept walking, soaked through and not caring the least, until he found the thing that he had asked for.

"You the guy I'm supposed to wait for?" said the man sitting in the driver's seat of a beat-up blue-and-white excuse for a cab. "Are you—what is it? Scribble-something?"

"Scrbacek."

"Scrbacek, yeah, that's it. What the hell kind of name is Scrbacek?"

"It's an old Apache name. It means 'lost no more.'"

"Funny, you don't look Indian." The taxicab driver gestured to Scrbacek's damaged face. "I hope the other guy, he looks worse."

"Does he ever," said Scrbacek as he opened the door.

When Scrbacek dropped into the seat, a wave of weariness flooded through him. He couldn't believe he could be this grievously sore, this tired, this relieved to be still alive. He leaned forward and checked that the face on the taxi license matched the face of the driver. It did. Jake Tomato. Nice name. He leaned back.

"Where to?" said Tomato.

Scrbacek reached into his pants pocket and pulled out a soaking wad of bills, all that was left of his glorious win at blackjack four nights before. He tossed the whole wet mass through the window in the Plexiglas partition. "Is this enough to get me to Philadelphia?"

The driver carefully extricated the bills one from another and smoothed them out on the seat beside him. "Yeah, it's enough. It's more than enough."

"Good," said Scrbacek. "Then let's do it."

Tomato started the engine. The cab, its shocks spent, jostled off and turned hard to the left. Scrbacek's head bounced to one side, bounced to the other. He had so much to think about, to digest, there was so much of his past he had still to pay for, but just then he didn't have the strength to review it all. He barely had the strength to close his eyes.

He awoke with a thundering panic as the cab fell in and out of a pothole. He looked out the window, desperately trying to figure out where he was. It was already bright. The sun glared from behind him. He was in a cab. He was bouncing through the air, soaring high into the sky.

"Hey, you're up," said Tomato. "Good. We're already on the Walt Whitman. Made damn good time."

Scrbacek leaned over and saw the gray Delaware River flash beneath him and the skyline before him and the morning light all around him, which looked as stark and fresh as a new beginning.

"It's a big city, Swifferdeck. So whereabouts exactly in Philly we going?"

"Chinatown, Jake. Let's start it over again in Chinatown."

ABOUT THE AUTHOR

Photo © Sigrid Estrada

William Lashner is the *New York Times* bestselling author of *Guaranteed Heroes*, *The Barkeep*, and *The Accounting*, as well as the Victor Carl legal thrillers, which have been translated into more than a dozen languages and sold across the globe. *The Barkeep*, nominated for an Edgar Award, was an Amazon and Digital Book World #1 bestseller. Before retiring from law to write full-time, Lashner was a prosecutor with the Department of Justice in Washington, DC. He is a graduate of the New York University School of Law as well as the Iowa Writers' Workshop. He lives outside Philadelphia with his wife and three children.